With You

Ellison Clark

Cover Design: Prince Enyiemah
Editor: Kirsten Rees | MakeMeASuccess
ISBN: 978-0-578-80391-3

Connect with Ellison Clark:
Instagram: ellison.books
Facebook: Ellison Clark Books
Email: ellisonbooks@gmail.com

To Tim, Lawson and Ellis, I love you.

Acknowledgments

A heartfelt thank you to my intelligent, lifelong friend, Amy Podrasky, who has helped me with just about every inch of this book. You may never know how truly grateful I am for your feedback and advice during this journey.

This book would not be what it is without the support of my husband, Tim, who occupied our children on long days when ideas just kept coming. Thank you for giving me the time and space to write.

To my parents, Dan and Brenda Dvorak, thank you for your unconditional love and support.

Finally, my appreciation goes out to my editing team. You are some of the smartest and most hard-working women I know. My mother, Brenda Dvorak; Amy Podrasky; my professional editor and coach, Kirsten Rees; Kira Doman and Brooklyn Smith. Thank you for everything you've done.

CHAPTER 1

I step onto the cool tile of the bathroom floor and look down at my feet. My polish is already starting to chip even though I painted my toes only two weeks ago. I guess when you walk around barefoot and dig your toes in the sand, it ruins your polish. Since I have a professional pedi booked for tomorrow morning, I remind myself I don't need to worry.

I fill my lungs and try to wake up, my eyes still squinting from the bright bathroom lights. My boyfriend is sound asleep in his bed ten feet away. He will wake in about thirty minutes when I start the coffee. I jump in the shower but make it quick. It's Friday, the week almost over. For the first time this morning, I feel some joy. All I need to do is make it through the workday and away I go.

Once a year I get away with my three best friends for a girls' weekend. We aren't really getting away as such, since we're driving less than two hours. Still, it's away from here, so I'm beyond excited. Just glancing at my suitcase puts a smile on my face. Even though I always look forward to this particular weekend, it's been on my mind more than normal the last few weeks. I head to the kitchen with a bounce in my step to throw my lunch together, just as Sai walks in.

"Morning babe. How did you sleep?" He asks and kisses my hair.

I clear my throat. "Fine, you?"

"Great anytime I can get you to stay over." His smile is loving. He's a hopeless romantic. "I never sleep well when you're not here."

"I know, it's just a challenge to get to work from here with the twenty extra minutes, when I'm always running behind."

He moves to the drying rack and grabs his favorite mug. "You must be really excited for your girls' weekend? I see you're already packed."

Over the last few weeks, I've started to leave extra clothes at Sai's. He's made a spot on one side of his closet for me to keep some things. It's come in handy the few times I came for dinner after work and then ending up staying because it got late. But as for this weekend's bag, it's been packed since Wednesday night.

"So ready. I miss the girls. Everyone seems to get busier every year," I say.

Sai pours his coffee, loads it with creamer and tells me to kiss him goodbye before I leave for work. I tell him of course I will and then think, *have I ever left without saying goodbye?* I'm slightly annoyed that he thinks he has to tell me. He will head out to meet with his new client before going to the gym, where he'll spend about an hour before returning home. He has worked from home since I met him eight months ago.

Just before we met, he hung up the normal forty-hour work week to try his luck in sales. Technically, he doesn't need to work. When his father passed away two years ago, he inherited a lot of money. He is set for life but chooses to work anyway.

I finish my breakfast and go into the bathroom as Sai steps out of the shower. As I brush my teeth, he asks if I will stick around awhile when I get back from work. He knows I finish at 2pm on Fridays, the perk of our new summer hours. I give him an apologetic smile, and tell him I'm only coming back to change before going to meet Kia for coffee. From there, we will make our way to the hotel. The plan is to meet everyone by 5pm to make dinner and evening plans.

Sai and I normally spend the entire weekend together, Friday afternoon until Monday morning. I feel bad that he will be on his own, but I also know that I need this, so, I shrug the thought away. He asks again if we're staying at Hotel Lotus in

Springbrook. I nod to confirm and tell him with a quick peck on the side of his mouth that I need to go before I'm late, again.

As I turn away, he yells, "I love you!"

I return with, "You too, sweetie."

Work actually flies by. Before I know it, we are cleaning up for the day and I'm talking with Emma about my weekend plans. As we head out the back door, hands full with bags of garbage, my foot catches the misplaced cinder block that is supposed to be holding the shed door closed. I wince in pain and look down at my big toe noticing a bubble of dark red blood forming at the top corner.

"Oh ouch, are you-"

"Ah, damn it. I'm fine," I say cutting her off. "I guess I won't be getting that pedi, after all."

"Are you going to report this?" Emma asks.

"Um, what?" I asked confused.

"Getting hurt on the job?"

"Oh, no." I take a deep breath since my toe is starting to throb and think of how Emma is somewhat of a rule follower.

"Okay, good," she says with a big sigh, "because we probably shouldn't have changed into our flip flops since we're still clocked in."

Smiling, I touch the back of her shoulder to help ease her worry and tell her it will be fine as we head back in.

Pulling up in front of Sai's house, I get a text from Kia.

Kia: So much to catch up on, can't wait, see you at Mocha Joes!

I feel myself relax. Enjoying this moment, knowing that the weekend is here, and in a short while, I will be with my closest girlfriends.

I beat Kia to the coffee shop, which is a super cute place I visit any chance I get. It's warm and colorful with local artwork hanging on display. It smells of strong coffee with an after hint of sugary pastries.

9

Checking the daily specials and reading Macadamia Nut Latte listed at the top, I stop and know that's my order. I either know what I want or have no idea at all and take a lifetime to make a decision. I head to an oversized loveseat in the corner of the room after my order is placed. There's a small shelf of used books nearby so I start looking through, reading the titles to see if anything sparks my interest. As soon as my drink is at the counter and they're calling my name, I hear Kia shriek.

"Jhett!"

I turn quickly, mostly because she startled me. She has a big smile and a devilish look in her eyes. She comes towards me and we embrace.

"Hello friend," I say, "the weekend is here!"

She takes a seat kitty-corner from me, after ordering a green tea. Each one of our knees is touching. Kia quickly catches me up to speed. She tells me that her parents listed their house for sale this week. After she and her sister moved out of the house, it felt too big and was too hard for her parents to keep up with. Her mom, Misty, is battling some bad arthritis in both knees and in her hands. Her dad, never making it past the first floor because of his bad back has been trying to convince their mom to move for years. Kia's parents are retired and are the oldest of all our parents, as old as some twenty-year-olds' grandparents.

After a few minutes of chatting, Kia's eyes wander to the counter.

"I'm going to grab a quick snack, since I skipped lunch. Do you want anything?"

"No, but thanks, I'm good with this," I say holding up my frothy drink.

As she walks to the counter I watch as she flings her long, shiny brown hair over her shoulder. I have always been envious of her perfectly thick hair. I notice a boy in his late teens look up from clearing a table and watch Kia as she walks past him. Kia is looking in the opposite direction, so she doesn't notice him checking her out. She comes back minutes later with a cranberry orange muffin. It looks and smells amazing. Instead of biting into it, she breaks chunks off.

"So, how's your man?" Kia asks with a questioning look.

"Sai? Good. Um, he's super great," I say, looking up and over to my right.

"He seems so fun! You guys are always doing something or going somewhere. You're so lucky!"

"Yeah-"

"What's wrong with him? Why are you not crazy about him?"

"No, I am. He is so sweet. He seriously is wonderful." I pause. "But, I don't know, maybe it's because he works from home and is always there-"

"Oh, yeah, he's too available." Kia states.

I agree with her and add how even when I go to my apartment, he's there. I tell her how I look forward to changing out of my work clothes, starting the laundry and getting a few chapters in before he comes over. But instead, he's in my apartment playing with Patches, my guinea pig, when I walk in.

"I just need this weekend away to get refreshed and I'm sure it won't be long until I'm missing him. It's just that I miss you guys more!" I laugh.

"Well hell yeah, we used to spend every weekend together," Kia says.

We chat for a while longer about my parents, work, and what we've been up to these last few weeks. We used to catch up weekly. Even if we couldn't see each other on the weekends, we would grab a drink after work on a weeknight to vent. It was rare for us to go more than two weeks without being together. Lately though, those weeks have turned into months.

After finishing our drinks, we head for the exit. Along the way, Kia points to an oil painting of a French Bulldog and says in the most serious voice, "That is the fucking cutest thing I've ever seen."

As she says this, the boy who'd been watching her every move from earlier runs over to hold the door open for us.

"Thanks, hun," she says in a sultry voice and winks at him. Then she tilts her head and flips her hair over her right shoulder. Instantly, his cheeks turn red.

Man, do I love this girl. Always so bold and blunt. I think to myself how I envy her 'don't give a shit about what other people think' attitude, and how it drives the boys wild.

I leave my car in the parking lot and jump into Kia's Jeep. She asks me to check in with the other girls. When I grab my phone, she asks, "When did you get that?"

I turn to her. "I didn't tell you? Sai got it for me."

"Are you fucking serious? He bought you a cell phone? And how long have you been dating, like four months?"

"It's been about six. I'm sorry, I thought I told you. It was only because he got a really good deal on it. Making a provider switch, I think."

"I wish James would buy me a cell phone. All he does is ask me for things. Lazy ass." Kia huffs.

"Is everything okay with you guys?"

"Normal. Shitty. I don't know. I swear he was flirting with the checkout girl at Walmart on Wednesday night. I said, 'you know she will always work here, right? Or some place just as pathetic.' He looked at me like he was disgusted and told ME to stop. He didn't want to fight. He said she was friendly, so he was being nice back. I told him, I know when a bitch is hitting on my man. And to do it right in front of me, she was lucky I didn't punch her in the face." Kia takes a breath.

I look over at her; suddenly she is wound like a jack-in-the-box. I giggle and say, "Sorry I asked." She busts out laughing, which makes me laugh.

As we make a turn, I hear my phone. "I got a text from Danielle; she's at the hotel and has us checked in."

Danielle had called in on a radio contest and won a weekend stay for four in the newly opened Hotel Lotus. It included a few meals at their in-house restaurant and a one hour massage for each guest. We were all beyond pumped to have our hotel paid for, and to get other awesome freebies. That meant more money to spend on shopping, alcohol, spa treatments, or whatever it was we felt like doing.

Danielle and I lived together for two years before I moved out and into the apartment I'm in now, one that is closer to my job and that happened to open up just as I started looking. Before, I was making a forty-minute commute to work. Sai had mentioned just taking a look to see if there'd be something closer. Of course, this benefited him as well. Danielle and I got along perfectly, but I was ready and excited for my own place. I wanted a place that I could call home for more than a year. I had been moving yearly since I was eighteen.

Moving was getting old. Just before driving over to sign the year lease, Sai joked about standing the landlord up and just taking all of my stuff to his place to move in there. I laughed and he followed. Part of me is still wondering if he was serious. We had only been dating for three months.

Shortly after Danielle's text, came Clarissa's.

Clarissa: I'm running late, please don't start the fun until I get there.

When we get close to the hotel, I let them know we are a few minutes away and that as soon as we are all together, the party will start.

Three minutes later I hear a giddy, "We're here!" from Kia.

I look up and see a beautiful building that looks nothing like your typical hotel. It's wide and short in height, maybe

13

only three floors high. The outside is tan stucco with white trim and white columns in the front. The bottom of the main level is a calico of stones. The structure resembles a celebrity's mansion.

The landscaping is immaculate; bright green grass, not a blade out of place, colorful plants and flowers everywhere. Giant ceramic planters line the entrance containing beautiful dark purple plants with long spiky tongues. Flowing around the base of the plant and around the top of the planter are long thin strands of ivy, green and white in color.

As soon as I read the words for valet parking, Kia wrenches the steering wheel, turning it in the opposite direction, my neck snapping around. Young and canny, especially when it comes to how we spend our money, there is no question, I would have done the same. She pulls into a parking space, and we climb out and grab our bags. I try to wheel my bag, forgetting that one wheel is broken. It wobbles and tips to the side, hitting Kia's bag.

"Looks like it's time for a new bag. Maybe you should tell Sai so he can buy you a new one, a nice one." She laughs.

"Ha," I laugh. "I don't need someone taking care of my every problem."

"Really? Because that doesn't sound so bad," Kia says, with an inquisitive glance.

Kia and I walk in and spot Danielle sitting on a couch in the lobby reading a travel magazine. Excitedly, we run over and hug one another. We decide to wait for Clarissa before going to the room, so we can see it together.

I pick up the room keys which are wrapped in a dark blue envelope. Hotel Lotus is written in silver letters across the front, with the image of a lotus flower. I unfold it and the inside reads, 'Executive Lakeside Suite'.

"Oh, sounds fancy!" I say and show the card to Kia. She takes a look then waggles her eyebrows and smiles.

14

We talk about whether we should use our dinner vouchers for tonight or tomorrow. After a few minutes, we settle on using them tonight. We decide to check out the nightclub in the next town over, tomorrow night. It would give us more time to get ready for the club the next night by using our vouchers today.

I notice Kia looking out into the parking lot and from the expression on her face, Danielle's eyes follow and mine trail as well. The three of us watch a young woman wearing a big sun hat walking towards the revolving doors. She has loads of bags. She stops, adjusts and looks up. Although she's wearing big round dark sunglasses, we know it's Clarissa. It looks like she could drop everything all at once but somehow she manages to get everything through the revolving doors. She does it in a way that is smooth, and not awkward at all. A bellhop hurries over to assist her. Clarissa hands over her bags so all that she's left with is her large black designer purse.

Clarissa is used to this sort of thing. She has grown up with money and is accustomed to nice things. To top it off, she is an only child. She's always admitted that her dad, who is someone not to be messed with, spoils her to the point of it being nauseating. She has it all. Clarissa is beautiful and confident, tall with a model-thin body, and the fake boobs to complete any man's dreams; she's the perfect ten.

She catwalks over and asks, "And why aren't we drinking yet?" She pauses then quickly adds, "Waiting for the fun to arrive I imagine." She smirks.

"You staying longer than us?" Kia teases and points to the bellhop loading her luggage onto a cart.

"I like to have what I need." She shrugs.

With purses slung over our arms or backpack-style, we head for the elevator. Once we find our room #300, Danielle waves the card at the door and a green light illuminates. She opens the door, which I can tell is heavy by the shouldering and light grunt she gives, and we all peer in at once. For most of us, this will probably be the nicest hotel room we'll ever stay in. It's huge. We branch off in all directions. The room is bright and twists and turns off into bedrooms and God knows what else. I head straight through to the floor-to-ceiling window to take in the view. Wow, is it pretty. Even though it's only been open for a month, you can tell this place is well kept. A few yards away where the grass ends, starts a sandy beach that leads into the lake; big, dark and beautiful. There's a dock off to the left that goes out into the water. There are canoes, kayaks, paddleboats, and not one, but three pontoons.

I text Sai.

Jhett: This place is beautiful, you should see it!

One of the things I love about Sai is that he understands the beauty in nature. We've been hiking the last few weekends and have seen some truly unique places. We can stand together and stare at a ginormous hundred-year-old tree for twenty minutes without either of us needing to say anything. He seems to enjoy the small things that make our world beautiful, and I really love that about him.

Sai: Glad to hear, send some pics! Tell everyone I say hi!

As I get ready to take a picture of the lake, I hear Kia.

"This room is unreal. I hope we don't get charged for fucking it up." She hollers from one of the bedrooms.

Danielle and I exchange a wide-eyed glance. She turns and looks at Kia who is now in the main area and asks, "How crazy do you plan on getting?"

"You never know." Kia shrugs.

"Well, keep in mind that although the room is free, I had to put my card on file, so please, let's not get too crazy," Danielle says in a serious tone.

Just then there's a knock at the door. Kia opens the door without checking the peephole; something I never do, even if I'm expecting someone. It's Clarissa, holding a stainless-steel bucket overflowing with ice which trails behind her as she walks in. She heads into the bathroom. I walk over to watch

16

what she's doing. She has filled one of the bathroom sinks with two bottles of champagne and a jug of orange juice and is covering them with ice.

Wiping her hands on a towel, she says, "Alright, these will be good in about twenty."

Taking a left out of the bathroom, I walk around a high countertop that has four stools lined beneath it and then head into the open kitchen. It's equipped with a full refrigerator, stove, and microwave. I pop open the fridge and see there's a row of bottled water on one of the shelves; nice touch. I walk back into the main area and stand in front of the windows. There is a dining table with six heavy chairs. Probably won't be using those. Going left is a cozy and intimate living space including a squishy, black leather, L-shaped sofa that looks so inviting I have to sit down. I sink in but not too deep. It's like getting the perfect hug; it has the right amount of pressure. Danielle jumps over the back of the couch landing on her back next to me.

"Thanks for winning this." I tell her. "And thanks for bringing us."

"Of course. Who else would I have invited?" Danielle asks. "You guys were my one and only thought."

I think of suggesting Ben, her boyfriend, but decide against it.

We sit across from a stone fireplace with a huge TV mounted above it. I stare at it. Danielle and I used to spend hours talking into the night about what our future might hold. Most nights our TV wasn't even on.

"Should we go check out the bedrooms?" Danielle asks.

"Yes!" I jump up and follow her into one of the bedrooms. The room is simple and bright and has two queen beds and a full bathroom with big fluffy white towels folded neatly on a rack. Bottles of shampoo, conditioner and body wash are displayed neatly next to the sink. I eye the bottles and notice the brand is of nicer quality then what I use.

We walk back into the main area to find that our bags have just been brought to our room. Clarissa hands a folded ten to the porter. He smiles, accepts the money and takes a small bow, then closes the door behind him.

Bags are grabbed off the cart and without words Kia and Clarissa head to the room that Danielle and I haven't been in. It's the first room on the right as you're first walking into the hotel suite. This room is also bright and massive. There's a king bed with a bench seat at the foot of the bed.

"We'll take this room," Clarissa announces. I assume Kia is sharing the room with her because her bags are already placed on a luggage rack that she must have pulled out and set up while waiting for our bags to arrive. Now it looks as though she is massaging the pillows with her hands. Maybe to check for firmness.

"Yeah, fine with us," I say, looking over at Danielle. She smiles and nods her head.

We carry our bags to our room and head to the living area where Clarissa meets us with mimosas. We make dinner reservations for 6:30pm and plan out our day for tomorrow.

2pm Spa - Manis, pedis, massages; I make a mental note to bring my book, no pedi for me

5pm Get ready - shower, makeup, clothes

7pm Dinner & drinks – restaurant still needs to be determined

9pm Nightclub - Club LuLu

We change into dressier clothes after our drinks and leave the room at 6:15pm. It's an elevator ride down and a short walk to BLU IRIS, a dimly lit dining room with high ceilings. We are seated immediately, and to no surprise, there is a bouquet of irises in the center of our table. Kia reaches out to touch them and grins when she finds out they're real. I look around and notice that each table has a different color; ours are purple. Colored lights change slowly from white to blue, softly showing through the clouded glass walls of the restaurant. Conversations are muffled by the running water that flows into an open trough. A nicely dressed man comes over and introduces himself as Walter, our server. He takes our drink order and returns minutes later with them; he then recites the specials from memory and asks if we have questions. When we say we do not, he bows and tells us he'll give us some time to look over the menu. It's small and lists only eight entrees. This tells me that what they do, they do well. I know this from watching restaurant makeover shows. Usually, the fancier the restaurant the fewer the options.

We place an order of bruschetta to share first. Clarissa orders lobster tail with a side salad and dish of macaroni and cheese. Danielle and Kia order one of the specials; fish tacos with a side of pineapple slaw, and I order a wild rice burger with a side of parmesan fries.

When we are finished with the bruschetta, our waiter comes over holding a tray of shots. Four shots we didn't order.

CHAPTER 2

"These are from the four gentlemen at the bar, ladies," he says.

We all turn at once and notice the men looking our way. They smile; one gives a little wave. We turn back to giggle to each other.

"What is it?" Danielle asks.

"Tequila Blanco, ma'am."

"Yuck, out of all the yummy shots we could take, they bought us tequila? Gross." Danielle whines. "It's my least favorite liquor, unless it's in a margarita."

"Actually, Tequila Blanco is quite smooth," Clarissa says.

"They're free shots, who cares!" Kia yells.

I glance over and see that the men are still watching us. Walter sets the shots down in front of us as Danielle asks, "If we take these, do we have to go over there and thank them?"

Clarissa looks at Walter and bluntly says, "Thank them for us."

He places a small white plate with four quartered limes near the center of the table, nods and turns toward the men.

"Are they watching us?" Danielle asks, her back to them.

"Yes," I say and clear my throat. "Well, what are we waiting for, with an audience or not, let's get it over with."

We each pick up a shot and all at once throw them back. I feel my face scrunch up and quickly get the lime to my mouth, sucking in hard. I don't look but I imagine the men are still watching us and probably laughing at the faces we've just unintentionally made. According to Clarissa, the men turn back around after Walter thanks them.

Our meal arrives and after a few bites, I feel the vibration of my phone. I discreetly try to read a text from Sai.

Sai: How's it going?

Jhett: Really good, out to dinner. I'll call when we go back to the room. Staying in tonight.

A *thumbs-up* emoji comes through in response.

I bring my attention back to the girls and hear Kia and Danielle ask Clarissa about her trip. She has just come back from a two week vacation with her parents in Barbados. She admits that at first, she was upset with her parents for not footing the bill for Max, her boyfriend of a year, to come along. It wasn't that he wasn't invited, because he was, but he could only go if he paid his way.

It turns out Clarissa met a local guy, Alejandro, on the second day, who she said was the sexiest man alive. So, she dropped her pouty attitude and started to enjoy herself. He took her all around the city during the day, and in the evening, he took her dancing in the local clubs. They spent all night laughing and flirting. She told us that he had kissed her one night and she kissed him back. None of us were surprised by this. If he was as appealing as she let on, I think we all would have been tempted by this man.

"It was all that happened and it's unlikely I'll ever see him again," she said. "But I won't be telling Max. It'll only create trust issues between us." She looks around at each of us as if asking for our silence.

Max was already the jealous type, so their relationship would be over if he ever found out. She had only been back in the States for two days and spent the entire forty-eight hours with Max at his apartment.

Clarissa has just finished her third year at Carroll University. It's where her mom went to college. She's majoring in business management. Her father's a lawyer and her mother, who worked less than a year before having

Clarissa, became a stay-at-home mom at the age of twenty-one, and pushes Clarissa to go into law like her father.

I'd always been good at visiting Clarissa on the weekends, usually once a month, or we'd meet for coffee when she'd come home. This last semester we were both so busy we weren't able to get together. So, in the past six months, we've only texted or sent silly pictures a handful of times each month.

Danielle looks at me. "How are things with Sai?"

"Things are good. He's a really good guy," I say.

"Still in the honeymoon stage?" She teases.

"I guess you could say that," I say. "We spend all of our time together. In the perfect scenario, I'd have more time by myself. Maybe just one afternoon a week to sit in a café and read my book while sipping a cappuccino. I feel the need for more girl time too," I say with a smile.

"Oh, I could always go for more girl time!" Danielle says brightly.

"Same! Let's promise to have at least one girls' weekend a year for the rest of our lives." Kia suggested.

"You know, I'm all for that, but what happens if one of us moves away?" Clarissa questions. We all pause and wait. "There's a possibility I'll go on to grad school."

I look at Clarissa a little stunned, about to ask for more details, but I stop when I hear someone clearing their throat.

"Excuse me, ladies?"

We turn and look; two of the men from the bar have come over to our table.

"Hi, I'm Jack. This is Roo," he says, placing a hand on his friend's shoulder.

They look to be in their late twenties or early thirties. They both stand about six feet tall and have a strong build.

"We heard Rio's rooftop bar just opened for the season. We're headed there for a few drinks." He pauses, I think to read us. We stare quietly and just watch him waiting. "The place is fun, great atmosphere; if you've never been you should check it out," he says with a nice smile and little nod. "It's right down the road."

I have heard of Rio's. My brother Beck has been there; it was one of the stops for his bachelor party. He raved about how fun it was, and I know they normally have bands on the weekends.

"Do they have a band tonight?" I ask.

"Not sure, but probably. You should think about coming down, you'll have fun."

"Yeah, maybe." I look around the table, the girls nodding like they might be up for it. "And thanks for the shots." I smile.

"Anytime. We hope to see you down there," Jack says. Then they turn and walk back to the bar.

"Well, what do you guys think?" I ask, feeling intrigued.

"All I know is that I don't want to be hungover for my massage tomorrow." Danielle states.

"I agree, but maybe we could go to check it out, stay an hour, and then come back early." Kia offers.

"I've always wanted to check it out, the place sounds fun." Clarissa adds.

"Okay, so let's go." And just like that, it's settled.

The air is light and cool so we each bring a thin jacket for the short walk to Rios. On the way, we agree to only stay until 10pm. We know all too well that once the night gets started, it can quickly turn into a drink-too-much, dancing-until-bar-close type of night. Then there goes most of Saturday either hungover, tired or both. We have too much planned for tomorrow to get carried away tonight. As for the weather, it's an unusually warm evening for the seventeenth of May in Wisconsin. The days can be in the 60-70s but it can drop to freezing at night. I check my weather app and it tells me that it's 62 degrees.

24

We can see the bar as soon as we turn the corner off the main road. Bright neon letters that read *Rio's*. Outside looks inviting, the type of place that draws people in.

It's loud and I can feel the beat of the music thump in my chest as I hand my ID to the bouncer. There's a small table open in the corner. We head towards it.

"Do you see the guys?" Kia asks over the loud music.

"They're probably on the rooftop," Clarissa says pointing to the ceiling. "Let's grab drinks and go up."

There are three large glass containers that resemble mason jars on the back of the bar. Only these look two feet tall and are filled with fruit and something else that I would imagine is mint or some other green edible. A small chalkboard leaning up against them reads, Blackberry Mojito, Apple Cranberry Vodka and Passionfruit Mango Vodka. A short blonde bartender with dreads down to her butt tells us they're made in-house and very popular; she can help us decide mix-ins if that's what we want.

I go with the blackberry mojito, something I've never tried before. It's served in a regular-sized mason jar. Chunks of the fruit and mint leaves sit at the bottom of my glass. I take a sip and notice some of it comes through the straw. I nervously swallow because I'm not sure what else to do.

Clarissa orders a local beer, Danielle gets a fruity drink, and Kia gets a vodka cranberry.

Together we climb the stairs. Once on the rooftop, we see the guys. They immediately wave us over, which I think we all appreciate because it's a little awkward searching for a seat when everyone in the crowded bar turns and stares. The foursome are seated at a patio set with a mishmash of different seats; some resemble couches that fit three and the others smaller, fitting two.

There is enough room for us but we have to intermingle between them. This makes sense to me because how often do you see three guys sitting closely on a couch when there are open seats around them? This way we will be sitting boy, girl, boy, girl. Clarissa confidently plops between the two men on the couch as if they are old friends.

"Hi, I'm Clarissa. Kia, Jhett, and Danielle." She points to each of us.

Without skipping a beat, Jack, who is sitting to her right, pipes up and says, "Mick, Graham, and Roo."

"Welcome ladies. Are you on a girls' weekend or having a bachelorette party?" It's Graham talking now, and I notice he's the only one with a wedding band.

A waitress comes over with a tray of bottled beers. She sets them down next to their nearly empty ones.

"Girls' weekend, we have one every year." Danielle tells them. "I won a stay at the hotel, so that's why we're here."

"Well lucky us I guess; we picked the right weekend," says Jack. "We're here to fish. We all live within two hours of here, so it's a nice meeting spot. We aren't staying at the hotel though; we just go there for the food. We're staying at that motel." He points up the road and we see what resembles a typical motel.

We slowly break off into conversations with the guy we're seated next to. I'm next to Mick. He tells me he was in the military for six years and now he works in his uncle's garage fixing vehicles. He's easy to listen to; he's charming and has a likable personality. He has a girlfriend named Rose that he's been with for three years and they've just moved in together.

"What about you, do you have a boyfriend?"

"Oh my gosh, I am so sorry, I'll be right back." I grab my purse and run down the stairs, heading for the exit. My heart is beating rapidly in my chest. I take my phone out and call Sai. He picks up right away. I apologize while trying to walk away from the bar as quickly as I can. The noise is making it hard to hear him.

"Where are you? Is everything okay?" I hear worry in his voice.

I wonder if I should have thought this conversation through before calling. I'm mad that I stupidly panicked. Sai is a worrier and doesn't like when I go out without him. I don't want to tell him about the guys because it will only make him worry more. I also don't want to lie.

"We're at Rio's. Remember that bar Beck talked about? The one he went to a few weeks before he and Morgan got married?"

"I thought you weren't going out tonight?" It comes out like a question.

"It's a block from the hotel…we all wanted to check it out. We aren't staying long, just one drink." I hear myself and I feel pathetic. I'm out with the girls and we made friends, big deal. But I know it won't seem that way to him. I remind myself to keep things short and simple. "Everything's okay," I say.

I feel a hand on my shoulder, it's Kia. I flash her the screen so she can see it's Sai. I hold up one finger to let her know it'll just be a minute. After convincing Sai we will head back to the hotel soon and promise to text as soon as I'm in bed, he accepts and we say goodbye.

Kia looks at me but doesn't say anything.

"I forgot to call. He was worried and was hoping we were still at the hotel restaurant. He's a little protective at times; it normally doesn't bother me," I say, feeling a little bummed out.

"You're still allowed to have fun. You know that right? You can talk to the opposite sex without something bad happening."

"I know. It's a good thing he doesn't know what happened on Clarissa's Barbados trip, because if he had heard that, I'm sure we would still be on the phone and I'd be walking back to the hotel."

Together we laugh as we make our way back to the group. A heat lamp nearby has been turned on. As soon as I feel the heat, I realize how cool it's gotten. Then I notice a full drink

27

next to my almost gone mojito. I feel eyes on me. It's Mick, his smile hesitant. He motions for me and pats the seat I'd frantically left earlier. I assume he has figured out why I left in such a hurry.

"Yes, to answer your question. Boyfriend, his name is Sai. We've been together six months."

We continue chatting. Halfway into my next drink I start to feel comfortable and know the alcohol has helped calm me down. I look around to see Jack and Clarissa giggling about something, their bodies turned towards each other. Kia, Danielle, Roo and Graham all look to be in deep conversation. Graham is telling a story.

We finish our drinks just before 11pm. By now, we've each had a number of drinks and it's apparent that everyone is pretty relaxed. Conversation is flowing and any onlookers would think we were pre-established friends. We've found out the guys are in their late twenties. Mick is the only one with a girlfriend and Graham is the only one married. Jack manages to mention that he and Roo are single more than once. After a while, it becomes a joke and he gets teased by the other guys.

They offer to get another round but we decline and let them know it's time for us to go back. The guys get up when we do and tell us they will walk us back. We almost too cheerfully accept their offer.

We're just out of the parking lot of Rio's when Kia shouts. "We should go in the hot tub when we get back!"

"Oh, we should, it will feel so nice. You guys should join us," Clarissa says confidently, looking back to Jack who is walking directly behind her. He gives her a slow pleased smile in return.

There's no way the guys would pass up the chance of joining us in the hot tub. They decided we could walk the last two hundred feet to our hotel by ourselves so they could run back to theirs to grab their suits.

It's not fifteen minutes later and they are at our hotel. If it would have been the other way around, we wouldn't have returned for an hour. Checking ourselves in the mirror again and again, squeezing red eye relief drops into our eyes and packing a change of dry clothes. Clarissa gets a text from Jack, forcing us to leave our room shortly after putting on our suits to head for the lobby. But before we reach the guys, I send Sai a text.

Jhett: All tucked in, gn, <3
Seconds later.
Sai: I love you. Be safe. Call me when you wake.

Glass is not allowed in the pool area so I grabbed eight waters from the fridge and threw them into a small cooler. I'm happy they were provided; we still might have a chance at feeling okay tomorrow. The pool area is open until midnight, leaving us with just less than an hour. There's a wide walkway of big round smooth stones that lead us to the pool. I have never been in or even seen an infinity pool in person before, so seeing this one makes me feel giddy. It really does look as though the pool is open on one end and the water just drops off over the side like a waterfall.

We claim a table by draping our clothes over it as we undress and remove our sandals. The guys being guys, whip off their shirts and jump in without a moment's hesitation; Roo doing a cannonball, Jack and Mick doing a shallow dive and Graham taking a simple hop off the side of the pool.

"I thought we came to use the hot tub," Danielle says.

"Look at this pool," says Jack. "How do you not want to come in? And...I think it's heated." He moves his arms around under the water. "It feels great, come in!"

An outdoor pool in May, in Wisconsin; it has to be heated. The four of us walk over and sit near the edge of the pool, dipping our legs into the water. It feels like warm bathwater. I like sitting here; it's peaceful and quiet. We have the entire area to ourselves. I can hear frogs, crickets and katydids in the distance, and here we are able to hear each other without straining.

I'm broken out of my relaxed trance when I hear Graham ask how we all know each other. He's looking at me. I start with how Kia and I met in the Girl Scouts.

"We went to different schools but we were both in the fourth grade. It wasn't until we were older that we discovered our schools were rivals! This made high school sports more interesting," I say and Kia smiles fondly.

"We convinced boys from each other's schools to take us as their prom dates so we could be at each other's prom. We traded prom dresses too, so we didn't have to wear the same one twice. I told them how once when Kia's school had their pep rally for Homecoming, I dressed as their school mascot and no one but her knew it was me."

Danielle jumps in to share how we met through a mutual friend that introduced us at her Halloween party. We thought it was a hilarious coincidence that we both dressed in all black like Sandy from Grease. We quickly became friends and soon found we had a lot in common. A few months later, we were both looking for a roommate so that's when we got an apartment together; it was as simple as that.

Clarissa and I had met two years ago. I babysat for a family that lived in the same neighborhood as Clarissa. Their oldest son was graduating from high school and I had gone to his graduation party. Clarissa was there with her parents. We were the only twenty-year-olds amongst fifty high schoolers. We talked briefly and went our separate ways. A week later, I saw her volunteering at the humane society. She was getting ready to walk one of my favorite dogs, which was the reason I was there. I went over to say hi and she asked me to join her. Later, she admitted that her being there to 'volunteer' was not her idea. She had a few hours of community service to complete. At the mention of this, the guys perk up.

"What did you do?" Jack asks excitedly.

"I caught my freshman roommate stealing from me, so I punched her in the face. Once for taking my stuff and then a second time because she had recently asked my boyfriend out behind my back. Before that, I had considered her a friend. I'd never do anything like that now, but she had it coming." Clarissa says it as if she has no shame. "Besides the community service, I also got a fine, but that was no big deal. My dad paid it."

"Oh, Daddy's girl huh?" Jack asks.

"Yep, only child," Clarissa says, as if she's bragging. She stands up and all eyes follow. "I'm going in the hot tub, who's coming?"

We all stand and make our way to the pool.

"Are those pontoons?" Graham asks.

The walkway leading down to the water has less lighting, making it hard to see the pontoons that are a bit in the distance.

"You bet they are!" Danielle says grinning.

"What are you girls doing tomorrow?" Not giving us time to respond, Graham continues. "We should rent a pontoon and go to that bar just off the edge of Kippers Island."

I've never heard of this bar, but I've never really spent much time around here.

"We don't really have any morning plans; we could probably go in the morning and still get back in time for our spa appointments," Kia says.

We agree, and I smile. I'm excited to know that we'll see these guys again. Spending the last five hours with them unexpectedly has made our night pretty enjoyable. It makes me feel like there's no way that tomorrow can be anything but fun. And sometimes, just flirting, knowing it won't cause any harm, is kind of exhilarating.

As we soak in the hot tub laughing, the guys tell embarrassing stories about each other. But soon enough, it's creeping on midnight and we know that the pool area is about to close. We're not getting kicked out, but hotel staff show up and patiently wait around until we pick up our things and leave. The guys walk us to the lobby, we confirm our pontoon plans for tomorrow, say goodnight and part ways.

There's small talk and tipsy giggles about the guys on the way to the room. It seems as though everyone is happy about our new friends. Once back in our room, I head into the bathroom to do my nighttime routine. I drink a second bottle of water and swallow a Tylenol just to be safe. I climb into bed and the moment my head hits the pillow I fall asleep.

CHAPTER 3

When I open my eyes, it takes me a few seconds to remember where I am. Eyes dry, I see a circle of drool on my pillow. I flip the pillow over and check my phone to see 8:06am. I feel groggy, but I know I won't be able to fall back to sleep. I wake up before 6am for work five days a week, so I know it's no use to fight habit and try to fall back asleep.

I notice that I forgot to charge my phone last night, or early this morning rather; I plug it in and look over to see Danielle still asleep. Quietly, I get up and go into the bathroom to splash water on my face. My hair is a mess and my skin looks blotchy. But I don't really care how I look right now, so I head to the kitchen. The coffee machine is on and Clarissa is at the counter with a cup of black coffee. She's scrolling through her phone.

"Morning. Is there any creamer?" I ask, opening three cupboard doors before finding the coffee mugs.

"The gross powdered kind. It's next to the sugar in the drawer just below. It's really good coffee though, if you can drink it black."

"Thanks. Anything good?" I gesture to her phone.

"A girl from my high school, married this military guy just after we graduated; they're pregnant with triplets."

"Ugh, let's hope they wanted a big family."

She puts her phone down, arches her back in a stretch and says, "Yeah, I hope I have one at a time." She cradles her coffee between her hands and takes a sip from the steaming mug. "Remind me, how did you and Sai meet again? Sorry for not remembering."

33

"It's fine." I laugh. "We go to the same gym. I had seen him a few times, but we never really made eye contact. Then I saw him at the cancer foundation 5k I do every September, the one in Falls. He recognized me and came over to say hi. While we were talking, it started sprinkling. He offered me his umbrella, and that's how it all began."

"Such a gentleman. How old is he?"

This is the most common question I get about our relationship. I don't know if it's because it's a normal question people generally ask, or if it's because they can tell Sai is much older than me and it piques their interest.

"He's thirty-three." I wait for her response.

Clarissa's face doesn't change. If she's judging me, she's doing a good job concealing it.

"So, that would make him eleven years older."

"Correct. But you know what they say, men take longer to mature, so I've found one that's at my same level." I shrug.

I taste my coffee. Clarissa, as ever, has impeccable taste; the coffee is delicious. I skipped the creamer and went for straight sugar.

Clarissa asks, "Would you like to see a picture of Alejandro? I was looking at his profile before you came in."

"Of course I do!" I grab her phone. He's hot. He's downright sexy. "Whoa." I swipe through a few more photos. "Did you ask him to come back with you? I would have."

"If only it were that easy. Besides, what would I do with Max? In a perfect world, I'd keep them both," she says grinning.

I run my fingers through my hair. "So, about grad school…are you planning on going somewhere out of state?"

"I'm not sure yet; I like to keep my options open. I'll finish out at Carroll for sure, then maybe go to UCLA, if I get accepted." She exhales deeply and looks at me.

Just the thought of one of us not being close by seems unreal. I know we can't make life decisions based on

34

friendships, but I feel like I need these girls, and I've always felt that they needed me. I'm not about to rain on her parade, though, so I smile. "Well, you know I'd come visit."

"What are you guys doing up so early?" We hear Kia calling from inside the bedroom.

"Sorry Your Highness, are we disturbing you?" Clarissa shouts back.

"I feel like shit, why do you both look and sound like you're fine?" Kia whines and is now standing slouched in the doorway.

"Um, because we are?" Clarissa raises her eyebrows. We didn't drink that much last night. Amateur."

"Yeah, okay, you drunk." Kia half-smiles.

"It is true, the more often you drink, the less severe the hangover," Clarissa says seriously. "I'm going to go put makeup on so I look halfway decent for breakfast. One of you should go wake Danielle so we have time to get ready before meeting the guys."

The food is set up buffet style. First, we see a table of beverages with five different kinds of juice, including something green and thick that is probably healthy but I imagine smells terrible. Kia goes for it. There's also a complete coffee bar. This one has flavored creamers and syrups. I take an orange juice and pour myself another cup of coffee and add hazelnut creamer. I follow Clarissa, who points to the back of the room.

The back doors are open and there are a few cast-iron tables unoccupied. It's bright and sunny. We take a table with four chairs. We set our drinks down and head back in to get food. I start by grabbing a handful of napkins; I almost always spill. The buffet line starts with eggs; I take a poached egg with hollandaise sauce, Clarissa takes a mini quiche, Danielle scoops scrambled eggs with bacon and onions onto her plate and Kia gets into line behind a woman to have an omelette made. Then come the meats. There are thinly sliced pieces of ham, steak, bacon and sausage links.

The smells make my stomach growl and my mouth has been watering since we walked in. There are a variety of fruits in a tiered basket and mixed fruit salad in individual cups. Next is bread, oatmeal, English muffins, rolls with butter, jam and honey and finally the pastry table which has scones, muffins, glazed donuts and something that looks like a homemade granola bar, Kia goes for this too. By now our plates are overflowing.

We eat until we are stuffed. Groaning, we slowly make our way back to our room. Kia goes off to shower; Clarissa and Danielle go into the living area, and I go to lie down. I reach for my phone. I know Sai is expecting a call but I don't have the energy right now. Instead, I text.

Jhett: GM, how was your night?

Sai: It was ok, I miss you. Did you just get up?

Jhett: I've been up for a bit, we just had the best breakfast! Miss you too. What are your plans for the day?

Sai: Workout…and not much else. Pretty pathetic Saturday.

Jhett: You should go on a hike. It's a beautiful day, get some sun!

Sai: Yeah maybe I will. Your plans?

Jhett: Beach, spa, dinner and club.

Sai: Which club?

Jhett: There's only one, Club LuLu.

I know Sai will be thinking of me all day, and it will probably drive him crazy to know we are going to a club.

Jhett: I'll text later, I need to get ready so the girls don't leave w/out me. Love you!

Sai: I love you, don't have too much fun without me!

A shower might refresh me, but I know I'll want one after my massage so I skip it. I don't want to do my hair and makeup twice, not that I wear much. I comb through my hair and throw it into a pony. After swiping on some mascara, I go into the living space. Danielle was smart and thought to call ahead to book a pontoon; there was only one left. Kia and Clarissa pack a small cooler of alcoholic drinks and a few waters. We grab our beach bags and head down to the lake. Looking for the guys, we spot them near the dock talking with hotel staff, getting instructions, I presume.

"Ladies!" Jack shouts, and waves to us.

All the guys look up and grin. We smile back and wave. They have a cooler three times the size of ours. I wonder if it's only filled with booze, and moreover, if we're safe with these guys we've just met. I take a second to gauge how I'm feeling. My gut's not yelling at me, and they're most likely harmless. I'd taken a self-defense class a year out of high school so I feel a sense of confidence.

"You ready?" Mick asks. "You look like you zoned out there for a sec."

I feel embarrassed; everyone is on the pontoon but me. "Yeah, let's go!" I smile and climb on.

Roo is driving and takes us on a ride around the lake. It's sixty-eight degrees and getting warmer but as we cruise the air feels cool and fresh. It takes about twenty minutes to get to Bob's, the bar off Kippers Island. As we get near, we can see there are two boats and four pontoons already there.

"Ladies, are we okay with dropping the anchor a few feet out just to float for a while before docking up?" asks Roo and we all nod.

Mick grabs the anchor and drops it slowly once Roo kills the motor and we slow to a stop. There are few clouds in the sky and a light warm breeze but the sun feels comforting on my skin. There's room on the pontoon seats to sit back and lounge. I remove my t-shirt so I'm wearing my swimsuit top and jeans shorts. Danielle does the same and Kia and Clarissa strip down to their suits.

The guys have already pulled off their shirts, Jack and Mick before we even stopped. My eyes skim over their nice bodies. Mick is the tallest and the most muscular, probably from his time in the military. Graham has a farmer's tan, pretty blue eyes, and light brown hair. Roo is the tannest, has big arms and nice hazel eyes. Jack has brown eyes, a strong jawline and confidence, making him the typical ladies' man; tall, dark and handsome.

I look down at my legs, they are embarrassingly pale. I've only worn shorts twice this Spring when Sai and I hiked through the dimly-lit woods. I look around, nobody seems to be blinded by my complexion.

I catch Jack looking at Clarissa. We all stare at Clarissa from time to time. When I do, it's usually because I'm imagining having a body that perfect. She eats and drinks what she wants, doesn't exercise aside from a nightly walk, and yet she doesn't have an ounce of fat or a hint of cellulite. And she's the oldest of us girls, so, we can't even tease it will catch up with her. She's tan from her vacation, and her body looks photoshoot ready, so I can't blame him for staring. She fluffs out a towel until it's just right, laying it on the floor of the pontoon and settles onto the middle of it. Kia, Danielle and I are sitting with our legs stretched out.

"Ladies, a beer?" Roo offers, holding two choices.

"I'll have a Spotted Cow," Clarissa says.

He pops the top before handing it off. The rest of us pass, holding our water.

"Maybe after this," I say, and give him a playful look.

"Well, aren't you all responsible," Jack says.

"They are, and they bring me when they're ready for fun." Clarissa smiles.

"So, some fishing trip?" Kia says.

"We went this morning actually. We did okay," Mick says, looking pleased. "Some decent brook trout."

"We're going again this afternoon. Might try a different lake this time," Jack adds.

"Does one of you own a boat, or are you charter fishing?" Clarissa asks.

"Graham brought his boat," Jack says, speaking for him.

After a half-hour of small talk, beer-drinking, and sunbathing, we notice a few more boats coming in, so we decide it's time to dock before there aren't any spots left. I decide it's time for some sunscreen. I take out the tube and rub it into my arms, legs and face. I hand the bottle to Kia and ask her to put some on my back and shoulders. She does, and I do the same for her. She tosses the bottle to Danielle.

"You don't really need to wear sunscreen, do you? With that gorgeous skin of yours," Clarissa asks Danielle.

"I can still burn. I won't get red, but my skin will still peel if I get too much sun," Danielle says.

"Can I ask, what's your ethnic background?" Jack inquires.

"My mom is Filipino and my dad is European."

Her skin is golden brown. She comes over to sit in front of me, and I rub the lotion where she can't reach. When I'm done, she hands off the tube to Clarissa who sits up, moves her hair from her shoulders and hands the tube to Jack.

"Will you get my back?" she asks with a sultry voice.

Kia, Danielle and I all look at each other. I whisper, "She's asking for trouble." They smile and nod.

Once docked, we climb out of the pontoon and head to Bob's. It's a bar with only three walls. Where the fourth wall would be, it's left completely exposed, facing the boaters so that it's very inviting as we walk up the beach. There are swings hanging from the ceiling on one end of the bar; I'm a bit disappointed to see these are all taken. Solid wooden stools line up next to each other, each in a different bright color. My eyes jump from the colorful flower pots to the hanging baskets, reminding me of the garden at my grandma's house, the one I used to help her with every Spring. I wander around the corner to check it out. This would be where most bar patrons would be coming into the bar if they did not come in off the beach. There are dragonflies and hummingbirds drinking from feeders. After a minute, I feel Kia grab my hand and pull me towards the bar.

"What can I get for you lovely ladies?" asks the middle-aged male bartender.

"Two piña coladas please," Kia says sweetly.

Walking back down to the beach, I see Danielle and Clarissa, each with a drink in hand. The guys are laying out a big blanket and a beach umbrella, something we did not think to bring. Mick and Roo carry the cooler over and set it near the blanket. Roo grabs beers from the cooler and passes them around. We join them on the blanket and sip our drinks, watching as people come and go.

Roo takes a seat next to me. He leans over and says, "Tell me something about yourself."

"Hmm." I try to think of something. "You go first," I say.

He thinks. "Well, I love reptiles. All animals, really, but reptiles are at the top. Snakes were my favorite as a kid. When I was ten my parents let me get a corn snake. His name was Ralph."

"Interesting. How long did you have Ralph?"

"Well," he sighs. "My dad died when I was twelve, so my mom had to sell our house and we had to move to an apartment. Ralph couldn't come with us. Not because he wasn't allowed, but because we didn't have the room or money to take care of him."

"Oh," I say quietly. "I'm sorry, about your dad and Ralph. It must have been terrible losing your dad at such a young age, and then having to give up your snake."

"It's okay, corn snakes are very docile and easy to care for. A kid from my class was happy to take him."

"Did you still get to see him?"

"I did," he says smiling, "I visited him a few times the next year. He lived in my friend's basement. I used to think Ralph remembered me, but then at the end of the school year my mom moved me and my brother again, and I never saw him

40

again after that. I was mad at my mom for a long time for moving us. Not only for making me give up Ralph, but because I had friends and did well in sports. We moved to a huge school. I didn't go out for football again because I knew that even if I made the team, I wouldn't be starting. And after starting every game the past two years at my previous school, it would have been impossible for me to just stand by on the sidelines waiting for the coach to call my name."

"Did you go out for any other sports?"

"I did play baseball. I made the varsity team my freshman year."

"So, you have some good memories," I say, trying to sound optimistic. "What position did you play?"

"I played shortstop all four years. And yes, I eventually stopped being mad at my mom when I made some new friends.

"I'm glad there was something good that came from you having to move and start at a new school," I say and he smiles. "You know, this makes me think of something. When I was in elementary school, I was a huge tomboy. The boys always played football at recess. I wanted to play with them, and they let me. I happened to be good enough that when we picked for teams, I'd get picked right away. I loved it. I asked my mom if I could play, to join the actual football team, but she wouldn't let me. 'I would get hurt' she'd say. Even though I was the same size as the boys in my class. I was mad for a long time because I knew I would have done well." I laugh. "I still love a good game of football...or almost any sport, for that matter. I have a competitive nature."

"Come on, let's go to that part of the beach," he says elbowing me gently and motioning to an open area, his tone enthusiastic.

"Why?" I ask curiously.

"There's a frisbee under one of the pontoon seats. Let's play!"

"Okay!" I say grinning. "Hey, who wants to play some frisbee?" I ask everyone on the blanket.

Clarissa and Jack join. They stand up holding their beers, and grab another for the walk over. Kia and Danielle are stretched out on the blanket, looking too comfortable to move. Roo runs to retrieve the Frisbee, and I run to the bar to get another piña colada for me and Kia.

We join up and walk to the open area. We take a few minutes to warm up, and it's a good thing because we all have a few crazy throws.

"So, do we want to make this interesting?" Roo asks, looking at the three of us.

"Of course we do," Clarissa says.

"We're a team," he says pointing at himself and then me, "and you're a team," he says, pointing at Clarissa and Jack. "Whichever team catches more passes after one minute, chooses which shot the opposing team buys them. We'll flip for who goes first.

Jack and Clarissa go first. A timer is set, and after one minute they have fourteen caught passes.

"We can do this!" Roo shouts across the sand between us.

I nod and give him a thumbs up. Clarissa gives us a countdown and starts the timer. We're off to a great start, but miss a few passes in an attempt to beat their number, so we get sloppy. I slow down my pace and Roo matches it. We start catching our passes again, and as we near the end we finally beat their number. Moments later, the timer rings; we've caught seventeen passes.

"What shot would you like, partner?" Roo jogs over to me, putting his hand up for a high five.

"How about a Kamikaze," I say, not wanting to pick something too girly.

"Perfect!" He turns towards Jack and Clarissa. "Well losers, our shots please." Roo waves a hand towards them.

Jack and Clarissa run off towards the bar, not bothered at all that they just lost. This is how I know I'm competitive. I would have yelled, 'best of three', the moment our number was beat.

"Nice work," Roo says giving me a playful smile. "I knew we'd win."

"Oh, I would have put money down on us," I say confidently.

Soon, we see Jack and Clarissa coming back holding the shots and laughing. Anyone looking at them would assume they were a couple. They are both beautiful people. Together they could walk the red carpet, or attend a yacht party full of celebrities, and nobody would know they weren't famous. Roo and I cheers, take the shots, and when we're finished I ask to play a round of boys versus girls.

This time Clarissa and I lose. The guys request shots of tequila. We oblige, but we're cruel and don't bring back limes. It doesn't stop them from taking the shots. We play a few more rounds, mixing up the teams. By the end, Clarissa and I have each taken three shots, and the guys, four. We walk back to the blanket to see snacks have been taken out of the cooler. I am so glad for this. Kia, Danielle, Graham and Mick are snacking on cheese and crackers, fruit and nuts. I take a water and drink half of it, and then take a handful of nuts and the bag of string cheese.

"Wow, what happened to you guys?" Danielle asks.

"What?" Clarissa responds, a bit snappy.

"You all look drunk; you were only gone for like an hour," Kia says, sticking up for Danielle.

"We had a few shots," Jack says holding his hands up theatrically, and all at once Roo, Clarissa, and I all burst out laughing.

"Guess we had to be there," Kia says in a mocking tone.

"I think we should be getting back soon. Would it be okay to wrap things up in the next fifteen minutes?" Danielle asks, looking at Graham.

He nods. He's clearly sober, and told us he would drive the pontoon back. They continue talking, but I zone out. My body feels light and heavy at the same time. I know I drank a lot of alcohol; I can feel it in my head. I'm relaxed and I love it here. I don't want to leave. I could come back with Sai. I shoot him a text.

Jhett: Just played some awesome games of frisbee on the beach. You should have seen me, I was on fire!

Sai: I bet you were, you're good at everything. Nice day huh?

Jhett: Gorgeous, love it here. Bring me back here PLEASE!

Sai: Are you drinking?

Jhett: Yes. Why?

Sai: I can just tell. What beach are you at?

Jhett: Can't remember, but the bar is called Bob's. We rented a pontoon to get here. We are heading back soon so we're not late for our appt's!

Sai: Enjoy the spa! I Love you!

Jhett: You too!

We start to gather everything up and head back to the pontoon. As soon as everyone's on, I walk to the front of the pontoon and loudly announce, "Everyone, look here!" I hold up my phone, everyone clumps together and smiles. I make sure to get Bob's in the background and snap the picture. I look it over; it's perfect, everyone smiling beautifully. I give a thumbs up and then stumble slightly from the movement of the pontoon and take a seat. I turn my body so that my legs are outstretched on the pontoons bench seat. Roo walks over and asks if he can join me. I tell him of course, but instead of sitting at the edge where the seat is open, he picks up my legs and scoots close to me, resting my legs down over his lap. There's a thrill of excitement that zips through my body at him touching my bare legs. It feels intimate. He rests his hands on my knees comfortably like we've known each other for a long time. I don't mind though, because the touch is comforting. He's kind and fun and very good looking. I'm finding that I like his company.

The ride back goes by quickly and before I know it, everyone's unloading.

"So, what are you ladies doing for dinner tonight?" Jack asks. His main focus is on Clarissa. "We have some fish we can cook up?"

Clarissa starts to answer, "We would-"

Kia cuts her off. "Thanks, but we're going to a pizza place called Basilico."

Danielle adds, "Their pizzas are made in a wood fire oven and the owners are from Italy. They've won a bunch of awards."

"When did we decide this?" Clarissa asks, sounding irritated.

"When we were at the beach. We met this nice couple that told us about it while you were off playing your game," Kia says in a somewhat bitchy tone.

"Okay well, we have your number, so why don't we text you later tonight. Maybe we can all meet back up?" I suggest.

"Crisis averted." Danielle whispers in my ear.

"Yeah, that's a great idea," Jack says, his hand out for us as we hop down from the pontoon.

"It's been a fun morning, ladies; we'll catch up later." Graham waves from the pontoon.

Roo and I lock eyes. He smiles and gives a light wave in only my direction. Without alcohol in my body I know I'd blush. I look away and catch the girls watching us, but because I've been drinking, I feel confident and I don't care who's watching. I turn back, smile, and wink before I turn my back and start up the walkway.

CHAPTER 4

We check-in at the spa and are shown to the changing area. Over by the sinks are five full-sized hair products; under the counter, placed in labeled baskets, are a hairdryer, a curling iron, and a straightener. We follow the polite woman giving us the tour to the small indoor pool and hot tub.

"When you are ready, your nail specialists will meet you here." She points to lounge chairs next to a small table, smiles, and bows before she walks out.

There's nothing for us to get ready for, so we take a seat and wait a few minutes until four women walk in and introduce themselves to us. After introductions, we follow them to a room with massage chairs.

One of the women walks over and holds out a drinks menu. "Can I get anyone a complimentary drink before we begin?"

I've been drinking water since we've come back from the island. I feel like my head is just about clear again. There are non-alcoholic choices at the top followed by several wine options.

Danielle asks, "Are any of these wines sweet?"

"It would be either the Pink Moscato or the White Zinfandel, ma'am."

I don't know much about wine, but Danielle and Kia order the Moscato so I go for it too, hoping I like it. Clarissa orders Chardonnay. Her parents are big wine drinkers, and I know she's been drinking it for years.

One of the women, Maria, beckons me to sit down.

"Oh, I will only be having a manicure because of my toe injury," I say and point to my foot. "I'm so sorry, I didn't think to cancel my appointment."

"Don't worry about it," she replies and shakes her head. She smiles genuinely and asks if there's anything else she can do before she leaves.

The woman who took our drink order returns with mini bottles of wine and gracefully hands them to us. I take a sip and am shocked by how much I like it.

"This is really good!"

"My mom drinks wine all the time," Danielle says examining her bottle. "I try it every so often and I'm usually disgusted. She told me that I should start sweet and eventually I'll be drinking dry like her. We'll see, but this is pretty damn good!"

"I'll be in the pool area. Can you come get me when it's time for our manicures?" I ask, holding up my book.

The girls are called over to their spots. They each take a seat and drop their feet into the water. I slip out, walking back to the pool area and sit in the comfy chair, pulling my legs in. Peaceful music is playing very low so that it's not distracting. I consider calling Sai, but quickly decide against it; I'm feeling more relaxed than I have in months and I have a feeling his questions would only bring me down. I open my book and start to read, when a thin piece of paper drops out. It's a note in Sai's handwriting, and it's written in Hindi, his native language.

Tum mere lie bahut maayane rakhate ho, main tumhaare baare mein gaharaee se paravaah karata hoon

Love, Sai

I smile. He's sweet. I reach into my small canvas bag and pull out my silenced phone. This isn't the first time he's left me a note to be deciphered. I look up the translation:

'You mean a lot to me, I care deeply about you.'

I need to tell him how thoughtful this was; after we're done here. I'm not ready to give up this alone time. I continue to read uninterrupted until Maria comes to get me. I join back up with the girls, taking a seat next to Kia.

"What did I miss?" I ask.

"We all chose which guy we would get paired up with if the eight of us got stranded on an island. You got paired with Roo. Hope you're okay with that," she says in a teasing tone. "You guys are so cute together, we didn't think you'd mind."

I laugh. "Thanks, I guess. Who did everyone else get?"

"Danielle with Graham, Clarissa with Jack, and me with hunky Mick," she says, sounding sassy.

"Honestly, I feel like we were all paired off like that today. Too bad Mick has a serious girlfriend," I say making a face at Kia.

"Yeah, I'd upgrade James for Mick in a heartbeat if he was single."

"Really?"

"No. James and I will get married…but it's still fun to pretend." There are a few moments of silence before Kia speaks again. This time her voice is livelier. "Oh, and did I tell you I left my Pinterest page up purposely so that he could see the types of engagement rings I like?"

"No, you didn't. Did he say anything?"

"He didn't right away, but eventually he brought it up. He said that if I wanted a rock that big, we wouldn't be getting engaged for at least another two years." She sighs. "But as much as I'd like to be married, he definitely needs to be more mature to be a married man. His mom still does his laundry."

"I don't care if it's a while before I get married." Clarissa chimes in.

"Well no, of course not, because then you'll be cut off," Kia says sarcastically.

"Well, I'll never get cut off completely." She laughs. "I'm just not in a rush, that's all."

"Same here, I'm in no rush. I don't even know if I believe that love can last a lifetime," I say.

"Wow, you sound so much like my cousin Jordan. I'm pretty sure he doesn't believe in monogamy. He's always bringing a new girl around. He doesn't believe in fate or destiny or anything like that," Danielle says.

"Whoa. I believe in monogamous relationships and in the past most of mine have lasted years, but fifty-plus years married to the same person, I just don't know. I get sick of spending time with the people I love just after a few days. I just need time to get away and be by myself to decompress or those little things start to bother me. I just want to be realistic, that's all. I don't know if love really lasts that long." I inhale deeply. "Danielle, what do you think?" I ask, looking at her.

"I think I'd be ready to be a wife, but not to Ben," she says. She and Ben have been together since senior year of high school.

"WHAT?" Clarissa shouts. "Then why are you with him?"

"Because I love him, I care about him. I just know he's not who I'm going to marry. I don't think he'll ever get married." Danielle's response is calm, and she's not at all bothered by Clarissa's outburst.

"Usually people break up when they know there's no future. That's how relationships end," Kia voices.

"Well, I guess I'm not ready to break up," she says, now sounding annoyed.

We're all quiet for a while. Then Danielle looks at me. "Do you think you and Sai are on the same page?"

I don't know if she's asking because she wants the pressure off her, or if it's because Danielle knows the most about my relationship with Sai. I take a moment to think before answering. "Sai is marriage material. He wants to be married and would make an excellent husband. He believes a couple can be faithfully committed to each other for their entire lives.

We've had conversations and I know marriage is very important to him-"

"Okay, so what does that mean for you and Sai?" she interrupts.

"Well, things are still early, I don't really know. I picture myself being married one day. I want kids and I'd prefer to do it in that order, marriage and then kids," I say, a bit self-consciously. "I mean, Sai's ready. He's hinted at marriage a few times, I think it's to gauge a reaction, but I usually try to stay neutral. I'm just not there yet. Maybe because he's older, he just knows what he wants." I shrug.

"It's all so mind-numbing. All the decisions. Stay together, break up, what a headache." Danielle groans. "Wouldn't it be nice to have someone tell you your future?" Now there's a trill in her voice.

"NO!" Clarissa frowns. "That would be so boring. Not knowing is what makes things exciting. Plus, that psychic crap is all a hoax."

I agree with Clarissa that not knowing the future makes the present more exciting, but I'm also intrigued by the idea of getting a peek into my future.

"Pff, I'm in, I'll go see a psychic with you Danny!" Kia says.

"Me too! That actually sounds like a whole lot of fun," I say.

All at once, we skim back over to Clarissa. She looks like she might take back what she just said. "I guess I could go along for the ride. I'll just sit back and listen as some witch woman takes your money and tells you made up stories," she says, smirking.

We start predicting each other's futures. Laughing more hysterically at each passing minute as we get more and more ridiculous. Our fingernails eventually get sprayed with a quick-dry finish and we're walked to the massage hall.

51

After the health and safety paperwork is complete, I'm given the choice of three oils to choose from, opting for a citrus blend. I disrobe and lay face down under the sheet. The woman returns with a light knock at the door.

She starts at my neck and shoulders and I immediately feel as though this is the greatest thing that's ever happened to me. I feel a deep calm come over me and suddenly nothing else matters. My mind has gone blank. I'm so relaxed, I think I might fall asleep. I focus on her hands working against the side of my neck, kneading her fingers into the nape of my neck then to the base of my head. Her fingertips are magic. My nerve endings tingle as she runs her hands against my smooth, oiled skin. She tells me to speak up if the pressure is too much but it's absolutely perfect as she moves from the top of my body down to my feet. After some time, she has me turn so that I'm on my back. I have no sense of time because I feel like I'm in a trance.

She continues kneading and rubbing muscles that I normally would not give a second thought about. A few times I become more aware when she slows to focus on an area that is not so relaxing. The feeling is a mix of pleasure and pain and I figure out that she's found a knot. She stays in the area and holds firm pressure. I focus on my breathing until she moves on. Within a minute or two, my breathing has slowed back down and I've turned into a melted lump on the massage table. Before I know it, she's resting her hand on my shoulder and telling me to take my time and come out whenever I'm ready. I can't believe it, I fell asleep. I'm annoyed with myself for not being able to enjoy the full blissful hour, but at least now I should be refreshed for our late night tonight.

I walk out into the hallway, my eyes scrunch into slits from the lights. Even though it's not abnormally bright, the room was dim so it takes a minute for my eyes to adjust. I find that I'm the first one out so I go to splash water on my face until I hear Clarissa and Danielle. I join them a second later, their faces look tired and relaxed, like mine. Kia appears a minute later. We make our way to the entrance, talking about how great the massages felt and how we need to get them more often.

Kia goes up to the desk first. She's about to remove her credit card when I hear the receptionist tell her something and Kia's hand stops. Kia says something in return that sounds like a question and looks surprised. The woman nods and I can read her mouth as she says 'yes'.

Kia twists around and says, "Sai paid for our nail appointments!"

"Wow, really?" I ask, surprised. I glance at the receptionist.

"Oh my gosh, I love him, he is the sweetest!" Kia says grabbing my shoulders.

"Wow! Please thank him for us!" Danielle says, a smile wide on her face.

"He also said if there is anything you'd like from our spa gift shop that you can add it to the tab." The receptionist informs us.

"Oh, thank you," I say, a bit speechless.

We go into the gift shop to look around. There is a line of hair products from the brand we noticed earlier. There are candles and oils and lotions. I check the price of the massage oil, the same citrus scent I had chosen for my massage, and my eyes widen in surprise at the price tag: $32. I love the smell but it's just too expensive for such a small bottle, even if Sai is willing to pay for it. We thank the woman and head back to our room. I text Sai along the way.

Jhett: You are seriously the best! The love note and covering our bill, what nice surprises! Thank you, thank you! <3

Sai: You are very welcome. Did you pick anything from the gift shop?

Jhett: No, but that was very thoughtful.

Sai: What are your plans for the rest of the evening?

Jhett: Going back to the room to get ready for dinner. Then we'll leave for the club from there. It's not far. Should I call when I get back? It might be late.

Sai: Yes, please call. What place did you pick for dinner? Did you have to make reservations?

Jhett: Basilico, an Italian pizza place. And yes, dinner at 7.

Sai: Have a good time. I'll wait for your call.

I feel a pang of guilt as I read his last text. He'll probably wait up all night watching TV or reading until I call. I know he'd rather I be there with him, while some men would go to the bar all night. I smile, thinking of how he is such a good boyfriend.

We all shower, do our hair and makeup, get dressed and request a car for pickup. The app tells us our driver will arrive in ten minutes. We head to the elevator wearing short dresses, high heels, and small wristlets in hand. We see our driver approach and climb into her SUV. There's a rap song playing with a heavy beat that instantly intensifies my excitement. I can tell the other girls feel the same because their bodies are already moving to the music.

Kia shouts over the music, "I texted the guys to let them know we are on our way to the restaurant."

"Are they meeting us there?" I ask.

"They're done with dinner, so they're going to sit at the bar and have a few drinks."

"So, are they planning on going to the club too?" Danielle asks, her voice hopeful.

"I'm sure, they can't stay away from us." Kia smiles and exaggerates blinking her long lashes at us. It makes us laugh.

"Nice. It will make the night more interesting. Maybe we should ignore them and find some other hotties to dance with to make them jealous." Clarissa suggests with a promiscuous look.

"I'm fine with just hanging out with them. I don't need any drama right now," I say.

54

We get to the restaurant and all pile out of the vehicle. We're a bit early for our reservation, but the hostess lets us know our table is about ready. There is a bench along the inside wall where I take a seat.

"Do you guys want to get a drink at the bar and say hi to the guys?" Kia asks.

"I'll stay here. It looks really packed in there and I don't even see them," Danielle says, her eyes searching the bar area.

"I'll wait with you." I tell Danielle.

"I'll go!" Clarissa says, and they head off towards the bar.

Danielle and I start talking about our old Italian neighbor who used to make us homemade meals when we first moved in together. In the middle of our conversation, I faintly hear a familiar voice, but it doesn't make sense in my mind. I'm confused and before I can register it, Danielle points to where it's coming from. I turn around and find Sai.

"What are you doing here?" I try to read his face. He's smiling, happy to see me. "Is everything okay?" I ask, feeling confused.

"Yeah, I'm fine. I just came to surprise you!" He says and then his face changes. "Why are you frowning?" He chuckles.

I'm sure I have quite the look on my face. Danielle gently touches my elbow and tells me our table is ready.

I turn to her. "I'll find you, I'll just be a minute."

Before I say anything to Sai, I pull him off to the side.

"Sai, what are you doing here? I'm here for a girls' weekend," I say annoyed.

"Why are you so upset? I thought you'd be happy to see me." Sadness falls across his face.

"I would be happy to see you if I had asked you to come here, but I'm here with the girls. You coming here is kind of weird."

He looks hurt. "You told me that I had to come see this place."

"What?"

"In your text, you said I should come see this place."

I remember now. I had texted him about how beautiful the view was from our hotel room. I take a deep breath, my body feels tense; my face is hot and I'm sure it's red.

"Yes, for us to come back another weekend. Not this weekend," I say trying to stay calm, but I'm sure my posture and heavy breathing give away that I'm upset.

Just then someone places their hand on my shoulder. "Jhett, is this man bothering you?" Before I recognize the speaker, I register the concern in his voice. I turn around; it's Graham.

"Excuse me, who are you?" Sai asks bewildered.

I put my hand up between them. "I'm fine, Graham, thanks. This is my boyfriend, Sai," I say feeling embarrassed. I hate causing a scene, especially in public.

"Who is this guy, Jhett?" Now Sai is upset and looking at me intently.

I give Graham a look that tells him I'm okay and he leaves turning into the men's bathroom.

"Sai, take a breath. He's someone we met yesterday. He's really nice and just happens to be here having a drink." I silently pray that the other guys stay in the bar and don't come over.

"How did he know you were here? He didn't look surprised to see you, did you come here together?" His voice accusing. It's starting to piss me off.

"No! Kia and Clarissa went to get drinks. They must have seen him at the bar. And he's married so you have nothing to worry about."

"Is that supposed to make me feel better? That means nothing, you know that right?"

"Well, it should mean something. I would hope that if we ever get married, I won't have to worry about you any time we're not together. And that you'd be able to trust me."

He seems to think about this for a minute. The bathroom door swings open and Graham comes out. He's holding his hands up as if he's surrendering and says, "Hey man, I'm really sorry."

Sai still looks mad but nods. Graham gives me a quick glance and then turns back to the bar.

"I'm going to go find the girls now; they're probably waiting for me."

"Yeah, okay. I just..." he lets out a deep sigh, "I just missed you and wanted to see you."

"Well, you've seen me and I'm okay. Are you going home now?"

"Yes. Still call me when you're back to the room, okay?"

"I will." He leans in for a hug and kiss. I don't want him knowing I'm still annoyed because I fear he will stay and want to talk about it. I hug him in return and let him kiss my cheek.

I walk him to his car and watch him pull away. I can still feel my heart beating in my chest and I feel anxious. I go back into the restaurant but instead of going to find the girls, I head to the bar. I spot the guys sitting at the far end in a corner.

"Hey!" I exhale.

"Hey!" they return.

"You okay? Graham said your boyfriend is here," Roo says.

"Not anymore. He left, everything's fine." I wave the bartender over. "Eight shots of tequila please." I don't know why I chose tequila, maybe because right now I don't care. My adrenaline is strong enough to give me the courage to do things I would normally hesitate to do.

"Okay," Roo says smiling.

I take my shot with the guys and suck hard on the lime. The shot tastes equally as bad as it did yesterday, but this time I expect the burn that follows and actually enjoy it. I feel like I've earned it. Even more, I suddenly feel bold.

I don't slam my shot glass down, but I don't gingerly place it on the bar, either. The guys set theirs down and wait for me to talk.

"All right, well, I'm sure you'll know when we're finished with dinner. I'm going to take these to the girls and we'll talk soon," I say with new energy.

Spotting the girls quickly, I walk over and set the shots in front of them.

"What are those?" Kia asks.

"Tequila," I answer.

"From the guys?"

"No, me. I already took mine, needed it after seeing Sai. I'm guessing Danielle filled you in?"

"Yeah, I told them. I also ordered you a vodka cranberry. I hope that's okay?" Danielle says.

"Yes. Thank you!" I smile.

The waitress comes over with our drinks and we place an order for two of their most popular pizzas to share.

"So, why the hell did Sai come here?" Clarissa asks.

"Honestly, I have no idea. My best guess is that he was bored and started to think about what I was doing. He was probably hoping I'd invite him to eat with us." I roll my eyes. "He said he missed me. Is it crazy he just showed up here unannounced?"

"Yes," Clarissa says nodding her head once.

"A little," Danielle answers nervously.

"I think it's sweet he's that crazy about you," Kia says.

"No. I don't know him, but that seems a little high school clingy to me," Clarissa says. "I can't imagine dropping in on one of Max's poker nights or surprising him while he's watching football at a friend's house. It's just not okay. He needs to trust you. And you know that's what this is about."

"Do you think that's why he came here? Because he doesn't trust you?" Kia asks.

"Sorry, I should clarify. It's not as much that he doesn't trust you, it's that he's insecure." Clarissa corrects.

"Maybe. This is the first time I've been out without him. It never crossed my mind before. Anytime we're not together I'm either with my family or at work."

"I wasn't going to say anything, but you have completely put all of your time and focus into him," Clarissa says. "We haven't spent time together in six months, and how long have you two been dating?"

Hearing this stings, and makes me feel a bit defensive. "Six months, but I've just been really busy."

"Yeah with Sai," Clarissa states.

I take a long drink of my vodka cranberry.

"Okay, I can see you're bothered by this. Let's just enjoy the rest of the night, okay?" Clarissa proposes.

"Deal." I'm happy to have the pressure off needing to defend myself or him.

We talk awhile longer before our food arrives, gossiping about the people we know. Once they've set our pizzas in front of us, we devour them, leaving two empty pie plates and a bundle of napkins in their place. It's too early to go to the club, so we head over to the bar and are happy to find it's cleared out since we arrived. We each order another drink and end up playing a few rounds of bar dice where I end up losing the second game - or winning, depending how you look at it. The shot is determined by Mick and paid for by Clarissa. It was a Boilermaker and absolutely terrible, though I'm sure everyone was entertained by my reaction.

By 9:30pm Kia requests a ride and we all leave the bar together. I'm grateful the weather is nice, because there's a short line outside the club where we wait for about ten minutes before the bouncer lets us in. It's crazy loud inside and there are people *all* around us.

Roo comes over and puts his mouth right to my ear. "Can I get you a drink?" he asks.

I rest my hand on his shoulder and go up on my tiptoes. The heels help with the height difference but I still can't reach his ear. He bends down to meet me, and I reach a bit further to get right up to his ear so I don't have to shout.

"Vodka cran, thanks." I smile and squeeze his shoulder.

He shoots back one hell of a sexy smile and heads to the overly crowded bar. I'm huddled together with the girls when I see Jack returning from the bar with a drink for Clarissa who is standing next to me.

"There's an opening," Jack points.

To me, it looks just as packed as every other spot. But Mick nods and Graham, Kia and Danielle follow to the bar.

I lean over to Clarissa, "Do you think they had the same conversation we did about being paired together if we were on a deserted island?"

She looks at me and smiles, "Probably not, but this is fun isn't it?" She whips around and starts dancing.

Clarissa is a great dancer. Jack moves behind her and puts his free hand on her hip. In a smooth motion, she adds her hand to the top of his. I can't get over how comfortable they are together. Everyone is back from the bar and on the dance floor. Roo has stepped in next to me, only a few inches between us. All eyes are on Danielle after Clarissa gently pushes her to the center of the circle. With her curvy body, Danielle is also a great dancer. We cheer her on as she dances solo. If it were me, I'd be too self-conscious; even with the alcohol in my blood, I'd dance right back into the circle.

After just a few songs, the club already feels hot and my cup is empty. The guys moved off one song earlier to see if they could find seating. Mick, being the tallest, waves us over a few minutes later.

"I'll get the next round," Clarissa shouts and walks off towards the bar.

There is an L-shaped black leather sofa just big enough for us, leaving no room for Clarissa, but she finds a solution as she walks straight over to Jack and throws herself onto his lap. She gives him a look which is met with a grin from him in return.

There are two platforms near us. Raised about three feet off the floor and two feet in diameter with a pole running up the middle that's attached to the wall. Two girls dance on one and three on the other. I've seen a few girls jump up from the dance floor, so I know they don't work here. The bartender comes over with the tray of drinks Clarissa ordered. She hands me my vodka cranberry and I gladly take a few sips, feeling some relief from the ice-cold liquid. When I go to set my glass down, I notice that it's already half gone.

My head starts to feel heavy and my body is swaying to the beat of the music. I look around at my friends and grin. The music is so loud that the couch vibrates from the beat. Every song makes you want to get up and dance. I grab Kia and Danielle by the hand and pull them up, making eye contact with Clarissa, motioning for her to dance with us.

The dance floor is packed. I feel sweaty bodies all around me, but I've had enough to drink that it doesn't bother me. The lights above flash and move from one corner to the next, dancing and moving with the music. I feel someone lightly touch my waist, and turn to see Roo; he tightens his grip as we make eye contact, as if waiting to make sure it's okay. I like his touch; it makes me feel secure. He brings his body in closer. His chest up against my back and his thighs are against my thighs. His face is so close to mine, I can feel his scratchy stubble on my cheek. He mimics my movements and we move in a fluid motion. I raise my arms up and arch my back.

The tips of his fingers graze the sensitive underside of my arm, lightly tickling my skin. He continues up my elbow and finally to my hands. I feel as though we have choreographed a routine and this is our performance. I look up and see Kia is watching us; she winks and I smile back at her.

We stay out dancing until we can't take the heat any longer. When we fall back to the couch, we finish our drinks and sit for a couple songs to rest our legs and feet. Mick orders another round and has the bartender bring waters to help cool us down. All the bodies make it hot and stuffy. It doesn't keep us away for long though. One of the platforms has opened up. Clarissa grabs Danielle, pulling her onto the platform. They start dancing and the guys are cheering. The girls whip their hair around, roll their bodies and move up and down the pole as if they know what they're doing. Roo wraps his arm around me and pulls me into him, his sticky sweaty, skin touching mine.

He speaks into my ear. "You said you're competitive, right? Here's your challenge." He nods in the direction of Clarissa and Danielle.

"Game on," I say, letting my lips just graze his ear.

Even though there's another girl dancing on this platform I pull myself up, Kia joining me, causing the other girl to leave. Kia and I grab the pole and use it to move our bodies in ways we otherwise wouldn't be able to. It's super fun, and makes dancing easier. Kia and I dance and bend, our bodies touching while we play in the spotlight. We playfully glance at Clarissa and Danielle as if we are having a dance-off. Their racy looks give me the energy to keep going even though the muscles in my thighs are exhausted and my calves are burning.

I feel eyes on us from all around the bar. I don't care about any of them but I scan until I find Roo. He's moved closer and his eyes are on me like I knew they would be. This makes my stomach flutter. He is so hot. He shoots me a sexy smile and I can't help but return it. We stay up dancing for another ten minutes before calling it quits.

Roo comes over to help us down. When he grabs for my hand he slides his fingers between mine interlacing our fingers and places his other hand on my back to help ease me down. Once my feet are both on the ground, he holds my hand for a second longer and gives it a squeeze. As he lets go of my hand, my eyes drift up but I keep my head forward and chin low so that I'm sneaking a glance at him. The corner of my mouth turns up into a smile. He catches me watching him and his grin turns into a deep smile. He gestures to let me walk in front of him, back to where the group is sitting and keeps his hand on the small of my back.

The club announces they'll be closing soon, so we call for a ride. We cram into the SUV, clearly supposed to seat five, but we make it work, though it doesn't stop the driver's annoyed glance. Everywhere you look arms and legs are stuffed and crammed into any nook and cranny. Our already hot bodies are smashed together, each of the girls sitting on a lap. Everything said seems to be funny and all we can do is laugh. We hear Jack announce to the driver to drop us all at Hotel Lotus. I know Kia had two stops planned when she booked the ride, but I'm happy when I hear his request.

"That's not a good idea." Clarissa states.

"Why, I think it's a fabulous idea." Jack returns; his words a bit slurred.

"Because…we all know how nights like these end."

"And?" Jack says into her neck.

"We're all taken. You can go back to your motel. Sorry, but I'm already sharing a bed with Kia."

"It's a king." Danielle shouts and then giggles. Clarissa shoots her a look, but struggles to contain a laugh.

"We'll just stay for one drink," Jack pleads.

Clarissa stands her ground, "No."

I'm surprised to hear this. Clarissa is normally the first to let loose and never wants a party to end. I look at Jack, the moonlight is coming through the window, illuminating his face. He's pouting at her and she gives him a playful slap.

Without looking up, Clarissa shouts, "This motel, stop here." Then slowly she leans in and whispers in his ear. "Sorry darling, the fun stops here." She kisses him swiftly on the cheek.

We all climb out and ask the driver to give us a few minutes, and realize this will be the last time we'll see the guys. I'm not sure what to say. The thought makes me sad, and I wish that we had more time with them. I suddenly feel like a child when I was told that my time of having fun had come to an end and it was time to go home. Clarissa acting as the parent, making it clear that we leave the guys here and go back to our hotel.

Kia is the first to address the topic. "It's been so fun hanging out with you guys this weekend. It's too bad we leave tomorrow."

"You ladies were definitely the highlight of our weekend," Jack says, speaking for the guys. He goes in to hug Clarissa first and then follows to the rest of us.

"Yeah, I don't think any fishing trip will ever compare to this one," Danielle says playfully.

"No way, unless by some miracle we run into you girls again," Mick says while making his rounds of hugs.

Graham follows and then Roo hugs me last. His arms completely envelop me and I can feel his chest thumping against mine. He holds onto me a few seconds longer than the hugs he's just given the girls. It's the kind of hug that makes you feel cherished. Before he lets go, he whispers in my ear. "I hope we get to see each other again. You're a really cool girl, Jhett."

I bring my eyes to his. "I hope so, too."

CHAPTER 5

I wake up and turn my head into the pillow, feeling overly tired and sluggish. Without standing, I can feel the fatigue in my leg and calf muscles. Moving my feet in the sheets, I'm reminded there are blisters on my heels, the result of wearing heels for the first time in weeks. I force myself to look at my phone, hoping it will cause a distraction from my hangover. Did I call Sai? No. Shit. I forgot. He's going to be pissed. Besides my queasy stomach and pounding headache, my brain now hurts at the thought of Sai. I groan and realize there's a possibility he's down in the lobby waiting to question me. I'm actually surprised he hasn't called fifty times, or texted me about being worried and that I need to call him ASAP.

I look over to see if Danielle is sleeping and see that her bed is empty. In all my worry, I hadn't even registered the time. I look back down at my phone, seeing it's already 10am. I haven't slept in this late since summer break back in high school; I hate sleeping the day away.

I force myself to get up and go into the bathroom. I undress and look at myself. Ugh. I can definitely tell I've been drinking for two nights. Not only do I look bloated, but my skin looks terrible. My eyes are puffy and bloodshot, and I have mascara smeared under my lower lashes. I need a shower. I let the hot water hit my back for a while before stepping out. After I'm dressed, I find Kia and Danielle sitting at the breakfast bar. They look a little tired but otherwise fine.

"Ouch, you look rough," Kia says.

"Thanks. I feel that way," I respond with little expression.

She laughs. "Sorry, that sounded bad."

"I really don't care. I'd just like this feeling to pass as soon as possible."

"Let's get some breakfast." Danielle suggests.

"Ugh, I can't even stomach the idea right now." I tell her.

"You'll feel better, just some toast or something light," Kia says.

"I'm going to wake Clarissa; we need to check out by 11am. We can get breakfast on the way back," Danielle says.

We're about ten minutes from the breakfast diner when a notification comes through on my phone. It's a request from a "Roosevelt Harris". There's a small picture next to the words, Accept or Delete. I squint at the picture and then click on it, opening the profile. It's Roo. I guess I never asked his last name or thought that Roo might be short for something.

"Why are you smiling?" Kia asks.

"Oh, am I? Roo just friended me."

"Well, I'm glad to see you finally smile this morning." She waits a beat and then asks, "What's bothering you? I know it's not just the hangover."

"Where to start," I say and think a minute before speaking again. "I don't know what to think about Sai. I feel both terrible and mad. I forgot to call him both nights, and I know if he was out and I was home expecting a call that never came I'd be mad too." I let out an exhale. "But then when he showed up at dinner and got so mad when he saw Graham…I thought he trusted me, but now I'm not so sure. I feel like he hovers over me. Agh, I just can't believe he showed up. I want to tell myself it was a dream, it was kind of mortifying."

"Did you talk to him this morning?"

"I texted him. I know, I'm a coward. I didn't have the energy. He wants me to come over as soon as we get back. He said he'd like to talk."

"Oh, that's never good," she says. Even though I knew that myself, hearing her say it causes a pit to form in my stomach. "Are you going?"

66

"I haven't decided yet. I'd like to go home and just get ready for the week, but I think avoiding him will make it much worse." I lay my head against the seat and close my eyes so I can think. I try to slow my breathing, something I learned in yoga to help calm my nerves. A few minutes pass by.

"So, what's making you smile now?"

"What?" I open my eyes and turn to her.

"You have a grin on your face. You're thinking about Roo aren't you?"

I blush and cover my face. "Oh my gosh, how did you know? And stop looking at me, focus on the road." I give her a light shove.

Kia laughs. "I'm your best friend, I know these things. And don't think I didn't notice you two whispering and touching all weekend." She teases.

"What? We were not," I say defensively.

"It's not me who you have to convince." She eyes me.

I glare at her and then look out my window. "These little memories of the past two days keep coming into focus. I can't stop thinking about him. He is pretty cute, isn't he?"

"Jhett, he is fucking hot. They all are. If only we were all single. Oh God, I wonder how the night would have ended!" She has a devilish look in her eyes.

We arrive at the restaurant and walk in shortly behind Clarissa and Danielle. The energy in the group has deflated since Friday afternoon. The waitress brings us glasses of water and takes our order. I force myself to drink the entire glass.

"Clarissa, what are your plans for the week?" I ask.

"Stopping in at Redds' tomorrow. I want to see if I can work there again for the summer. Not much else."

"Would you want to get together one night this week?"

"Sure, so soon?" she says hesitantly. "What are you thinking?"

"I've thought about what you said, and I want to make up for not coming to visit you this last semester. Maybe we can walk dogs at the shelter?"

"Yeah, I'd love that."

"Okay, how about you two, what are your schedules like?"

Kia and I make plans for a jog Saturday morning. Danielle and I talk about getting together the following week.

We eat, say our goodbyes, and before I know it Kia is dropping me off at my car. Throwing my bags in the backseat I wave to Kia as she drives off. A wave of anxiety washes over me. What am I going to do? Where am I going to go? I want to go home, but I know that Sai and I need to talk. I don't feel ready to see him and I'm running out of time. I can't stall any longer; a decision needs to be made. I dial his number.

"Hey," he answers. "Are you on your way over?"

"Hi," I take a moment to steady my breath; I feel nervous. I know I'll upset him. "I'm not going to stop over. I'm…"

"What, why not? You said you would." There's no anger in his voice. Instead, he sounds a bit desperate.

"I know. But I really need to go home. I'm tired and I need to get stuff ready for the week."

"You have clothes here you can use for work tomorrow, and I already have groceries to make dinner tonight."

"Can you save it for tomorrow? I'll come over after work."

"Will you spend the night?"

There's a short pause. I don't want to make any promises and I don't know if I'll be up for it. I'm unsure of where our talk will take us.

"Maybe. I don't want to think right now. I'm hungover and really tired." As soon as the words leave my mouth, I wish I wouldn't have said them.

"How much did you drink last night?" Now there's a hint of annoyance in his voice. "How long did you stay out?"

"Sai, this is the reason I don't want to stop over. We can talk tomorrow. I'll answer any questions you have, okay?"

"Okay." He exhales loudly into the phone.

"And," I lower my voice slightly and say, "don't stop over tonight or anything, okay?"

"Yeah, okay." He sounds irritated. "I'll see you tomorrow. I love you."

My throat feels tight as I say, "Love you too."

CHAPTER 6

My alarm goes off and instead of hitting snooze once like I normally do on a Monday, I get up right away. I had a string of weird dreams and feel like I'd like to take a sick day. But I won't because I don't even like calling in when I'm genuinely sick.

I munch on a bagel and sip my coffee after I finish getting ready, and update myself on the news while holding Patches. I send out a text to Jillian, my neighbor, and thank her for looking after him this weekend. We've been helping each other out since I moved in. I check in on her cat anytime she's away overnight, and she looks after Patches. While I'm on my phone I look to see if there's a text from Sai; there's not. I'm not sure if I should be disappointed or relieved. Maybe he'll call when I'm on my way to work. It's unusual for me not to have heard from him by now.

I get to work five minutes early so I sit in my car. A text comes in. Subconsciously I'm thinking it's from Sai, but it's actually Kia.

Kia: How did yesterday go? BIG blow-up?

Jhett: I didn't go. And I don't feel much better about it. I was hoping my anxiety would fade but it hasn't. Going after work.

Kia: Good luck hun, call if you need to talk!

Jhett: Thanks! Xoxo

I head into work and prepare for my typical routine day. I say hi to Emma and she asks about the weekend. I fill her in as much as I can before we are called to morning huddle. As a group, we discuss our appointments for the day. Our head receptionist gives us a heads up on new patients and on ones that need to pay before service, as well as anything else that is out of the ordinary. At the end of our huddle, our boss tells us we are bringing on a temporary consultant. They've met a few times; we will love her.

"She will be with us for a few weeks starting next Monday, and will be here to improve work performance." Not much else is said and we branch off in different directions.

Emma follows closely behind me. "A consultant. Why do you think we need a consultant?"

I consider this. Our branch has been in the top three since I've started. "Not sure," I say. "Maybe boss man wants to finally hit that number one spot and he thinks bringing her in will do it?"

She looks worried. She's so sweet and I wonder what it would be like to have this much anxiety all the time.

"I wouldn't worry about it; it probably won't even affect us."

"Yeah, okay." She nods and nervously looks away.

After a pretty smooth morning, we break for lunch. It's a gorgeous day, so Emma and I decide to take a walk. We punch out and I check my phone for the second time since I've been here. Still no text from Sai. I decide to text him.

Jhett: We still on for tonight?
Sai: Yes, I hope so! See you around 5?
Jhett: Yes

No other replies. So unlike him. I put my phone away and Emma and I pick up from where we left off this morning. When I'm finished filling her in, I ask about her weekend. She spent it with her parents and it doesn't sound like they did anything very exciting. Emma moved into her own apartment a few months ago because her therapist and mom both agreed she should try being more independent.

Emma has relied on her parents from when she was a child, up until she moved out. Her mom made her breakfast, lunch, and dinner every day; she did all her laundry; and even cleaned up her room. I would never judge her for this, but I think Emma and I are in agreement that it's a good thing she moved out when she did. Her new place is only about five minutes from her parents' house. She still goes to their house most nights for dinner, but she's been trying to gather inspiration to make her own meals by watching cooking shows. But, as far as I know, she buys premade meals and other easy-to-heat foods that require no prep at all.

Emma also tells me that she's been debating downloading a dating app. I'm surprised and glad to hear about this; it's a big step for her, and I encourage her to do it. Just before I was hired, she had broken up with the guy she'd been with since high school. We weren't close right away, so I didn't know why she was always so upset and I didn't want to come off as nosey. I'd felt sorry for her because most mornings she would come into work with red swollen eyes; it was obvious that she had been crying either all night or all morning, or even both.

Eventually, I felt comfortable enough to ask why she was upset, and everything came pouring out. Damien was the only boy she'd ever dated. Her first love, her first everything. She thought they would get married and have a bunch of kids; she even had a list of names. Then one day her best friend, Julie, asked her to come over. She said they needed to talk. Emma could tell by the tone of her voice something was wrong. Her mind started to imagine terrible things, maybe Julie was moving away or maybe one of her parents was dying of cancer.

When she got there, Julie hugged her and they went into her basement where she told Emma to sit down. Julie confessed to having slept with Damien while Emma was away with her family on vacation.

Emma remembered in great detail how Julie's face was blotchy and how she spoke with tears in her eyes. Julie apparently told her it was definitely over between them.

She looked at her like she was supposed to accept her apology so they could move on and all be friends again. Emma's mind was understandably all over the place. She didn't know what to say, even if she could speak.

As she was about to get up and walk out, Julie stopped her because there was one other thing she had to get off her chest. After a full minute of stammering, she finally choked out that she was pregnant.

Emma had run as fast as she could out of the house, slamming the door behind her. As soon as she got outside, she threw up all over the front porch. Not bothering to clean it up, she got into her car and drove off. She needed to pull over twice to catch her breath and clear her eyes from the stream of tears. She was relieved to see her parents weren't home when she arrived. She wanted to be alone and didn't want to have to relive the revelation to explain it to them. The humiliation was so unbearable she felt like she wanted to curl up and die. Adding to the pain, she got a text from Julie.

I am so sorry. It was honestly all a mistake and Damien and I both know that now. I need you in my life, Emma. You are my best friend. My parents don't even know yet and I don't think they'll support me in keeping it. Please call me.

Emma blocked Julie's and Damien's numbers. She burned everything Julie and Damien had given her and left a note for her parents that if either called or stopped by the house, they were to tell them to never contact her again. Emma wrote that she would tell her parents what happened as soon as she was ready. Her parents were loyal and did so without asking questions. They had some idea since Emma didn't want to see Julie or Damien, but were shocked to hear about the pregnancy. Some time had passed and Emma's mom grew concerned when she noticed Emma losing weight. She knew Emma was still struggling but had wanted to give her some space. But hearing her daughter crying at night eventually became too much; Emma started therapy the following week.

Emma and I are back to work when I tell her that it won't hurt to see who's out there. She looks optimistic upon hearing my support. I noticed that over the last few months she's been happier than when we first met. I really hope she finds someone great because she truly is a sweet, genuine person. She leans in and thanks me. I hug her tightly and wonder if I'm Emma's best friend.

We make it to the end of the day and after I punch out, Emma and I walk to our cars together. "Would you want to get a drink together after work sometime?"

"Yes, that would be so fun!" she says enthusiastically.

Because of her after-work therapy twice a week, we settle on Wednesday next week for Wing Wednesday at Marco's. My favorite bar-restaurant near my apartment.

I start the car and turn in the direction of Sai's. I have a few things packed if I decide to stay but I'll make that decision later. I feel a little better than I did this morning; my head feels clearer about what I'd like to say. About a half-hour later, I pull up to Sai's. I swallow and make my way to the door. Sai is there waiting for me. He hugs me tightly and I return it. I don't like confrontation so this helps to settle some of the tension between us.

"Come in, tell me about your day."

There's a fabulous smell coming from the kitchen that's so distracting I walk towards it and stroll over to the stove. "Is this your mother's famous Tandoori chicken? And naan and hummus?"

"Yes and I made the hummus this morning and I have laddu for dessert."

"Thank you for cooking." My stomach growls. "My mouth is watering; can we eat?" I didn't have much of an appetite at lunch; I only ate half my sandwich and an apple.

"Yes, please." He grabs the dishes and brings them over to the already set table. There's a candle lit in the center of the table and he dims the lights. He does romantic gestures like these all the time. As we fill our plates, there's a bit of a silence. He must be noticing the same because he turns on some music.

"I must say, I was a bit surprised you didn't call or text this morning," I say.

"I wanted to give you some space. I know you've said before you like time to yourself and I could tell when we spoke yesterday that you needed it. It was hard, don't get me wrong. Especially since I wanted you here with me." He stops and smiles. "I'm going to try to back off. I trust you and I don't want to jeopardize our relationship. You're too important to me."

"Thank you. And I need to apologize for not calling. I would have been worried, too, so I'm sorry."

We continue to talk over dinner. Sai's asking questions, but not as many as I thought he would. He doesn't ask for a lot of detail, either, which is something he normally would do. I feel like it may have something to do with me being here and in one piece.

I take a few more bites and my plate is nearly empty. Sai gets up and carries the dessert over.

"The girls told me they miss me hanging out with them. We've agreed to plan some time each week to visit. I'll make sure we still have our time together though." I smile.

"Okay, just let me know what days you'll be with them and I'll plan to keep myself busy. There was a booklet at the coffee shop of summer classes that are being offered at the local college, and there are a few I'm interested in."

"Really? That's great, like what?" I ask curiously.

"There are a number of painting classes, beginner level for me, of course, and Intro into Musical Instruments. I think that may be for younger students but it got me thinking that I should get back into piano. I absolutely hated it as a kid but once you perfect a piece, it's very rewarding."

"It would be so nice to hear you play," I say while taking another bite of the sweet laddu.

I thank him for making dinner and I clear the table. Together, we load the dishwasher and talk about plans for next weekend's hike. We'll camp and hike as much as we can Friday afternoon until Sunday. I'm excited to picnic on the beach and ID birds with Sai. He packs his *Native to Wisconsin* bird book for every hike.

Sai looks at me sweetly and says, "So will you stay the night?"

I feel like tonight's conversation could have gone one of two ways, and it definitely went better of the two.

"Yes, I'll stay." I smile, hopeful that with a little space in our relationship, things will be better.

After returning from a walk around the neighborhood, we get our pajamas on and climb into bed. Sai turns on the TV and starts to search for a movie, and I set my alarm and lay down close to him. I must be exhausted because my eyelids feel like they're being weighed down, and before I know it my alarm is waking me up.

Friday

Clarissa and I have plans to meet up after work, so I text her before I clock in.

Jhett: What time do you think you'll get done?

Clarissa: Depends on how busy we are, yesterday I was done at 2. If I get done early, I can pick you up. Still thinking Margs, chips and salsa after walking the pups?

Jhett: Yes! We have CPR training until 4.

Emma and I both fall behind with our first patients and it throws off the whole morning. I usually try to help her out by taking a quick appointment, but I just can't manage it. I'm hot and feeling overwhelmed and I just wish it was the end of the day.

I get a quick peek at Emma as I walk my last patient to the front. She's getting her room ready for her first appointment after lunch. Her last patient of the morning canceled, giving her a few minutes to catch her breath. Her hair looks frazzled and it reminds me of what mine looks like after a crazy night out. It's only the two of us in the basement lunchroom. As she walks closer, I can tell she's upset. She grabs her lunch from the fridge and thuds her yellow daisy lunch tote onto the table, cracking open a Diet Coke as she slouches into her chair.

"So, have you chosen a dating app yet?" I try to distract her.

"Yes, I have ... I was meaning to tell you this morning, but I didn't want the other girls to hear." Her voice is neutral. Today's workload must have really gotten to her, but I bet if we continue on this topic, it will brighten her mood.

"I went with Romeo and Juliet. I signed up last night."

"Have you looked at any profiles yet?"

"Yes. I was up until almost midnight and you know me, I'm usually in bed by nine." She gives me a sideways glance and I see a hint of a smile.

"Wow, yeah, that's crazy. I'm guessing you must have seen some good contenders then?"

"There are a few guys that I'm interested in, but I want to wait to see if they message me first."

"Really? Why wait? You can make the first move."

"Me?" she says, touching her chest. "I feel like I would come across as desperate."

"Or confident."

"I'll give it a few days and if I don't hear anything, I'll reach out."

"Promise?"

There's a low groaning sound coming from her throat and then a smile, "Okay, yeah."

"That's my girl!" I smile enthusiastically.

I ask details about her perfect guy, and she lists hair and eye color, height, teeth and skin color. I laugh when she tells me he has to be tan. We discuss what his personality must be like and from all the information I've gathered, I'd say Emma has high standards, and she should. She's super smart, and if I'm remembering correctly she told me she was the valedictorian of her class. She's attractive, but so shy, and because of her reserved behavior she tends to fall unnoticed from time to time.

Because she's quiet on top of being shy, it makes keeping a conversation with her difficult. But it doesn't take long for her to open up once a bond is created. That's when you get to see the true, wonderful Emma. The type of guy she is describing would be one of those heartthrob romantics that has huge muscles and treats his woman like she's the only female left on the planet. I can't say I blame her. I think most girls dream up some similar version of this dream man at some point in their lives.

It's not until the early adult years, sometimes sooner, sometimes later, when we realize there are a good handful of scumbag cheaters out there. Unfortunately, she's already experienced it with Damien. I think it's great that after all she's been through, she still has hope. From my experience, I have the real deal with Sai. He's a romantic and is constantly looking for ways to surprise me. He's not much for big muscles, but what he lacks in physical attributes he makes up in great boyfriend qualities.

Emma deserves a man who will treat her the same way Sai treats me, and she knows this. She's always saying something like, 'I hope I can find someone that cares as much about me as Sai does for you' or 'I hope to get that lucky one day' whenever he's brought up. After our break, but before we part ways I make her promise to keep me in the loop. She agrees, and as I thought, she's back to her usual happy self.

Our afternoon goes smoothly, and the morning chaos is nearly forgotten. I get a text from Clarissa letting me know she got done early and will be waiting for me in the parking lot after work.

I change quickly and jump into Clarissa's SUV and we take off.

"So, how were your first couple of days at Redd's?"

"Boring, but good. I remember it being more fun last year." Clarissa complains.

"Was it because the owner's son was there? Drooling over you and telling you how hot you are ten times a day?" I ask, setting my purse and lunch bag on the floor of the backseat.

"Ha," she laughs. "Maybe I just need to find something else; I'm not cut out for reception. When it's pretty slow I can be on my phone if the owners aren't around, so that's nice, but I just don't think I have the patience for the people anymore."

"Don't take this the wrong way, but aren't receptionists normally outgoing, friendly and generally like people?"

"I am definitely none of those things, gag." She rolls her eyes.

Clarissa doesn't need to be a people person; her beauty draws not only boys and men in, but also women. She's like a mosquito to a shock light. Just like the zap the insect receives, Clarissa will give you one of her dagger stares that tells you that you are an idiot if you ask a stupid question or make a ridiculous comment. She won't even waste her breath on you. The look alone will make you second-guess everything. I've heard people pathetically apologize to her; it's like they want her approval. It's a pretty great superpower.

We pull up to the humane society and go directly to the dog area. We've volunteered many times in the past two years so most of the staff know us by name. We take two dogs that are side by side in kennels; one is a black lab mix named Hank, and the other is an Irish Wolfhound mix named Leroy.

Clarissa and I love big dogs and most times take the largest in the kennel. We sign the dogs out and head for the three-mile dirt path we always walk.

"How are things with Sai? Did you get scolded for having fun?"

"No, not at all. I went to his place Monday after work and I think it just really helped to have that time to think. He made dinner and it was a really nice evening. There was no argument."

"So, he wasn't mad about the guys?" She eyes me, not buying it.

"Well, when he came to the restaurant, he only saw Graham…so, he doesn't know about the other guys."

"Oh my gosh, he doesn't know?" Her voice excited.

"No, did you tell Max everything we did?" I don't need her to respond; I know she didn't.

"Of course not. When he asked how my weekend was, I said it was awesome and that's all he needed to know."

"And he didn't press you for more details?"

"Oh, he knows if I say something like that, he gets nada. So, what did the two of you talk about if you left all the fun out?"

"I told him everything we did, but left the guys out of it. Technically I didn't lie, I just happened to leave out some details. You know, kept it simple."

"I think I'm rubbing off on you. I love it."

"Don't make me feel guilty." I grin and change the subject. "How are you and Max?"

"He was a little weird when I first got back from my Barbados trip; I think he was still mad that he couldn't go. But now things are fine." Clarissa shrugs.

"Has he brought up moving in lately?"

"Not for a while now. I think he finally gets it. He knows that I'm cut off if I move in with him before marriage. That's one rule my dad won't back down on."

"I mean, I get it, but is it really that bad?"

"Makes the family look bad. You know, people might talk. 'Arthur Thomas's daughter moves in with nobody boyfriend'," she says in a mocking tone.

"I just don't think people care about that. Everyone is so busy these days, they don't give a flying you-know-what about two twenty-year-olds moving in together. It's not like you're sixteen."

"Fuck. They don't give a flying fuck. There, I said it for you, and you're right. People don't care about who's moving in with whom," she says shrugging. "But truly, it's less pressure on me. I think it would be fun to live together, but financially we would struggle if my dad keeps his word. Besides, this way I can go from my place to his anytime I want. And there's that sushi place I love right next to his, and the art shop across the alley!"

"You'll have to bring me some time; I'd like to see it."

"Tomorrow?"

"Kia and I are jogging in the morning. Do you want to join us, we could go after?"

"Hell no. This is as far as my exercise goes. What about going at one?"

I shake my head. "Sai and I have plans to go to a street fair near his house. We're going around lunch to eat the terrible-for-you-but-ridiculously-good vendor food. After lunch, I was planning on bringing him to this hiking place I found."

"Sunday?" Clarissa asks as Hank yanks her back hard. I turn around to see Hank hunched over doing the one thing we hope doesn't happen when anyone else is around. Luckily, it's just us today. A little plastic dog bone hangs from the leash loop filled with tiny waste bags. Clarissa slowly scoops it up so that nothing comes into contact with her hand.

"Going to my parents' house. I haven't been over to see them in a while," I say.

"How about I call you the next time Max and I plan a date night and you and Sai can join us. It will be nice to meet him."

"Yeah, that would be fun."

We stop for a margarita at our favorite Mexican restaurant after we've finished walking the dogs. Every month they have a featured flavor, this month is watermelon; I decide to go for it. Clarissa orders raspberry lime, our usual go-to.

For the last two years, the four of us would meet here during the summer on every second Friday. The rule was at least one person had to order that month's flavor, and only once we were disappointed. It had been my turn and the flavor was banana. I should have known when I ordered it to have low expectations. It tasted artificial and was way too sweet. Even with the girls trying to help, we couldn't finish it.

I make a mental note to suggest starting our tradition back up in June. I think we've just all been so busy that it slipped our minds. It was Clarissa's idea to come here tonight; she said she missed it and that the one near her campus just doesn't compare.

Our margaritas are delivered and the watermelon is pink, like I expected. I'm pleasantly surprised I like it as much as I do; the right amount of sweetness that goes perfectly with the salty bottomless chips and salsa we've been binge eating. Clarissa's cousin, Olivia, planned a last-minute trip home and wanted to meet up with Clarissa while she was in town, so we take off shortly after we finished our margaritas. She drops me at my car and I head to Sai's for the night.

Saturday

It takes me a minute to realize it's Saturday when I wake, and a moment of gratitude comes over me. I get ready for the day wearing a razorback 'I <3 Wisconsin' top and yoga shorts. My hair is in a pony pulled through my baseball cap. I grab a hoodie for later. I've learned to always bring backup because Wisconsin weather can change on a dime.

I pour coffee and creamer into a to-go mug and throw my water bottle and tennis shoes into a backpack. Giving Sai a kiss, I tell him I'll be back after my run with Kia, then I slip on my sandals and head for her place. She lives minutes from Lake Michigan and there's a newly paved trail that provides some nice shade, making it nice for a 9am run on a warm morning. Kia is the perfect running partner. We've been going together on weekends since middle school when we were in track. Sometimes we chat the entire time and others we stay silent until we've ended.

Running along the lake is a favorite. The sound of the waves crashing against the rocks puts you into a bit of a trance. One of my favorite runs was last Fall when we watched massive gray cumulonimbus clouds come in. As soon as we noticed the sun slipping away and the sky turning dark, we decided to turn around; we didn't want to get stuck in a downpour. Every time we looked over our shoulders it seemed as though the clouds had gained measurable distance on us. When the first few drops landed on our heads, they felt cold and heavy.

Kia and I looked at each other with big eyes, and without speaking we took off in a sprint. It was the fastest we've ever run in the long-distance back to our vehicles. By the end, we were soaked to the bone. We sat in my car with the heat on laughing our butts off for ten minutes. I don't know why we thought it was so funny, maybe because we thought we could outrun the rain, maybe because it made us feel like kids and we enjoyed every minute of it. We both went home and took a hot shower, the only thing we knew that would take away our chills and goosebumps.

Typically we walk to the lake from her duplex, but since we both have places to be, we drive there. We change into our running shoes and take off in our usual direction. There's a particular route we run because there's a tree branch sticking out as if it's going to give you a high five. Once we reach the branch, we high five it then turn around. There was controversy over having the branch removed because it could be harmful to someone not paying attention, but the people in this town went as far as petitioning to keep it. Kia and I both signed to keep it. From where we start, it's about forty minutes there and back. After our jog, Kia and I stop in at a smoothie shop to grab some carbs.

The shop opened two years ago, shortly before the trail was finished. It offers protein shakes and healthy, vegan smoothies. There is also The Carb Counter, where you will find an assortment of baked goods. Some are good for you, and some are most certainly not, but they taste really good. Little paper signs are propped up next to each selection with nutritional information. Both are equally popular and the place is always at least half full. Kia orders a green smoothie and a banana bread muffin. I order a blueberry scone with lemon glaze from the unhealthy side.

"Run again next Saturday?" Kia asks, breaking her muffin in half.

"I can't; Sai and I will be hiking up north all weekend. How about the Saturday after?"

"I think that should work." I see her tap her watch; she's checking her calendar. "Yeah, I'll put it down. But hey, I have to take off, I told my mom I'd help her with the garden. She just picked up her flowers."

"Okay, I'll walk you to your car." We stand, grabbing what's left at our table. "How are your parents?"

"Not great. I brought my dad to his last appointment and according to his doctor, most of his aches and pains are from being overweight and old. Not his exact words, but that's basically what he meant. My dad went in wanting more pain meds, but the doctor recommended physical therapy. If after three months he's still in a lot of pain, he'll re-evaluate his meds. My dad laughed in his face. I'm sure he'll be switching doctors soon."

"It's too bad he's in so much pain. How terrible to be so uncomfortable."

"I know, my parents are always complaining about the pain." She holds up her smoothie. "Maybe that doesn't need to be me though. They've eaten terribly their whole lives, so I hope this makes a difference.

We approach Kia's car. "Please tell your parents I say hello."

"I will. You should stop by sometime; they adore you."

"The feeling is mutual. They've always been my second set of parents," I say.

"Oh, I know. Every time I got into trouble, my dad would threaten to replace my name with yours in their will."

"That's hilarious. You never told me that!" I laugh.

"I'm sure it's because I was afraid there was some truth to it."

We hug. "Thanks for the jog date," I say.

"Anytime, love." She winks and gets into her car.

When I approach Sai's place, he's standing outside talking with the neighbor. He heads for my car as soon as I pull up, opening the door and getting in quickly. I hear the neighbor call out as Sai shuts the door, barely giving me enough time to wave in response.

"He's so nosy. Drive before he walks over."

I hit the gas a little too aggressively. There's no squeal but my car lurches forward as if I'm trying to make a getaway.

"Well, that was embarrassing. I hope he wasn't watching." I groan. I check the rearview mirror and unless his eyes were closed, he saw. He's still looking in our direction.

"What was he asking about?"

"Us. How old you are, how old I am, how we met, what your parents think. It's a bit rude, don't you think?"

"Besides asking what my parents think, those are commonly asked questions when someone's trying to get to know you," I say, trying to justify it.

"Well, it sounded like he was digging. I was grateful when I spotted your car," he says patting my knee.

I wonder if he had time to answer all the questions. Did he answer the question about my parents and their thoughts on our relationship? I'm not going to ask. It's always been a touchy subject.

"How was your run?"

"It was great. Actually, I was thinking about changing when I got back, but I guess I'm staying in these clothes now."

He looks me over. "Did you get sweaty? You don't even look like you ran."

"There was a nice breeze, so I didn't get too hot."

There is parking near the street fair and already tons of people around. The tent vendors and food trucks line both sides of the street, and Sai makes a beeline for the mini donuts. I can't resist ordering a cob of butter-drenched corn. I add pepper and salt, even though it probably already has a whole day's worth of sodium from the butter. We get a lemonade to share and find a picnic table near a few kiddie rides. There are kids anxiously waiting in long lines, dancing around as if they have ants in their pants. While eating, we watch the younger ones so innocent and cute, while the older ones whine impatiently at their parents.

"How many kids do you want?" Sai asks.

"Hmm, I'd like one of each for sure," I say casually. I've known since we met that he wants kids. "You?"

"At least two. I'd be happy with either, but I've always pictured myself having girls. But we can have as many as you want." He looks me in the eyes and smiles.

I return his smile and take one of his donuts, looking back to the kids. Sai has always talked of the future, as if we were already married, even since our first month together. One time he got upset because I referred to my bed as 'mine' and not 'ours'. I've always thought he was more like a girl in that way.

He cares about how things are said and pays very close attention to how I answer questions about us.

"Hey, remember that waterfall I was telling you about?"

"Yeah." He nods.

"It's actually only thirty minutes from here."

"That's great, when do you want to go check it out?"

"Maybe when we're done here? After all the food we're eating, I'm going to want to get some more exercise." I chuckle.

"Yeah, and we can finish planning our trip for next weekend, too."

"Great." I smile. "Let's finish up here and we'll head out."

We walk to the end and back, and I find a few pieces of jewelry that catch my eye. I buy a small pair of natural stone earrings. Before leaving we order a basket of fried cheese curds, a turtle caramel apple and a bag of taffy to snack on for the week.

We drive just under thirty minutes to a place we didn't know existed until two weeks ago. There's a gravel parking lot with a few vehicles that I pull into. The information sign tells us it's approximately one mile to the waterfall.

The dirt path is easily two-person wide. We stop to take pictures along the way. The weather is perfect, seventy-five with a light breeze. There's plenty of shade coverage too so the sun's not beating down on us. The waterfall stands before us, and though it's only fifteen feet tall, it's beautiful. It's loud at first but after a while it becomes background noise and you barely notice it.

Another couple makes their way towards us from behind the waterfall. When they pass us, Sai takes my hand and we go to explore it. The mist settles on our arms and legs, the little water droplets give me goosebumps. We pose and take a selfie. I tuck my phone away and use my hands to guide me along the wet wall of rock behind the waterfall. It's so much louder up close and the mist is thick, causing my clothes to cling to my skin. On steadier ground, I snap a few more pictures. We continue along a thin ledge to the other side, moving slowly so as not to slip from the slick surface. We spend another half-hour walking around before walking back to the car.

I get on the interstate and drive south to Sai's. Once we get back I plan to shower, make a packing list for next weekend and make salads for dinner. Sai grabs the bag of taffy from the floor of the car and offers me the bag. I take one and set the bag in my lap.

"What time are you going to your parents' tomorrow?" Sai asks.

"Late morning. I'll probably sleep in and leave after breakfast."

"Great, I'll make us breakfast. Eggs? Pancakes?"

"Let's have both." I grin.

"You got it!" He says placing his hand on my knee. "Do you want me to come with you? It's been a while since I've seen your family."

"Nah, that's okay. Thanks for asking, though," I say, trying to make it sound casual.

"Hey, do you mind if I send myself those waterfall pictures?"

"Yeah, of course. Here." I hand him my phone, unlocking it.

"So, for Friday, I'll have everything packed and ready. When you get to the house we should be able to leave. It will take about five hours with stops to get there so I'll get food and snacks while you're at work. Let me know what you want for the car ride so we don't need to make extra stops." He smiles at me and then goes back to the pictures.

"Oh, I already know what I want; chocolate covered almonds, string cheese, those extra thin mint..." I trail off because I can tell somethings wrong. Sai's looking out the window and I can tell by his body language that he's upset.

"What's wrong?" My eyes shift down to see my phone open to a photo. It takes me a while to recognize it. When I do, I think my heart stops for a moment. It's the selfie I took last weekend on the pontoon in front of Bob's. I see Jack, Roo, Graham, Mick, and the girls. All eight of us are smiling happily and mixed together on the pontoon like we've been friends for years. I forgot all about the picture. How could I be so stupid? I close my eyes for a second, and feel my face burn. I know it's flushed red.

"What's wrong? Are you kidding me?" He says in a low voice. "You *lied* to me."

"Sai, I'm sorry." I nearly whisper. I have no idea what to say or how to get myself out of this.

"How could you lie to my face? I trusted you. You told me in the restaurant that that guy," jabs his finger at my phone, "was married and I had nothing to worry about. Do you know how shitty I feel right now? I don't think I've ever been so hurt."

"Sai please." I feel my throat tighten as I try to swallow. I wish more than anything I wasn't driving right now, I wish we were at his house or any place other than in the car. I'm so mad at myself for not deleting that picture.

He doesn't say anything and it's quiet for a few minutes. Too quiet.

"Are you even going to your parent's tomorrow?" He suddenly asks. His tone is accusing and I'm appalled.

"You think I'm making up trips to see my parents?" I answer a bit snappy.

"How am I supposed to know? Did you even jog with Kia this morning? Do I need to ask her?" He takes out his phone.

"Don't you dare get her involved." I push his phone and it lands on the mat of my car.

"Why, is she keeping a secret for you?" He asks, raising his voice.

"How dare you. Don't make stuff up. The picture is all it was. That's everything. Don't overthink it!" I say feeling heated.

"Jhett, right now I can't believe a word you're saying. You make me sick to my stomach!" He yells.

I slow down by nearly slamming on my breaks.

"Get out!" I yell.

"Are you crazy? Bring me to my house!"

"I can see a gas station. You can walk, figure it out. And to answer your question, NO! I'M NOT CRAZY, YOU ARE!" I yell back unbuckling his seatbelt.

He gets out and slams the door. I drive off frantically, glad there are no cars around to witness what just happened. I fight myself to keep my eyes forward. I glance up after about half a mile to see just a small figure in the rearview mirror. My phone rings. It's Sai and I automatically swipe to dismiss it. I turn the ringer to silent and then a second later decide to shut it off completely.

As soon as I'm in my apartment, I lock the door behind me and then remember Sai has a key. My heart has been racing since I drove off, maybe even sooner. For good measure, I prop a chair against the door. Not because I'm afraid of him, I just don't want to see him or talk to him for a long time. This way if he tries to come in, I'll hear him trying to enter and I can tell him to leave. I sit on the couch and cover my face with my hands. I take one deep inhale and just like that the tears flow. I cry hard and fall into a couch pillow, letting my tears soak into the fabric. I stay there all night. I cry myself to sleep.

I hear my back pop as I stretch myself awake. My neck feels kinked and I begin to remember all of what happened. I need to distract myself. I go over to Patches and take him out of his cage, bring him over to the couch and cuddle him. It feels good to hold his little body in my hands. He squeaks at me and then gives a grunt when I rub the spot on the top of his head between his ears. I lay on my back and place him on my stomach. I have a slight headache and wish I hadn't made plans to visit my family today. I don't want to talk about what happened, but I know they'll ask how things are going. I'll text my sister, tell her Sai and I got into a fight and to please tell Mom and Dad not to ask or bring him up. My phone slowly comes to life and I'm greeted with three voicemails and a handful of texts from Sai. I ignore them, but open a text from my sister, Kate.

Kate: Sorry, I won't be able 2 make it 2day...got called into work.

Nooo. What am I going to do now?

Jhett: Damn, I needed you today.

Kate: Reschedule, nxt Sun?

Sai and I would be hiking at St. Peters Dome and the surrounding waterfalls all weekend, but that is definitely not happening anymore. I can't even stand to think about him right now, let alone sit in a car for five hours with him after what happened yesterday.

Jhett: Sure, I'll be there

CHAPTER 7

I plug in my phone and turn on the news. I feel my stomach growl and I'm reminded I didn't eat last night. I get up to place Patches in his cage and empty some treats into his bowl, he hurries over and starts to nibble on them. I take a long, hot shower. I wrap my hair in the towel and dress in jean shorts and a t-shirt. I walk into the kitchen and pull open the fridge. I stare for a while and tell myself to focus, grabbing the cream cheese and last cinnamon raisin bagel.

The bagel has undoubtedly gone stale, but I can't bring myself to care at the moment. I fill a large glass with water while my bagel toasts and start to drink slowly. The toaster clicks and my bagel springs to the top, I remove it from the toaster and frost it. It's a bit dry but I pick at it until it's gone.

I look at Sai's name next to the unopened texts and feel a pit in my stomach. I'm so mad. I don't want to hear his voice or read anything he has to say. I'm afraid he might even stop by to talk, so I leave early for my parents' house.

I arrive at my parents just before 10am. I'm greeted with hugs and loving smiles, and force a smile so that it's not blatantly obvious I'm upset.

My dad always asks, and he doesn't disappoint today, "Can I get you something to drink sweetheart? I just started making your mother a Bloody Mary, would you like one?"

"Yes, actually that sounds great." I smile.

He smiles and turns away from me heading into the pantry. My mom and I walk through the house and onto the deck.

"It's so nice out," she says as she shoos a few chickens off the steps. "Oh, did you know, Kate can't make it today; she has to work."

"She told me. But we made plans to come here next Sunday. If that's okay." I look up.

"Of course! You never have to ask."

"Well I guess we made the plans without asking if you'd be here."

"Where else would we be on a Sunday morning, besides church I mean?"

"I don't know, sometimes you surprise me. You could be flying."

"Your dad and I haven't been going as much as we have the last few years."

My dad got his private pilot's licenses a few years ago and has been out flying at least twice a month since. It's usually a short trip, to the Flyer's club where they meet for brunch once a month, or to a small island a few hours away.

"I've noticed. Why is that?"

"You know, I don't know, you should ask him." She starts picking at her hanging baskets, deadheading the old buds to make room for the new. A moment passes before she adds in a more upbeat tone, "Did you hear your brother and Morgan are stopping over?"

"Today?" I look up and she nods. "No, I thought they were out of town and wouldn't be home until later."

"I guess they stayed home. They should be here within the hour."

My dad comes out of the house carrying a little tray with our Bloody Marys. He looks them over and hands me one. Cheese whips, a beef stick that I'm sure is jalapeno cheddar, two green olives and a pickle spear. He remembers exactly how I like them. He makes them all custom to our liking.

"Nice tray," I say.

"Thanks." He smiles and looks proud of it.

Never in a million years did I think my dad would be serving me a Bloody Mary on a tray. He was pretty strict with us growing up, but I suppose age has softened him, and now he seems to like serving us instead of the other way around.

We hear a door shut from inside the house, followed by a few voices.

"They must be here." My mom says, leaning over to look through the doorway.

My brother Beck and sister-in-law Morgan walk out onto the deck, prepared for the welcoming hugs from the rest of us. Morgan said the first thing she noticed about our family is that we are very huggy people; the first time she came to a family reunion she said it was a bit overwhelming because she hugged at least thirty people in the first five minutes. She joked she was nervous it would never end.

Morgan walks over and sits in the open seat next to me.

"How have you been, Mo? I didn't think I'd be seeing you guys today," I say.

"Good, really good. How have you been?"

"Yeah, same." I try to sound convincing but my energy just isn't there. My brother cuts in, which relieves me, I don't want to talk about my life right now.

"Yeah, we canceled our trip. We've just been so busy. And, you know, not having anything to do for one weekend has been so great. I feel so refreshed."

My dad comes out with a platter of mixed cheeses and crackers.

"I got these from the cheese store, the one with the giant cow out front," he says, pointing down the road as if we needed to know the direction.

"Yeah, we know the place you're talking about, Dad. We've all been there a handful of times," Beck says in a teasing tone and we all share in a little laugh.

"Is Kate still coming over?" Morgan asks.

"Oh no, she had to fill in for someone at work." Mom answers.

"Oh, that's too bad," Morgan says disappointedly.

"She'll be here next Sunday if you want to see her."

"Oh, yes, well…" she trails off. She looks at my brother and he nods. "We, so…um," she clears her throat. "We're actually here to tell you all, that we're pregnant!" Her face goes from unsure to relieved to exhilarated in a matter of seconds.

"Oh my gosh!" My mom screams and it startles me half to death. She runs over and hugs and kisses them both.

"Mom, are you crying?" Beck asks.

"Tears of joy, tears of joy." She sobs and wipes them away.

Dad and I are up congratulating them too. I'm so happy for them; they've been married for two years and have been trying for just as long. They were looking into options to help them conceive if it didn't happen by Fall; Morgan is a bit older than Beck and it had been a big worry for them.

"How far along are you? When is the baby due?" My mom asks, standing only inches from Morgan.

I get up and sit next to my dad, and my mom jumps into my chair without taking her eyes from Morgan.

"This will keep her busy for a while," I whisper to my dad. He nods and I can tell he is equally enthralled.

"I was twelve weeks on Friday. Baby is due at the beginning of December." Morgan says cheerfully. "Since Kate's not here, will you please keep it to yourselves until we tell her? We also need to tell the rest of my family. We told my parents last night so you're the only ones that know so far."

"Of course." My mom says. "Will you find out the gender?"

"We aren't sure yet," my brother says looking at Morgan. "We can't agree," he says with a chuckle. "I want it to be a surprise, she wants to find out."

All at once, Mom is saying, "find out!" and Dad and I are saying, "keep it a surprise!" We all laugh because we know this is no help to them.

"I want to start shopping." Mom says, looking worried, as if you can only buy baby items if you know the gender.

"If we do find out, it will be after the shower. A friend of mine got a ton of baby clothes because they knew they were having a girl, and not much else, so she suggested if we want to find out, to do it during or after the baby shower."

As they continue talking, I notice my cell phone light up next to my mom. I sneak over to grab it while everyone is distracted with the baby news. Just as I hoped, my movements don't seem to faze anyone; I'm probably the furthest thing from their minds. I see it's another missed call from Sai. At least he's not leaving voicemails anymore. As I'm about to shut it down, something on my screen catches my eye. I do a double-take and notice the bubble at the top of the screen, and excuse myself to the bathroom. There are many questions to be answered by Morgan and Beck so I know I can get away for a few minutes. I lock the door and take a seat on the side of the tub. I look at the bubble again, my face breaks into a smile as I read Roo's name.

Hey Jhett,

I hope all is well with you. I just wanted to share that I reconnected with my old friend. The one that took Ralph, my pet snake. He was on my mind after we talked so I searched for him. He remembered me and told me that Ralph lived with him until a few years ago. He sent a few pictures; Ralph looked exactly as I remembered him. Anyway, it was nice to find out what happened to him, it was closure I didn't know I needed.

Oh, and last weekend…it was great. The guys and I would have had a good fishing trip no matter what, but you made it unforgettable. I'm still hoping I get to see you again.

I read it a second time. The smile still on my face; the ending is my favorite part. I'll respond later when I have more time, for now, I should rejoin the baby conversation. There is so much love here and the vibe is great; it's a good distraction from my current mess with Sai. I leave after lunch, and though my mood is better I feel exhausted.

When I get inside my apartment I decide it's been long enough without listening to Sai's voicemails.

Jhett, please come back. We can talk. I'm at the gas station.

His voice shaken and pleading. I feel a pang of guilt leaving him roadside. Then I remember how he accused me of lying about my jog with Kia and my plans to meet with my parents today. I hope he didn't wait long before calling a ride. My guilty feeling is quickly gone.

Delete. The next message comes through.

Jhett, please call me. We need to talk. Please. I know you're upset. I said some things...we need to talk to clear the air. I'm sorry.

This time his voice is calm. There's no anger but I can hear the sadness. The next message, less than an hour later:

I miss you. I know I need to give you space, let you cool down, but it's really hard. I just want to be with you. I'm going crazy.

Listening to his messages bring up mixed feelings. I know it's not fair to fall off the face of the earth but there's no way we can have a conversation right now. I feel on edge and emotional.

The next one starts. It's from this morning.

What's going on, Jhett? Please call me back, or answer when I call. This is driving me nuts. I need to know what you're thinking. I didn't sleep at all last night.

Panic and worry is in his voice. He sounds like he's suffering. I delete them and go to my texts. It's all the same. Some sad, some pathetic, and some irritate me. I groan to myself and think maybe if I send him a reply he'll stop blowing up my phone.

Jhett: I'm not ready to talk and I don't want to see you. I need time to clear my head. I'll let you know when I'm ready.

Not even a minute later comes his response.

Sai: Thank you for breaking the silence. Every second that drags by feels like hours when I don't know where you are or who you're talking to.

Jhett: Who I'm talking to?! You're referring to the group of guys aren't you? This is why I'm so mad. You think I'm doing stuff behind your back.

It's bad timing that I had just got a message from Roo, but I'm not going to worry about that. A minute or two passes before I get a text back.

Sai: You lied to me. You didn't mention you were off flirting with a group of men all weekend who wanted nothing more than to hook up with you. I know how they think. Most men are pigs. Even if they know you're taken, nothing stops them from trying. I can't help but worry about you. Men stare at you all the time. Most of the time you don't even see it, but I DO. It drives me nuts when you're somewhere without me.

Jhett: Sai, I'm shutting my phone off. You'll hear from me when I'm ready. And in case you're wondering, I will not be hiking with you this weekend, the trip is off.

I don't actually plan to shut my phone off but I do want him to understand that I will not be responding to any future texts. He texts back anyway like I thought he would.

Sai: I need to see you. We can meet for dinner tonight. You don't have to come here if you don't want to, I'll meet you anywhere. Please Jhett, I love you.

I exit out and shut my screen off. Even though I have little energy I walk to Jillian's apartment and knock on her door. She opens and smiles when she sees me.

"Hey Jillian, would you be up for a walk?"

"Yeah sure, I was just thinking of going outside, it's so nice out. Come in, I'll be just a sec." She goes into her room and returns carrying socks. She unfolds them, slips them on and slides her feet into her shoes.

"So, how've you been?" She asks.

"Okay." I sigh. She waits for me to continue. "Sai and I got into an argument yesterday and things are not going so well."

"Hmm." She has a look on her face like there's something on her mind. "You know, I thought I saw him drive past last night. I was on my balcony watering my flowers. He was driving by really slow, which is why I noticed in the first place. I wasn't sure if it was him but then I saw him again this

99

morning. Really early, like before 6am, but this morning when I waved he sped off. I thought it was a bit weird and so unlike him. He's usually so friendly."

I feel heat rise inside my body. I take a deep breath and can feel Jillian looking at me. I clear my throat. "He didn't mention that when we talked. I'm glad to know. I had a feeling he'd try to come over but I didn't know he was checking up on me." I feel so irritated that I'm tempted to call him right now.

"Maybe after our walk we should have a drink?" She suggests.

I lightly shake my head, "No, thanks though." I muster up a little smile.

I change the topic and start asking what's going on in her life, hoping I can concentrate enough to keep my mind off Sai. It doesn't really work; I can't help but let my mind wander back to him, and I have to ask her to repeat herself a few times. I feel guilty but she doesn't seem to mind. After a forty-five-minute walk, I feel slightly better. I thank Jillian for keeping me company and for letting me vent. We part ways and once I'm inside my apartment I text Danielle.

Jhett: Still up for meeting on Tuesday?

Danielle: Yes! I was going to text you, a bubble tea shop just opened a few blocks from my apartment. Want to check it out? 5:30?

Jhett: Sure, sounds interesting

I look at my gym bag sitting next to the front door. I try to work out three to four times a week. Sai joins me most nights after work, and come to think of it, I've never gone without him after we started dating. Now I just don't want to run into him. I search on my phone for in-house workouts, and after looking through a variety of workout plans I end up doing a series of push-ups, crunches and planks. My anger towards him fuels me and I push myself harder than I have in the past few months at the gym. By the end I'm breathing hard, sweating and feeling satisfied. I wander into the kitchen to refill my water, and check my grocery status while I'm at it. My fridge is nearly bare, and unfortunately the cupboards seem to be as well. I've been spending so much time at Sai's that my apartment hardly looks lived in when it comes to food. I open my grocery app and make a list for the week. I'll go to the store tomorrow after work.

I normally wouldn't go on a Monday since it's my least favorite day of the week, but Sai knows this, so he won't be expecting me to go there. We typically avoid the gym and grocery store and treat the afternoon like a Sunday. I'll take my gym bag too since he most likely won't be there either. I go into the living room and sit; my muscles are tired. I know that if I were to lay down now, I would end up falling asleep. I force myself up to take a shower. Once in, I realize it's exactly what I needed, the water feels amazing running down my body. The smell coming off my skin is a mixture of sweat and that sun smell after being outside for hours. I close my eyes and let my head drop back, feeling the water saturate my hair while I listen to the relaxing sound of a thunderstorm from my playlist. After a long while I turn the water off, dry myself and wrap the towel around my hair. I dig for my softest and most comfortable pajamas. I've owned these clothes for years and I would be embarrassed to be seen in them. I climb into bed stuffing extra pillows behind me. I pick up my book off my nightstand and read until I fall asleep.

Monday

Everyone is huddled at work getting ready to meet our new short-term consultant. She walks up with our boss and at first glance she looks like one hard-ass woman. Her frame is strong and she has a man's build. Her name is Geri Oles. Our boss gives a short introduction and talks about changes we'll see around the office put in place by Geri. When she starts to talk it seems as though she is struggling not to yell. She gives us a quick background and the first thing that sticks out is when she tells us she was a Lieutenant in the military. I should have seen that coming; if I had to guess, I would have predicted she had a military background.

"Finding problems in this office is why I'm here. When a change needs to be made you need to accept it. What may seem normal to you, because it's what you know or how you've always done it, does not mean that it is the right way or the best way. You will dislike some of these changes. You may even learn to hate me," she says and then busts out into hacking laughter. "But I am here for a reason and I will do everything in my power to bring this business from subpar to supreme by the time I leave."

I glance at Emma, she looks intimidated, and everyone in the office is still and quiet, except for our boss who is beaming at her. If I had to guess I'd say he may have a crush on her. She towers over him and he seems to like it. We break away after a few uncomfortable minutes to prepare for our patients. As I'm about to turn to discuss the meeting with Emma we nearly collide. She places her hand on my shoulder and whispers so quietly that I can barely hear her. "She is so scary. I thought we were told we would love her?"

"Bossman must have meant *he'll* love her rather than *we* will. Did you see the look on his face? He was smitten." I shudder.

"I guess everyone has their type," Emma says, shrugging. "I'm just going to steer clear."

"Hey, speaking of that. Have you found anyone who fits your *type?*" I ask.

"I've gotten two emails!" Her eyes brighten with excitement.

We're each leaning halfway into the door of our first patients' rooms when I see Geri coming towards us.

"Okay, fill me in at lunch!" I say.

As soon as I say it, I hear Geri's deep voice. "We're having a mandatory meeting over the lunch hour today." No smile, no hint of approachability. I nod, feeling stupid. She stops in front of me, her eyes stare into mine as if in a challenge." Don't you have a patient to call back?" She questions, her face flat.

"Yes ma'am." I shudder. Why am I so frightened of her? As I leave, I can feel her eyes on me. I hope this woman doesn't stay long; I dislike her already.

My day continues with the same uncomfortable feeling anytime I see or hear Geri in the office. When I'm finished with work it takes no time at all to decide that the gym and grocery store will have to be postponed. The stress of this woman being in our office has mentally drained me. I can't wait to get home and just unwind.

Tuesday

After another ruthless day at work, I feel good knowing I'm about to see Danielle. She's already waiting outside for me when I get to her apartment, extending something out to me wrapped in a paper towel.

"What's this?"

"It's a buffalo chicken wrap with pickles," she says. "Medium heat."

"Wow, thanks."

"I thought you might be hungry."

I take a bite as we sit down at a picnic area behind her apartment.

"This is really good! Thanks for thinking of me."

When Danielle and I lived together we shared meals all the time, even when we couldn't eat at the same time. She worked a lot of afternoons and evenings so if she made something during the day, she'd leave a dish for me and I'd do the same for her. Typically, we'd get to eat together twice a week. Our go-to takeout was from our favorite pizza place only minutes away. We chose their mouthwatering taco pizza or incredible

BLT pizza. Other nights we'd search for a meal idea and then cook it together. I've missed dinners with her.

"How are things with Sai?" She asks.

"Not very good. His jealousy is a bit out of control and it concerns me."

"Is he controlling?"

"A week ago I would have said no, but I think I've been blinded by some of the things that I thought he was doing to be sweet. Now I've been thinking his actions were just due to his own insecurities. His constant need to check on me has always been annoying, and when I mentioned it a few weeks ago I thought he would try to make some progress." I shrug.

"Did he slowly go back to his old ways?"

"Yep, right back to constant calls and texts anytime I wasn't with him. He plays the guilt card if I plan to do something solo, and I cave." I look at Danielle with a guilty face. "But to make things worse, he saw the pontoon picture. The one with all of us, including the guys. Trust is out the door." I wave my hand. "I can't blame him for being hurt, but before we would have been able to talk and resolve the problem. But on Saturday he accused me of lying amongst other things."

"Wow, not good. So, what now?"

"I'm waiting for the right time to talk to him. I care about him and we have fun together..." I suddenly remember what Jillian told me, and my anger comes flooding back. "Oh, I almost forget to tell you!" I half shout. "He was spying on me. Sunday night and early yesterday morning my neighbor saw him driving slowly past our apartment complex. Danielle, he was checking to see if someone was there with me. I know him. I guarantee he checked the cars in the lot."

"Jhett, that's pretty bad."

"Agh." I rub the back of my neck with my hand. "If I say, I wish things were easy, would that make life boring? I've had a constant headache since Sunday."

"No, I don't think what he's doing is healthy," Danielle says sadly.

I know she's right, but I'm ready to move on from talking about him. "Let's go check out the bubble tea place. And you can fill me in on what's going on with you," I say, wrapping up what's left of my wrap.

"Okay." She agrees and we stand. "Hmm, well," she pauses, "I think Ben and I are done."

"What? Really?"

"I wasn't ready before, but I think I'm ready now. I'm going to break up with him."

"What was the turning point?"

"A lot of things. He's a guy's guy, ya know? I'll never come first, and I was okay with that for a while." She waits a beat and then adds, "I think when we first started dating, I just assumed his behavior and our relationship was normal. He chose his friends over me all the time. But it never got better, he still does that and he never sticks up for me. He'll choose their side over mine every time and it feels immature, and makes me feel shitty."

"Danielle, that's awful, he shouldn't make you feel that way."

"I know. It's just really hard, we've been together for six years. I don't know what it's like not talking to him. He's my best friend."

"I know he is. But," I try to say this softly, "you wouldn't be friends with any of us if we treated you like that or made you feel that way, right?"

"Right, but it doesn't make it any easier," she says.

"You just call and I'll be there, okay? We can do anything to keep your mind off him, just name it."

"Yes, we'll have to." Her eyes look towards the bubble tea shop. We're stopped at the corner across from it. "Shall we?"

"Yes," I say. "Now tell me, what is bubble tea?"

"So, I read about it. It's a drink made of tea, milk, sugar and flavoring. You'll see little balls or squares, moving around at the bottom, those are made of tapioca. They're small and jelly-like and they come through the straw."

"Hmm, interesting." We walk up to the counter and read off the flavors: strawberry hibiscus, lavender, matcha, coconut nectar, desert pear, mango milk, and taro, and in parentheses, it says cookies and cream.

I order the Taro and Danielle gets the Strawberry Hibiscus. We take a sip and I wait for her reaction.

"It's good, in a weird way, right?" Danielle asks.

"Yeah, I like it. Good flavor, just different." I answer with a shrug. "Are you chewing the ball or swallowing?"

She laughs, "The pearl, you mean. Sorry, I just remembered they're called pearls."

"Ha-Ha, just tell me how to eat it." But now I'm laughing.

"I think if you chew you get more of the flavor. I'm pretty sure they're soaked in the flavoring."

"Right." I take a drink and chew, but I'm unable to hold in the gag that escapes.

"Oh my gosh," she's laughing even harder now, "did you just gag?"

"Yes," my hand up to my mouth, "but I'm fine, I was overthinking it. I'm pretty sure I like it." I take another sip to convince her, "Want to try mine?"

She nods and we swap cups. Hers is sweet and fruity. Mine is chocolaty and creamy. I certainly like the flavor but it's the texture that first threw me off. After playing with the texture of the pearl, I feel like it's growing on me.

I break our short silence. "So, I haven't told anyone yet, but Roo sent me a private message."

"What did it say?" She looks excited.

"Just small talk. He mentioned something we talked about on the beach. Danny, he's on my mind all the time."

"What did you say back?" She asks eagerly.

"I haven't yet. I'm hesitant because I feel like it's crossing a line. Sai and I are still together," I say like it's obvious.

"Come on, you have to write him back, you can't be rude." She teases.

"True. I can keep it friendly. You know, no flirting."

"If you can help it." She smiles at me. "And are you?"

"What?" I ask confused.

"Together, with Sai. Or, are you on a break, or 'timeout'?" She says searching for the right word, using finger quotes.

I squint at her and giggle, "A timeout, really?" I consider this. "I didn't say anything about us not being together, but it feels like we're taking a break." I frown. "I honestly don't want to be his girlfriend at this moment." I rub my thumb up the side of my plastic clear cup, pushing the condensation away. Danielle's eyes are glossed over, as if her mind is off in another world, and I wonder if that's the same look I had on my face when Jillian and I went on our walk. "When do you think you'll tell Ben it's over?"

"I can't do it over the weekend, so I think I'll do it on a Monday. If my mind is busy at work, I'll get through the week easier. If I don't have a set schedule, I'll be miserable. I'll think and overthink like I did when we broke up two years ago. Remember that? I just kept second-guessing myself. I don't want to take him back this time. I'm ready to move forward."

"I can tell you are."

"What if I can't find the courage to do it? What if I chicken out? Breaking up is so hard."

"Remind yourself why you're doing it, you're not happy with him. I know it's hard losing the person you've been so close with, but it will get easier each week." I reassure her.

"Well that's the thing, I don't feel like we're that close anymore. I feel like we've been drifting further and further apart, and I just don't care anymore."

"Should we make a plan to come over after it happens? You can send a group text and we'll be there."

"No, that's okay, but thanks. I don't think I'll want to talk about it right away."

"Okay. Just know that if you change your mind I'll be there. I can spend the night, or you can come to my place."

It's Danielle's apartment but Ben stays over almost every night. He claimed his parent's basement after his older twin brothers moved out, but he still spends most of his time at Danny's and has quite a collection of his belongings at her place. I imagine the break up will be drawn out and he'll be back daily for something he forgot.

Then, as if she read my mind, she says, "I think I'll box up most of his things while he's at work. That way I don't have to see him again and again. There's nothing harder or more awkward." A look of dread washes over her face.

The walk back to her apartment is silent, I think we both have a lot on our minds. When we get back to her apartment, I suggest, "When you do it, try to have something you can focus on. Find something that interests you, like a new hobby, to pull your mind away from the overthinking. It may help."

She smiles, but her eyes look sad. "Okay, I'll try. And Jhett, I know it will be okay. I just need the courage to do it and then make it past those first few weeks."

I give her one last hug before leaving, and can't help but see the similarities with her situation and mine. Thoughts of my relationship with Sai bounce around in my head, and I find it funny how it's so easy for me to give Danielle advice about her relationship when I feel so lost in my own. I wonder what she'd tell me if I asked her to give me her honest opinion about my relationship with Sai. I wonder if deep down I really want to know. I know he's done some questionable things, but I also know I'd end up defending him. I already know that my parents don't care for our relationship. I wonder how many of my friends question it, too?

When I reach home, I open my tablet and pull up Roo's message. I read it again and then view his profile. To my surprise, he is friends with my cousin Angie. This makes me curious. She's a small-town girl who has never moved away and spends all of her time with the same two best friends she's had since high school; someone I do not peg Roo to particularly mesh with. Plus, they live hours apart. I suppose I could be wrong; she could have moved away temporarily without me knowing, or he could have lived near her. He did say his family moved around a lot. I could just ask her; she's always been an open book. She's constantly posting her weekend plans on social media, backyard parties, beach get-togethers, bartending photos with her regulars, or her newest guy are always popping up. We used to be much closer when we were kids, always excited for the next time we'd see each other. We have a big family reunion every Fourth of July and we would spend every minute glued to each other. She was sort of a trouble maker. She'd talk back to her parents and push the limits. Naturally, I looked up to her bravery and confidence. As we got older, though, the 'don't tell me what to do' attitude started to look immature instead of cool and I felt like she was trying too hard. I remember thinking she was loud and bratty, and I was not as fond of her as we became teens. She shared details about her boyfriends and each year she seemed to go through them faster and faster. I always thought she was a bit slutty but I enjoyed hearing about the drama and the details about her sex life. It was good enough for me to look forward to catching up each summer.

After eagerly swiping through Roo's photos, I have the itch to message him now.

Hey!

I think it's really great that you reconnected with your old friend. It must be comforting to know Ralph had a nice long life with him.

I entirely agree about the weekend. It was a lot fun and I'm glad to have met you all! Whoever's idea it was to send us the shots, smart move. And I'd be happy to see you again too.

It looks like we have one mutual friend. How do you know Angie Thor?

My subconscious tells me that sending this will only fuel Sai's anger, but I feel so strongly about seeing him again that I send it anyway. I know I need to be productive so I grab my purse and keys, and decide it's finally time to stock my fridge. I'm surprised by how dead the lot is when I'm able to get a spot right up front. The inside of the store matches the lot and I'm able to move quickly through the aisles. After my cart is more than half full, I figure this should at least get me through the week, and head to check-out.

When I get home, I unload my bags and take a treat out for Patches, dropping a carrot and piece of lettuce into his dish. He scampers over and starts to crunch his treats. I finish putting away my groceries, wash my hands, and go back to pick up Patches. He squeaks for more. I put a few lettuce leaves on my stomach and let him munch on them, scratching the course hair on his back and smile as he grunts in satisfaction. My phone rings, pulling both of us out of our relaxing state, and I roll my eyes at Sai's name flashing across the screen. He can go to voicemail.

CHAPTER 8

Emma and I walk into Marco's and take a seat at the bar. Demi, my usual bartender, walks over with a smile.

"What can I get you ladies?" Demi asks.

"I'll take a summer hummer." It's my typical go-to when I'm here.

"What's that?" Emma turns to me.

"It's vodka and lemonade. That's the traditional way, or you can get it with raspberry lemonade to make it a pink summer hummer; both are super good!"

"Okay, I'll try that." It almost comes out like a question as she turns to Demi.

"You'll like it. It's a very popular summer drink." Demi smiles at her. "Wings too?"

"Yes, thanks," I say.

I turn to Emma, "What do you normally drink when you go out?"

"Um, I don't go out really. Sometimes I'll go out to dinner with my parents and occasionally I'll have a sip of my mom's beer. She'll order one and drive us home. My dad will order a bitter dark beer or an old fashioned; I think both are terrible."

"Hmm. Well, bartenders are really good at suggesting drinks if you're ever stuck on what to order." I wait a moment and then ask, "Are your parents okay with you drinking?"

"Oh yeah, my mom is always telling me to order something when we're out to dinner. Most things I've tried I just haven't liked so I feel bad if I don't finish it."

I look at her with curiosity. I didn't know Emma in high school but if I had to guess, I'd say she was the teacher's pet. I love the girl but she is definitely not one to take risks.

"So, tell me about these guys! I can't believe I've had to wait this long. I'm dying to know!"

"I know, I don't like that we weren't able to talk much this week." Annoyance shows on her face, but quickly turns to excitement, "So, there's Logan and JJ. I really like them both and I've been texting with them almost every day. They're both really good looking, too, so it makes it really hard."

"But that's the fun. Options! You can go on dates with both!" I wink at her.

She giggles. "I suppose, but what if I can't decide between them? They are so different from each other. They're both really sweet in their own way. And they both make me laugh."

"Well of course, they're trying to impress you. Time will tell, and if you go on a couple of dates you'll feel a stronger connection to one of them."

Demi carries over our drinks and seconds later brings plates and a stack of napkins. She also places a drink chip next to each of our glasses, reminding us it's double bubble, meaning you get two drinks for the price of one, until 7pm.

Emma and I grab our plates and move to the wing table, piling our plates and then taking our seats back at the bar.

"So, describe them to me."

She's just taken her first bite so she swallows, wipes her mouth and then clears her throat. "Logan has more of a baby face and JJ has a mature face with a square jawline. JJ is really hot and Logan I'd describe as cute, but I'm very attracted to both."

"Yeah, you've made that pretty clear." I tease. "What else?"

"Well, I know they are both taller than me. Logan is lean and I can tell he is really smart. He's going to school for computer science, and has a year left. He kind of takes his time when replying, so I think he'll be a bit quieter and shy when we meet. JJ is witty and quick with his replies. I know he works out and he seems to have more confidence." She's smiling.

"When do you get to meet them?"

"I'm going out with Logan on Friday and JJ on Saturday. They both wanted to meet sooner but I didn't want to go out on a weeknight."

"Wow, how fun! Aren't you full of anticipation?"

"Well yes, of course! I'm a nervous wreck!" Her eyes are wide.

We both laugh and I notice our drinks are about gone. I tap my glass to hers. "Ready for your next one?"

"Sure! You were right, these are really good!"

She picks up her glass and sucks, draining the remainder of her drink until I hear air come through her straw. I motion for Demi at the end of the bar and she brings us another round. Our plates are empty too so we go over and grab a few more wings.

"These are so tasty!"

"I know, it's why I work out." I tell her. "Although I've been slacking the last two weeks. Time to get back on track before I fall off completely. It doesn't take long." I give her a goofy smile as I pick up my next chicken wing to take a bite. She laughs and does the same. "What are your date plans?"

"Logan is meeting me at the botanical gardens, and then we're going to trivia at this bar he likes. JJ's picking me up on Saturday for dinner and then we're planning to go to a movie after."

"Sounds like a really fun weekend!"

We sit and sip our drinks, pick at our wings, and talk for the next two hours. Although I know we could easily spend another two hours talking, we decide it's time to head home; we do have to work tomorrow after all.

"I can't wait to get all the details of your dates!" I say, unlocking my car.

"I'll tell you everything!" She says.

As soon as I'm back at my apartment I change into my pajamas and go to plug in my phone. I see the familiar bubble at the top of the screen once again, with Roo's face filling the circle. I smile eagerly, I've been waiting for his reply.

Hey Jhett,

How have you been? How's the start of your summer going?

Jack and I went disc golfing a few nights ago and we had some pretty great weather. No wind and no bugs. We had a few drinks so naturally Jack and I started talking about the fishing weekend and, of course, your names were brought up ... Not that I minded. ;) He told me that he's been texting with Clarissa. He wants us all to get together again. I told him I liked his idea but I don't know how easy that would be now that summer is here. Weekends are filling up fast, and I work every other. I don't think I ever asked, what do you do for work? I'm a financial advisor at a car dealership in Wisconsin Rapids. And, it just so happens my coworker went home with the flu so I have the opportunity to come to Sheboygan for work tomorrow and Friday. I haven't spent any time there and was hoping that if you'd be around maybe we could meet up. What do you think?

Yes, I know Angie. She dated my college roommate. How do you know her?

I'm excited at the thought of seeing him again, but in the next second my mind bounces to Sai. Is this crossing a boundary? I'm certain Sai would be furious. I'm sure he's going crazy right now because it's been days since we've last talked. I don't feel guilty about wanting to see Roo, but will I feel guilty after seeing him and flirting with him. Our banter is so flirty, that I have to take a moment to weigh the options between Sai's feelings and my own. It doesn't take long; I've made my decision. I want to see him, so I will. I write back.

Hello,

I've been good. I've gotten together with the girls a few times since our girls' weekend. How long have you been disc golfing? Are you any good?

114

Is that why you won the most rounds when we played on the beach? That's a bit unfair don't you think? ;)

I would really like to meet up. There are some cool local places that I'd be happy to show you. What time will you be done Friday?

I'm an LPN and I work at Lakefront Dermatology.

Angie is my cousin.

Minutes after I hit send, I hear my phone chirp. I skip over to it, and find that once again I'm smiling, seeing a new message.

I think it's cool that you girls are so close; in proximity and friendship wise. I wish the guys were closer. We generally get together twice a year, once in Spring to fish and once in Fall to hunt; we rent a cabin up north.

Haha, I have disc golfed twice in my life before last week. In all fairness, throwing the frisbee on the beach was the first time this year.

I'm glad to hear you can meet. And even happier to know I'll be shown around by a local!

Even without hearing him say it I can tell he's teasing me.

I'll be done around 5. Would it be possible for us to get dinner? Do you think your boyfriend would be ok with that? I don't want to cause any problems.

Too late, I think. I wonder if he's really asked to find out my current dating status. Maybe he's hoping I say that we aren't together anymore, or that I'm not telling him about this whole thing? I'm not sure how I should answer, maybe, I'll just tell him the truth. I sigh and stare out my window.

There's a gentle breeze and I see two birds flying happily around each other. One bright in color, I'm sure this is the male, the other is dull in color, most likely the female. Watching them, I understand the expression 'love birds'; they look so carefree. Do all birds mate for life like penguins and geese? Suddenly the male bird flies into my glass window, making me jump. After making sure he's okay and watching him fly away, I type a reply.

Yes, to dinner. Things are complicated with Sai. I guess you could say we're taking a break. He won't know we're going to dinner unless I tell him.

Let's plan to meet at Howard Park. I'm done early on Fridays so I can meet any time after 2…in case you get done early, otherwise I'll see you just after 5. I drive a black Impreza.

His immediate reply back:

Can't wait ;)

Thursday drags on and I find myself thinking of Roo most of the morning. I think of Sai too, but it's only because I know I need to face him eventually. Hushed whispers and excitement come from the front desk as I walk my last patient out. There's a lively bouquet of flowers sitting in front of our desk receptionist, Ruthie, and she smiles broadly at me. Her eyes shift back to the bouquet, and I know now the flowers are for me. I walk over and take the envelope which has my name written out on it and pull out the card.

I love you. I miss you. I'm sorry. Please call. Love, Sai

I feel a moment of disappointment. I thought for a brief second that they could have been from Roo. But now I feel foolish. He hardly even knows me and he knows that Sai is still in the picture. Why would he send me flowers? As I stand at the front desk I can feel attention on me. I'm not very close with the receptionists, and aside from them knowing that I'm in a relationship with a man named Sai, they have no idea what else is going on.

I move my eyes up and smile as sweetly as I can, trying to convince them that the flowers were a sweet surprise, and not sent in the form of apology. I take the bouquet and card and go down to the breakroom. I place the flowers on the breakroom table, and rip the card in fourths before throwing it in the trash.

Checking my phone, there's a voicemail from Sai. I delete it without hesitation. I remove my lunch from the fridge and sit at the table. Emma was running behind with her patient so I'm alone, and for once I don't want to be. I'd like to fill her in on my dilemma with Sai. It's cool and windy today so my plan of us walking is out the door. I hear footsteps on the stairs and hope it's Emma, but I hear muffled voices round the corner and see Emma joined by Ruthie.

"Oh, how beautiful!" Emma beams. "Are they yours? Sai sent them?"

"Yes, they are pretty." I admit.

"What a lucky girl you are," Ruthie says. Ruthie is an older woman who's been married for over thirty-five years to her high school sweetheart.

"I've always wanted flowers sent to me, but it's never happened. My husband is just too cheap. They lift your mood, don't you think?"

"They do!" I agree and smile, trying to cover the fact that I'm not particularly happy with who sent them. I plan to tell Emma everything as soon as Ruthie leaves, but she stays and spends her entire lunch break with us.

We finally make it to the end of the day, and the only thing that's been keeping me motivated is thinking about tomorrow with Roo. I try to think of where to bring him, and a small wave of anxiety hits me. What if it's awkward and he's not at all like I remember? We were drinking the entire time we were together. After a minute, I tell myself that I'm overreacting. Even if he's not as I remember, it will still be fun to play tour guide.

I have my gym bag in the back of my car and feel like I have the energy for a good workout, I just hope Sai won't be there. I drive the entire lot and breathe a sigh of relief when I don't see his car. I change and glance around again when leaving the locker room just to make sure.

I place my earbuds and start my three-mile workout on the elliptical. I zone into a reality tv show and before I know it, I'm nearly finished. I catch an arm-waving towards me from my peripheral vision, and my stomach drops as I register who it is. It's Sai and he's coming towards me; a desperate grin showing on his face. I feel anxiety hit me and a pit starts to form in my stomach. I slow the machine, hitting pause, to step off of it.

"Can I hug you?"

And before I can even process his question, I'm wrapped in a deep hug. I feel claustrophobic and uncomfortable.

"Why are you resisting me? Can't I give you a hug?" Hurt fills his voice.

I take a deep breath, feeling awkward about us meeting like this in a public place, hoping to God no one is watching us. For a Thursday afternoon, it's slower than usual and I don't see anyone looking in our direction.

"Let's sit down." I motion to some chairs off to the side. "I didn't plan on seeing you here. I'm sorry that I didn't reciprocate the hug. It's just…" I trail off not knowing what I should say. "I came to get a workout and didn't want to think about much else."

His hands go up to cover his face and he lets out a deep sigh. "I miss you so much." It's almost a whisper. "I don't care about anything. Not the picture. Not the married guy in the restaurant. I just want us to be okay." His words are tender and soft. "I haven't slept since you left. I don't have an appetite; this is the third time I've been here this week…" he trails off.

I know he's telling the truth; his eyes are bloodshot and he looks like he's lost weight.

"You've been working out but not eating? That's not healthy," I say.

"No, I haven't had the energy for that either."

"Then why did you come here?"

His face changes and he knows he's just been busted. If he's not working out that means he's been coming here to run into me. I try to keep my voice even and fold my arms across

118

my chest. "Did you follow me, or have you been coming here every day looking for me?"

He's slowly shaking his head but doesn't speak.

"No?" I'm surprised by my own voice. Not loud but firm. "Tell me which it is?"

"I've come here only the past three days." He swallows. His head turns down, he sounds like a child that's just been caught doing something naughty and is trying to justify himself with a weak explanation.

"That's not cool. I told you to back off for a while. Doing this makes me want to take a step back, you realize that, don't you? I can't even miss you because you're always here." The words are harsh. And I can tell he's crushed.

"Have you been coming to my work or my apartment?" I question, already knowing the answer.

There's a second of hesitation and then he says "No, this was it."

I feel my jaw tighten as I clench my teeth; I stand up. As calmly as I can, I say, "You're lying. Do not call me or drive past my place again. Now, please leave so I can get back to my workout."

He gets up without saying anything and leaves with his head down. I feel so much anger inside me. I head back to the elliptical and stab at the buttons. I do another two miles at a greater speed and incline. I'm hot and winded with sweat dripping down my face and body. I go to the free weights and lift for forty minutes until my entire body feels like a wet noodle. I've never been so tired or so sweaty in my life. I can't help but think that anger is the key to a complete body workout.

By the time I get home, I'm cooled off and my hair is halfway dry from my lukewarm shower before leaving the gym. All I can focus on is how tired my leg muscles are as I walk up one flight of stairs. I go into my apartment, feed

Patches, and get into my pajamas. It's 7:45pm as I crawl into bed. I wake to my alarm the next morning.

Friday

The first thing I notice when I wake is a message from Roo. This immediately lifts my spirits and puts me in a good mood.

Good morning. Looking forward to seeing you this afternoon!

It's short and simple, yet it makes my heart beat faster in my chest.

By the time I get home I've worked up a mixture of nerves and excitement. I take a quick shower and dress in shorts and a tank top and try to do something with my hair. After ten minutes I settle on leaving it down. I try to keep myself busy until it's time to meet up, I switch the laundry and water my plants, but I keep running out of things to do. I grab my book and message Roo, letting him know I'm heading to the park early.

I park where I told him we could meet, and see someone making their way to my car as soon as I pull in. A big smile comes across my face when I realize that it's Roo walking towards me. He's smiling too and he lifts his hand to wave.

"Hey!" I say as I climb out of my car.

"Hi, how are you?" Roo asks and leans in for a gentle hug.

"I'm good. I didn't expect to see you here already."

"Ahh, I was bored out of my mind. I couldn't stand sitting there another minute knowing I could be outside with you. I left as soon as I got your message." He smiles his beautiful smile at me.

It's contagious and I feel myself turn into a ball of mush when he holds his gaze for an extra second. I try to bring myself back down so that it's not blatantly obvious that I have a crush on him. I'm pretty sure he feels the same pull of attraction that I do because I've felt it since the day on Kippers Island. "Will you get in trouble?" I ask.

"Maybe, but I'm not worried about it."

"Well, I really hope you don't. Have you walked around at all?"

"No, I wanted to wait for you, and I've only just beat you here. I did see a couple kids fishing down by the water. It was fun watching them get so excited pulling up the little fish they were catching. Reminded me of when I was a kid."

"Well let's go then!"

We walk towards the path and I explain how this park had been restored within the last few years, and how local artists compete to have their sculptures up along the walkway. We stop at the first of nineteen to read the plaque next to the piece; listing the artist's name, inspiration behind the piece, and a quick description of what we're looking at. Many of them have historical meaning. The first one stands about nine feet tall and is made of different metals. It's an old fisherman holding a net filled with fish. There are twelve kinds of fish to spot; each represents a species that you will find in Lake Michigan.

Roo starts naming off the fish without looking at the plaque.

"I thought you might like this one," I say.

He nods, grinning. "This is really cool. I can't wait to see the rest."

I have the urge to reach for his hand, but I quickly remind myself that we aren't a couple. My nervousness had dissipated the moment he said hello because it feels so natural to be near him. I laugh at the thought I had yesterday, thinking he wouldn't be what I remembered. In fact, he seems better. We continue until we reach the next statue. This one is of a girl and her mother holding hands and enjoying a day at the beach. The little girl is holding a bucket filled with shovels and scooping toys, the mother is wearing a big floppy sunhat and holds a picnic basket in her free hand and a blanket under her arm. Their smiles are big and joyful, and when looking at them you can't help but smile yourself.

We walk to the next statue. It's a beautiful mermaid made of copper. The details are exquisite. There's a pattern of colorful jewels of purple, green, blue and teal that cover her chest as if she's wearing a strapless bikini top. Just below that to the lowest part of her midsection starts a thin layer of tiny square glass pieces that reflect light from the sun. A few inches below her belly button starts her mermaid tail, which includes the same colors as the top but with less specks of purple. I run my hand over her body. I can't help but touch her.

"She's my favorite," I say staring at her.

"I can tell." He laughs.

"If you come after dark on a night when the moon is bright, she has this radiant glow."

"That would be cool to see."

We continue around the path, stopping at each statue to admire it. We talk about his job, my job, our friends, and places we've been. Once we're finished reading about the last statue, we take a seat at a nearby bench. We watch as two old women in windbreakers hustle by, they've lapped us once already on the path.

"Must be getting their steps in." Roo motions with his head in their direction.

"Yeah," I chuckle, "I think I'm going to be like that when I'm old, or I hope I am. I want to be able to keep up and get outside with my girlfriends, to walk the neighborhood. Do you ever think about what you'll be like at that age?"

"Well, first of all, I hope I'm still alive." He laughs. "Most of the males in my family haven't been so lucky when it comes to a life of long prosperity. Secondly, if I do make it that long, I better be retired by that age. I'll most likely fish, play cards and drink coffee like old men do."

"That sounds like a pretty relaxing life." There are a few moments of silence, but it's pleasant and not uncomfortable. "So, what do you say we move on?"

"Sounds good!" He says and we stand, making our way back to my car. He points to his car and I see it's only three spaces past mine.

"How would you feel about following me to my apartment, parking there, and walking to Marco's?"

"Sure, it's a nice afternoon, we should take advantage of it."

We get to my lot and park. Roo meets me and we move to the sidewalk. There are kids playing outside, dogs barking, flowers blooming in windowsills and in flower beds, sprinklers running, and there's just something in the air. It's a flawless summer afternoon.

"So, Marco's, what kind of place is this?"

"One of my favorites!" I say. "It's a bar with great food and great specials. Tonight, they will have a pizza buffet. And it isn't crappy bar pizza; their pizza is top-notch."

"I wasn't worried. Have I told you pizza is my favorite?"

"No," I laugh. "But, since most Americans are fans, I didn't think you'd oppose.

I automatically start towards my normal barstool, but Roo stops me by saying, "How about this table?" He motions to one alongside the wall, away from all others.

"Sure." I turn and follow him to a high, two-person pedestal table. Demi comes over wearing a playful smile.

"Nice seeing you again," she says, looking at me. "What can I get for ya?"

"I want to try the house sangria."

Roo clears his throat. "I'll try that coffee beer you have on tap."

"Sure thing. Are we having pizza?"

We nod. She turns around grabbing the plates and napkins that she had set behind her.

"She knows me well. I was just here on Wednesday with my coworker," I say, leaning into him.

"What's in the back?" He asks.

"Oh, it's so fun out there!" It used to be an old parking lot and now they have a volleyball court, horseshoes, cornhole, giant Jenga, and beer pong. There are leagues for volleyball and beer pong, which I think are taking place tonight.

"Wow, this place is cool, no wonder it's your favorite!"

Demi brings over our drinks. "There ya go, enjoy!"

"Thanks," we say in unison.

Roo and I take a drink and I motion over to the pizza buffet. "Ready?"

"Always!" He says.

Little signs sit next to the pizzas with their description:

Meat: Pepperoni, sausage, bacon, prosciutto, mozzarella & red sauce.

Margherita: Bruschetta tomatoes, mozzarella, basil & garlic olive oil.

Veggie: Roasted Cauliflower, broccoli, carrots & onions, five blend cheese & mascarpone garlic white sauce.

Spinach and Artichoke: blackened chicken, spinach, artichoke, onion, provolone & asiago white sauce.

Mediterranean: Olives, artichoke, tomatoes, feta cheese, olive oil & red sauce.

Fire House: Spicy jerk chicken, chili flakes, pineapple, onion & fiery red sauce.

Roo's looks me. "You didn't say gourmet! Oh man, my mouth is watering."

We fill our plates and head back to the table.

"If I don't eat too much, I'd love to beat you in a game of cornhole," he says.

"Don't be too confident. I won the last three games I played here."

We chitchat over the next hour with another round of drinks. I stay with the sangria, while Roo tries two other beers on tap.

Finally, when we've sat for a while after finishing our pizza, I look at Roo. "Want to go play a game?"

"You're on!" He says.

We head out to the back and see there are games of volleyball and beer pong going on, as I had thought. There are four guys playing horseshoes and two couples playing corn hole.

"I guess we're left with the giant Jenga," he says.

We stack them up to three feet tall as neatly as possible.

"Rock, paper, scissors for who goes first?" I suggest.

He nods.

"One, two, three and then shoot." I demonstrate so there's no confusion.

"Got it," he says a bit mockingly but gives a cute smile.

"Okay, ready?" I say. He nods and gives me a serious look, making me laugh. Our hands are out in fist form. "One, two, three."

I play scissors and he plays paper. I act out the motion by cutting his paper hand with my hand scissors and grin. "Wow, that was easy, I already beat you at our first game."

He smiles back. "And that's where it stops."

I win the first game in ten minutes, to which he quickly demands a rematch. "Go again?"

"Of course!"

"Do you want to stack while I get us another drink?" He asks.

"Yes!"

I'm finished before he's back so I take the time to check my phone. I'm excited to see a new group chat started by Clarissa.

Clarissa: Can anyone meet for brunch tomorrow?
Kia: I can make it! Jhett are you still hiking?
Danielle: Me too!
Jhett: I'm in. Canceled hiking trip with Sai. Where should we meet?
Clarissa: Little café down from my place, 11?

Kia: sure thing
Danielle: I'll be there!

I'm about to send another text when I hear Roo's voice, "Wow, did it get busy in there, sorry about that. Our table has been taken so you're stuck out here with me."

"You know, it's not that terrible." I toss my phone into my purse and look up at him.

"You go first this time."

We play two more games and Roo wins both. The horseshoes open up, so we play two games there.

"How about I grab the next round?" I offer and he agrees. When I get back Roo is seated next to a heat lamp. The sun is setting now so the temperature has started to drop a bit. We sit and talk for the next two hours and I'm surprised by how fast the time flies. When I look at my phone it's 9:30pm.

"Should we get going?"

"I'm fine with that. But only if we can come back to play cornhole sometime."

"It's a deal."

We shake on it. Feeling a little tipsy, I steady my balance for a moment before we move from the table. I wave goodbye to Demi and she shoots me a wink. As we walk back to my apartment, we talk about our plans for the following weeks; he tells me that he's coming back to Sheboygan in two weeks for a minor league baseball game with two friends. As he talks, our hands lightly brush against one another. The feel of his skin makes me tingle, and I have to force myself to resist taking his hand in mine. He asks if I've ever been to a minor league game and I tell him I haven't; I've only been to the major league games.

"Will you tailgate?" I ask.

"Oh, there's no other way." He pauses, "You know it's pretty easy to pick up another ticket. Would you want to come?"

126

"Oh, thanks, that would be so fun, but I have plans to go to Brat Fest that same weekend." I leave out the part of having made the plans with Sai. I wonder if we will actually keep those plans. It's not something I want to think about right now. "Do you have plans for tomorrow, or will you head back right away?"

"I wish I didn't, but my brother and his girlfriend are visiting for the weekend, so I'll probably take off in the morning."

We come up to my apartment, but I'm not ready for him to leave. I really don't want the night to end. "Why don't you come up for a bit, at least until the alcohol is out of your system."

He seems to like this idea because he smiles and says, "Yeah, okay." He stands close behind me as I work the key into the lock. There's so little space between us that I can feel the heat of his body. I'm reminded of the dance floor at the nightclub and my stomach does a flip.

After we walk in, he takes a seat in the corner chair of my living room while I get us glasses of water. I go over to the couch and lean back onto the pillows so I'm facing him. He gets up to join me on the couch, and lifts my legs like he did on the pontoon, placing them over his lap. My stomach tightens when his hands touch my bare legs, and he gives me a flirtatious smile. I return it. I turn and try to concentrate on finding something on the TV that we might both like. I land on Cupcake Wars; one of my favorite baking shows, and turn to him, "How's this?" But I blush as I notice he hasn't been looking at the TV, he's watching me.

"This is good," he says seductively.

I don't know if he's referring to my question about the show or if it's in response to how we are seated together. He's still looking into my eyes and he leans down slowly so that he is lying next to me. He entwines his legs around mine and pulls them closer to him. My body starts to tingle. He reaches for one of my hands, but to my surprise, I'm already moving my hand towards his. When our fingers touch, my breath quickens. He slowly interlaces his fingers with mine and moves towards me, lightly brushing his lips against my cheek. The touch gives me goosebumps and the soft slow movement tickles my skin. My body reacts instinctively, drawing closer to him, and I want so badly to kiss him, but I can't, I turn away slightly. His lips move to my neck so that I can feel him breathing heavily against it. He brushes his lips up my neck to my ear, inhales and then stops.

He whispers, "I'm sorry, I couldn't help myself."

I groan softly and move my face back towards his; his face is buried in my neck. Every bit of me wants to be with him but the smallest bit of my subconscious reminds me this is wrong.

My right hand goes to cradle the left side of his face. "No, I'm sorry," I whisper in his ear. "I want to, but I can't."

He pulls me in, wrapping me in a hug. There's so much magnetic energy between us that it takes all of my will power to keep from kissing him. His right hand is around my back holding me close to him. His left has moved down to my thigh, softly resting there, his fingertips a few inches from my shorts. I like how his hands feel on me.

After laying like this for a few minutes, he clears his throat, "I should probably get going."

As much as I know it's a good idea, I want him to stay here with me. It takes me a while to say anything but I finally spit out, "Okay…" I pause, "I'm sorry."

"Please don't apologize. I know you're still figuring things out with your boyfriend."

He sighs and we sit up. I move off the couch and walk him to the door, feeling awkward for the first time tonight.

"Are you okay to drive?"

"I'm fine, my hotel is ten minutes away."

I don't know what to say. Tonight wasn't a date but it felt like one. I have no idea if we'll even see each other again, but I know I want to. All I can think to say, is a pathetic, "Goodnight."

"Goodnight Jhett." He rests his hands gently on my upper arms and leans in to kiss my forehead. A warm sensation courses through my body. I don't want him to leave, but then he gradually turns to open the door, smiles and walks out. I close the door slowly behind him, lock it and go back to the couch. It's still warm. I pull a blanket off the back and cover myself.

CHAPTER 9

I wake the next morning on the couch with a stiff neck. I hear a muffled beep coming from my purse. It's my phone's warning that the battery is about to die. As I bring it over to my charger, I see I have a message from Roo.

I want you to know I had a great time. I don't know when I'll see you again, but I'm going to make it happen. I know you are currently taken, but I like you, and in case you haven't noticed, I don't give up without a fight.

Enjoy your weekend, and until next time…

Holy crap! I am so beyond excited. I take a moment to enjoy his message.

Danielle and Kia are already seated at a small table when I walk into the café. Four mimosas are sitting in front of them.

"Morning. How are you both?" I say cheerfully, picking up a mimosa.

"Relieved to be out of the apartment," Danielle says with an eye roll. "Ben has been driving me nuts. I filled Kia in, so she's all up to speed."

"Now you'll only have to tell Clarissa once she gets here," Kia says sarcastically.

"Have either of you heard from her?" They shake their heads. "And I thought you'd all be waiting on me."

"So, what's up with you and Sai?" Kia asks. Just as I'm about to answer, Clarissa walks in.

"Sorry I'm late, did I miss anything?"

"You missed how Ben's about to get kicked to the curb. And now we're getting the scoop on Sai," Kia says looking at Clarissa.

"Oh, I don't want to miss this."

Suddenly I feel pressured; all eyes are on me. I feel a little self-conscious because I know I should have an answer for them. Will I stay with Sai or are we breaking up? Only Danielle knows about my messages from Roo. I adjust myself in the chair and run my fingers through my hair hoping it will buy me time, but instead the silence hangs in the air, adding more suspense.

"Well?" Kia says.

"Um, so, Roo came to see me yesterday. We spent all afternoon together and I invited him to come up to my apartment." I blurt out.

"Hell yes, you go girl!" Kia says, laughing, and gives my shoulder a little shove.

I shake my head. "I mean, he came for work, he was already in the area. And he did come up to my apartment but only for a short while." I look around and everyone is beaming.

"Oh, come on, more details!" Clarissa smirks.

I relax a little and feel the hint of a smile. Telling the girls about Roo makes me feel giddy, like I'm reliving the time we just spent together. "Okay," I say, and the girls move closer to the edge of their chairs. "I'm starting with Sai." I fill them in on the pontoon picture that started the fight, how he accused me of lying, and that he'd been driving past my apartment and the gym. They make comments about Sai but I can tell all they really want are the details from last night. I tell them about our walk around the park and pizza at Marco's, which is followed by even more comments and a handful of questions.

"I can't believe you didn't kiss him! It's not like you and Sai are currently together," Clarissa says.

"Well we didn't break up, either," I say looking at her. She doesn't say anything but the look on her face says it all. I can tell she's disappointed.

"Some of us have morals," Danielle says sticking up for me.

"When Sai and I started dating, there wasn't much of a spark. I knew he was interested, and he kept asking me to hang out. Eventually, I agreed. Feelings did come, and I clearly care about him but ... it's just not enough. With Roo, I can't wait to hear from him. I get so excited just seeing a message from him. And when I see him, let's just say there are strong feelings."

"You and Roo are really cute together. You just fit," Kai says. "I can tell you have chemistry."

I think of how Sai and I must look together; it's like we have to prove to people we're a couple, that our relationship *can* work. Sometimes I think the only reason I want to keep the relationship with Sai is just to be able to say onlookers are wrong. They see the age difference and think it can't work. I've always acted like it didn't bother me but deep down it does. Maybe I was only making it harder for both of us by prolonging it.

"Do you miss him?" Danielle asks.

"Who?" I ask. Not sure which guy she is referring to.

"Sai, do you miss him?"

"I miss things about him, but being apart isn't as painful as I'd thought it'd be."

"Well that should tell you something right there," Clarissa says.

I let her words sink in, and I know she's right. I should want to be with the person I'm dating. If after all this time I'm not miserable, then we're not meant to be together. I shouldn't be constantly thinking about someone else. I spend more time daydreaming about Roo then worrying over what's going on between me and Sai. "It's over between us. I'm going to end it."

"Welcome to the club," Danielle says. "When is it going to happen?"

I empty a second mimosa; this would have been Clarissa's, but she doesn't protest, she knows I need it more than she does right now.

"Today," I say. "I'll go straight from here."

They all look at me a bit shocked. But this is not something I want to overthink. Deep down I know ending our relationship is something that I've thought about too many times already.

"Is there a reason you wanted to meet today?" I ask, glancing at Clarissa.

She starts to nod. "So, I've applied to UCLA."

For a few moments, it's quiet. If she gets accepted, she will be on the other side of the country. The thought makes me sad and a bit uncomfortable. I try to read her face; she's waiting for one of us to respond. But it's more than that, it looks like she's waiting for approval or maybe acceptance. "When will you find out?" I ask, trying to sound happy for her but my words come out monotone.

"Six to eight weeks is the norm," she says, her voice even.

"Well, we might just have to have our next girls' weekend out there I guess," I say.

"Yes!" She says looking a bit relieved. "It would be the perfect place to have a girl's weekend! And you know, I've always pictured myself somewhere busy, full of life. I want to live on the beach, if I can find a place my dad will approve. I'll be furthering my education, so I'm sure he'll be okay with it." She takes a moment before continuing. "Can you imagine being able to get up on a Saturday and going surfing? Or walking down the boardwalk on a sunny afternoon with the sound of waves crashing in the distance? The sunsets, the salty smell..." She's looking off into space like she's describing her latest daydream.

"Um, maybe you should just take us up on that jogging offer? We run right next to the lake, it's gorgeous," Kia says. "You can have all that right here."

Clarissa shrugs as if it's not enough.

"It does sound pretty amazing," Danielle says, "but, I would miss you like crazy. It would be so hard not having you here. It sounds like you've already fallen in love with it. Is this just for school or are you planning to stay longer?"

"Whoa, I haven't even been accepted yet," Clarissa says laughing, putting up a hand. "Just dreaming about the possibilities. And wondering how you guys feel about it."

The waitress carries a large tray over one shoulder and sets it on a brown folding stand. She dishes out our plates and leaves after we order another round of mimosas. "Anyone want my pickle?" I say, holding it up on a small plate.

"I'll take it!" Clarissa grabs it.

"You won't believe how good this strawberry French toast is. Anyone want a bite?" Kia offers.

I lift my fork and cut off a corner. She's right, it tastes like dessert. I take a few bites of my sandwich and pick at a handful of fries before realizing I'm not even hungry. Knowing I'm going over to Sai's has made my appetite vanish. I think about texting to give him a heads up but decide to call him as soon as I leave the restaurant. We finish eating and I leave cash for my share of the bill. "Okay, wish me luck," I say. I get pitiful glances from them and a few words of encouragement.

"Let us know how it goes. I can meet you later tonight if you need it," Kia says.

"Thanks, I'll let you know."

I take out my phone and dial his number. He picks up on the second ring.

"Hey Jhett!"

135

"Hey Sai, do you think you can meet me?" I ask, my voice soft.

"Yeah, of course! Where are you thinking?" Sai asks enthusiastically.

"Used book store, the little red brick one on the corner?"

"Yeah, I can meet you there, what time?"

"Um, are you free now? I ask.

"Yes, I can be there in fifteen minutes."

"Okay, thanks, I'll see you soon." I hang up before he has a chance to say goodbye. I just can't stomach hearing an 'I love you' right now.

I chose the used book store because I want to be in a semi-public place. The back area is open but fenced in so there is some privacy. People seem to mind their own business and it's always been a pretty quiet place. When I get there, I walk straight through the store to the back. I see a few people shopping but no one is outside which is a bit surprising because it's really nice out. Soft music is playing and I can hear a sprinkler in a nearby yard. I sit in an old wicker chair in the back corner. There's an identical chair inches away for Sai.

As soon as he spots me, he's all smiles. He has big, dark bags under his eyes that make him look even older. He still must not be sleeping. I watch him walk over, it doesn't look like he's blinked once since spotting me. I slowly lift a hand and give a weak wave. I don't know how to act and I feel a bit nauseous. Seeing his big grin makes me want to return with a smile but I don't want to give him false hope. It's difficult but I try to leave my face neutral. I get up when he reaches me and we embrace. He pulls me in as close as he can and tightens his arms around me. It's a real, deep, loving hug, lasting more than a few seconds. I relax and I let my arms go around him. If there's one thing I can do, it's to give him a genuine hug.

"How are you?" I say as soon as we sit.

He lets out an exhausted breath, "I'm a wreck, to be honest."

136

"You look thin and tired," I say.

"Yeah, well, I am. I haven't eaten much in the past couple weeks and it's the same for sleep, haven't gotten much."

"Have you signed up for one of those classes at the local college yet?"

"No, I haven't. I've been trying to read and I've been walking a lot. I think I will sign up though, I need something to keep me busy." He waits and then rubs his forehead. "Jhett, I can read you. Tell me why we're here?"

I think of my body language and how uncomfortable I'm feeling. I sigh. I feel like my throat might close up on me. I don't know if I've ever had to do something as hard as this in my life. I've broken up with boyfriends before but this just feels different; it feels harder. Maybe it's because I know how deeply he feels about me; I know he's had marriage on his mind shortly after we started dating. My hand goes up to my temple and I start to tug at the tiny hairs there, something I do when I'm nervous. "I've been thinking about us." I take a breath. "I…"

"Just say it, Jhett. Just say what you need to say," he says when I stall. His eyes are closed and his head is tilted down.

I swallow. "I don't want to do this anymore. This isn't what I want. I'm sorry." It comes out a whisper.

"Is there anything that I can do, anything that I can say? I just want more time with you. Even if you need more time apart. I'll do anything to keep us together." He gestures to place his hand on mine but I recoil and he pulls back.

"Sai, I'm sorry. I really am."

His hands go up to his face and he turns towards me. His shoulders are slumped forward. "I knew that's what you were going to tell me. As soon as you called, I knew. I guess I was hoping for the small chance that we could work through it." I look at his teary eyes, and feel mine well up too.

"I guess I should get my stuff from your place," I say quietly.

He drops his head and I see a single tear fall to the ground. It makes me feel ill. I start to feel a burn in the back of my throat and tears start to build around my lids. I can't imagine how he must feel.

"I'll stop by sometime next week," I say and my voice cracks.

He nods but doesn't say anything. I see him wipe his eyes.

"I'm going to go now." I slowly stand and he does the same.

He mutters, "Can I walk you to your car?"

"Of course," I say quietly. We don't talk until we reach my car, where he reaches out and places his hand on my shoulder and strokes up and down, lovingly.

"Let me know if you need anything, okay?" He says.

I nod. When I turn to get into my car he leans in for another hug. This time I feel the weight of him as he leans into me. I feel his body start to shake and I hear sobs escape from his throat. Tears of my own start to fall. We stay like this for a few minutes until he lifts his head and wipes his face. He looks into my eyes and all I can see is hurt and sadness.

"Goodbye, my love."

If I hadn't been able to read his lips, I wouldn't have heard his whispered goodbye. He releases me and gradually turns to his car. I climb into mine and slowly drive away. When I get to my apartment I collapse onto my bed, feeling miserable and relieved at the same time. I text Kate.

Jhett: We still on for tomorrow?
Kate: Yes! What time will you be there?
Jhett: 10?
Kate: K, can't wait to see you!

This makes me feel good. I feel like I need family right now.

Jhett: Same, miss you! <3

I send a group text to the girls.

Jhett: It's done, we're broken up. There were tears, but overall, I feel relieved it's over with.

Kia: So proud of you! Breaking up is so hard!

Danielle: Love you!

Clarissa: <3 call if you want to talk.

Jhett: Thanks for the support, love you guys

CHAPTER 10

Sunday

I have my second cup of coffee down before 8am. The caffeine has kicked in and I'm starting to feel jittery. At least I can use the energy to go for a run, since I won't be able to comfortably use the gym. I change into workout clothes and take off towards Howard Park. Starting with two laps around the statues, I then make my way along the lakefront trail for another thirty minutes. I walk the last few blocks to my apartment feeling satisfied, and leave the house by 9:30am. I dial up my mom's number as I pull out of the driveway.

"Good morning!" She answers.

"Hi, whatcha up to?" I ask.

"Your dad and I are in West Bend. We had breakfast this morning with the Flight Club, and we're just sitting around talking now," she says cheerfully.

"Oh, I didn't know you were going."

"It was a last-minute decision. I actually asked your father last night when he was planning to fly again and it led to us to going out this morning."

"Oh, that sounds nice. Well, I'm heading to the house now, and wanted to know if you needed anything."

"We're all out of fruit if you'd like to grab some? And we should be home a little after 11am."

"Sounds good. I'll see you when you get home."

I stop at the grocery store near their house. I grab a pineapple, purple grapes and a mixed tote of apples and oranges and head to the checkout.

My sister is already at my parent's house when I arrive.

"Hey, am I glad to see you!" I say.

"Yeah, sorry, I've been so busy lately with work."

"It's fine, I just feel like I have a lot to fill you in on."

I hand her the bag of grapes and she takes them over to the sink to rinse them. I start cutting the pineapple and place the chunks in a bowl. While she takes a fruit bowl from the cabinet and fills it with apples and oranges, I fill her in on everything.

"Wow. I did miss a lot," she says sitting on the barstool next to me. "So, this Roo guy, when will you see him again?"

"I'm not sure. I really like him, but he lives two hours away."

"Yikes, that's not fun. But it's not the worst thing." She shrugs. "And don't take this the wrong way, but I didn't think Sai was a good fit for you."

Even knowing that myself, it's still hard to hear. "I know," I say.

"Are you going to be okay? Breakups suck."

"Yeah, I'll be fine."

"Oh, and I know about Mo and Beck's baby! Mo called me Wednesday because she couldn't wait any longer," she says excitedly.

"Can you believe it? We're going to be aunts!"

"I know! A little Christmas baby!" She says.

Kate stands and gestures to the deck, "Want to get the grill going? I saw some burgers and hot dogs in the fridge."

"I could eat." I nod.

After we finish eating, Kate takes the tray of uneaten food in the house. We stay out on the deck until our parents show up. When they finally arrive, I tell them about Sai, and can't help but notice the look of relief they seem to share.

"Well, let us know if there's anything you need," my mom says.

There's an awkward silence until Kate pipes up, "Look, Mo and Beck posted their baby announcement!" She passes her phone around the table.

It's quite adorable. Mo has her arms wrapped around Beck's neck and she's holding the ultrasound photo; Beck has his back to the camera and is wearing a baseball cap that reads "Dad".

"Aw, it's really cute," I say and pass her phone to my mom.

We talk about Mo and Beck and the baby for the next hour. My mom and sister already have ideas for a baby shower, and when they start planning a food menu I decide it's my time to leave. Overall, the day went better than I thought it would, but I cannot wait for a relaxing night with my book and blanket.

Monday

Emma and I break for lunch and quickly change into our tennis shoes. She waits no time at all to spill the details of her dates.

"So, on Friday, Logan met me at the botanical gardens. It was beautiful! We held hands, and walked through the flower trails, and he asked all about my family and life. It was so sweet. We talked about traveling, and apparently he's never even been out of Wisconsin; I asked about places he wants to go someday and by the end of the night he asked if I would like to go on a day trip with him to Chicago! He's always wanted to walk Navy Pier and visit Shedd Aquarium!"

"What did you say?"

"I told him I'd love to!"

"Oh, that's great. Did you guys make it to trivia?"

"Yes, it was really fun and we did pretty good. That lasted about two hours. We stayed after and had burgers."

"It sounds like it went well. Did he kiss you goodnight?"

"No, at first I thought he might because he looked a bit nervous when we walked to my door, I probably did too, but

143

he hugged me instead and said he couldn't wait to see me again," she says looking pleased.

"So overall it went well?"

"Very well. I really like him, he's easy to talk to. We had a few quiet moments but eventually, he'd just ask me another question. He's very calm and gentle. He's almost the opposite of JJ."

"Hmm, okay, tell me about JJ."

"JJ picked me up on his motorcycle! My parents would have freaked if they found out."

"Were you scared?"

"At first! I've never been on one, but it was so fun!" She turns to me, "Have you ever been on one?"

"I have, but only because my dad owns one. He used to run me to and from softball practice on it. I loved going for rides to get ice cream on summer days too." I reminisce. "So, where did he take you for dinner?"

"He took me to a hookah bar!" Her face looks shocked. "Can you believe it? But it was actually super fun!"

"That's cool, I've never been to one."

"The Mediterranean food was amazing. He ordered for us because I didn't know what most of it was, but he let me pick the flavor of tobacco. I was a little nervous but it was kind of exciting to try something new. He said he usually only goes a few times a year."

"Fun, what flavor did you pick?"

"Dragon's blood. It had a little asterisk next to it, saying it was a fan favorite. I thought it smelled and tasted like fruit punch; it was pretty good. He warned me my throat would probably feel kind of scratchy the next day, and it was."

"And did you go to the movies?" She doesn't say anything but instead gives me a look and smiles. "How was it? Based on that look I'd say it was good?"

"I couldn't even concentrate on the movie. He reached for my hand as soon as it started. And he was stroking my arm.

Ugh, he is so hot, all I wanted to do was kiss him, finally somewhere in the middle of the movie, we made out! I felt like we were teenagers. I could have stayed there all night. Then when he dropped me off, he suggested that he come in! He started kissing my neck at the door and he was very handsy."

"Wow, that's bold, did you let him in?"

"No, and it was hard telling him no."

"They do sound like opposites, one that was too nervous to kiss you and one that was hoping for more."

She blushes when I say this. We only have a few minutes until the end of our break but I fill her in on the breakup. She has always liked Sai, even though she's never actually met him. She has seen him a few times at the office when he's taken me out to lunch or when he's dropped something off. She sounds sympathetic but it's only moments until she brings up Roo.

"Have you spoken to Roo lately?"

"No, but I'll message him tonight. He's on my mind all the time."

"That's how I feel about JJ. I daydream about him constantly. I think of Logan too..." She trails off.

"So, do you think you like JJ more?"

"It's so hard to tell. There's so much I don't know about them. I think I'll have a better idea after going to Chicago with Logan."

We get back to work, switching back into our work shoes. "Do you have plans to see JJ again?"

"Nothing scheduled yet, but he's pretty busy. I'm sure we'll make plans soon."

I see Geri coming down the hallway so I give Emma a more serious look. "I guess we can talk later."

"Excuse me ladies," Geri says with her deep stern voice, "I hope I'm not interrupting." Emma shakes her head quickly. "Emma, I'm going to be spending the afternoon with you."

Emma looks quickly at me; she looks terrified. "And don't think you're off the hook," Geri smirks, shooting a glance at me. "I'll be with you tomorrow." She's holding a clipboard and motions to Emma to get moving. We break off into our rooms. I'm worried for Emma. I pray that she doesn't get nervous and make a silly mistake. I start to think of Geri watching me and how intimidating it will be. For the entire afternoon, I overanalyze everything I do. I'm glad I have time to prepare, but I feel bad for Emma because she wasn't so lucky. After work I ask, "How did it go?"

"It was awful, I'm still shaking," she says holding up her hands. "That woman is the worst."

"I know," I say. "What did she do?"

"She stood in the back of the room and would write on her clipboard every few minutes."

"Try not to worry about it. It's just part of her job. She's probably just trying to figure out ways to improve the schedule."

Tuesday

Just as I knew she would, Geri walks into my room shortly after I've finished setting up. I try concentrating on what I am doing and try to do it confidently. My first patient has been a patient at our clinic for years. I know her well and we have a good relationship. I call her back and we start talking. The appointment is going well until we get into the room. I feel awkward with Geri listening so I decide to introduce her. At this she takes over and asks if it's okay for her to be present for the appointment. I am hoping she gets a no, but my patient isn't the least bit shy and as soon as Geri asks, she gets the okay to stay.

It's my patient's third round of hair removal on her legs. I review her chart, have her sign a waiver and dim the lights. I remind her to speak up if she gets too uncomfortable. Whenever I see Geri make notes on her clipboard, my heart starts beating faster. The rest of the appointment goes as well as it can and I dismiss my patient.

I bring back my final patient for the morning and get on with the appointment. When I finish and return to my room, it's empty. I feel like I can breathe for the first time today. During morning huddle, we were told we would be having a meeting during the lunch hour. It turns out to be a forty-minute video on teamwork and efficiency. I personally feel like it's a waste of time. I think we make the best of our time and everyone helps each other when they can. I wonder what Geri's report will be at the end of all this. I've only seen small changes so far. By the end of the workday, I feel mentally drained. Roo hasn't heard from me in three days and his last message was really sweet. Driving home, I think of the message I will send him.

Hey there!

I'm really sorry I've been MIA lately. How have you been? How was the visit with your brother and his girlfriend?

I have some news! I'm going to be an aunt! I'm beyond excited! I've known for about a week, but now I have the ok to share. I've been trying to focus on that lately because Sai and I broke up a couple days ago. Which also reminds me that I no longer have plans next Saturday.

I make a quick meal of spaghetti and garlic bread for dinner and hit the couch with a book. Twenty minutes in, I hear my phone buzz. I'm hoping it's a reply from Roo. When I pick up my phone, I'm surprised to see that he's calling. I swallow and take a breath to calm my nerves.

"Hello?" I say, and it comes out more like a question.

"Hey Jhett, it's Roo, how are you?"

"Hi," I say smiling, "I'm good."

"Good. Are you busy?"

"No, no, I'm at home, not busy at all," I say, hearing myself sounding a bit too pretentious. I tell myself to slow down.

"Oh good, I thought it would be nice to hear your voice."

"Yeah, I'm glad you called. How are you?"

"I've just found out some pretty great news, so I'd say I'm doing pretty good." His voice is light and flirty. "First of all, congrats aunty, that's awesome!

"Thank you!"

"Second, I'm sorry about the breakup, even when you know it's for the best it's not easy going through it."

"Yeah, it did suck, but I'm glad it's over with."

"Well, that brings me to what I'm about to ask next," he pauses so long I'm about to ask if he's still there when he finally speaks. "I'd really love to see you again and I'm hoping that this time around when I ask, you'll say yes. Would you want to come to the baseball game with me next Saturday?" Before I can answer, he speaks again, "unless it's too soon, and I totally respect that if you aren't ready."

I feel myself smile. He's sweet.

"Roo, I'd love to see you again, and yes I'll go to the game with you."

"Ah, thank you. I don't think I could have handled being turned down a second time, I would just feel like an idiot." We both laugh. "The game's at 7pm, and just to remind you, two of my buddies will be there. We'll probably start grilling around 5pm. Can I pick you up?"

"Sure, that would be nice."

"Okay, great. Well, I'll be in touch, I'm actually still at work so I better go."

"Sounds good, thanks for calling," I say joyfully.

I walk into my bedroom and put my phone on my nightstand. I lay across my bed and my mind takes me to the beach on Kippers Island where I first got to see his playful, flirtatious side. Then I think of us together on the dance floor in the nightclub where it became very apparent that we were attracted to each other. I think of this past Friday at my apartment where we shared the couch and laid next to each other; suddenly it makes my stomach flutter.

With my eyes closed, I picture his face, his suntanned skin, and attractive hazel eyes. I imagine him wrapping me up in his strong arms, and how his face was so close to mine. Our breaths were so in sync and I know he would have kissed me if I hadn't turned away. I can't believe I didn't let him kiss me.

Without meaning to, I fall asleep and dream of Roo. He takes me to a skate park and he teaches me to do the halfpipe. I master it on the first try, which must be beginners' luck, I guess. Afterwards, we get ice cream and he surprises me with the news that he's moving to the area. I leap into his arms and he swings me around happily. He kisses me goodbye when dropping me off hours later. When I walk into my apartment, I'm surprised by hundreds of sticky notes stuck all around the apartment. Sweet Roo, when did he have time to do this? My hand goes to my heart as I reach for one. To my horror, though, they aren't from Roo, they're from Sai. They read: I miss you, I love you, and I want you back. There are hundreds, everywhere I look. I hear my bedroom door creek. The inside of my room is pitch black. The door is slowly moving and I see a hand wrap around the side and slowly pull it open. It's Sai but he's not smiling. I'm sweating and my heart is pounding out of my chest. What does he want, why is he here? He starts walking towards me in slow motion but I can't move, my feet are steeled to the floor and I'm stuck in place. I scream and suddenly I'm awake.

I feel dazed. I turn on my lamp and check my room. Nobody is here but my heart is racing and I'm sweating. I go to open my window but I'm too freaked out, so I turn on a fan instead. I feel the need to check the apartment. I check the bathroom and kitchen and the locks on my door. I make a mental note to email the landlord for new locks. Heading back into my room, I try to slow my breathing. I read for an hour until I relax and finally drift back to sleep.

As I get ready for work, I think of my nightmare. What does it mean? I know I'm not afraid of Sai; he wouldn't hurt me. And the notes? Why did it have to turn so ugly? Especially since I was in such a good place with Roo. I turn on my playlist hoping it will distract me.

Just before I'm about to head out the door, I get a message from Kia.

Kia: Join me @ MMA tonight?
Jhett: MMA?
Kia: Mixed martial arts…duh!
Jhett: LOL, yes, I need to cancel my gym membership
Kia: YAY! Starts at 6, meet me at Power-Up gym
Jhett: See you then

I see Kia getting out of her car. She's wearing a black tank with gold lettering reading, *'Don't fuck with me'*.

"Hey girl, you ready to kick some ass?" Kia yells from a row away.

"More like get my ass kicked," I say.

After a quick warm-up, we jump right into the class. It's intense and I feel muscles ache in places that I didn't even know I had muscles. The ripped instructor shouts encouragements, my favorite being, *'imagine what you want your ass to look like, now make it happen!'* Everyone cheers. The positive energy definitely motivates me. We kick, we punch, we jump rope. By the end, we are all dripping with sweat and bent over trying to catch our breath.

"Holy balls, that was tough! Kia says.

"No, kidding. But I'm happy I did it," I say wiping my face.

"So, you'll come back?" Kia asks.

"No way, one and done." I laugh.

She gives me a disappointed look.

"Okay fine, now that I know what I'm in for, I'll be better mentally prepared."

She smiles. "Maybe this can be our new thing?"

"Yeah, you make a good workout buddy. You're motivated and I need that. Are we still on to jog this Saturday?"

"Yes!" She pulls a protein bar from her workout bag and breaks off a chunk. "Here, my new favorite, mint chocolate cream. It tastes like ice cream."

"It's good," I say, but all I can taste is artificial sugar, or maybe it's the whey. I've never been a fan of protein bars; they all have the same aftertaste.

"Any word from Roo?"

"Yes, he called last night. I'm going to a baseball game with him and his friends next Saturday." I share happily.

"Oh, how fun, I wish James would want to do something other than go to movies or dinner. He's just been so boring lately."

"Why don't you make plans and just tell him he has to go?" I suggest.

"Oh, you know him, he'll just bitch or sulk the whole time, and then I won't have fun."

"Okay, so why don't we plan something. All the girls. If you can't have fun with him, you can have fun with us."

"Okay, I'll find something for us to do. I'll keep you posted."

We say goodbye and I return home. As soon as I walk in the door, I get a message.

Kia: Psychic reading this Friday! There's a place outside Port Washington. Who's in?!

Jhett: ME!

Danielle: Me too!

Clarissa: I don't believe in that crap but I'll go along for the ride.

Kia: YAY! I'll book the 7pm spot, we can grab dinner at 6 in PW.

Clarissa: Let's meet at the park-and-ride at 5:30, I'll drive.

CHAPTER 11

Friday

The week flew by and I can tell everyone in the office, aside from our boss, is over-the-moon happy that today is Geri's last day with us. We've had lunch meetings every day this week. Most of the changes around the office have been minor and easily adjustable, from tweaking our dialogue on how we explain procedures, to getting a patient to book their next appointment before leaving, as well as optimizing the new layout in our patient rooms. I feel grateful that Geri has stayed away from me the past few days and I think it's part of the reason why my week hasn't been so bad.

When I get into the office, I look for Emma, I know she's here because her car is parked in the lot. I go about my normal routine and meet everyone for huddle at our scheduled time. She is still not around. I hear voices and turn to see our boss, Geri and Emma for a split second, just before they move out of eyesight into the back hallway. I wonder if she is being given a new task or maybe getting a raise. Minutes later, only our boss returns. Our meeting starts and I can't seem to focus on anything. Why isn't Emma here? Something feels off. My boss looks like a deflated balloon. There is no mention of Emma and as soon as we're finished, I hurry to my purse and grab my phone. I go into the bathroom.

I text Emma.

Jhett: Hey, are you feeling ok? What's going on?

I wait three whole agonizing minutes before I make the decision that she isn't feeling well and had to go home. She probably hasn't taken her phone off silent. On the way to my room, I pass my boss who I smile at. Instead of looking directly at me, his eyes shift quickly to the ground which only makes me feel a bit uncomfortable. I walk over to the reception area but go straight to Ruthie before calling my first patient back.

"Hey Ruthie, do you know what happened with Emma? She was here this morning." I ask in a quiet voice.

"No, I'm sorry I don't," she gives me a sad smile.

I wonder if she really does know something but isn't telling me. Ruthie is the first one here every morning and it makes me think that if anyone knows anything it will be her. "Before morning huddle, I was asked to reschedule her patients," she says shrugging.

"Okay. Thanks Ruthie," I say.

After my second to last patient, I finally get a message from Emma.

Emma: Jhett, I GOT FIRED! I've been crying since I left and I can't even talk to my parents I'm so upset.

Jhett: Oh my gosh, wth happened? I'm so pissed for you! Who did it?

Emma: It was Geri, she did all the talking. I don't even remember what she all said.

Jhett: Can I come see you? I have one patient left; I can be to your house by 2:30.

Emma: I booked an emergency appt with my therapist. I'm going to ask my mom to drive me and I think I'll just go back to their house and spend the night.

Jhett: Please let me know if there's anything I can do.

I put my phone away and stand against the counter in disbelief. I wish I could have gotten the reason as to why. I hear a gentle knock at the door.

"Jhett, I just wanted to let you know your last patient is here," Ruthie says in a gentle tone.

"Thanks, I'll be right up. Hey Ruthie, before you go," I pause trying to search her face for a reaction, "Emma got fired today." I whisper.

"Oh dear, I'm so sorry, I know the two of you were close." She's not surprised.

"Ruthie, did you know about this?"

She glances away from me briefly, "I had an idea. I overheard Geri talking yesterday morning. I don't think she knew I was here. I heard her say something like, 'the weakest link' and that's when I knew I shouldn't be listening so I went straight up front. When I heard Emma get called into the office this morning, I just had this awful feeling. I'm sorry sweetie," she says and touches her chest. "I'm going to miss that girl."

As I head home, I try thinking of my friends, hoping it will lift my mood. Patches is extra squeaky when I walk in so I go over to him. I cradle him in one arm while I take carrots out of the fridge with my free hand. I go outside and walk over to a shaded area where I sit crossed legged and place him on the grass. He sniffs around and scurries from edge to edge in the little open area I've allowed for him. His happiness is rubbing off on me and I'm starting to feel slightly less irritated about work. After a half-hour, we head back inside. I look at my phone, I have a missed call from Sai. Part of me is glad I didn't take it with me outside. I listen to the voicemail.

Hi Jhett. I have a few things here that are yours. I put them aside. If you could call me back to arrange a time to come get them, that would be great. I'll be here all weekend. Okay bye.

His voice is soft and calm. I know I have a few things of his so I walk the apartment and put anything I find in a laundry basket. Then I make a pile of anything he's ever given me that I no longer want so I can dispose of it. I'd read somewhere that getting rid of anything that reminds you of your ex is the best way to move on from a breakup. I should pick up my things from him sooner rather than later so we can make the exchange.

I send him a text.

Jhett: Hey, I can stop tomor. When is a good time?

Sai: How about mid-morning?

*Jhett: I'm jogging with Kia at 9…*I start typing but decide less detail is better. *I can do 11?*

Sai: Yes, thanks, and if there's anything of mine that you want to bring over that would be great.

This surprises me. I was thinking he'd want to come here a different day to pick up his things just so he would have an excuse to see me again. I guess he's doing better than I thought he would.

Jhett: Doing that right now.

I move on to sending Roo a message. We have been messaging daily since his phone call.

Jhett: Hey, how's your Friday going?

Roo: It's ok. How was your last day with Geri? Did anything exciting happen?

Jhett: Not exciting but shocking…I was so ready to see her leave but that terrible woman fired Emma today. It was awful. I don't know much about the details, but Emma will get a hold of me when she's ready.

Roo: That's terrible. But, don't let that ruin your plans for tonight. I hope you have a really good time having your future read. I'm sure seeing the girls will make your night better.

Jhett: Thanks, I'm sure it will. Is there anything I need to know about you? Any secrets that could be revealed tonight?

Roo: I guess I should tell you now that I'm a wanted man. Roosevelt Harris is just my alias.

Jhett: Haha. I'll let you know if she mentions that.

Roo: I can't wait to see you next week.

I blush.

Jhett: Me either!

I'm the last to get to the park-and-ride so Clarissa pulls up alongside me. I jump in beside Danielle; Kia is in the front with Clarissa.

"Hey, you ready for this?" Danielle asks excitedly.

"Yeah, let's do this!" I say.

Clarissa takes off in the direction of the restaurant, which is a little hole-in-the-wall place with great reviews.

We order our food and get our drinks. I start to feel better about the day. I'm still thinking of Emma but something tells me everything will be okay.

"I read online that with a group reading she'll do a short reading for each of us, give us some insight into our future and allow us to each ask one question at the end." Kia informs us.

"Good to know," I say, trying to think of what I should ask.

"I can't believe how serious you're all taking this. You know this is fake right? She's probably searching you all online right now."

"You might think that but she doesn't have any of our names," Kia says smartly.

"How did you pay for it, with a credit card?" Clarissa says and then adds. "That has your name on it."

"Okay, so she has *my* name. Big deal, she doesn't know who I'm bringing."

"Hmm, you booked a group reading, and I'm sure if anyone looked at your most recent photos on any of your social media sites, the majority will be of us."

Kia looks annoyed now.

"Stop being such a Debbie Downer. It's just for fun," I say.

"As long as you know that it's just for fun," she says with a smirk. She turns to Danielle. "What's the latest with Ben, are you going to ask when you should dump him?"

"It crossed my mind, but no, I think that would be wasting my question," Danielle says seriously after considering her question. "Whenever he's at the apartment, I find myself wanting to leave."

"How are you and Max?" I ask.

"Fine," Clarissa says quickly with a shrug.

"Really, that's it?" Kia frowns.

157

"Yeah, things have been good since I've been back."

"And what about you and James?"

"Things have been good..." Kia says but she doesn't seem so sure.

"You don't sound like you actually believe that," Clarissa says.

Kia's lips part as if she's about to say something but then she frowns and sighs. "It's like we have one really good day and then we'll have two or three really shitty days. It's like I can't ask him anything or if I try to make a plan he can't commit. I just don't know what's with him. He's so moody all the time."

"Hasn't he always been like that?" Clarissa asks.

"A little, I guess. It's like we go in phases." Kia sounds annoyed with the question.

"Maybe the honeymoon stage is over and this is just how it's going to be."

"That's a terrible thing to say," I say, giving Clarissa a look that says back off.

"Not if it's true," Clarissa says scowling back at me. "Are you still talking to Roo?"

"Yeah, we talk every day," I say.

"Doesn't he live like two hours away?"

"He does, but it's nothing serious." But as I say the words, I feel a pang of sadness. "I like him and I guess in a perfect world, I'd prefer he was much closer."

"I was in a long-distance relationship once. I was a junior in high school and my boyfriend was a freshman in college. We had been dating a year when he left. He was three hours away. It's not fun and it's not easy," Clarissa says.

I take in what she says but before I can respond she says, "Of course that was a high school relationship, those never work out."

"Hey!" Kia yells. "Danny and Ben are high school sweethearts!"

"Oh right. My point exactly. She wants to break up with him." She laughs lightly.

"Can you be just a little more sensitive?" Kia asks.

"Okay, sorry." Clarissa gets up to use the restroom. "Check please." She yells to our server.

As soon as she's out of view, Danielle says, "What's with her tonight? She's usually more fun."

"I don't know, I think she's always like that," Kia says.

We finish up and drive a few minutes to the psychic's house. It's a small house with green vines climbing up one side. There's a stone pathway that we walk which leads to a side door where we will enter. We follow Kia and when she is about to knock, we hear, "Come in."

It startles me and I notice Danielle jump. I see she is seated near the open window. Kia pulls on the wobbly thin screen door that creaks when it opens. The first thing I notice is the smell of something familiar. When I step into the house I see a diffuser a few feet away. The room is dimly lit and I notice little statues all around the tiny room.

"Hello, my name is Regina," she says standing a few feet from us. She motions to the space she had just come from. "Please take a seat."

I expected to walk through a beaded curtain and into a dark room. I had also envisioned we'd be seated across from a woman sitting behind a table draped in a tie-dyed cloth, wearing a goofy hat. But instead, there is a loveseat and two wooden chairs on the opposite side of her. She takes her seat behind a small table; there is no table cloth but rather, a small simple white candle. There is natural light coming through the window so it's surprisingly light and airy with the window open.

Clarissa picks up a wooden chair and places it against the back wall, she sits. "I'm along to listen, I don't want a reading," she says.

159

Regina nods politely. She closes her eyes and starts mumbling to herself, it sounds as though she's saying a prayer. I hear the words, 'healthy positive energy'. It's still and quiet while we wait. I feel like we're all on pins and needles. Regina slowly opens her eyes and raises her head so that she's looking at us.

"I will be getting images; I will relay those onto you. You may not fully understand what they mean now, but they might make sense to you tomorrow, next month, or years down the road. For example, if I see a blue tandem bike it could mean you will be gifted one, your neighbor owns one, you run one over with your car, etcetera. The information is usually something significant, even if in a small way. The possibilities can be endless, so try not to spend too much time thinking about what you hear; try not to base your life around it." She brings her fingertips together.

"Dear, can I hear your voice," she says looking at Kia who is seated to my left.

"Um, sure." Kia swallows. She looks nervous. "I'm Kia."

Regina nods. And after a moment says, "I see a lot of animals. Dogs. Cats. Some other rodents."

"Ugh, I hate cats, and rodents? Are you sure?" Kia says wrinkling her face. "What does that mean?"

"Keep an open mind. It may mean you may work or volunteer at a pet shop, it might mean you buy a hobby farm, it could mean any number of things." Regina interlaces her fingers. "I see that health is very important to you." Kia nods in agreement, and looks like she's in a trance. "You will spend a lot of time helping people feel better." Regina smiles and moves onto me.

"Hello, how are you?"

"I'm good." I'm curious if she is asking to hear my voice.

"I see travel."

My first thought goes to Roo. Long drives to visit him? I want to ask if she sees me with him but I wait.

"You will come into some money," she says. This is shocking to hear and I look wide-eyed at the other girls. Regina looks like she is uncertain. Maybe she's thinking or waiting for images to come. The anticipation is making me anxious. I want to know more but I try to let her talk instead of interrupting.

"You will have a health scare in a few years. It is blood-related and is not life-threatening."

"Oh wow, that sounds real fun," Clarissa says from the back of the room.

Regina looks at me and says, "Everything will be okay in the end, just remember that."

Regina moves onto Danielle who says, "Hi, I'm Danny."

"I see a roller coaster of events in your near future." Regina waits. "I can see that you worry, but know that things will settle and be okay for you too. I see the color green, which usually means growth. You will need to be patient."

"Agh, I hate being patient," Danielle says under her breath. I can't help but smirk because she's the calmest and most patient person I know.

Regina then moves on to the second part of the appointment. She gives each of us a message or two from a past loved one. We all seem to know who is sending us a message. It's pretty cool and I wish we would have more time to spend on this part of the appointment.

"Now, you are all allowed one question. Who would like to go first?"

Kia raises her hand but doesn't wait for Regina to say anything. "Which one of us will get married first?"

It's quiet and all eyes are intently on Regina. It's quick but her eyes glance up to Clarissa and then over to the rest of us.

"Danny," she says.

We all whoop and holler and make remarks. Danielle is blushing but is smiling sheepishly like she's surprised and happy by the news.

"How many kids will we have?" Danielle asks.

"You will have two. Kia will have one and you," she says now eyes on me, "will have two as well."

"What about Clarissa?" Danielle asks.

Regina looks at Clarissa. "Do you want to know?"

"What the hell," she says shrugging.

"You, you will have three."

"Ha, no way! No offense but there's no way," she says with a smirk.

I look at Regina's face to gauge her reaction. She doesn't look offended. In fact, she's pretty good at keeping a straight face.

"What is your question dear?" Regina is looking at me. I have no idea what I want to ask. I'd like days to think up my question, not a mere hour on the drive over when I'm engaged in conversation.

"Do you want me to give you a few examples of questions that are commonly asked?"

"No, thank you. I think I know." I look back to Clarissa and then to the other girls. "Will any of us move away? Like far away?" I hope Clarissa doesn't hold this against me. The sooner I know the better prepared I'll be when she packs her bags.

"Yes, but not permanently." I'm sure Regina can easily read the look on my face because I'm sure it's clear that her response doesn't tell me much. That could mean Clarissa moves away for a year or half a century. Or that I move to be with Roo, something that I would not dare tell the girls or anyone for that matter. It's a bit premature thinking like that since we aren't even a couple. It has crossed my mind because I'm starting to really care about him and I don't like the thought of long-distance. And I'm pretty sure the feelings are mutual. I decide not to say anything and leave it be.

"Oh my gosh, that was crazy. What did ya'll think?" Danielle asks.

"That didn't sound like me at all!" Kia says laughing.

"Three kids? Shit Clarissa," Kia says.

"No fucking way. That's what I was saying, sorry but that was all of a bunch of BS."

"Okay, but did you guys have fun?" I ask.

"Oh yeah. No matter what she said and what happens, I thought it was great. I'd even do it again," Kia says.

"I liked it too." Danielle adds.

"It's too early for the night to end, anyone want to stop for a margarita?" Kia asks

"I'm in! I was hoping we'd get back to our margarita tradition," I say.

"Me too!" Danielle says.

"Are you okay with it Clarissa?" Kia asks.

"Yeah, of course we can stop. I'm not really feeling a margarita but I'm fine driving you alkies around." Clarissa answers.

"Well how mature, thank you," Kia says.

"Yeah, I'm trying to behave. I don't want anything getting in the way of me being accepted to UCLA. And I must say, I feel like I've been pretty tame since my DUI last year," Clarissa says.

"Good for you. Most people do not learn," Danielle says.

The weather takes a turn. We make it into the restaurant just before the rain comes pouring down. We see loads of people from the patio area hustling into the restaurant. That distinct smell of rain from a heavy storm hits my nose as we take our seats. I look outside the double doors just before they're closed to see the sky has turned dark.

This month's flavor is strawberry pineapple. The bartender explains that local strawberries are added to the pineapple mix. Kia says it's her turn to order the flavor of the month but we tease her because who won't want to try this combination.

The point is that it's a gamble. You just hope to get lucky and get a good month. Since this is the first time we'll all here this year, we tell her it doesn't count because it's too safe a combination. She rolls her eyes and flips us off.

"What question would you have asked, Clarissa?" Danielle inquires.

"Hmm, maybe who will be the first to die?" She says with a smug look on her face.

"Shit, you're awful." Kia gives her a shove.

"Wow, that is not funny," I say and Clarissa is laughing to herself.

"What can I say, I know my sense of humor is twisted. It's the first thing that came to mind just now."

We're all still pretty full from dinner so it's the first time in history our chips basket is not empty by the time our margaritas come. We stay for about an hour talking about what paranormal we believe in before Clarissa takes us back to the park-and-ride. Thankfully, the rain has slowed to a sprinkle as we climb into her SUV.

"Kia, we still on for our jog tomorrow?" I ask.

"Sure are!" She chirps.

"I'm stopping at Sai's afterwards to grab my stuff."

"Ugh, yuck, I hope it doesn't turn into a thing where he wants to talk," Kia says.

"Me either. But I think it will be okay. When I talked to him last, he seemed okay."

"Just know that a guy like Sai just doesn't move on quickly, if at all," Clarissa says.

"You never even met him. Why do you say that?" I ask.

"Jealous boyfriends…or I should say ex-boyfriends have a hard time letting go and moving on. And from what I've heard, especially the part where he was ready to marry you, I'd say he won't be healed for years."

"Well, I really hope it's as painless as possible. I already know it will be somewhat awkward when I hand him his box of possessions."

"Do you want me to come with you?" Kia offers.

"No, but that's sweet, thank you."

We head our separate ways and when I'm home I phone Roo. We talk while I lie on my bed. The rain started back up shortly after I returned home. Now, there are bright bolts of lightning flashing across the sky.

"Do you have lightning there?" I ask.

"No, but it's raining pretty hard."

"I love the sound of rain, especially this loud stuff. I'll probably sleep great tonight. And this lightning is pretty crazy. I have a great view from my window."

"I can hear it. And, I wish I was there."

I ache to see him. It crosses my mind that I could go see him now. It's just after nine on a Friday night. But I wouldn't get there until after eleven and he has to work tomorrow. I'd have to cancel with Kia too and I don't like the idea of that, although I know she'd understand. I imagine what it would be like surprising him.

I've never been to his place but I imagine it's clean and simple. I picture a bowl of apples on the counter, a neat stack of mail off to one side and a throw on the back of his couch. But in reality, there are probably a couple empty beer bottles where the imaginary fruit bowl is. A clean apartment for a bachelor is probably pretty rare.

"Me too, and I'd love to stay awake with you all night," I say in a low voice.

He groans, "I wish you weren't so far away; I'd drive there right now if I didn't work tomorrow."

I smile. "I believe you. But to look at the bright side I will see you in a week."

"One week and a day. I have a countdown," he says.

I can tell he's smiling.

165

"What time are you planning on getting here next Saturday?" I ask.

"Well that depends on whether you have plans during the day," he says in a playful voice.

"I don't, and I'll make sure to keep the day open if you can be here!"

"Alright, let's plan to have lunch then. I'll leave by ten."

"Perfect!" I say twisting a chunk of hair around my finger.

"I want to hear about the psychic; tell me how it went."

I fill him in on everything I can remember. I give him the details about my grandma who came through. Regina brought up things that shocked me. Like that my brother liked chocolate milk from the jug but I preferred the powder mix so she would have both when we'd stay over. And the time she took me to get my ears pierced. I also told him about the questions we asked and how Clarissa sat out.

Close to eleven, we say goodnight. I fall asleep almost as soon as I close my eyes.

I wake up feeling energetic and like a million bucks. Kia meets me by our favorite trail and looks to be in a good mood too. We take off with a bounce in our step. I bring up Roo before she has the chance to ask and tell her about our plans for next weekend.

"Oh my gosh, are you guys like a couple?" she asks with interest in her voice. "I mean, I get it, he's super-hot, but I guess with the two-hour drive I just didn't know if you were going to pursue it."

"Well it's kinda hard to just shut off feelings. I think about him constantly."

"Well good for you." She takes in a breath. "Do you think if things get serious, he'd consider moving here?"

I don't tell her that I've considered the move myself. Instead, I say, "If things get serious, then he'd better be open to a move. He seems pretty easy going."

166

Kia invites me to grab a smoothie but I decline, I'd rather just get my stuff from Sai's so I can be done with it. We make a plan for a weekday workout and part ways.

My stomach feels a bit off but I brush it off to it being nerves. When I get to Sai's place, I have to talk myself into getting out of my car. I slowly start up his driveway and notice movement past the front window. He's at the door before I knock.

"Hi," he says, a bit quirky.

"Hey." I respond with a friendly smile.

"Come on in. How are you?" His tone and body language are welcoming.

I never know how to answer a question like this to an ex. "I'm okay. You?"

"Yeah, good, real good." His expressions match his words.

I relax. "That's really good to hear. What have you been up to?"

"I signed up for the class I was telling you about."

"Great. Which one?"

"Piano. I started in the beginner's program, but after the first class the instructor pulled me aside and said it was too basic for me. So, I actually dropped the class and hired him for private lessons twice a week."

"Wow, look at you! I bet in no time you'll have something memorized."

"That's the idea."

He's smiling happily at me, so I politely smile back. Then he comes over and hugs me. It surprises me. I pat him on the back as if we were old pals, making sure not to give him mixed signals.

"It's so good to see you. I've missed those eyes," he says, pushing me back gently so we're an arm's length apart. His hands rest on my shoulders and he's intensely looking into my eyes.

I'm not sure where to look and my eyes shift around a bit. His eyes don't move from mine and it feels like he's trying to look into my soul. I don't know how much longer I can keep this half awkward smile on my face. Just then, he seems to read my mind.

"I'm sorry, too much…" He trails off and I wonder what he was going to say. "Can I get you something to drink?" He motions to the kitchen. "Or to eat?" He adds quickly.

"No, I'm fine, thank you." I had purposely left his things in the car. I thought it would be a kind gesture if I didn't just run them up to the door, grab my things, and peel out. "Um, I'll go grab your things now if that's okay?" I say gently.

He nods. "Yeah, and I'll grab yours."

A few minutes later, I'm back in his living room with the laundry basket in my arms. "I think this is everything, but if I happen to find anything around the apartment, I'll make sure to get it back to you." I gesture to hand it off to him and he reaches to accept it.

He glances at it quickly and turns away. I see sadness on his face as he nods again and bites his lip. He turns and picks up a box sitting on the table behind him.

"Here's your box. Would you like me to carry it out for you?"

"No, I got, thanks," I say, taking the box.

I turn my body so that I'm facing the door. His arm stretches out. His fingertips graze my arm. "Can you stay a few minutes longer?"

The moment I've been dreading. I almost thought for a minute that he was going to be okay, but I realize now that he hasn't moved on at all.

"I really shouldn't stay," I say quietly.

"Oh, are you meeting someone?"

This irks me, but I try not to show it. Immediately, I think he is referring to a guy when he uses the word someone. I need to keep my composure to keep things from escalating.

I slowly shake my head. "No, I should just get going."

"I just..." he takes a deep inhale. "There's some questions I've wanted to ask, and I think that if I get them off my chest, then maybe I'll have some peace."

I close my eyes and breathe. I slightly nod. I know this man is still in pain. I can at least hear him out, let him vent, or do whatever he needs so he gets some closure.

"Thank you." His expression is grateful.

I follow him to the couch. He takes a seat in the middle. I sit next to him but turn my body so that I'm facing him and opening the space between us.

It's quiet and I wonder what's going through his mind. The silence moves on and it's becoming clear that he probably has so much to say that he might not know where to start.

"Sai, I just want you to know, I didn't cheat on you. Whatever you think might have happened, didn't happen. Please don't overthink that weekend."

He's quiet for a moment, but I give him time.

Finally, he speaks. "Why? Why did we really break up? I feel like there needs to be more. You told me you loved me. If you were truly in love with me, we still have hope; we can make this work."

This is so much worse than I thought. "You are a great person, and we have some common interests, but overall, I think we are very different from each other. Our age difference also made things harder."

"How so?"

"I could never see us long term. Marriage. It was something you talked about right away, and for me, I felt nowhere near it. I've always felt that you have been more confident in us. For a while, I was hopeful it would come because I know you'll make a great husband and-"

He raises a hand to stop me from continuing.

"Okay," he says in a whisper.

I hope it's because he finally understands and not because he can't take any more pain from my words. His face is flushed and his eyes look like they're about to spill over with tears. I place my hand down on top of his.

"I'm sorry Sai."

I'm about to stand but he takes my hand into his and brings it to his faces. He starts to kiss my hand. My hand catches a tear as I pull it away. I pull it in close to my body and dry my hand, the feeling of his lips still lingering on my hand. I'm once again uncomfortable. Now I stand abruptly and I know it's time I go. I grab my box and hurry to open the door. He stays on the couch but calls after me, tears are streaming down his face.

"Please Jhett, please! I just need to tell you one last thing!" His face is so pained and there's so much compassion in his voice. "There will never be a man that loves you as much as I do. There will never be a man that will treat you like the princess you are. Not like I can and will."

I turn and walk out the door. Tears in my own eyes start to form. Quickly rushing down the steps, I get into my car. I wipe away the few tears that have rolled down my cheeks from a deep pain of sadness in my chest. I start my car and I drive.

CHAPTER 12

I pull up to Emma's apartment. She had a session with her therapist this afternoon and asked me to come over after work. I'm surprised by how well she looks.

"Hi, how are you?" She asks in a sweet voice, and throws her arms around me in a big hug.

"Hi, it's so good to see you! Here, I brought this for you." I hand her a bottle of Moscato d'Asti, the only gift I could think to grab last minute. "I think you'll like it; it's sweet like juice."

"Oh, that's so sweet. Should I open it now?" She asks as she holds out the bottle to read the label.

"Whatever you want."

"I had a really good appointment today; I feel like we should celebrate!" She waves me in towards the kitchenette. "And things are going really well with JJ too."

"Good!" I say cheerfully. "Does that mean you're not seeing Logan anymore?"

"We are still talking but I told him I wanted to slow things down. No more dates, at least not while I'm seeing JJ." A big smile comes across her face and it makes me smile, too.

"Does JJ know about work?"

"I told him last night. He was really supportive and I think it helped with my session today." I watch as she winds the corkscrew down the middle of the cork and starts to lift the cork from the bottle. "So, what about you? Dating that hunky guy yet?" She asks, grinning.

"Nothing official but he's taking me out this Saturday. Should be fun!"

She hands me a glass of wine and raises hers. "To new hotties and a better life!" She says with a grin and we clink our glasses.

"It's really good to see you this happy," I say after tasting my wine.

"I know, I feel like a weight has been lifted. I didn't realize how much I hated that job. I still have anxiety, but it's weird, it almost seems more manageable and I feel it way less often."

I nod, understanding what she's saying. "So, what's next?"

"I dropped off a few resumes, and that new restaurant on the other side of town already called me this morning for an interview. I went before my appointment and before I left, they were asking when I could start!"

"That's good, something to get you through for a while."

"Right. My first day will be Friday. And of course, now I'll be working nights, weekends and holidays but I've waitressed before and the money is usually pretty good. I'm just a little bummed because that means JJ and I can't go on normal dates. But he was really sweet and said that he'd take me out during the week so we could still spend time together."

Emma and I continue talking about JJ until it's time for me to go. When she told me about her dream man weeks ago, I thought she had set the bar too high. I thought she'd be disappointed that her real dates were nothing like her fairytale daydreams. But for the last hour, hearing her talk about JJ she sounds like a girl falling in love. Before I leave, she makes me promise to tell her all about my weekend with Roo, which is easy because Emma is a hopeless romantic. I can be sappy with the details and I know she won't judge me for it.

Saturday

I wake up in a great mood, knowing I get to see Roo today! After starting some laundry and cleaning Patches' cage, I realize the morning is going by more quickly than I thought it would. I run to the grocery store so it looks like I actually live here. I put together a 'pick six' pack of beer I think Roo might like and buy a pack of black cherry hard seltzer beverages for myself. After finishing the laundry, I get a text from Roo.

Roo: Over halfway, see you soon!

Jhett: Yay! I'm so excited to see you!

I hop in the shower and use the rest of the time getting ready. I just get done lighting a candle when I hear a knock. I want to shriek out loud in excitement. I half run over to the door and swing it open.

"Hey!" He says with a giant grin. He scoops me up and swings me around in a big bear hug.

"Hi! I'm so happy you're here!"

"Oh man, this day couldn't come soon enough!" He says. "And the drive seemed to go in slow motion." He keeps his hand in the small of my back. "So, what are you thinking, you ready to get lunch?"

"Sure. I was thinking we could go to this burger place. It's not far from here; they have like twenty-four different kinds of burgers."

"That sounds amazing."

We take a table outside on the patio and look over the menu. We order pretty normal burgers, except mine is served on a pretzel bun, and his has peanut butter in the sauce.

Roo looks at me with his intense eyes. "Tell me about your week."

Gosh, he's cute. It's hard not to gawk at him. I'm glad he's asked me a question because I have an excuse to stare.

"So, Danielle…do you remember she was in a relationship with a guy named Ben?"

"I knew she was in a relationship. Trust me, it was the first thing I can recall from the weekend. As soon as we found out you were all taken, we were a little bummed." He shakes his head. "And we didn't think you guys would ever show up to

173

Rio's bar." He laughs. "Man, it makes this seem surreal. Anyway, I did not remember her boyfriend's name."

"Well, that's okay because they broke up. She ended it Monday."

"Really?" He says with a look of surprise and excitement.

"Yeah, I'm pretty happy about it, too. It was long overdue."

"How's she doing?"

"We all got together on Tuesday night. She seems to be doing okay."

The waitress wiggles between us and places two baskets in front of us, and plops a bottle of ketchup down before walking away.

"Oh man, does this look good!" Roo says grinning. He got the steak fries and I ordered the seasoned waffle fries.

"Would you like to try my fries? They are so good!" I say, holding one up.

"Oh yeah? Mine are pretty good, probably better than yours." He teases and then gives me a playful smile. He dips one in ketchup and holds it out in front of me.

I feel silly biting for it midair but do it anyway. "Mmm, it's good," I say and he starts laughing.

"What?" I say and wipe my mouth, suddenly worried I have a mess on my face.

"You're cute," he says with a smirk.

"What? Are you laughing at me?"

"Not at all. The opposite actually. I think you're really fun. You have really contagious energy," he says and then snatches a fry off my plate.

"Oh, well in that case, thanks," I say, smiling up at him. He winks at me.

"So, what are we doing after this?"

"I don't really have a plan; I was thinking we could just wing it."

"Hmm, okay," he says as though he's thinking. "I'm up for whatever, as long as we get to the park by 5pm."

"What do you think about paddleboarding?" As soon as I ask, I realize he probably didn't bring swim trunks.

"I'd love to! Today, after this?"

"Well yeah if you'd want to go. I probably should have asked you to bring a swimsuit. Your shorts will probably get wet."

"I could use another pair," he says shrugging.

"I hate to sound like such a girl, but I love shopping. We can go after we're done here!"

"Is it hard, paddleboarding? I've always wanted to try it."

"If you have decent balance, you'll do fine. Start on your knees, and eventually, slowly, you'll be able to stand once you're feeling confident."

"Oh, now I can't wait for my first lesson."

Roo grabs the check and sets his card on top of the receipt without looking at it, and hands it back to the waitress.

"Thanks for lunch."

"I will gladly take you out anytime." His direct gaze mixed with his sex appeal makes me blush.

We take a short drive to an outdoorsy shop near the lake where we can shop for swim trunks. The shop door opens with a ding and we are welcomed in by the woman behind the counter.

"Hi there! Please let me know if there's anything I can help you with," she says with a smile.

"Men's swim trunks?" I ask.

She points to a rack in the back. We look through them, and Roo holds up a few pairs to ask what I think.

"I like the green pair."

"That's what I was thinking. They go good with my eyes, right?" He uses a serious voice and holds them up to his face. We both start laughing.

"Perfect!" I say mockingly, but they really do make his hazel eyes look greener.

"What about a suit for you?" He asks.

"I always have one in my workout bag. You just never know when you might need one."

"You come prepared; I like that."

I grab my suit from the bag and we head to the rental shop. I bought a punch card at the beginning of the summer for ten rentals. I have them punch two for me and Roo. We are fitted for our boards and change into our suits. We walk our boards down the beach to an area that is normally quiet. I see two people off in the distance in kayaks. I walk a few steps into the lake. The water splashes up against my ankles and the cool temperature makes me flinch.

Following me he says, "Water feels good."

"Yeah…it's a little cold but I'm adjusting."

We set our boards on the water; they lift slightly from the small current.

"You ready?" I ask looking at Roo.

"I am. Let's go!" He moves quickly, pushing his board out before climbing on. "And don't fall in, water's much colder when you get waist-deep." He swiftly boards, starting on his knees and placing his paddle in the water, trying it out.

"You're a natural, are you sure you haven't done this before?" I ask, watching him. Just then he teeters and almost loses his balance.

"Don't jinx me," he says, smiling. "If I fall in, guess who's coming with me?"

"No way. I do not plan on getting soaked today. This water is far too cold to swim in this time of year."

"What if you fall in?" He asks.

"Well, for starters, I don't plan on falling in. I've never fallen in. So, if I end up in the lake because of you, I will not be happy with you," I say threatening him.

"Okay…" he says nodding.

"Why do you have that mischievous look on your face?" I ask.

"I don't. That's just how I look." He brings his paddle up to splash me. A few droplets land on my board and a couple on my arm. When he sees that the water has splashed my arm he tries to quickly paddle away.

I fail terribly at trying to splash him back. My attempt makes my board rock side to side and I almost lose my balance.

"Where are you going?" I shout.

"To someplace a little more secluded."

"There is no secluded place. We're in the middle of a lake."

"We'll see." He shouts over his shoulder.

Roo slows and gradually starts to stand. I catch up to him and we call a truce. He happily agrees since standing is more difficult.

We paddle for the next thirty minutes. We get to a spot that looks shallow; here you can actually see the sand through the dark blue water.

"Should we stop?" Roo asks.

"And do what?"

"I'm pretty sure we're over a sand bar," he says.

"Are you getting off?"

"Maybe," he says looking over his board contemplating his next move.

"Be my guest," I say gesturing to the water as I drop down to sit.

He drops down to a seated position with both legs hanging off one side and then just slides off his board and into the water. He's standing waist-high in the lake.

"See I knew it!" He says raises his hands up. "Come in!"

"I don't know, it's probably really cold," I say skeptically.

I lean forward to allow my fingertips to touch the water and before I know it, I'm sliding off my board with no hope of stopping and in a split second, I'm in the water. I struggle to keep my head above water and gasp for air as I'm submerged chest-deep in a shock of cold water as I try to find my footing. Roo had tipped my board just enough for me to slide not so gracefully into the lake.

"What the hell?" I yell and splash him.

This time I'm pleased as the water hits his body. He flinches and turns his head to the side. He has a huge grin across his face when he turns back to me. He comes towards me and scoops me up in one swift motion. He throws me over his shoulder.

"I can't believe you just threw me off my board! You are in so much trouble!"

My hands grip at his arms and shoulder for support as the fear of being dropped back in the water makes me hold on for dear life. He slowly works his hands over my body until we are face to face. He lowers us down into the water so that the water is to our chest.

My breaths are shallow and quick but his are more controlled, as if the temperature doesn't bother him. My arms are wrapped around him and his are around me. I wrap my legs around his waist and he lowers us even more so that we are gently bobbing along with the waves. I gasp as the cold-water slaps against my back and feel goosebumps cover my body. He brings his face closer to mine and looks at my lips before looking back at me. Butterflies flutter from deep in my belly and rise up through my chest. His eyes twitch for a splint second and then his lips are on mine. My hands move over his muscular back.

A flash of warmth comes over me and I feel myself relax and give in to the kiss. My fingertips find the base of his hairline and I lightly pull at the tiny hairs. His breathing amplifies and his hands move around my waist, where I feel him hold me securely. He tugs at the bottom part of my lip before pulling away slightly. He lets out a deep sigh and looks up at me with the most beautiful smile. He moves his right hand to the side of my face and rests it on my jaw.

"I have been waiting so long to kiss you…and God does it feel good."

"Me too," I say whispering into his ear.

"It was worth every minute." He pushes a piece of hair off my face and kisses my forehead softly for more than a few seconds and gives another deep exhale.

We get back to my apartment just after 3:30pm. Now when we get out of my car he reaches for my hand and we walk together up the stairs. I have a chill from the lake so I tell Roo that I'll take a quick shower before we leave for the game. I head into the bathroom and peel off my still damp suit. When I see steam, I pull back the curtain and step in. A couple minutes later, I hear a light tap on the door and then Roo clearing his voice.

"Is there room for one more?"

A moment of shock comes over me. Did I just hear him right? I wasn't expecting this. I pause for a second before sliding open the curtain to peek at him. He's so hot. I pull back the curtain a few inches more revealing my wet shoulder. We lock eyes and I motion him towards the shower letting him know he can come in. Even as I do this my stomach is doing somersaults at what is taking place. He drops his suit and steps into the shower.

Focusing solely on me, he takes my face in his hands and slowly kisses me. Because of our plans, we only spend the next few minutes kissing before he hops out. As soon as he does, I feel myself shudder from realizing that we were just standing naked in the shower together. When I hear him leave the bathroom I get out and dress quickly. I catch my reflection in the mirror, the grin on my face widens as I take in this new euphoric feeling that I've never felt before.

I walk into the kitchen wearing a Milwaukee t-shirt and short jean shorts that are frayed at the bottom.

"Wow, you look hot," Roo says, placing his baseball cap on backwards.

"Thanks, so do you." Feeling more confident, I walk up and kiss him before opening the fridge. "I got these for you, I hope you like them," I say, holding up the beers I had bought earlier.

"That was sweet, thanks babe." He glances at the labels before placing them in the cooler.

I hand him the ones I've bought for myself along with some cheese curds and a bag of chips.

"This is great, we'll just need to stop for meat on the way. You ready?"

I reach for his hand. He grabs the cooler and we're out the door. On the drive, Roo fills me in on the friends I'm about to meet. He gives me a little insight as to how they met, too.

Roo drives to where his friends are parked. When we emerge from his vehicle, he grabs the cooler, then walks over to meet me and reaches out to take my hand. Coming here, I was slightly nervous that I was crashing a guys' day, but something about his confidence and the look on his face when he looks over and smiles reassures me that being there with him is exactly what he wants.

From a few parking spots away, I see a plastic white folding table filled with all things tailgating. There is queso dip, salsa, a jar of jumbo dill pickles, watermelon slices, cookies, and a big plate of brats surrounded by bottles of condiments and a cooler off to the side.

"Hey guys!" He says excitedly and gives my hand a squeeze before releasing it to hug his buddies.

"Hey man, how are ya? Who is this beauty you have here with you?" His first friend asks.

Turning back to welcome me, he places his hand gently on my lower back. "This is Jhett," he says as if he's announcing me onto a stage to perform.

"Nice to meet you. I'm Roger. Roo and I played baseball together in high school."

"I heard about that on the way over. It's nice to meet you too," I say, extending my hand to shake his.

"And this is Sam."

"Hi, good to meet you. I've heard a lot about you," he says reaching to shake my hand.

"You have?" I say surprised and turn to look at Roo.

"Only good...so far," says Sam teasing. "Maybe we should start with one of these to formally welcome Jhett," he says picking up the cooler.

"What's in there?" I ask.

"We sort of have this tradition; anytime we get together for a game we make pudding shots," Roger says.

"Oh yum! What flavor did you make?" I ask peering into the cooler.

"We have chocolate and grasshopper," he says offering me a brown and green cup. "Good together or by themselves."

I take one of each just like Roo had. "Cheers!" I say as we raise the cups. I take the chocolate first. "Is that vodka I taste?" I ask surprised by the pungent taste.

"Yeah. The chocolate are a bit on the strong side. I made those first." Roger says making a face himself. We all pop the top on the grasshopper and slide our tongues on the inside of the cup like we did with the chocolate. This one is much better and doesn't have a shock of strong booze to follow.

"What did you think?" Roo asks.

"The grasshopper is so good!" I say and Roger offers another. "No, thank you. Maybe in a bit."

I sit on the tailgate of Roger's truck with a drink in my hand while Roo roasts the hot dogs we picked up on the way over. Roger and Sam sit in lawn chairs drinking their beers and bring up the funny or embarrassing stories they can think of from Roo's past.

"Try all you want, but I'm kind of boring. There shouldn't be anything too crazy that will scare this girl away. Well, at least I'm hoping," Roo says wrapping his arms around me and kissing my cheek.

I smile and feel myself blush. I really like how laid back and easy it is for me to be with Roo and his two friends that I've just met.

After eating, we take another two pudding shots and have another drink before making it into the game. We have bleacher seats so we're able to sit together. The game goes by quickly and by the end, I've learned more about Roo's friends and a whole lot more about Roo. We win by two and Roger and Sam try to convince us to join them for celebratory drinks at a nearby bar. Roo declines but promises that when he's in town again he'll let them know. They both wish me good luck and tease that they hope I know what I'm getting myself into. I feel like the day couldn't have gone better, and from everything they've told me, what you see is what you get with Roo.

Roo and I walk hand in hand back to his vehicle. "Did you have fun tonight?" he asks.

"Yes, are you kidding, I had a great time! I loved hearing all the stories and your friends are great," I say, beaming up at him.

"Good, I was hoping so. It's always great seeing those guys but I'm really glad they got to meet you."

"Really, why?" I ask as I pull open the passenger door and slide onto the seat.

Suddenly Roo is quiet. I turn to see if he's heard me. He's sitting still and looking down at his hands. I wonder what he's thinking, and the quiet stillness between us makes a lump form in my throat. Just as I'm about to ask if everything is okay, he turns to me.

182

"Jhett, I'm crazy about you. I can't stop thinking about you and all I want is to be with you all the time." His voice is serious and I can tell he's nervous. "I haven't been in a serious relationship since high school, and that was so long ago. I dated a few girls here and there but up until I met you, I thought I had too high of expectations or I was jinxed at picking the wrong type of girl." He takes my hands in his and squeezes. "I just want you to know that I'm serious about us. I'm not here to play games. These last few weeks of getting to know you have been amazing, and I thought I should tell you because I've felt a really strong connection to you since we first met and I feel like it's only getting stronger."

"I know I made it hard in the beginning. I really like you too," I say and can't help but smile. "And I love that you're here and I'm getting to know you even more. That's the coolest part. I want you to know everything about me and my childhood and my passions and I want to know the same about you."

"It's so good to hear that," he whispers and runs his hand up the side of my arm pulling me toward him. He kisses me, then breaks away slowly and holds my gaze for an extra second before grinning and saying, "Let's get out of here.

He quickly puts the vehicle in reverse. The drive back to my apartment seems to take forever. We practically run into my door because the pressure of getting the key into the lock quickly makes me fumble, and takes twice as long to unlock it. I slam the door closed once inside and when I turn Roo is there. He pushes me up against the door and my head hits it lightly.

He scoops me up so that my legs are wrapped around his waist and my back is pressed firmly against the door, his hands are cupped under my butt. We're breathing heavy and kissing like our lives depend on it. My hands are holding firmly onto his back and I can feel taut muscle. He tastes so good. His lips are soft and feel like they belong against mine. I feel him shift his arm so one is under me, holding me up and the other has moved to the back of my hair. He runs his fingers through it and tugs gently.

He carries me into the bedroom and slowly drops me down in the middle of the bed. He's heavily panting and I realize my breathing is the same. He slowly lifts his shirt and pulls it over his head. Instead of being modest like I was at the beach and in the shower, I stare. I stare at his smooth rapidly moving chest for a few beats and then bring myself to look him in the eyes. I flash him a playful smile and I curl my finger up to motion him over. He drops his shirt and with his other hand, he grabs the door and swings it shut.

CHAPTER 13

I wake up the next morning in Roo's arms. Our bodies are entwined and the sheets are a twisted mess. Sunlight is pouring in and I know it must be past 8am. I turn, reaching for a glass of water. Roo inhales deeply and stretches, opening his eyes.

"Hey." He smiles.

"Good morning," I whisper. "Did you sleep well?"

"Best night of my life." He is still grinning.

"What do you want to do today?" I ask.

"Hmm. Breakfast...and maybe just lazy beach day?"

I nod. "I'll make us some breakfast burritos, sound good?"

"Sounds amazing," he says running his fingers through his hair.

A short while later, I set two plates down on the counter.

"Filled with scrambled eggs, caramelized onions, crispy bacon, and loads of cheese," I say. I add an extra piece of bacon on each plate. I set two glasses of orange juice between us and take a seat next to him at the counter.

He leans over and kisses my forehead before taking his first bite. "You're the best. Thanks babe."

I smile and wish that time would slow down. It's painstakingly hard knowing I only get somewhere between twenty-four to forty-eight hours with this man before having to wait another five to six days to spend time with him again. "What time do you have to head back today?" I ask between bites.

"I guess that's more up to you. Do you have any plans?"

"Nope, I'm open all day," I say cheerfully.

"Great, probably sometime in the early evening then. I'd love to take you to dinner before I go."

"Really? That would be awesome."

"There's nothing that I want more than to spend a few extra hours with you."

After breakfast, we take our time getting ready for the beach. We plan to spend a few hours there, have a light lunch and then go to dinner around 5pm. I make turkey sandwiches and find out quickly that Roo does not like mayo; he's very serious when telling me that it makes him gag. Luckily, I have some mustard in the fridge. I pack my portable Bluetooth speaker and have Roo add a few of his favorite songs to my playlist while I finish packing up.

"Hey Jhett, a text just came through."

"Who is it from? One of the girls?" I say, walking towards my phone.

"Um, Sai," he says, sounding a little uncomfortable.

I swallow and feel a bit unsettled. I look at the screen and see the message is unopened. I'm thankful he didn't read it out of curiosity. This text could mean any number of things coming from Sai. I sit across from Roo putting a little distance between us so that he's just far enough from the screen. I don't want to hide the message, but this way I'm hoping I can sum up the text and deflate anything alarming. I tell myself it's no big deal and to stay calm, if I freak out, he might freak out. I open the message.

Sai: Jhett, I've been trying my hardest to accept the fact that you have moved on, however, I am having a very difficult time. I think I need closure to help me move forward. Would you please consider meeting for dinner this week?

It's so formal and I don't know what to think. I don't know what to tell Roo either. Why did he have to send this message right now and ruin this perfectly wonderful morning.

"Is everything okay?" Roo asks, breaking me from my concentration. "You look really concerned."

"Yeah, um, it's fine. Sai asked if I'd meet him for dinner this week so he can get closure," I say.

"Okay, so what are you thinking? Do you want to see him?"

"No, not really. I think it will do more harm than good."

"Okay…" Roo looks like he wants to say something more but holds off. Now he has a look of concern on his face.

I move over to sit next to him. "I think it's important for you to know that I don't have any feelings for him whatsoever. Things were actually over for a while before the breakup. And I really don't want you to worry."

I reach for his hand. He smiles at me but it's not his normal genuine one.

"Has he been bothering you?"

"No. I randomly get a text from him but it's just little things. Not at all like this. I just blow them off, and most times I don't respond." Saying this makes me feel guilty that I sometimes do respond, and realize how much that probably hurts to hear.

He nods. "I can say something to him," he says with some sternness in his voice.

I stop him. "Oh no, I think that would make things worse. When I respond, I'm going to let him know that if there will be a conversation, it will be further down the road and not over dinner." I shake my head and make a face. I take a deep breath and stand, pulling Roo with me. "Let's go to the beach and get back to enjoying this day." He looks at me for a few seconds, smiles, and leans in to kiss me. And, just like that, the butterflies are back.

We spend the next five hours at the beach. The majority of it is spent laying on our backs or stomachs soaking up sun. We share our lunch and spend some time reading. I'd packed an extra book for Roo, the only one I could find that I thought he might like, which happened to be a murder mystery. We walk part of the beach searching for seashells and sea glass.

Roo finds a smooth green piece of sea glass that he thinks looks like a heart. I don't see it but he's sweet for giving it to me. We make a small sandcastle that's not very impressive. Of course, the fact that we don't have the proper bucket, shovel, and scoops makes it hard to design something that we can actually be proud of. Eventually, we give up when we run out of beach treasures to decorate it.

After getting back from the beach we shower and change into dressy clothes. Roo searches for a nice restaurant and settles on one not far from my apartment. It's certainly a place you could bring someone for a date with its dimmed lighting and a relaxed, romantic atmosphere.

When we get there, Roo holds out the door for me and we walk in. We are seated in a small quaint area all to ourselves.

"So, I forgot to tell you, while you were in the shower, I watched a video that Roger and Sam sent last night. It was hard to hear because they were in a bar and also because they were pretty smashed, but they gave you two thumbs up, literally. They also had big dopey grins on their faces," he says smiling.

"Oh, so they approve. I'd like to see this video if you still have it."

"Well, of course they do. They'd be idiots not to," he says reaching for his phone.

This is when I realize I've only seen Roo on his phone a handful of times; otherwise, I've had his complete attention. I like that about him and hope that he's not one of those guys that has his phone glued to his hand once he gets comfortable. I hear my phone ping and a banner across the top of the screen lets me know that a media message has come through from Roo. He puts his phone back and turns his attention to me.

"I've been wondering if you have plans for next weekend."

"I don't, would you like me to come visit?" I ask sweetly.

He dramatically puts his hands over his heart and falls back into his chair, "Yes! That's what I was hoping you'd say. I don't think I can handle going two weeks without seeing you." He reaches for my hand and grazes my knuckles with his fingertips. "Actually, I haven't told you yet, but I have some flexibility with my schedule. On the weeks that I work Saturday I get to choose my weekday off. I normally take Wednesday since it's the middle of the week, but I could take Monday off the weeks I come here so we can have an extra morning together, or I could take Friday on the weekends you come to see me. You get done at two, right?"

"Yes, that's great! This makes me feel better about our situation. I've been wanting to talk to you about that," I say and my voice goes quiet towards the end.

I see his face change. He usually looks optimistic with just about anything I say, but his look is serious now. "Are you worried about being in a long-distance relationship?" He asks.

"I can't say that I don't think it will be a challenge. How do you feel about it?"

"Well, I'm definitely not a fan, but it could be worse."

I laugh lightly. "I know, and that's what my sister said, too."

"Oh, you've told your sister about me?" He asks, looking amused.

"Yeah of course, and actually, before I forget, I have this family thing coming up. First weekend in July. I know there's a chance you might have to work. I just thought it'd be a good idea to mention it now so you can request time off…if you'd want to come. I know it's kind of soon, but I really want you there."

"Absolutely. I'd love to. I already have off for the Fourth so I'll drive down Thursday."

"Oh! I like knowing I get you for a long weekend!"

Our food comes and we devour it. Roo offers me a taste of his tilapia and I offer him a bite of my pasta. Both are mouthwateringly delicious.

"Now that's good, but I don't think I'd be able to drive home after eating it. It would put me right to sleep," he says seconds after taking the pasta off my fork.

"Are you more of a morning person or night owl?" I ask.

"Night owl for sure, especially when I was in college. I don't stay out as late or go out as often anymore. But definitely still an owl. What about you?"

"If you asked my friends, they'd say morning person. I'm usually the first one up in the morning and the first to request leaving a bar or club on a night out. So, I guess that makes me a morning person. Generally, I don't sleep past 8am on the weekends."

"Oh, you mean like today?" He teases, being well aware we got up later than that.

"Well when someone keeps me up late," I pause and stare at him for a second before adding, "I like to sleep in just as much as the next person." I shrug playfully.

I see something twitch in his eyes and he gives me a sultry smile. He picks up my hand and kisses the inside of my wrist.

"We should finish up here so that I can bring you back before it gets too late," he says and I know exactly what he means. I feel my stomach tighten, and I feel my face flush. We box up the rest of our food and head back to my apartment where Roo practically rips my clothes off.

"I don't want you to leave," I say as he starts to get dressed.

"I know, I really wish I could stay another night with you," he says, taking a seat on the edge of the bed. "I want to ask you something." He pauses. "Jhett, I want you to be mine, all mine. Will you be my girlfriend?"

"Yes, of course!" I say, beaming.

I get up and throw a baggy V-neck t-shirt on. I walk over and take a seat on his lap. He clears his throat. "I will always be honest with you, and I won't play games," he says in a solemn tone.

I kiss him. "I know."

Roo takes my hand and grabs his bag with the other. We slowly walk to my door. He slowly turns to me and says, "See you next weekend."

We embrace for a long hug. Many times this weekend I wished for time to slow down or to stop all together but now I wish I could go back to yesterday when he first showed up so that we could do it all again.

"This week better fly by," he whispers in my ear. He brings his lips to mine and kisses me goodbye.

I slowly close the door behind him, keeping my hand on the door for a few seconds after it's closed. I think of how different this goodbye was from the last. Even though it couldn't have gone any better, I have the same craving for him as I did last time. I smile a sad smile knowing I just have to wait to be with him again. I walk to the window and watch as his car pulls out of the parking lot.

I scoop up Patches from his cage while checking my phone and notice I've missed a whole conversation with the girls. Scrolling up to the first message, I read through to the last chuckling and rolling my eyes at some of their messages. There are a few comments asking where I am, followed by the girls taking turns uploading GIFs making fun of me for not responding. I laugh at them because they are pretty accurate. They have made plans to meet up on Tuesday at Marcos. I'm relieved when I see this because the thought had crossed my mind that they might tell me that I was doing the same thing with Roo as I had with Sai, spending all my time with him and falling off the face of the earth. This is somehow different though.

With him living two hours away, and weekends being the only time we can spend getting to know each other, it doesn't seem right for them to be upset if I dedicate my weekends to him. At least not in the beginning. I make a mental note to schedule another get together on a weekday before leaving Marcos on Tuesday.

My phone pings and I glance to see there's a message from Roo.

Roo: Missing you already…and did you know we met one month ago today?

It seems like our girls' weekend was not that long ago, but the fact that I've known Roo for only a month seems unreal to me too. Maybe because he consumes my every thought when my mind wanders, and because we've been talking so much it feels we've known each other for months.

Jhett: That was some wknd…almost as fun as this one!

Roo: ;)

I write back to the girls, letting them know I will meet them on Tuesday at Marcos. I decide while I'm at it to text Emma too.

Jhett: Hey Em, how have you been? Let's make plans!

An almost instant reply. I don't even know how she could have typed so fast.

Emma: HI! So good! JJ is amazing, I can't wait to tell you more about him! Can you meet Friday after work? I don't start till 5. How are things with Roo?

I consider this and know that if my boss leaves at 11am like planned, I can make it to Roo a little after 1pm on Friday.

Jhett: Fri is no good, Thurs? Things are great with Roo. He came to visit this wknd and we had a really good time…and I'm his gf!!

Emma: WOW! I'm happy for you! I can do Thurs, I work the day shift, can you do 5:30pm?

Jhett: That will be perfect! See you then!

Tuesday

"Hey bitches. I'm starving. We ready to eat?" Clarissa says loudly not bothering to care about the other people surrounding us. Eyes around the bar look up; women frown and men hold their gaze a few seconds before looking away.

"Yeah, so are we, what took you so long to get here?" Kia asks.

"Well I didn't tell you to wait," Clarissa says with a look of annoyance on her face.

"We waited to be polite." Kia turns away from Clarissa and rolls her eyes at me.

After a few minutes of small talk, Danielle says, "I want to share with you all that I'm in the process of buying a house." She sounds a little unsure.

"Hell yeah, that's great, I had no idea you were looking," Kia says.

"Well it all happened really fast," she says shifting her eyes to me, "Jhett advised me to focus on something to help me from thinking of Ben after the break up. It started with me thinking about moving into a new rental. As you all know, everything is getting crazy expensive around here so I started looking at houses just for fun. My dad was really supportive about it and we looked at my budget to see what I could afford. We just went to see this one house for the second time last night."

"That's awesome, so did you put in an offer?" I ask.

"Yeah, I did this morning," Danielle says cheerfully.

"Well, I think we have to toast to that!" Kia says raising her glass.

We cheers, ask a bunch of questions, and ask to see photos.

Kia passes over Danielle's phone so I can look at the photos. "It's so cute, I love all the character!" Kia says.

"Thank you. I know it needs some work but my dad will help with all that. It's nice knowing I'll be out of the duplex in less than two months."

I hand the phone to Clarissa and hope she doesn't say something that will offend Danielle.

"So, when's the housewarming party?" I ask excitedly.

"Well if all goes well the closing is at the end of July. The couple I'm buying the house from is moving out of state mid-month, but they've agreed that I can move my things into the garage on the twentieth which will make moving in less stressful."

"Cute, can't wait to see it," Clarissa says in a positive tone.

I glance at Danielle and she has a proud smile on her face.

"Thanks!" She says setting her phone down.

"So, how was everyone's weekend?" Danielle asks.

"Nothing as exciting as buying a house; well, at least not for me." Kia states. "Is Ben leaving you alone? It's hard for me to picture that he is."

"Um, well, not really. He texts me every day. Most of it I ignore but it's really hard for me not to read his messages. And then I usually get suckered into responding."

"He knows what to say to get you to respond. Have you thought about changing your number?"

"My dad suggested that too," she says shrugging. "He saw him driving past when we were leaving the other day; it was a bit scary. My dad turned red and I had to tell him to calm down. He wanted to call him and after I talked him out of it, he mentioned I get a restraining order."

"Are you serious? Is it that bad?" I ask.

"Well, my landlord changed the locks last week, and Ben got really wasted and tried getting in Saturday night. He did a lot of damage to the door."

"Oh my gosh!" Kia says dramatically.

"Why didn't you tell us?" Clarissa asks.

"He was just drunk. He left after the neighbor threatened to call the cops if he didn't stop making so much noise." She speaks matter-of-factly and pulls all her hair over one shoulder. "But enough about Ben, what about you Jhett? How are things going with Roo?"

"Yeah, I want to hear all about you and that hunky man," Kia says friskily.

I think about where to begin. Before I can say anything Clarissa says, "Oh my gosh, you are smitten with him," she says teasingly. "I've never seen you speechless."

I know I'm probably blushing. I can talk to these girls about anything individually but it's more intimidating talking to them all at once. "Okay, so yes, I really like him."

"He spent the weekend, right?" Kia asks.

"Yes, he got here Saturday and left Sunday evening. We got lunch and went paddleboarding and I met two of his friends at the baseball game. It was all really great. I'm really excited about him."

"Well yeah, it's clear to anyone that you two have chemistry."

"Thanks," I say to Clarissa, knowing if she sees it, it must be true. "I love how he zeroes in on me. It's like all his focus is on me in that very moment and he gives me all his attention. He's been the one to initiate holding hands too. It probably sounds dorky but it means a lot because it makes me feel like we're on the same page. And I know Sai did that stuff, too, but it's different. Sai did it because he wanted people to know we were together and that I was his. Roo does it when we're alone and when we're in public."

"Oh, I love that. It shows that he's mature and doesn't care what his friends think. James rarely holds my hand. I think he thinks it makes him look weak, which is just stupid."

I tell them how he asked to join me in the shower when we got back from paddleboarding. They get all excited and giddy. Shivers tingle down my spine as I share how we raced back to my apartment after the baseball game and he kissed me against the door. I give them the gist of what happened next, purposely leaving out the extra details. I know I wouldn't want Roo sharing that type of stuff with his friends.

"Wait, wait, go back. You mean to tell me, while you were in the shower, all you did was make out?" Clarissa asks.

"Yes." I nod. Clarissa has a look on her face like she doesn't believe me.

"Did you at least sneak a peek? How could you not." Kia asks.

"Um, think about it, we were facing each other. There was no way for me to sneak a peek, and I would have been mortified to be caught looking."

"Because if you would've looked and he caught you, guess what? Then he would have known it was okay to stare back, sister," Kia says in a fiery tone.

Danielle is laughing and I feel like rolling my eyes at these two.

Clarissa is looking right at me. "Tell us more about the hookup."

"All I will say is there was passion," I say back to her. I wait a moment and then add, "Okay, I will say there was a LOT of passion."

The girls love this and they start making moaning and other embarrassing sounds.

"Hmm, I wonder if it was because you've wanted to jump each other since sitting together on that pontoon," Kia says.

I shrug, smile, and say, "Yeah probably." Now we're all laughing.

"And he calls you babe, that's so cute. I didn't get a pet name for, like, months," Kia says.

"Maybe it's time we trade in," Clarissa says looking at Kia. "Max has been a huge ass lately. He told me I was being really bitchy the other day, and he will not talk to me like that. I told him to get the fuck out of my house and go back to his shitty apartment for a few days. I'm so sick of his shit."

"Yeah, James is so damn disrespectful all the time. I threaten to be done, and then he'll turn it around and treat me like a queen for like a week and then it's right back to the same ole shit."

Clarissa and Kia go on venting about how unhappy they are with their boyfriends. I zone out and start thinking about Roo. Danielle offers to buy me a second drink but I know it's time to call it quits.

"Sorry ladies, it's time for me to leave."

"Yeah, we know, you have to get up early," Kia says, making a pouty face. "I should probably leave too."

"What about a workout class this week?" I ask Kia.

"For sure, but it needs to be before work because I'm working late all week." She reads my facial expression. "Supposed to be the best way to start the day."

"Okay, I guess I can try it," I say wondering if I will regret committing.

"Can I join you?" Clarissa asks.

"Really? I thought you hated working out," Kia says.

"I do, but it's good for you right? And I gotta keep this bod looking hot," Clarissa says, gesturing to her body with her hands.

"Oh geez," I say, shaking my head. "You are always welcome. Danielle, you wanna come too?"

"Thanks, but I'm content sticking with the Y, I really like their new Pilates classes."

We all walk out together and say our goodbyes. I get into my car and drive the few short minutes home. By the time I get out of my car, I'm on the phone with Roo and we spend the next two hours talking before going to bed.

The rest of the week goes more quickly than I thought it would. Kia and I worked out as planned in the morning class. Clarissa stood us up with a text.

Clarissa: Way too tired, not going to make it.

197

Neither Kia nor I were surprised. Although it was hard for me to get out of bed, I felt more awake and better all day because of the early workout, just like Kia had said. Since I probably won't have Saturdays to jog with Kia for a while, I agreed to one early morning workout a week.

I meet up with Emma on Thursday and we talk about her waitressing job, JJ, and Roo. She seems to be doing really well and thinks that JJ is going to ask her to be his girlfriend soon. She is still seeing her therapist twice a week and spends her two free nights with JJ.

Checking my work schedule, I notice the last two hours are blocked off. I know the only way they will open up is if an emergency patient gets added. I see the new girl, Abby, that was hired in Emma's place walking down the hallway towards me.

"Hey, it's Friday!" she says with a big smile on her face.

"Yes, I can taste the weekend," I say taking a few boxes of gloves out of the storage closet. "I see you have a full schedule, ready to be on your own today?"

"I hope so, things have been going better for me this week."

"You're doing great. I'm sure you'll be fine. Let me know if you need anything." As soon as the words leave my mouth I cringe inside. Why did I offer to help? I should have said, 'I'd like to slip out as soon as possible to visit my boyfriend; who lives two hours away, so if you happen to get a cancellation, it would mean the world if you could take one of my patients.'

When I get to work I miss that comfortable relaxed feeling I used to get when I saw Emma. I miss having a close friend in the office. Abby is nice but it's just not the same.

Now that time has passed, I know why she was let go. I suspected it all along but since her leaving I've had my performance review and it clarified my suspicions. My boss shared our workflow stats. It revealed how many patients were seen in a day, time spent on scheduled and emergency appointments, what procedures took in the most revenue, how the company is expected to grow based on Geri's changes, etcetera.

I was employee 'X'. Next to my marks on the graph was employee 'Y'. Without him telling me, it was very clear that Emma had been employee Y. I was shown that by using a program on our software, he could pull reports showing different stats. He explained what the chart outcomes and numbers meant. The first number he pointed out showed all patients that were assigned to me on any given day. Next was the actual number of patients that were seen by me. Because we have to login using our passcode, it linked me to the patients that were scheduled with Emma. He told me that he looked into each patient's chart just to make sure there were no errors, and on average I took two extra patients per workday who were not assigned to me. I had no idea it was that much or that often. In the end, I was given a two-dollar raise, which made me ecstatic, but it also meant that I could handle more patients. My schedule would be adjusted the following month. This gave me the time to finish training Abby. I'm lucky she's a quick learner; otherwise, there'd be little chance of me getting out early.

By the end of my last appointment, I can feel a surge of energy start to fill me. I check in with Ruthie to make sure it's safe to leave before taking off. I had thrown my overnight bag in this morning so I'd be ready to head north straight from work. I load Roo's address into my GPS and hit start. I'm not even thirty minutes in when I decide to call Roo.

"Hey, are you getting close?"

"Ugh, I wish. I have another hour and a half."

"Oh, so you just left."

"Yes, but remember some Fridays I work until two, so I guess getting there at two isn't so bad."

"Yeah, I guess. But anyway, I have an idea for this evening…is there anything you'd like to do until like four-ish?"

"Hmm, what's this idea?"

"It's a surprise, I can't tell you."

"How do you know if I like surprises?"

"Well, even if you don't, too bad, I'm not telling you."

I laugh which makes him laugh.

"Well, I'm trying to be creative but there's one thing that I can't seem to push out of my mind." I pause a moment and then add, "I think you know what I'm thinking."

"Oh, I know all right, and I guess I should have mentioned that the first thirty minutes of you being here is going to be spent in my bedroom. Sorry, should have made that clear."

I feel myself blissfully grin. I notice the stoplight turn to yellow so I pull off to the side. I take a picture of myself biting my lower lip while Roo rattles off suggestions. I send it to him without saying a word. Within seconds he gets the message.

"Did you just send me something?"

"I did."

A pause and then, "You just made the next hour and a half so much harder for me. Get here as fast as you can, but safely."

"Okay, I will. Do I have to knock or can I just walk in?"

"I'm setting a timer; I will be waiting at the door for you."

I chuckle and we say goodbye. I must have been daydreaming so hard that I hadn't noticed for a good ten minutes that I was driving in silence. I turn the radio up and try to focus on the lyrics instead of how much longer I have. It works for a bit because while scanning for a new station I find a Christian rock station that has some pretty awesome songs. They're all new to me so it makes a chunk of the trip pass by quickly. The anticipation of getting there is making me crave a snack.

I stop to fill up, use the restroom, and grab a bag of nuts. I see a sucker stand on the counter and start to read the flavors as I wait. I grab blueberry cheesecake. Then I think about it and replace it with a dreamsicle; I don't really want blue lips when Roo first sees me. I'm back in the car in less than ten minutes. I get through the bag of nuts and move onto the sucker. I concentrate on making it last as long as possible. Thirty minutes later and it's a small pea-sized ball hanging off the edge of the stick.

Finally, I make it to Roo's place. I park and look up to see if I can see him. It's hard to see but I think I make him out in the window. I stare a moment longer and then get embarrassed when he's clearly in the window staring back at me. He's moving his arm motioning me in. I hop out quickly and grab my bag from the back.

He swings his door open. "Get over here! What's taking you so long?" He says, smiling at me.

"Hi!" I say as he swallows me up in a hug. He takes my bag and slings it over his shoulder. Then he kisses me; it feels so good. I kiss him back and he walks with his arm around me into his place.

"I'm so glad you're here. It seemed like it was taking forever." He gives my hand a squeeze.

"I know, why didn't you tell me the drive would be torture?"

"Because I wanted you to visit!" He says with a serious look.

He shows me around his apartment. It's nice, a little bigger than I expected, and not at all what I envisioned. It is clean; well, it is guy clean. My guess is he probably spent the last hour or so picking up. We walk into the kitchen and just as I thought, there are dishing in the drying rack. I think it's sweet though. He cleaned up so it would look nice for me. I hear the dryer buzzer go off in the background.

"Towels are dry." He states and for the first time, there's a bit of an awkward silence.

"Want me to help you fold them?"

"No way," he says grabbing me and pulling me close for a kiss. "I have other plans for you." He whispers in my ear.

His warm breath tickles my neck and I feel goosebumps climb up my skin. His mouth stays near my ear for a moment longer before he pulls away. Instead of finishing the tour of his place he leads me to the couch where he takes a seat and then pulls me onto his lap so that I'm straddling him. I lean down for a long kiss. I love the way his hands move around on my body. His fingertips softly pull me into him. We make out on the couch like a bunch of crazy-in-love high schoolers until finally we get up and go into his bedroom.

Twenty minutes later Roo and I are panting heavily, lying side by side on his bed. He reaches for my hand and brings it to his lips to kiss each one of my fingers.

"Have you decided what you want to do?"

"It looked like something was going on downtown, do you know what that is?"

"Oh yeah, the farmer's market. Great idea, I could use a few things."

I'm impressed that Roo has reusable bags in the trunk of his car. He grabs two and we walk towards the first stand.

"I can't wait to show you my favorite stand, there are lots of samples!" He says, his facial expression like a small child getting excited about something.

We pick up some strawberries and fresh herbs for his mom. He said he gets them for her every time he comes.

"Okay we're getting close, close your eyes."

"What, are you serious? I'll walk into something, or someone."

"You'll be fine. Stand here. Close your eyes; the stand is right around the corner." He waits for me to close my eyes. I hear Roo's voice and I can tell he's talking to someone. The conversation is hard to make out but I hear his name so this tells me he must be a faithful customer.

"Okay, keep your eyes closed and open your mouth."

I shake my head. "Um, I need a little description or a hint. Is it like a pretzel with dip? Something sweet or savory?"

"Sweet!" He says. "You will like it, I'm sure of that."

I open my mouth and something smooth and sweet hits my tongue. I bite down and taste more sweetness and then the perfect balance of salt.

"Salted caramel chocolates?"

"Yes! Dark chocolate sea salt caramels. I went with something safe." He leads me around the corner and says, "This is Jhett, my girlfriend."

"Oh, how nice to meet you." A man and woman a few years older than my parents don't just shake my hand but come around their booth and place both hands around mine to welcome me.

"Oh, hello dear," The woman says in a soft motherly tone.

For a moment I wonder if this is his mother and I've missed something.

Her husband says, "I've always wondered when we'd get the chance to meet the special woman in Roo's life." Wow, this has to be a relative.

"This is Martha and Frank. They own the best sweets shop in town."

"Roo, you are too kind. I think he's the reason our business does so well. We see him just about every other week." She smiles.

"I like to bring cookies or turtles for my coworkers every once in a while," Roo says.

"Frank, put something together for them." Martha tells her husband. Without a moment's hesitation, he pulls a small white box from beneath the table and starts placing truffles and other goodies inside the box.

"Oh, throw some of those in," she says pointing. "Those are his favorite."

"You don't need to do that," Roo says. "I was planning on buying a box anyway."

"Oh, I don't doubt you were, but this is a special day meeting your lovely girlfriend," Martha says, patting his upper arm. She continues pointing out to Frank what he should be packing into the box until it's full.

"That is so nice of you. Thank you Martha, thank you Frank," he says and leans in to hug them.

"Yes, thank you. Your chocolates are amazing!" I say. Touching my fingers to my lips, I swallow the chocolate covered cherry that Frank had handed me.

"You are so welcome my dear." She hugs me and adds, "Please take good care of him."

"I will," I say when I meet her eyes.

She returns with a heartfelt smile. Frank hands the box to Roo and claps him on the hand. This couple adores Roo. Their generosity makes me curious to know if they are like this to all their loyal customers or if there's something more. If they were related, wouldn't Roo have mentioned it when introducing us? Once we are out of earshot, I look over at Roo. He's beaming, with the same look on his face as when he first told me about bringing me to his favorite stand.

"So fill me in."

"On what?" His look tells me he has no idea what I'm talking about.

"Martha and Frank."

"Oh, they're great, right?" He says smiling. "Can you believe this?" He says holding up the box.

"Yeah, they were like the nicest people I think I have ever met. How do you know them?"

"Well like they said, I go to their shop a lot. I wasn't expecting to see them here, so that was a nice surprise. They

204

usually stay at the shop and have one or two of their employees work here at the market."

"Okay, so they're just that nice? I thought she was your mom or aunt at first."

He laughs, "Oh, well, no, no relation. It's sort of a long story." His voice turns solemn. He's looking straight ahead but I can see the creases in his forehead.

"What? Can you tell me? I'm confused," I say slowly.

"Let's go sit over there." Roo points to a lone picnic table and we take a seat.

He rubs his forehead and takes his time getting the words out.

I see him swallow. "Martha and Frank lost their son a few years ago. He was killed in a motorcycle accident. He was their only child. I had gone to their shop for the first time a few weeks after he passed. Anytime I'd come into the shop Martha would come out from the back. She always waited on me, and she was always so sweet. I could tell each time something was on her mind. Finally, one day when Martha wasn't there, her husband came out to talk to me. He apologized for her behavior. I thought it was silly because she never bothered me. I had asked him why she always came out from the back; I never saw her do that for anyone else. He told me that I look just like their son. He told me about the accident, and said that every time I walked in, she felt like she was seeing him. I'll never forget the look in Martha's eyes the first few times she saw me." Roo inhales sharply and pinches the bridge of his nose. After another inhale he continues.

"I asked to see a picture. Frank was so, so happy that I was okay with all of it. He handed the picture over and their son looked just like me. More like me than my own brother; it's like we were twins - same age and everything. After that, I couldn't stop going because I knew how much it meant to Martha. I had gone about once a month before, but now I go every other week. I visit them on his birthday. We have lunch and sit and drink coffee and they share stories about him."

I lean over and hug him. "That's so sad, but how sweet of you to stay in their lives and be a part of this." Now what I had seen back there made sense. "How long ago did this happen?"

"He's been gone for three years now. It's kind of strange; although I've never met him, I feel like I knew him."

"You are amazing," I say. "Do you know what a gift you are to them?"

"I think I do. That's why seeing you was so great for them today. They want me to be happy." He smiles. "I'm sorry I didn't share this with you sooner. I had actually planned to take you there for a date sometime, but didn't know I'd get the chance to introduce you this weekend."

"I'm glad I got to meet them."

"Frank was finding one way or another to ask me if I was seeing anyone just about every time I walked into the shop. Like I said, I haven't had a serious girlfriend for some time so they've been waiting a while for this day."

My heart feels full, and I think that if I wasn't already falling hard for Roo, I am now. We leave the market and walk to his vehicle. He opens the door for me, and before closing it, he kisses me but it's different. It's slow, and somehow it feels like Roo and I have just connected on a deeper level.

CHAPTER 14

It's Sunday afternoon and I feel depressed. All I can do is think about Roo and how much I want to be spending another day with him. I turn onto the interstate and decide to call my sister.

"Hey," she answers. "What's up?"

"Hi. I just left Roo's and now I'm on my way back. Thought I'd give you a jingle. Are you busy?"

"Not at all. How was your weekend?" I hear the interest in her voice.

"Great, but it went too fast. We don't get much time together and it's really hard to leave."

"Ah, yeah, that sucks. When do you get to see him again?"

"Next week thankfully. Oh, and he took off for the Fourth so we will get to spend a decent amount of time together, and he's coming to the family reunion!"

"Awesome, I can't wait to meet him!" I hear the smile in her voice. "Did Mom tell you Molly will be there too?"

Molly is our first cousin who we are closest with. She's a few years older than me. She babysat us and we've always looked up to her. She travels with her husband all over the world and tells the best stories.

"She didn't, but that's awesome, I haven't seen her in ages. I'd love to hear what she's been up to."

"Yeah, well Mom heard they want to start a family, so maybe we'll see them around more."

"Speaking of, have you seen Morgan or Beck recently?"

"No, I stopped by Mom's today for lunch, and she said Mo has been really sick. I guess the morning sickness didn't stop after the first trimester like it usually does."

"Ugh, poor woman. Hopefully, that doesn't happen to us."

"I'm a long way off from having to worry about it, but..." she trails off for a second. "Maybe not you?"

"I just started dating him. There is no talk of kids."

"Yet." She throws in.

"No, it's way too early."

"Ha." She laughs. "So, what did you do this weekend?"

I fill her in on the farmer's market and the story of Martha and Frank. "He took me to a drive-in movie theatre last night, it was so cool. I didn't even know they still existed."

"Fun, neither did I. What did you see?"

"This World."

"Oh yeah, I've seen the previews, was it good?"

"It was, I really liked it, but there was no kissing in his vehicle like you see in movies. You could see into all the cars around you. It would have been awkward."

"Yeah, I'd imagine that'd be pretty weird to look over and see the neighboring people looking back at you. What else did you do?"

"He made me breakfast this morning - chocolate chip pancakes and sausage links. Then we took a walk around his neighborhood before going to the zoo."

"Oh my gosh, that is so sweet. He sounds like a keeper Jhett."

"Oh, he is. I don't plan to give him up," I say. "Anyway, what's new with you?"

"Hmm, same work crap, but actually things have been going well lately. I did take off for the Fourth and I already have the weekend off, so I should be there both days. Do you and Roo plan to go both days?"

"Yeah, I'd imagine so. That way we won't miss those who can't make it on Thursday."

Our family reunion started with our family getting together on the Fourth each year, but because so many have moved away or still have to work on the Fourth, it's been extended to two days now. It's near the beach and there's a large park for the kids so there is plenty to do and see. A few families even camp there for the weekend. Yard games are set up and before long someone starts a drinking game. Things get fun and crazy really quickly.

"Great, I will too." Kate adds.

"Good, it's more fun with you there! I'll see you Thursday then!"

"See you Thursday!" She says and I hear the click disconnecting the call.

This week goes by slowly, which is surprising because it's a short week. The clinic is only open Monday through Wednesday. Today, I eat my lunch with Abby and Ruthie. Ruthie asks a hundred and one questions when she gets the chance, so I get to know Abby pretty quickly. It helps to pass the time because Roo is coming tomorrow and I can't stop thinking about it.

I joined Kia at this morning's workout class, and I swear each week gets harder and not easier. Clarissa promised she wouldn't bail on another class but once again we were not shocked when she didn't show. She did text me later asking if I'd meet her for a dog walk later this week. Even though she stood us up more than once, I feel bad telling her that I have plans with Roo and it will have to wait until next week. It's hard with her, she'll either give me a hard time or act like she doesn't care at all. By the end of the day, her reply text comes.

Clarissa: *no biggie*

I'm relieved even though I know it was silly to worry.

Thursday

While Roo makes the drive to my apartment, I put together a pasta salad and cookie bars. I pack my trunk with a cooler, picnic blanket, utensils and a Frisbee. I smile when I place it in the trunk remembering the first time we played on Kippers Island. By the time Roo gets to my place, I'm ready to go. He greets me with the biggest grin and one of his huge bear hugs.

"Hello beautiful," he says.

"Hi there," I say softly, looking him in the eyes. "You ready for this?"

"Meeting all of your family at once? Your parents, siblings and grandparents...Yeah, not nervous at all," he says sarcastically.

"Add aunts, uncles, and cousins," I say smiling apprehensively. "It's a family reunion."

"What? You said 'family get-together'." A look of worry crosses his face.

"Did I? I'm sorry, I didn't mean to mislead you. There will be over sixty people there."

He just stares at me with a dumbfounded look on his face.

"They'll love you. There are newbies every year so you won't be the only new face. Plus, Mo and Beck will be there, and I'm sure they will get most of the attention with their baby news," I say, planting a kiss on his cheek.

Roo adds his things to my trunk and we take off for the park. For the first time since we've met, Roo looks uneasy.

I pat his knee. "It'll be okay." He smiles but it's not convincing. "We can have a drink as soon as we get there if you want." I suggest.

"Yeah, that might help." He nods.

I see Kate as soon as we pull up and she heads for my car. I think breaking the ice meeting one family member before we jump in might help Roo relax.

"Hey, you must be Roo," my sister says, extending her hand to Roo.

"Hi, and you must be Kate." Roo says taking her hand.

We chitchat for a few minutes near the car before heading towards the park where my family has gathered for as long as I can remember.

I slowly introduce him to my immediate family first. I think it goes well because the conversation flows nicely. Two aunts walk over and introduce themselves to Roo.

"Hi, I'm Aunt Phyllis."

"Who do we have here?" My Aunt Lu asks, practically cutting off Aunt Phyllis.

"This is Roo, my boyfriend," I say leaning gently into Roo.

"Oh, hello there," she says slowly. She has an unusual look on her face but she has always been a bit weird. "Welcome."

"Will you all be here tomorrow?" Lu asks, looking back to me.

"Yeah, the whole family will be here today and tomorrow."

"Oh good, Angie can't make it today, but she'll be here tomorrow. She hates missing out."

"I know, it's only once a year that everyone gets together," I say.

"We'll talk later; we have to go make the rounds," she says, gesturing to more cousins a few feet away.

The next few hours go like this and it seems that Roo is doing fine. The three of us change into our suits and take a walk down to the beach. The water is still cool but it's a gorgeous sunny day so we walk out to the sand bar.

"So, are you looking forward to seeing Angie?" Kate asks.

"Ha, not particularly."

"Oh, I know, but I just love how she clings to you like you're still best friends."

"She doesn't cling. She just likes to gossip and talk loudly," I say dipping my hair into the lake to smooth it. "Oh, and just so you know, she dated one of Roo's college friends, so they met a few years ago."

"Oh really? Actually, I'm not surprised, she gets around." Kate says, making her eyes big. "I bet she brings a new guy tomorrow that she just met last week."

"I will not take that bet because I think you're right."

"Roo? Ten bucks she brings a new guy?" Kate asks.

"No thanks, I agree with Jhett." He smirks.

We hang out for another hour before walking back. The grill is going and food has been placed out buffet style. More people have joined the group and kids are running everywhere. Games are set up and there are clusters of relatives talking in groups all around. Mo and Beck have arrived so we walk over so I can introduce them. At dusk, Roo and I retrieve the blanket from my trunk. He takes my hand and for the first time since we got to the park, he kisses me. My skin prickles from his touch. I feel myself relax. I knew Roo was holding back and not fully being himself, and it had created a little tension between us.

"I've missed those lips the past few hours," I say.

"I know, I'm sorry," he says and kisses my forehead.

Although I can't blame him for being a little nervous about meeting a crazy number of my relatives, everyone has been welcoming and I thought it all went really well. He's still a little quiet but more relaxed than he was when we first got here.

I lay the blanket off to the side, toward the far end of the area we've claimed, so that we can have a little privacy. We pull our sweatshirts on and lay on the blanket. I curl into his side and he wraps his arm around me as the first fireworks start to explode in the sky. He pulls me closer to him and turns to spoon me. I feel him press his nose into my hair and inhale. It makes me smile and I squeeze his arm. We stay like this for the next thirty minutes and it's absolutely perfect.

The next morning, I start to get ready as I had the day before, packing the cooler and getting things ready for the park. Roo slept in and is now slowly starting to come to life.

"Hey," he says reaching out for me from the bed when I walk into my room, "what if we go somewhere today."

I take his hand and sit next to him. "What?" I ask, confused. "We're going back to the park, remember?"

"I know. I just thought it would be really nice to have you all to myself. We don't get a lot of time together. I thought maybe we could do something spontaneous, take a mini road trip, and come back Sunday."

"Roo, that sounds amazing…but," I trail off.

"Come on babe, we can start driving and stop wherever we want." He slowly starts kissing my knuckles.

"There is nothing that sounds more appealing than a road trip with you, but, maybe next weekend?"

"We have a long weekend off together right now. Let's do it." His eyes are pleading.

"You're making this really hard. I love your spontaneity, but I see most of these people only once a year. Some of them even less often."

He looks a bit crushed.

"You know what, why don't we go for a few hours and take off early." I suggest, squeezing his hand.

He smiles. "Deal."

I go into the bathroom to grab my toiletries and start packing my overnight bag. I'm just about finished when I hear a can crack from the kitchen. I wander in and see Roo drinking a beer.

"Whoa, starting already?"

"Yeah, why not, it's the weekend!" He shrugs.

"I guess, but hey, I'm not driving the whole trip, so when we decide to leave you need to start drinking water so you can take a turn when I get tired."

"Of course, my lady."

"You're such a dork," I say and we both laugh.

I text my neighbor, Jillian, to ask if she can check on Patches while we're away. She replies immediately saying she can.

"Alright, I think everything is taken care of!" I say, smiling at Roo.

We get down to the park and the food tables are already out for the day. It looks like four or five families stayed to camp. We can tell who stayed because we got a downpour last night. The parents look rough and the kids are less energetic, so I imagine they didn't get a good night's sleep. We set up our chairs in a little circle and I see my cousin Molly coming towards us. I wave and smile.

Kate says, "Hey, Molly's here!"

We hug and start catching up immediately. First, we do introductions and then we move on to her latest trip. I take mental notes and even add a few locations into my phone under, *Places to Visit*. Then, out of nowhere, Roo, who is sitting in a bag chair next to me, gets half body-slammed and half hugged from behind by Angie.

"It is you! How have you been?" She says so loud half the family looks over to see what's going on. I can tell she's already been drinking and I can tell by the look on Roo's face that she's scared him half to death.

He clears his throat, "Hey Angie, how's it going?"

She immediately ignores him and walks over to me. "Does he belong to you now? What a small world."

This is pretty normal behavior for Angie so Kate, Molly, and I all stand to hug Angie.

"Hey Angie," I say, "Yes, small world."

"And you guys are going to be aunts! There's so much we need to catch up on," she says elbowing me in the ribs. "But I just got into town and I promised my mom I'd come over and say hi as soon as I got here so we'll have to do it later. Her tent is right over there," she says pointing.

"Yeah, we'll be around, just come find us," Kate says and I know she's really thinking she'd be perfectly content if she didn't see Angie again all day.

As soon as Angie walks away, Roo says, "I'm getting another beer, can I get anything for you ladies?"

We shake our heads and continue where we had left off. Mo and Beck add to the circle and I notice Roo signaling for me from behind a tree. I excuse myself and meet him.

"What's up?"

"Are you ready to get out of here?" He says hooking his finger into the belt loop of my jean shorts, pulling me towards him.

He's so hard to resist. I find myself biting my lower lip. Together we wind our way around from group to group having quick conversations with as many of my relatives as we can. It takes about an hour before we finally sneak away. I apologize to my mom and Kate and tell them that I thought I told them about our road trip plans and we're sorry but we need to get going. They take it pretty well and I'm grateful for the amount of people who weren't here yesterday that they can now keep busy with.

Roo and I take turns calling out the next turn. The anticipation of not knowing where we're going and it not mattering is sort of exhilarating. We've been driving for three hours and so far we have mostly traveled southwest. This is sort of the only direction I thought we'd go since East takes us to Lake Michigan and Roo probably doesn't want to go North anywhere near his turf.

"Should we stop in the Dells? Go to a waterpark?" Roo asks.

"That sounds fun but I kind of just want to keep going," I say.

"K. It's your call next anyway."

"I do think we should stop in the next two or three hours though, it would be nice to relax in a hot tub with you."

He winks and says, "Absolutely, that sounds perfect."

When it's my turn to drive, I hand Roo my phone. He reads the heading out loud.

"'Road trip questions for couples.' You want me to ask you all these?"

"Not just ask me them, I want to hear your thoughts."

"Okay, first one, what is your ideal weekend? Hmm, that's really easy, can I go first?" He asks.

"Yeah, let's hear it."

"This."

I laugh, "More details, please. I really want to know what your perfect weekend would be like."

"Okay, so, my perfect weekend would be a long weekend. Thursday night, you'd be with me, we'd have a great meal, and go back to one of our places and get super comfy on the couch. We'd watch a really good comedy, one that makes our faces hurt from laughing so hard. Sex. We sleep in the next morning and wake up refreshed. Sex again, and then we'd do some kind of activity where I kick your butt."

I turn to playfully glare at him and in return he's looking at me with a mischievous smile on his face.

"You are competitive, aren't you? I can't even mention beating you at something without getting a look."

He playfully pokes my thigh. Without saying anything, I flash a flirtatious grin. He stretches his arms out in front of himself and continues.

"After spending all day in the sun, with perfect weather of course, we find a bed and breakfast for the evening. More sex. We eat breakfast in bed and just spend the rest of the time relaxing. That's why this weekend is so special," he says stroking my knee. "We get more than two days together."

"I know, hopefully you don't get sick of me," I say smiling.

"That is not possible." He takes my hand. His voice goes from playful to stern, "Jhett, you are incredible. I think about you all day every day, and it's really hard not seeing you during the week. I care about you a lot." He emphasizes the last part. Hearing this makes me swoon. I've only known Roo for six weeks, but our connection and feelings are growing fast, and they're stronger than anything else I've ever felt.

I wish I wasn't driving during this conversation. I wish we were sitting or walking or at least parked somewhere. I decide to tell him how I feel anyway, looking over at him every few moments.

"Roo, you are amazing, and I love the time we get to spend together. You are the subject of my daydreams all day, every day, and I'm crazy about you too."

He squeezes my hand and smiles at me. He continues reading off the questions and we take turns with our answers. In the middle of Roo answering where he sees himself in ten years, my phone rings.

"It's your sister, should I answer it?" He asks.

"Nah, I can call her back later. It's probably not important, just family drama or something she forgot to tell me."

After driving four hours, we stop to get gas, stretch our legs and plan our stop for dinner. There's no voicemail from Kate so I decide I'll call her back when we stop for the night. Roo and I talk about driving to Springfield and spending the night there. Roo found a restaurant an hour away from the hotel that he'd booked for the night.

My phone beeps and I see a text from Kate.

Kate: Hey, I need to talk to you ASAP. Preferably while Roo's not around ...

Jhett: What's going on? We just got back on the road.

A few seconds go by and each one makes my heart beat a little faster. What is taking her so long? I text again.

Jhett: Kate! What!?

A minute later comes her response.

217

Kate: Sorry, I needed to get away. Lu was acting really strange since you left. Angie was talking to her and a few other people, whispering, and I noticed they kept looking over at me. After Angie got done talking to Molly, I asked what they talked about…apparently Roo and Angie dated?! Did you know?

Jhett: WHAT? No, she dated his college roommate.

Kate: Maybe you should check with Roo, Angie is clearly upset and things are kind of awkward around here.

I feel my cheeks start to burn. My mind starts racing with questions. My stomach twists at the thought of Angie and Roo together. Is this why Roo suggested taking this road trip? To get us away from my crazy, slutty cousin? Did he not think I'd find out? I clear my throat as a knot starts forming and try to swallow it away.

"Roo, I need you to pull over," I say, trying to keep my voice steady but instead it's shaky.

"Yeah, are you okay?" He asks, concerned. "You look sick." He immediately starts to slow.

"Not here, the exit," I say pointing ahead to the off-ramp. "I need some air."

My hands are trembling and I feel ill. The vehicle is quiet as he pulls off and before he's in park, I'm getting out. Roo jumps out and trails a few feet behind me.

"Hey, Jhett, what's up? Did something happen?"

I try breathing and staying calm but when I open my mouth to talk my words come out sounding anxious. "What's up with Angie? She's telling everyone you dated?"

He shakes his head but I notice recognition in his face. Now his breathing changes. He inhales sharply, closes his eyes for a second, and says, "Let's sit." We walk a few feet to sit on some grass. My heart aches and my gut is telling me that if he has to explain anything, something happened; my stomach twists.

It takes Roo a long time to get his thoughts together. I look at him and without speaking he knows he better say

218

something and fast. "Angie dated my college roommate, like I told you, but a few weeks after they broke up, I saw her in the bar we used to all go to together. She was hoping to find him there but he purposely stayed away knowing she'd be out looking for him. She was upset and I listened. A couple weeks went by and the next time I went there she was there again. She looked like she was doing a lot better and we talked again. We ended up having a few too many drinks and…" He trails off.

I bite my lip trying to compose my feelings but tears burn at the back of my eyes and start to pool around my eyelids.

"Jhett, I'm sorry this happened, but it was years ago. I never had feelings for her, and I didn't even think I'd ever see her again."

"Really? You knew she was my cousin. Why didn't you tell me about this when I asked how you knew each other?"

"Because I really liked you. I didn't want there to be anything that got in the way of seeing you again." He shakes his head. "It was a mistake and I've regretted it ever since."

"Did she try reaching out to you after?"

"I knew she wanted more. I copped out and told her I couldn't see her because it would ruin my friendship with my roommate."

"Have you talked to her since?"

"No. That was the last time."

"Well, it sounds like everyone knows that you've slept together, which, quite frankly, is disgusting because I know she's been with a lot of guys, Roo. Now my whole extended family has you linked to Angie."

"I'm so sorry." He reaches to touch my back but I pull away.

"I need to take a walk." I huff.

"Okay." He nods and stands with me.

"No, by myself."

"I'll be at the car." He murmurs.

My head aches as much as my heart does. I clench my jaw and within seconds the tears roll down my face; it's a silent cry. I'm hurt but I just can't take a few days off from seeing Roo since we're hours from home. I walk down a hill and see a stream. I find a large smooth rock and take a seat. I sit for a while watching the water, trying to figure out what to do. Some time passes and the wind picks up. I feel goosebumps lift on my arms and legs. Behind me I hear a stick break and turn to see Roo walking down the hill towards me.

"Hey, can I sit?" He asks gently.

"Sure."

"I just want to check on you. You've been gone an hour and I was starting to worry, especially because you left your phone behind," he says softly, "I canceled the room in Springfield. I figured you didn't want to continue driving."

I nod.

"Jhett, I'm so sorry. I'm such an idiot. I feel so bad and it's killing me that you're mad."

"I'm not mad." I snap. "I'm hurt because I care about you and this sucks. I know this happened before you met me and there's nothing that can be done to change it. I hate the fact that everyone knows about it and they heard it from Angie. Who knows what she's told them. Even though most people know she exaggerates, they won't know what's true and what's not. And I'm hurt that this trip away was planned because you didn't want to see her and for me to find out."

"You're right," he says, and hearing him say it makes it hurt even more.

"When your aunt said she was coming today, I panicked. I didn't know when or how I should tell you. But truthfully, I would rather spend a weekend away with you and I hope you know that."

"Yeah, this ideal weekend doesn't seem so perfect anymore," I say.

220

He pulls me in for a hug. As much as I want to pull away, he's the only comfort I have, so I let him hold me.

With his arms wrapped tightly around me and whispers, "You have no idea what you mean to me." He rests his head on top of mine.

Another tear drops. I know how he feels because it's how I feel about him.

"Do you want to stay here tonight or drive back?"

"I'd like to go back." As crappy as it is to cut the weekend short, I'm too hurt to forgive him for having me find out about him and Angie this way. I know I will fixate on this far too much and I'd rather just be by myself then carry on with conversations pretending like everything is just fine.

We start back up the hill when Roo reaches for my hand. I pull away and without looking directly at him I know this pains him.

The drive back is quiet. The radio is on and each time a love song comes on, Roo changes the station. I'm glad for it because they're too hard to hear.

I have a slew of messages from Kate. Most of them are just checking in to make sure I'm okay. I let her know that what she heard is mostly true and that I'll fill her in later. I hear my stomach growl and Roo must have heard it, too.

"Should we stop for something to eat?"

"Sure," I say in a monotone voice. We've only been driving for an hour and have another five to go. I feel exhausted and I'd like to get out and stretch again. It's a little past nine and although I don't have much of an appetite, my stomach tells me otherwise.

Roo spots a sign for a Mexican restaurant and after checking with me he takes the exit. We are the only customers and are seated in the middle of the restaurant. We order and sit without talking until the server brings over the margarita I've ordered. Roo looked surprised when I ordered it and he looks surprised now while I finish it. I feel it go straight to my head but I don't care, I just hope it helps to calm my thoughts.

Our food comes out quickly and it's then I realize it's been hours since I've last eaten. I eat half my meal. I glance at Roo's plate and it looks like he hasn't taken more than three bites. I can tell he's too upset to eat. The food feels heavy in my stomach and I start to drift off shortly after we're back on the road. When I wake up, we are stopped at a motel in a city I've never heard of.

"Sorry, I don't think I can drive any further. I'm really tired," he says in a low voice.

I stay in the car while he walks in to get us a room. When he returns, he heads straight for the trunk to get our bags. We walk to door five and Roo hands me the key. I open it and we walk in. He places his bag on a bed and I take mine, setting it on the other. I grab some clothes and my toiletry bag and walk into the bathroom. When I come out, he is in his pajamas and sitting on the edge of my bed.

"Can we talk?" He asks.

"I'm really tired, and I really don't know what to say." I get into my bed.

"Okay." He whispers and moves to pull back the sheets of his bed. He turns the bedside lamp off and gets under the covers. The room is eerily silent. I hear him toss and turn for what feels like an hour, which means I'm fully awake and unable to fall asleep. I turn from side to side, unable to get comfortable. A few minutes later, when I think he must have fallen asleep, I hear his bed squeak and know he too must be feeling as miserable as I do. There's an aching inside me. I want him to hold me and I want everything to be okay.

I start to think of Angie but push the thought away, and before I can talk myself out of it, I get up to crawl into bed with him. He pulls me into him instantly and wraps his arms around me. I feel a jolt of jitters from his touch. I lay with my back pressed against his chest and I can feel his heart pounding against my back.

He rests his cheek against mine and kisses me just below the cheekbone. He tightens his grasp on me and butterflies flutter in my stomach. I turn my face to meet his and kiss him. Warmth fills me. I feel like I'd been holding my breath since our rest stop and now I can breathe again. His hands move all over my body and he starts to undress me. Soon our clothes are off and we are making love. It's slow and passionate and different from all the other times. He kisses me softly, keeping one hand on my face.

I don't know if it's the sex, the cut of tension that was between us, or the fact that I really can't be away from him, but surprising myself I say, "I love you Roo."

Even in the darkness of the room I can see a look of relief and happiness spread across his face. "I love you Jhett, so much!" he says with a trembling voice.

CHAPTER 15

We wake up to sunlight shining through a crack in the curtains. I rub my eyes and turn to look towards the light. Roo stirs and slowly opens his eyes to look at me. A big smile comes across his face.

He gently rolls me on my side so that I'm facing him. He brings his lips to my ear, "I love you," he whispers.

I smile back and look at him. "I love you too," I whisper.

"Do you still want to go home?"

"Yes, but I'd like for you to stay," I say in a low voice.

"Okay," he nods. "Let's get in the shower."

He pulls me up and we walk naked into the bathroom. We get into the steaming hot shower where we keep the passion going.

"I've decided that I'm going to take you anywhere you want. A long weekend for the two of us to get away and do this right, whether it's a road trip or a plane ride. We can go wherever you want to go, and do whatever you want to do."

"That sounds really nice," I say and I mean it.

"Great. We can discuss ideas on the way back."

We pack up and make the drive to my apartment. This time we talk and finish the list of questions that we had started from the day before. Roo makes fettuccine alfredo with chicken, carrots and broccoli, a side salad, and garlic bread for dinner. I make cheesecake for dessert and pick out a movie to watch after dinner.

"I know we talked about you coming to visit next weekend; are we still on for that?" Roo asks.

"Yeah," I say.

He still seems a little unsure when it comes to us being okay. A thought about Angie creeps into my mind. I try hard to dismiss it. I know it will take time to get over the image of them together, but I remind myself that everyone has done things they later regret; it helps to know he never had feelings for her.

"My mom will be selling pies for the church all day Sunday. I'd like for her to meet you, if you'll go with me." Roo looks hopeful.

"I love pie and I'd love to meet your mother," I say cheerfully.

"I wish I didn't work Saturday but I should be done by three."

"That's fine. I plan on checking out the shops in town. I'll probably bring a book and sit in a coffee shop. Don't worry about me. I'll be fine."

The rest of the weekend continues without conflict and Roo leaves Sunday afternoon as originally planned.

Monday through Thursday go by normally. I didn't feel like talking to the girls about Angie so I've kept it to myself for now. Kate and I talked on Wednesday and I told her everything. She was supportive but something told me she was holding back. I think it's hard for her not to be a bit protective. Even when we were in school and fought and argued like crazy, we always had each other's back.

Tonight, I'm picking up Emma and we're going to Marco's because she has the night off. JJ is picking her up around nine.

Emma looks like she's doing well and she can't stop talking about JJ.

"I can't wait to meet him! It's so great that you found a good guy." I smile at Emma.

"He's amazing! I can tell he has a hard time sharing his feelings but he has a way of showing me that he cares. It's all about the little things."

"How did Logan take you canceling the trip to Chicago?"

"Okay, I guess. He was really bummed but he said that if I didn't feel it, then there was nothing he could do about it."

"I'm glad he didn't give you a hard time, and that brings me to my next question. Are you and JJ official?"

"Well, he's never outright asked me if I'd be his girlfriend, but you know how sometimes when you start seeing someone for a while you just become a couple?"

"Yeah, for sure." I nod.

"He asked last week if I was only seeing him, and when I told him yes, he said, 'good, because I don't like sharing'. He knows I uninstalled the dating app a couple weeks after I met him. I guess I would pick that day for our dating anniversary."

"Nice, it's fun that we're both in new relationships and have ourselves some keepers," I say but as soon as I say it, I'm saddened by the thought of Angie again.

After a few drinks, I can't hold it in any longer and tell her about Roo and Angie. She listens and is understanding like I knew she would be.

"I'd be upset too, but Jhett, he sounds really great and I can tell you really care for him. In time, it should get easier and soon it will have little impact on you. Talk to him when it bothers you. You might be surprised but this could strengthen your relationship."

I wonder if this is something she's learned from her years of therapy.

"Thanks Emma," I say.

Emma's phone pings and she looks down at it. "As planned, JJ will be here around nine!"

"Great! He's staying for a drink, right?"

"Yeah, I've been excited all week for you to meet him!" Emma is glowing.

"Do you have any pictures? I noticed he's not on Facebook. Not that I've been creeping." I smile.

"The ones I have aren't very good. He doesn't like having his picture taken. Here are a few, I took them when he wasn't paying attention so they're kind of far away." She slides her phone over.

I look over the photos. They're either too dark, profile shots, or taken from multiple feet away. "Camera shy, huh?"

"Yeah, he said his mom constantly had her camera out when he was a kid and it traumatized him. Which is too bad because I'd really love just one good photo with him," she says.

"I can help with that. Before you guys leave, I'll take one of you. He can't protest if he's just met me, right?"

"Great idea!" She lights up.

When nine o'clock rolls around, Emma checks her phone every couple seconds. She's like an eager teenager. At 9:05pm the bar door swings open. A man dressed in all black and wearing a helmet with the visor up calls over rudely to Emma. "You ready or what? I texted you." He walks back out.

"Oh shoot, he's here." She looks down at her phone. "How did I miss his text? I've been watching constantly." She seems disappointed.

"I thought he was going to come in." Anger starts to bubble inside me as I think of how rude and disrespectful he was to Emma.

"Oh, he texted saying we can't stay. It came through one minute ago." Her brows come together and she hesitates before saying, "Sometimes he gets in these moods. I should get out there."

"Emma, I was really hoping to meet him," I say it sounding sad, but that's a cover for the fact that I'd really like the chance to tell this ass how lucky he is to have her.

"Another time, I promise." She jumps off her stool, hugs me, and is out the door before I can get out what I want to say.

I sit for a minute feeling dumbfounded before Demi walks over.

"What was that all about?" She asks.

I shake my head. "Between us, it's a good friend falling for an ass."

"Yeah, he looked like trouble." She takes Emma's glass and wipes the water mark away. "And your friend, she seems really sweet. It's hard seeing a good friend with a douchy guy."

"I was not expecting that. She made him out to be so wonderful."

"Love is blind. You know you can't say anything, either, because she'll defend him."

I know she's right and it saddens me. "You ready for your next one?" She holds up my glass. I hesitate just long enough for her to say, "You look like you could use another one. I got you."

"Thanks Demi." I half-smile. I know I should go home because I work in the morning, and because I have tons to do before I leave for Roo's. I decide to leave after this next drink. The bar is unusually quiet for a Thursday night. I move to the bar and sit near Demi making my drink. I bet she'd be fun to hang out with if she ever got nights or weekends off.

"Do you own this place?"

She laughs, "God no. My uncle does, and my boyfriend is the manager, so we pretty much live here."

"Who's your boyfriend?"

"Ed, the dirty hippie with the dreads. He bounces on weekends."

I nod and laugh, knowing who she's talking about.

Someone from down the bar yells for her. She heads to the cooler, grabs a bottle of beer and plucks it open. I take the moment to check my phone and see that I have a message. I can't tell who it's from until I open it. My stomach instantly feels sick. Angie. I open the message and read.

Hi Jhett. I know we didn't get the chance to talk before you left...there's something on my mind and I think it's only right if you know.

I stop and look up to the ceiling, not sure if I should commit to reading her side of things or if I should just delete the message and move on. Demi is still down on the other end of the bar talking to the man who ordered the beer. I close my eyes and know that I'm not strong enough to ignore the message. I need to see what she has to say. I read.

I dated a friend of Roo's many years ago. I got to know Roo and we became friends. After the breakup, Roo and I started hanging out. Mostly it was just drinking at the bar, but he took me to dinner and things started to take off. After a few weeks, he told me that he couldn't continue seeing me because it wasn't fair to my ex, who still had no idea.

You know I've had a lot of boyfriends in the past, but Roo is different. I fell really hard for him. I didn't date anyone for months afterward because I hoped we'd get back together. Even though I reached out after the breakup, I don't think he ever knew how much I cared for him. Recently I started thinking about getting back in touch with him. As you can imagine it was a major shock when I saw the two of you together, not to mention painful.

I need you to know that I'm not over him…

Dot, dot, dot? How can she end it like that? And a breakup? Dinner? Roo said it was one time, didn't he? I read the message again and again. Breaking my concentration, Demi asks, "You okay?" After lightly shaking my head she adds, "Is it your friend, the one from earlier?"

"No." I swallow the last third of my drink and slam the glass down harder than I intend to. "I have to go, sorry."

I grab my things and walk out. Instead of getting into my car, I walk home. I make myself a drink once home and slam it. Liquid spills out from the side of my mouth and runs down my chin. My nerves and mind and stomach are going crazy.

I go into my bedroom and change into yesterday's workout clothes, not caring that they are dirty. I do what I always do when I start to feel out of control. I run. I run the fourteen blocks to the park where Roo met me the first time he came to visit. I see the park a block away when out of nowhere I feel a hot acidic sensation rises up my throat. I heave sideways throwing up all over someone's front yard. I wipe my mouth with the back of my hand and spit before standing and walking the rest of the way to the park.

I hadn't noticed until now how much the temperature has dropped since I've left the bar. I look up at the sky and take in how big and bright the moon is. Last night was a full moon so it's still quite large. I walk to my favorite mermaid statue where I plan to sit. To my surprise, someone is already occupying the bench. I feel disappointed and start to walk past when I hear my name.

"Jhett?" The voice is deep and sounds surprised.

I turn and take a few steps closer. "Yes?" I say hesitantly.

"Hey." After hearing him again, I realize it's Sai. "I didn't expect to see you here."

"Oh, hey," I say and without hesitation, I take seat next to him.

He wraps his arms around me in a side hug. "You look cold. What are you doing out here?"

"It's a mess." I mumble.

"What is?" He asks, turning his body to look at me.

"My life." I grumble and drop my head back which hurts and I regret it immediately. "Ouch!" My hand goes back lifting the crown of my head. Sai places his hand under mine.

"Be careful," he says kindly.

"Why are you here?" I ask, confused.

"I like how the mermaid shines when the moon is bright," he says looking at the statue.

"No, that's me," I say seriously and then start to laugh. Sai follows and I lean my head on his shoulder. It feels easy and there's a comfort to it. I close my eyes.

I can tell Sai is about to say something because I feel him move as if he's about to talk. He hesitates.

"What?" I ask.

"Did you get sick?" He waits a second before adding. "I smell something."

"Oh, yeah, sorry." I do a quick check of my shirt, shorts and lastly my shoes where I see remnants of my vomit.

Sai goes to his car and comes back offering a water bottle. After a few sips he rinses off my shoes.

"We should get you back. You're going to freeze." We walk to his car and he pulls the door open for me, something he always did. When his car is in motion he asks, "Do you want to talk about it?"

I rest my head against the window.

"No." I mumble.

It's quiet during the few minutes it takes to get to my place. He walks me up to my door and extends his hand out to retrieve my keys to unlock the door. I know he's noticed but he doesn't say anything about the new lock that I had changed after the breakup.

"Can I get you a glass of water?"

"Yeah, thanks. I didn't think I drank that much," I say.

"Did you eat any dinner?"

"Emma and I shared an appetizer."

"Well, there you have it," he says matter-of-factly. He walks into the kitchen. I hear the refrigerator door open, then the cupboard doors. "I'm making you a quesadilla."

"Thank you." I take a sip of the water and stumble into the bathroom. I strip off my clothes and stand slumped with my head hanging down and my arms dangling at my sides. I pull back the curtain and feel the temperature of the water before clumsily stepping in. I stand facing away as the hot water hits my back. What normally feels enjoyable feels heavy tonight. I wash my hair and body and step out. I impatiently start combing through my hair.

"It's ready." Sai calls.

I give my hair one final squeeze with my towel before opening the door.

"Jhett, you okay?" I hear him ask.

"Yeah, coming." I holler back.

Saliva instantly fills my mouth at the glorious smell of food. The quesadilla is cut into triangles with toppings off to the side. Sai was always good at whipping a meal together. I take one big inhale as I take my seat on the barstool. Sai is leaning against the counter across from me watching my every move.

"Thank you," I say and I mean it. I think of how kind he's always been. He's a natural nurturer, and he's always made me feel safe when we were together. I think of the last couple of weeks we were together before I ended it and how harsh I was towards the end. Just when I'm about to tell him how great he is, he clears his throat.

"I'm glad I ran into you, or actually, you ran into me...you get the idea." He chuckles and shakes his head. "Without food in your stomach and hydrating, you would have been pretty hungover in the morning. Do you work?"

"I do." I moan.

He walks over and gently rubs my shoulders. When I'm about finished eating, he says, "Let's go relax in the living room." I get up and we walk to the couch. He takes the remote, turning the TV on.

"Your favorite baking show is on," he says cheerfully.

I wrap myself in a blanket and curl up on the couch. Sai goes into the kitchen and I can hear him cleaning up. I hear drawers and cabinets opening and closing and I know he's putting the remaining food into containers and into the fridge. I watch him cross the room and reach into Patches' cage, and gently pet his back. Patches comes to life and is squeaking happily. When Sai looks up to me, I pat the cushion next to me. He closes the cage and walks over. He sits and I lean into him and rest my head on his shoulder.

The next morning, I wake in my bed with Sai sleeping next to me. I jolt up and cause such commotion that I wake him.

"Why are you in my bed?" The words come out rushed and accusatory.

"Nothing happened," he says nervously. "When I put you to bed, you asked me to stay. I asked if you were sure and you said yes."

I didn't think I drank that much and I can't believe I don't remember going to bed. I rub my head. I relax a little learning that we didn't sleep together. As that thought starts to diminish, it's replaced by the awareness of a sour stomach and throbbing headache in my forehead and temples.

I sit quietly since I'm not sure what to say to Sai. I know it wouldn't be fair to get upset with him after his help last night. He doesn't say anything else but instead walks out of the bedroom and goes off into the apartment. I check the time. It's thirty minutes later than when my alarm normally wakes me. I search for my phone and find it next to my purse. The battery is drained. I plug it in and go into the bathroom to check my reflection in the mirror. It's funny that before looking, I can tell that my hair will be a disaster based on how I am feeling. I try to see if there's any way I can fix my crazy, matted hair.

"You showered last night." Sai reminds me and hands me a glass of water and two Ibuprofen.

"I remember that, but have you seen my hair?" I say sarcastically.

"Don't you have a straightener?"

I'm a bit annoyed that he's right. At this point, it's the only thing I have time for.

"Thanks for your help. I'm not being sarcastic; I really mean it. Thank you."

"You don't have to thank me. It was really good seeing you…even with puke on your shoes." We both laugh even though it hurts a little. "I'll get out of your hair so you can get to work on time."

"Thanks again," I say.

When I look away to grab the next chunk of hair to smooth, Sai kisses me on the cheek. There's something very tender about it. He turns away without saying anything else and leaves. I'm looking back at myself in the mirror and even though I feel like complete shit from the hangover, a gentle smile falls across my lips.

When I walk out of the bathroom, I see he's placed the leftovers from last night along with an orange by my keys and purse. A note is sitting under the orange when I pick it up.

Your car's in the lot; I grabbed it from Marco's last night. Have a great day my sweet fighter Jhett. You are stronger than you know. If you ever need to talk, I will always be here. Love, Sai

Appreciation fills me. I know he could have kissed me last night and possibly gotten away with more, or simply dropped me off in the parking lot since he has no obligation to help me. I consider the idea of getting dinner with him like he'd wanted, maybe as a way of thanking him for being so respectful. Hopefully, in return, I could give him the closure that he needs. I wonder how Roo would feel about that.

Then for the first time, I think about what Roo would think about Sai spending the night. My sensitive stomach suddenly hits me with a wave of nausea at the thought of telling Roo. I grab a package of saltine crackers and my phone, seeing that it's only at fifty percent. I power it on and see missed calls, voicemails and a message from Roo. I open the message first and see a long message from him. I'm confused until I scroll up to see that I forwarded Angie's message to him. Until now I had completely forgotten that I sent it to him. This makes my head spin even more. I know I don't have time to read and respond so I decide to leave the messages until my lunch break when I can focus. I listen to his voicemail on my way to work.

Jhett, I have so much to say and I'd rather not leave a message. Please call me as soon as you can.

It's the only voicemail from his three calls. I think about calling him right now, but I don't know how to tell him I'm upset about Angie's message and that also, my ex slept in my bed last night. The feeling of guilt starts to overwhelm me. I decide it can wait.

Work is thankfully a good distraction and I'm grateful to see the majority of my appointments are easy ones. At lunch, I read over a new message he's sent. He denies they had anything special. As for the dinner, they were at the bar and she was hungry so they left to get food. They went to a place she picked. In his eyes, it wasn't a date. He never invited or met her anywhere other than the bar or her apartment. When I read that part, I feel sick. She was nothing more than an easy hookup. For a split second, I feel bad for Angie. How could she be so blind? Never in a million years could I picture Roo treating a woman like that … even Angie.

Towards the end of my lunch break, a nagging pang sneaks up on me. My sudden impulse to speak to Roo is so strong, it's all I can do to keep from calling him to tell him how awful he was to Angie. Instead, I keep my thumb pressed hard against the side of my phone, resisting the call back icon. I know what happened with Angie is in the past, so I need to forgive him. As I get to the top of the stairs, a text comes in from Roo.

Roo: I'm working till 3, then coming to see you. I'll take a sick day tomorrow. I need to see you.

I respond back quickly.

Jhett: No. I don't think it's a good idea.

I hit send before I can change my mind. He calls immediately but I let it go to voicemail and this time he leaves a message. I drop my phone in my purse and tell myself to focus on my patients.

Clarissa: I'll be there!
Kia: Same, see you soon, xoxo

236

Danielle: Me too

I read the responses from the girls after setting four bottles of our new favorite Moscato wine in the trunk. I had texted '912', which is our code for boyfriend trouble. They've all come through, agreeing to meet at my place.

When everyone arrives and finds a spot in my living room, I hand out glasses of wine. Me, on my third, I set it down on the coffee table with a brash clink. The sound is loud enough for my subconscious to become aware that I need to slow down.

Gradually, I tell them everything. By the time I'm done, my eyes are red rimmed and swollen from tears.

"Sweetie, I'm really sorry. I know how much you care about him, but he lied to you. I don't know if I'd be able to forgive him. I know that's all I'd ever think about," Kia says.

"He didn't really lie about anything...he just kept the hurtful parts to himself. If Angie is the worst thing in your relationship, you're doing good," Clarissa says.

"I'm sorry, but knowing your boyfriend slept with your cousin, even if it is in the past, is a big deal and takes time to get over," Danielle says.

"So he has some baggage with Angie, big deal!" Clarissa shoots back.

"She's in love with the guy, which complicates things even more." Kia snaps in my defense.

So many thoughts make my head spin. I drop my head into my hands. "I miss him. Like right now I just want to be with him. I wish I could forget all of this, or be with someone who makes me feel the exact way Roo does but doesn't have a past with someone I know. It's all I can think about. Even though I know he didn't have strong feelings for her, they shared time together. They must have had some fun. It went on for a few weeks, or maybe even a few months, I don't even know."

"Weeks or a couple months is not that long. It was probably just the convenience of having someone. I mean, I

237

know it's going to take some time, but don't dwell on this shit," Clarissa says, as if it's that easy.

I lift my glass and tip it back to find it's empty. I see Clarissa hasn't finished hers yet, so I finish it and put the glass down again. Danielle jumps up, runs into the kitchen, and returns with the next bottle of wine. She walks to each glass, filling them.

Clarissa waves a hand over her glass. "Nah, I'm good, this shit is too sweet for me and I already have a headache."

I take Clarissa's glass and let Danielle fill it up so that I have two full glasses in front of me.

"You keep that up and you'll have a headache too," she says, giving me a look.

"I'll take my chances," I say, bringing one to my lips.

"What does this mean for Sai? I'm sure he still has strong feelings for you." Kia asks.

"I've gotten a few messages from him, checking in, saying he's available anytime if I need to talk."

Clarissa rolls her eyes. "Oh, I'm sure he is. He'd do anything to be with you again, but that should not happen. You'll only be leading him on. Even if he says it's a friendship thing, don't fall for it."

"What's your plan?" Danielle asks as she takes her seat on the couch next to me.

"I'd thought about talking with Sai to at least thank him or give him closure or whatever, but I know it won't do any good for either of us. I just haven't made it clear to him yet. With Roo, my feelings are so strong." I feel an ache rise in my throat, and my voice goes high when I squeak out, "This sucks."

Danielle scoots closer and places her hand around my shoulder. I look to the ceiling, hoping I can stop the tears.

In an unsteady voice I say, "He told me he loved me, and I know he does, but it doesn't take the pain away." I let out a breath of frustration. "Up until last week, things were freaking perfect."

"Maybe you should just give it some time," Kia says gently. "You probably both need it since I'm sure he's upset about Sai staying over."

"Actually, I haven't told Roo about that yet."

I see their eyes go wide as they glance around to each other, and Danielle murmurs, "Oh boy."

CHAPTER 16

At ten, Clarissa and Kia take off. Danielle stays and I lean into her on the couch. We watch a movie and finish the last bottle of wine just before midnight.

"I kind of want to call him." I look at Danielle but can't read her neutral face.

"What would you say?"

I consider this, and I have no idea. "I don't know. I just want to hear his voice," I say softly. "I miss him so bad."

"I know you do. It's hard."

There are a few moments of silence before I say, "I'm going to call him."

She nods. "Do you want me to stay?"

"No, I'll be okay." I hug her tightly and lock the door behind her when she leaves. I walk into my bedroom and press the green phone icon next to his name. He picks up on the first ring.

"Jhett." He sounds relieved.

"Hi." I close my eyes. My heart aches for him. I want him here to comfort me.

"How are you?" I can hear the tenderness in his tone.

"A mess, and heartbroken, to be honest."

"I miss you so much. I want you here with me." Hearing him say this makes me miss him even more. "I want to fix this. Please let me come to you. I will leave right now." His voice is eager.

"No, it's late, and I need to swallow this if we're going to move past it."

"If I can come see you and we talk, I promise things will be better. Please let me come."

"Roo, no."

"I'm sorry, but Jhett, I'm afraid if too much time passes, you'll move on and I'll lose you." Silence weighs between us for what feels like a full minute. I hear him exhale before he speaks again. "Jhett, it feels so right being with you. The past few weeks have been amazing and you're what I've been searching for these past few years. You make me feel whole. I feel that with you, I-"

I cut him off. "Don't even tell me this right now." My voice shakes. "I don't want something with so much meaning to come out during this…fight."

"Why? I'm trying to tell you how much you mean to me."

"We haven't even known each other for that long and we live two hours apart." I immediately regret saying it. He goes silent and I think how he's always been worried about how I felt about the distance.

"It doesn't matter how long we've known each other. We have a connection and, it, you, us… it just feels right. I…" He stops short and I push my ear harder into the phone waiting for what he's about to say, but he doesn't say anything. Silence is between us once again. I want to ask what he was going to say but I don't. I feel like I want to keep him at arm's length until I figure out if I can get past this. I swallow hard when my conscience brings Sai into my mind.

"There's something I need to tell you." Involuntarily my lips pinch together as if my mind is telling me to keep quiet when it comes to mentioning Sai. I know it will only make things more complicated between us and I know it could make it hard for him to trust me. I swallow hard, "Before I forwarded Angie's message on Thursday night, I was out with Emma. We had drinks and shared an appetizer. I was pretty buzzed when the message from Angie came through, so that only made things worse. I went home, had another drink, and went for a run."

"In the middle of the night? Wasn't it late?" Roo asks.

"I don't really remember the time. It wasn't that late, maybe ten. Anyway, I ran into Sai." I wait a moment before continuing as dread fills my chest. "I had thrown up from the run, the alcohol, or both, and he helped clean me up and eventually he brought me home. He made me something to eat and I fell asleep on the couch."

"Did he stay?" I hear uncertainty in his voice.

I rack my brain to think of a quick response or an excuse. Should I say what happened was due to too much drinking and exhaustion? Will that soften the blow? I can't do it. I can't lie or give a shitty excuse. I know I'll be a hypocrite if I don't tell him everything. Imagining how Roo must be feeling, I feel sick with myself, and to make matters worse my guilt has been growing since I've told the girls. What I did was worse than his leaving out a few details about his past, and it's just now sinking in.

It's so quiet on Roo's end of the line that I swear he's able to hear my heart pounding. He waits some time before making me jump when he frantically yells, "Jhett, say something!"

"Nothing happened…" I swallow hard, "but when I woke up, Sai was lying next to me in bed." I blurt out. The pounding from my heart feels as though it's moved into my ears and the sound intensifies as I wait for his response.

"Are you kidding me?" There's anger in his voice. "Do you know how wrong that is?"

"Yes, yes, I do, and I feel awful." My voice cracks.

"You feel awful?" He says surprised. "I felt so bad about Angie, about someone who I never loved, never had feelings for, and you tell me your ex-boyfriend brings you home and gets into bed with you? Someone who is still madly in love with you?" He takes in a sharp breath.

"Roo, you know I'm over him." Tears are falling from my eyes as I can only imagine the pain he feels.

"That doesn't matter. If Angie found me drunk and upset last night, would it be okay for her to take me home and crawl into bed with me because I don't have feelings for her?"

"NO! Roo, it's not like that. Please, I'm sorry. I'm so sorry." My apology comes out in broken sobs.

"How could you be so upset with me and then turn around and do something like this?" He breaks for a moment and can tell he's started crying. "I gotta go."

Before I can say anything, I hear the click of the call ending.

I lay into my pillow and cry. If I wouldn't have been so sensitive to his past with Angie, I'd be snuggled up against him in his bed. I don't know what this means for us, but suddenly the reality of my mistake comes into focus and I see that I have unknowingly sabotaged my relationship with Roo.

CHAPTER 17

I've reached out to Roo every day for the past two weeks. The only response I've received was Roo telling me he needed some time on day three. I've never made a mistake this huge in a relationship before, so I don't know what my next move should be.

I have called and left voicemails. I texted a simple 'good morning, I'm thinking about you'. I've sent long and short apologies. I've even written him a letter telling him how much I miss him and what he means to me. He should have received it in the mail two days ago, but I have no way of knowing because he hasn't said anything. If this is his way of punishing me for Sai staying over, I can deal with it and I accept it, but I don't know how much longer I can take it. Each day that this goes on, my anxiety intensifies.

Kate, the girls, and even my parents and coworkers, who I try to hide my sadness from, can see that I'm struggling. The thought of not being with Roo is so unbearable that my appetite has plummeted, my energy has dropped, I've stopped all forms of exercise, and depression has taken over. Everyone tells me to stay positive and that they are all here for me any time I need them. They have proven it thus far by letting me cry, vent, and whine about him for the past two weeks. But even I'm starting to get sick of the tears, my poor mood, and the buzzkill that I've turned into.

Danielle's housewarming party is just days away. I haven't made my mind up if I should go, or if it'd be better for everyone if I just stay away. I don't want to sit there faking a smile, but I also don't want to stay home with the girls texting and calling. Either way, I feel like I will be ruining the party. When Danielle had finally picked a date for her housewarming party, I'd already had multiple ideas of what I'd bring for a gift. I had thought about what desserts and appetizers would be most loved from my favorite baking book. Most importantly, though, I had envisioned walking up her driveway with Roo by my side. Thinking about it now just reopens the wound and reignites the deep ache in my heart.

CHAPTER 18

The morning of Danielle's party I wake up feeling a little more optimistic than I have the previous days. I try to focus on ways I can help her get ready. I start by wrapping her gift; a hand-carved wooden platter and matching fruit bowl I found at the farmer's market. I wrap them in bright lime green tissue paper and tuck them into a violet and green striped gift bag. I send her a text.

Jhett: What time should I come to help set up?

Danielle: How about 2? I'm still cleaning and I feel like I might not be ready in time!!

Jhett: Don't worry, we will get everything finished well before people arrive!

Danielle: You are a lifesaver! Xoxo

I take the beer cheese dip and beef sticks out of the fridge and grab the family size bag of pretzels and pack them in my travel bag. I drop two ice packs inside and zip it closed.

I fill up my water and grab a banana for the car. I call my mom to let her know I'm on my way over.

When I get to my parents' house, Beck, Morgan and Kate are all there.

I walk in a bit confused. "Hey, I wasn't expecting everyone to be here?"

"Well hello to you too sister." Beck smirks.

I smile back annoyed.

My mom comes over to greet me with a hug. "Good morning." After she releases me, she says, "I just told them you were stopping over and everyone just happened to be free so I told them to join us." They smile weakly at me.

247

"This just feels a bit weird. And I'm hoping this doesn't turn into an intervention or something." And as I try to make it sound like a joke nobody laughs. Suddenly I'm very uncomfortable and I think it may be why they're all here.

"No." Kate says, allowing me to breathe again. "But...we weren't sure if we should bring up Roo. You know, like, we want to ask how things are going, but if you don't want to talk about it, we get that too."

"Oh yeah, no, that's fine, I um- I'd rather not talk about it," I say looking towards the floor, tucking hair behind my ear.

"Okay!" My mom says a little too enthusiastically. "Dad made omelets if you're hungry?"

"No thanks, I had a banana on the way over," I say.

"Oh man, all you ate for breakfast was a banana? Gosh, I am hungry All. The. Time. That would be a snack between my breakfast meals. I eat two breakfasts now." Mo says laughing.

"She does. She's not kidding." Beck says with wide eyes.

"Please tell me more about the baby," I say, wanting to hear some good news.

"Well baby is the size of a mango, and kicking like crazy! I love it!" Mo says putting her hands over her belly.

"Beck, can you feel the kicks?" I ask.

"Not yet, she tells me when it's happening but I haven't been able to feel them."

"We can find out the gender at our next appointment!" Mo says gleaming.

"Have you decided what you're going to do?" My mom asks.

"I think we have." Mo looks at Beck and grins.

Beck says, "we're thinking about doing one of those gender reveal parties. We'll either do it at the end of the baby shower or at our house with less of a crowd- parents, siblings, something low key."

"Fun, I like both ideas," Kate says. "How will you keep it a secret until your party? Don't you think you'll slip up? I know I would."

"We might just have to wait until the party to look ourselves," Mo says eyeing Beck. "I think with this pregnancy brain I'm bound to have at least one slip up."

"She had that all the time with you three; I think it got worse with each kid," my dad says.

My mom frowns as if she's offended and makes a tisk sound with her tongue. "Well I was a very busy mother so of course it got worse with each one." She turns and grabs a small planner from the computer and looks at Mo, "Now, let's talk about the shower details."

After an hour or so, my mom has come up with individual lists for me and Kate. I read my list.

Jhett
Melting Chocolate for fondue
Fruit & skewers
Bottled water, Champagne & orange juice
Cups & champagne flutes

"Do you really think we should have alcohol for a baby shower?" I ask.

"Most people dread showers so having some alcohol will be nice." My mom says.

"You get to play games, eat some really good food and see family and friends. What's not to like?" I shrug.

My pocket vibrates and I see a text has come in. Every single time this happens my heart skips a beat until I read the name and see that it isn't Roo.

Danielle: My cousin just bailed on grabbing the keg. Any way you'd be able to pick it up? I don't think I'll have time to get it.

"Hey dad, will a keg fit in my car?" I yell into the living room where my dad sits looking at an airplane magazine.

"Yes it should, why do you ask?"

"Danielle needs me to pick one up for her party, I just don't know how big it is."

"Take my truck. It'll be so much easier getting it in and out."

"Thanks!" I say and he nods. "I'm going to take off then, I'm helping her set up. Can I bring it back tomorrow if I stay the night?"

"Of course. And please be careful." He wraps me up in a hug.

On the way to the liquor store, I think about Roo. He knew about this party because I told him about it multiple times through the voicemails and texts. I daydream about him showing up to surprise me. It is all I want. It's what I want more than anything I've ever wanted. It feels so petty now; the anger I had about Angie. I'd like to call him but I talk myself out of it. Instead of trying to get ahold of him all the time I need to stop reaching out. I need to let him miss me. Suddenly my phone rings making me jump. It's Kate.

"Hey, what's up?"

"I just wanted to say I'm sorry," she says with a heavy sigh.

"What?" I ask a little confused.

"About Roo. I'm really sorry for what you're going through. And I can see how much you're hurting."

"Oh thanks," I say quietly. "Is it that obvious?"

"I'd like to say I just know you really well, but yeah, I can see it in your eyes." She waits for a breath and then continues, "If you ever want to get out of the house, talk, I'm here okay?"

"I know Kate, thanks."

I know they're all there for me. But, no matter what they do or say, it doesn't stop me from feeling completely alone.

As we hang up I pull into Danielle's driveway. She's carrying a box into her garage when I jump out of the truck.

"Nice, upgrade," she teases.

"Yeah, I wish. My dad thought it'd make the hauling a little easier."

"And, how was it?" She asks peeking around the truck to look at the keg.

"Fine. The guys at the liquor store loaded it and everything. Went great," I say opening the door to grab my appetizer and dessert. "How's it going here?"

"Feeling better about it. I have a few boxes left if you wouldn't mind carrying them into the garage?"

"Put me to work."

She smiles. "Can I get you a drink before we start?"

"Um, yes, if you'll have one with me."

"Actually, I already started."

We walk into her house. It's so adorable. "Oh my gosh, Danielle, it looks so different," I say with an impressed tone.

"I know, my dad helped a ton. And I didn't want to tell you guys everything we did because I wanted you to be surprised."

"It's so bright and inviting. I love all the sunlight coming through." I look over at her and she's beaming. She turns and with a skip in her step grabs a red plastic cup.

Placing it under the nozzle of a giant container she twists the tap and out pours a light pink liquid.

"Here, try this," she says, handing me the cup.

I take a sip trusting her; since we've met we've always liked the same drinks.

"It's really good, what is it?"

"It's a punch recipe I found online. There's rum, vodka and a bunch of juices in it."

"Yeah, I'm gonna want the recipe. And if this is strong, I can't tell."

She laughs and says, "I know when to cut you off."

We put on quite a show to anyone who is lucky enough to witness us move the keg from the truck. The shape of it makes it hard to maneuver and we can't help but laugh. Once it's sitting in the plastic container in the garage we surround it with ice.

"So, was your cousin Jordan supposed to pick this up?" I ask.

"How'd you guess?" She rolls her eyes. "He didn't even give me a reason, just said he couldn't get it. Then he had the nerve to tell me to get it on ice right away so it'd be cold when he gets here."

"Wow, what a jerk."

"Yeah that's Jordan, I'm pretty used to it. I mean we were joined at the hip when we were kids so I guess you could say he treats me like a sister. Sometimes he can be a real ass but, I know he'll always have my back."

We finish setting up ten minutes before Kia shows up. I bring three cups of punch into the living room where Danielle and Kia are talking about the house. Within the next few hours, there are easily fifty people spread about the house. Danielle has been running from group to group trying to greet each new carload that shows up; thankfully her dad is helping by taking family around the house for tours.

Clarissa, Kia and I have moved into the garage and have dibs on the next game of shuffleboard. Clarissa walks up to us with a look on her face that I've seen before; she's about to reveal something. Danielle is on her heel, they take a seat next to us.

"So, before James and Max get here, there's something I need to tell you," she says with a mischievous grin.

"Ooo what?" Kia says.

"You know I've applied to UCLA…well I've been accepted!" Clarissa says with the biggest smile I've ever seen on her face.

I swallow hard and take a shallow breath. "Wow, that's great," I say and hope that my lying has gotten better over the last few weeks.

"Congrats hun!" Kia says and hugs Clarissa.

"Oh, I'm so happy for you!" Danielle says.

"Thanks guys," Clarissa says looking at each of us. "I wanted to tell you before the guys show up because, um, Max doesn't know yet. I'm waiting for the right time."

"He knows you've applied, doesn't he?" I ask.

"He does, but he knows he can't afford it out there. And you all know how my dad will not allow us to move in together so we'd be in separate apartments. So, we said if I got accepted we'd cross the bridge when it happened and not worry about it before then."

"Okay, so you have your last semester at Carroll and you'll move out there a few months after?" I ask.

"That was the plan originally, but that's not what I'm doing." Clarissa tips her cup and drinks while we all wait in silence. She's always been really good at keeping us on the edge of our seats. I feel my mouth go dry and take a drink of my own. "I'm moving out there in a few weeks," Clarissa says and each one of our mouths drop open. I feel myself tense up and as I'm about to open my mouth to ask if she's joking she speaks again.

"I know it's really fast and you weren't expecting this, but I just can't sit around here any longer," she says gesturing with her hands. She takes a deep inhale. "I'm finishing my last semester out there online so I don't have to wait." She licks her lips and sets her cup down. "Ever since I submitted my application it's been on my mind twenty-four seven. I wake up and I'm thinking about it." She looks at us and takes in what she sees, a crease comes across her forehead. "You guys, I really need this. I know it's going to be hard to leave so please don't make it harder."

I let my face fall, "I'm not going lie, I'm going to miss you like crazy," I rub my hands over my face and look at her, "but you need to do what's right for you. And, I'll support you."

Clarissa relaxes and with an upbeat tone says, "You know how much fun it will be to visit?"

"Oh, hell yeah, I'll take a week of vacation to sit on the beach with you!" Kia says smiling.

"I haven't stopped thinking about learning how to surf since you've mentioned the idea," Danielle says.

Just then a girl calls over to us, "board is yours," she holds up the metal shuffleboard puck and waves it at us.

"Thanks, be right there." Clarissa yells back.

We stand and start to walk over to the board. I reach to check the time and realize my phone isn't on me. "I'll be right back," I say. I walk into the house first, as I cross the threshold a guy turns the corner and nearly smacks into me. "Oh hey, excuse me," I say startled. I don't recognize him or the girl he's with. He shoots me a look and says, "Oh no, excuse me." And smiles. They walk past me and I continue searching around the house and try to remember the last time I had it. I spoke to Kate in the truck on the way to the liquor store. I turn and head back outside. Danielle and I make eye contact as I walk out of the house. The guy I had just ran into nods at me and leans into Danielle. He asks her something. She lightly shakes her head and shrugs. I tear my gaze from them and go to the truck. I find my phone between the seats. I check the screen. Only a text from Sai. I roll my eyes. As I walk back into the garage, I see that Danielle is saying goodbye to the couple. I watch as he hands a helmet to the girl he's with. They start walking my direction.

"Nice truck," he says confidently and winks at me.

"Thanks," I say hesitantly.

The girl behind him glares at me and I look away. A few moments later I turn to see them climb onto an all-black sports bike.

"So, it looks like you've met my cousin," Danielle says walking over.

"That's Jordan?" I ask surprised.

She nods.

"What did he say to you?"

254

"He asked if you were available," she says with big eyes. "And trust me, I just saved you. I can't believe he had the nerve to ask when his girl was ten feet away."

"Wow," is all I can say.

"Who was the hottie?" Kia asks.

"Oh, don't let him hear you say that. He's ego's big enough already," Danielle says walking back to the shuffleboard table. I glance back again when I hear the bike start. I see them both lean forward and the bike moves forward smoothly. Then in a split second, a high-pitched sound comes from the bike and they are off down the road.

"You ready?" Danielle says looking back at me.

Max and James show up shortly after nine.

"Where have you been?" Kia snorts at James.

"Relax, we stopped at a few bars on the way here," James says.

"You said you'd be here around seven, have you eaten anything?" Kia asks in an accusing tone.

"No, not really, we had some stale bar popcorn."

"That's not funny." Kia yells and walks away crossing her arms. James follows her into the house.

"Max, you are supposed to be my DD tonight. How much did you drink?" Clarissa asks.

"I'm going to stop now," he says as he drops the red plastic cup back down on the stack he was pulling it from."

"What the fuck! I'm the responsible one. I asked for one night!" Clarissa shouts.

"Hey, you guys can spend the night. It's totally fine," Danielle says trying to de-escalate things.

Clarissa ignores the offer. "I already have one DUI, do you not care? Is it really that hard to skip one night of drinking?"

"Babe, it's fine. I'll go eat something, and I'll be fine to drink…I mean drive." Max corrects.

"You're ridiculous, you can't stand or talk straight and you think I'm going to let you drive us?" Clarissa rolls her eyes and turns away from Max and mumbles under her breath, "Men are such ignorant assholes. He is so lucky he got here when he did, I was just about to get another drink." She reaches into a nearby cooler for a bottle of water. I watch her as she glances over at him, pure rage comes over her face. Her eyes narrow. "He's finding out tonight," she says.

"Are you sure you don't want to wait until you're both sober? Things might go over a little better," Danielle suggests gently.

"No. Honestly, it's always like this. He's either drunk or short-tempered and complaining that he needs a drink."

"Really?" I ask, surprised. "I guess I didn't know that about him. He always seems to be in a good mood, he's either laughing or joking.

"Because he'd probably been drinking," she says seriously.

Danielle and I exchange glances and the conversation ends.

By ten all guests have left. Clarissa and Max were still fighting when they got into Clarissa's vehicle to leave. Kia and James were doing the exact opposite when they left. Initially, Kia had stormed out the front door and started walking down the street right after their spat in the garage, but James had caught up to her and begged her to come back. An hour later they were making out on the couch.

Danielle and I cleaned the entire party zone which took until one in the morning. We were so beat that we ending up falling asleep in her bed minutes after starting a movie. The reason I know this is because we got a group text from Clarissa ten minutes after one that we didn't see until the morning.

Clarissa: Max's ass got kicked to the curb...he made it easy for me.
Kia: So you told him about California and then ended it?!

Clarissa: Pretty much…it was a 3-hour yelling match but that was the end result.

After reading the messages, I look up to see Danielle roll her eyes as she walks away from the window. Her fingers had been pressed down on the blinds as she peered out the window.

"What? More mess to clean?" I ask.

"No, I just saw Ben drive past. I noticed he drove past twice last night too. He's lucky my dad didn't see him."

"He's still coming by? I thought he stopped that?"

"He only changed his drive-by schedule after I called him out on it. He said he has a friend that lives around here but every time I see him, he's always gawking out the window."

"So maybe that restraining order's not a bad idea. I don't think he'd do anything but it's just creepy he's always driving by."

"Yeah, I might look into it."

We say goodbye and I get into the truck and make my way towards my parents' house. I think about calling Emma. She has attempted to get me out of the apartment on more than one occasion, but instead of keeping plans, I'd blown her off or made excuses that later made me feel like a shitty friend. Instead, I call Clarissa.

"Hey, whaaat's up?" Clarissa answers not sounding so hot.

"Hi, good morning," I laugh. "You okay?"

"Yeah, fine. Just feeling shitty. I have a throbbing headache."

"I'm sorry to hear that."

"Hey, can I call you back? My cousin Olivia is calling."

We hang up and my eye catches the familiar green siren logo, and I instantly crave a cup of coffee. I swing into the Starbucks drive-through and order my usual. As I pull out into traffic, my phone rings. It's Clarissa.

Clarissa starts talking before I even say hello.

257

"So, Olivia just suggested something that you might think is insane, but it's actually a great idea."

"Oh yeah." I chuckle. "What's that?" Noticing Clarissa's tone has dramatically improved.

"She has invited us to her place. Don't say anything. Just think about it. I know you need a distraction, so please just give it some thought…and then decide to come with me," she says in her most charming voice.

"Okay, I'll think about it. When are we talking?" I say hesitantly.

"Next weekend."

"No way, that's too soon."

"That's not a good enough reason not to go. If you had plans then at least you'd have an excuse. Seriously, consider it," she says more firmly.

"I thought you had plans for next weekend," I say, trying to buy some time.

"Max and I were going to go to the cabin, but now I have new plans."

"Tickets are going to be crazy this last minute."

"Stop trying to come up with excuses. And you have to come because Danielle won't be able to get out of work and Kia has plans with her extended family."

I allow the idea to slip into my mind. "Let me think about it, and I'll let you know as soon as I can."

"She makes it hard to say no to her," I say as I sip my coffee.

"I think you should do it," my mom says, surprising me.

I turn to look at her. "Really, you're serious?"

"Why not? As long as work is okay with it, I think it's a really good idea," she says removing dishes from the counter.

"I guess the idea excites me a little."

"Where does her cousin live?" My dad asks, peering out momentarily from the Sunday's paper.

"New Orleans."

"Oh yeah, you should go," he says and snaps the paper back into place.

"Why are you hesitant?"

"Well for one, I wasn't expecting you and dad to be so gung-ho about it. I thought you'd tell me it was a dangerous city or something. And secondly, the last-minute thing just makes me a little uneasy; I'm a planner," I say rubbing the brim of my coffee cup.

"Well then, maybe that's why you should go; get out of your comfort zone, nothing wrong with that. Let Olivia do the planning and just go along for the ride. Then there's no reason to stress," my mom says, her eyebrows arched encouragingly alongside her caring smile.

"Yeah, you're right. I should go." I nod and smile.

Thirty minutes after my boss approved my long weekend away, I'm on the phone with my mom. "I'm not going. The tickets are over six hundred dollars. That's not in my budget. Even with free housing, there's food and drinks and…well, I can't think of what else right now but I know there will be other expenses," I say panicked.

Calmly my mother says, "You shouldn't have many other expenses. They have those street cars that pretty much run all over the city for cheap transportation."

"I think Olivia has a car. I just don't feel like spending the money right now," I say moping.

"Jhett, we'll cover half your plane ticket. We know how much you need this, and it can be an early birthday gift."

"Mom, that's too much."

"Jhett, go!"

Clarissa and I sit and wait for the announcement to board the plane. I get up one last time to use the bathroom and ask Clarissa to watch my stuff. When I get back I notice the line that has formed and passengers are beginning to board.

Because of the last-minute booking, we are a few rows apart. I make a pouty face as I walk past her row. She makes a silly face and then grins at me. I take my seat next to the window and pull my murder mystery book from my purse. I get as comfortable as I can and go to power my phone down. The background picture catches my attention. It's a picture of the four of us from Kia's birthday last year. I'm confused for a brief moment before I realize that Clarissa must have changed it while I was in the bathroom. As if she can read my mind, when I inch my body up and see over the seat she is turned back looking at me. She smirks and turns back around. A text comes through.

Clarissa: You can't move on from Roo if you are constantly seeing a picture of him.

Jhett: It wasn't a picture of him! I type out somewhat annoyed. How dare she change my picture.

Clarissa: It was a picture of your feet and his feet in the sand, please don't fight me on this…It's time to start moving on. Let's have fun this weekend and try to forget about the breakups…let's do this together.

Jhett: OK. I'm turning my phone off now :P

My anticipation has grown over the last few days and I've had to try a little less each day to convince myself that this is what I need. I open my book in the hopes that I can focus on the story enough to forget that I'm crammed next to a stranger. Picking up from where I last left off, a new character is introduced. He immediately reminds me of Jordan. He's mysterious and sexy and of course confident. Each time I read about the character I envision Jordan's face and I start to feel intrigued by the idea of him. From what I've gathered, he's the typical bad-boy type. And that is not my type; normally. This also encourages me just a little, I wonder what it would be like to go out and just have fun. For there to be no emotional connection.

I must have daydreamed so long that I'd fallen asleep. I jump when the pilot's announcement comes in that we are twenty minutes away from landing at the Louise Armstrong airport in New Orleans.

Olivia cheerfully greets us curbside after we leave the baggage claim. She hugs us and thanks us for coming. We load up Olivia's SUV and pull away from the airport.

"I have a great weekend planned for us!" She says happily. "I kicked Allen out of the duplex so it will just be us girls!"

"You didn't have to do that," I say.

"Oh, I'm sure he will be happier staying with his buddy. Not a big deal." She says, turning onto the freeway.

"So, what's the plan?" Clarissa asks.

"We'll hang around the neighborhood tonight and do the local hot spots. Dinner, drinks all that kind of stuff. Tomorrow, we'll go into the city. We'll take the streetcar so you can see more of the city. Parking downtown can be a nightmare. And Monday we'll go to my favorite brunch place before I drop you back at the airport. Now is there anywhere you want to see or do?"

I shake my head even though she's not looking at me. "Nope, I'm along for the ride so I'm good with whatever."

"Same," Clarissa says sipping water from her bottle.

The two of them start talking about an ill family member I don't know. I take the time to find Jordan Reyes on Facebook. I try different spellings of his first and last name. I can't find him and I wish I could ask Danielle.

We get to Olivia's place which is in a cute neighborhood in the Garden District. When we walk up the sidewalk I notice Mardi-gras beads everywhere. They are hanging from the trees, bushes, front yard fences, and pretty much any surface that a strand of Mardi-gras beads can hang from.

Olivia reads my expression, "Oh, they are a big thing here!" She says touching a strand that's wrapped around her mailbox.

She unlocks the door and we walk into her small but nice two-bedroom lower level duplex. She shows us to the spare bedroom where there is a queen bed for Clarissa and I to share.

Clarissa throws her luggage down. "Traveling sucks, I'm already exhausted."

"It's probably the humidity," Olivia says. "It sucks your energy. You want some coffee?"

"No, I'll be fine. Although I'd like to take a shower, I feel really gross."

Olivia takes us on a quick tour of the duplex and hands Clarissa a towel when we get to the bathroom.

"I have to send a quick work email, are you okay for a bit while I do that?" Olivia says looking at me.

"Yeah, I'll be fine," I say and as soon as I'm alone I go to my phone. I look at the picture of us girls and think that it was the right move for Clarissa to change the picture. I still love him but I think I need it gone for my own sanity. I search again for Jordan. I try Instagram and after seeing a few photos, I think I've found him. There aren't many but I recognize his bike which is in every picture and decide to follow him. Before Clarissa is out of the shower, I get a message from him requesting I add him on Snapchat. His username is ridiculous and feel somewhat foolish typing it into the search bar but I do it anyway. Within seconds he sends me a message.

Jord@n69: Hey girl, how've you been?

Jhettskii: hey, I'm good. How are you?

Jord@n69: Really good, especially since I found out that Danny lied to me…she told me you were taken.

Wow, he's not afraid to jump right in.

Jhettskii: Actually, I think she told you I wasn't available?? And speaking of taken, who was that girl you were with? She looked like she was, or at least thought she was your girlfriend.

Jord@n69: No girlfriend. She does want me…but what can I say, who doesn't ;)

Jhettskii: Oh my gosh, are you seriously that vain?! Do you think all women want you?

I start to wonder if I have just made a huge mistake by starting a conversation with Danielle's egotistical cousin, the same one she warned me against.

Jord@n69: I'm starting to think you do…

Jhettskii: Wait backup, how did you know I was single if Danielle didn't tell you?

Jord@n69: I don't have FB but a friend does, I looked you up after the party and saw that you weren't listed in a relationship.

Jhettskii: That doesn't necessarily mean I'm not seeing someone

Jord@n69: Are you?

I wait a few seconds then decide to just tell the truth.

Jhettskii: no

Jord@n69: Anyone that is in a serious enough relationship has, "in a relationship with" as their status on FB.

I think about how he's probably right. If a person likes someone enough, they will want people to know they're exclusive. If they don't think the relationship is going anywhere, they probably won't take the time to post. I think about what Jordan and I would be. There would be no way in hell I'd consider posting "In a relationship with Jordan Reyes" since I only intend to have a little fun.

Jord@n69: so you see what I'm saying? Btw, I see how you changed the subject when I asked if you were into me. So, comment or not, I know the answer ;)

I'm getting ready to reply with a witty response when Clarissa swings open the door scaring me enough that I jump. I make it too obvious that I'm trying to hide the screen. She rushes over and tries to snatch my phone away.

"Who the hell are you talking to?" She demands.

"No one!" I yell.

"If you are talking to Roo, I'm going to kill you." A deep frown sets between her eyes.

"I wasn't," I say sternly and I can tell she believes me.

"Okay, well good. I don't want you taking a step back." Her voice softens. And her eyes look away like she feels guilty for accusing me.

"I haven't heard from Roo at all. And I'm proud of myself, even though it's been really hard, I haven't tried contacting him since I agreed to come on this trip."

She bites her lip. "You looked guilty with whatever you were doing. Were you looking at porn?"

"No!"

"Well, I don't know. What were you doing?"

"You just scared me," I say, trying to be convincing.

"Yeah, okay," she says, not buying it.

"I noticed you sending messages so I guess I could ask you the same thing," I say crossing my arms over my chest.

"It wasn't Max." She hesitates. "Remember the guy from Barbados? The hottie, Alejandro that showed me around all week?"

"I do," I say scrunching up my face. "You guys are still talking?"

"He's been a nice distraction."

"You guys almost ready? Oh, and don't wear anything too nice or light in color." Olivia shouts from another room.

"We'll be right out," Clarissa says then drops her towel. She stands in her bra and underwear and picks through her clothes holding up different tops. After she's dressed and ready, we head for the city.

"I'm taking you to my favorite crawfish spot. Have you ever had crawfish?" Olivia asks looking at me.

"I haven't, but I've heard seafood is big down here," I say and I really don't know anything about crawfish.

"Oh yeah, there's a lot of great seafood here but Captains is hands down the best."

We are seated at a table that's covered with a red and white buffalo plaid polyester tablecloth. It's not at all what I was expecting. I guess because of all the nice dinners I've heard

Clarissa's family went to I was picturing something other than a greasy, smelly, overly crowded restaurant that uses paper towels in place of plates. Olivia orders ten pounds of crawfish and my jaw drops.

"Are we taking some home with us?" I ask.

She laughs. "No, we will eat every last bite. Trust me."

"I'm just going to have a salad." Clarissa tells the waitress.

"Are you crazy? You did not come all this way to get a salad," she says, looking up at the waitress.

Clarissa shakes her head and shrugs at the waitress, "scratch that I guess."

After the waitress walks away Olivia asks, "A salad?" Her eyebrows furrowed.

"I'm feeling puffy." She shrugs.

"Are you kidding me? You're the tiniest person I know." She picks up the glass pitcher of water and an empty glass and fills it. "The heat and humidity are making you swell. Start hydrating."

In less than ten minutes a waiter dumps bright red crawfish, potatoes, chunks of garlic and quartered cobs of corn from a boiling pot onto our table. Steam rolls from the mound of colorful food and the smell of salt and butter hits my nose. My mouth instantly starts to water.

Olivia wraps her hair into a low bun. "Ready to get messy?" She smiles. "Let's dig in!"

As intrigued as I am to jump in like our neighboring tables, I'm equally mortified at the thought of sucking off the tiny little bodies in front of me. I pick one up and even though I know it's dead it looks like it's looking at me with its black beady eyes.

"Don't think about it, just do it." Olivia says picking up her second crawfish.

I start with a small piping hot potato that tastes like it's been soaking in juices and spices all day. I mash up two more and add a chunk of garlic and it's the best potato mash I've ever eaten. I pick up a crawfish and watch what Olivia does. Forcing myself to stop wasting time and just do it already I follow her steps: crack away and bring the sea urchin to my lips. I suck the meat out and feel the juices run down my hands and arms. The taste hits my tongue and the flavor is exquisite. It's tender and tastes far better than I had imagined. After I devour five more, I start to feel a burn on my lips. The heat from the spices get more noticeable with each bite. I switch to a cob of corn hoping it gives my lips a break. It doesn't. I go back to the crawfish and eat as fast as I can before I can't take it anymore.

"Pretty amazing right?" Olivia asks.

"So good, I can't stop," Clarissa says. "I don't think I've had crawfish since I was a kid. I forgot how good they were."

We lean back in our chairs and breathe deeply.

"I'm so stuffed," I say. "Thank you, this was an experience."

"You can't come to New Orleans and not go to a crawfish boil. And lucky for you, all the food here is lights out, you can't go wrong." As we get ready to leave, Olivia tells us about her favorite bar; the one she'll be bringing us to.

"Ugh, I seriously don't think I can consume anything more. I feel sick, I ate too much." Clarissa complains.

"Aw, come on. We can go buy you some bigger shorts."

"No, really, I feel sick."

"You look like you have the food sweats." Olivia says with sympathy. "Did any of them taste rotten? Sometimes a dead one gets mixed in and it can make you sick."

Clarissa groans and holds her stomach. "Ahh, I hate you right now, why didn't you tell us that earlier?"

After sitting for two hours back at Olivia's to let our feast of crawfish digest, I start feeling fairly energetic. I'm not ready for the night to end and even though Clarissa went to lie down, Olivia and I decide to go out for one drink. We leave a note for her to call us when she gets up.

The bar Olivia takes me to feels welcoming. The people look friendly and the bar staff smile when we walk in. We walk to the middle of the bar and sit at a small round table with two bar stools.

"So, tell me, what's your dating plan? You gonna stay single for a while or try to get back out there?"

I shrug. "I've met someone who is not my type at all, but, there's something about him that makes me a little curious."

"What makes him not your type?"

"The easiest way to describe him, I'd say he's a player. He's hot as hell and super confident, so also cocky. But I kinda find myself having a crush on him...and I know, I know," I stress, "he's not boyfriend material. And I'm one hundred percent okay with that. Which also excites me because I've never had a no strings attached relationship."

"You should go for it!" She says eagerly. "What do the other girls think?"

"Oh, they don't know. He's related to Danielle and I think the girls would try talking me out of this. You know, they probably think I'll get hurt, and they'll want to be protective. But I'm excited to try it. I need to move on. Honestly...I miss Roo, but I think because he hasn't forgiven me by now, he's not going to. I don't want to sit around waiting, I've seen other girls do it and it's sad. I don't want to be that."

"Right, and you should have some fun, you're young and it might be nice to date around a little." She smiles. "You want me to be your wing-woman? We can start tonight?"

"No, please don't." I laugh. "I think a little fun with one guy is all I can handle; no one-nighter with a random stranger."

Olivia and I get a text from Clarissa saying she feels better, but is going to bed early and we should stay out if we're enjoying ourselves. So, we do just that. We stay out laughing and talking for hours until bar close. We call for a ride and stumble up the walkway to her duplex trying to be as quiet as possible.

The next morning I wake up feeling awful from drinking too much. I hear noises coming from the bathroom and notice Clarissa is missing from the bed. I pull the pillow over my head and try to fall back asleep but the noise seems to get louder. It sounds like deep laughter and I wonder if she's on the phone. But in a moment my heart sinks and I'm suddenly fully awake. I sit up and swallow hard when I realize Clarissa is not laughing, she's sobbing. I start feeling guilty that we stayed out all night instead of checking on her. Maybe she wasn't sick at all, maybe she's taking the breakup harder than she let on. As Clarissa's closest friends we know that she hides her emotions and it's hard for her to open up.

My foot catches on the sheets and I stumble out of bed. I land on my hands and call out for her. "Clarissa, I'm coming," I say trying to find my voice. It's scratchy and horse. She sounds uncontrollable, and the sobs are getting even deeper than they were a minute ago.

"Clarissa!" I yell out and reach for the handle. I turn the knob and swing the door open. She's crouched between the tub and the toilet with her head between her knees. Her hands are covering her eyes. She slowly shakes her head.

"Clarissa, what's wrong?" My heart feels like it's pounding out of my chest.

"You're scaring me!" I quickly get to her on the floor. I notice she's changed out of her pajamas and into shorts and a t-shirt. I survey the bathroom. There's a plastic bag with red lettering printed on the side. She's gone out this morning.

"Clarissa, say something!" I demand. She lifts her face only enough to look at me for a split second. Her eyes are so bloodshot and swollen from crying that I feel my own eyes start to ache with tears. I reach for her hand. She's holding something but quickly hides it from me.

"Stop, I'm trying to help you. Talk to me." I reach for her hand again and yank. I look down, and, in her palm, she holds a white stick that all girls are familiar with by the time they are a teenager. It's the most commonly used gadget when two people are either trying to conceive or when a woman realizes she's late on her period. And in the moment it takes me to understand, I read the unmistakable bright pink plus symbol in the clear window of the pregnancy test.

CHAPTER 19

"What the hell is going on?" Olivia bursts into the bathroom looking sickeningly concerned. It's not until I see her face that I know she is as pained and hungover as I am. My symptoms have seemed to take a backseat until now and I feel my stomach turn. I watch Olivia hurl herself onto Clarissa, she tries pulling her out from the corner. I reach inside the plastic bag and find the opened pregnancy kit. I pull it out and discreetly show it to Olivia. Her eyes widen and she covers her mouth with her hand. The three of us sit on the floor for some time. Besides Clarissa's sobs, it's quiet. Olivia has both arms wrapped around Clarissa and I'm lying on the ground with my head near her feet squeezing one of her hands. Olivia tries comforting Clarissa by telling her it will be alright but it only makes her cry harder.

The three of us jump when a phone rings. It's Olivia's fiancé. She slowly walks out of the bathroom and takes the call.

Clarissa looks at me. Her face is red and blotchy. I've never seen her look so helpless.

"Please don't tell anyone," she says in a scratchy, barely audible voice.

"Of course not," I shake my head, "I won't." I bite my lip. "How did you know?"

"Headaches, being tired all the time, feeling sick."

I nod. "I thought you were on the pill?"

Max and I were fighting a lot and we weren't having sex. My birth control was still giving me bad side effects, so I got off it."

"Oh. I guess I knew you guys had a few fights but I didn't know it was that bad."

"You know I don't like talking about that stuff."

"So, what now?"

"I don't know. And fuck, we just broke up. But, what's going through my head right now, is not that I'm pregnant and single, it's that California is off the table. I feel like my dreams have just been taken from me." Her bottom lip quivers and tears start to fall again.

Growing up Christian, I know I would not even consider getting an abortion. If she thought it were an option, she would have brought it up by now and California would still be on the table.

"Let's take a walk, get some fresh air," I say standing.

Olivia takes us on a walk around the neighborhood playing tour guide. I'm not sure how much it's helping but it seems like a good distraction to me. The houses are truly breathtaking. Some of them are hundreds of years old and have quite the backstory. The gardens and landscaping are also magnificent. After we finish a few blocks, we spot a juice bar.

"Can we stop?" Clarissa asks, almost embarrassed. "I get tired so fast; I feel like all my energy has been sucked from me."

"Of course!" Olivia says. And at this point, we are both so happy that the tears have stopped that we will do anything to make her happy.

We order three frozen blended drinks and take a seat in the window. Clarissa gets up to use the bathroom.

"Does she seem a little off? I mean besides the pregnancy?" Olivia asks looking at me.

"I'm sure she has a lot on her mind. The breakup, a baby, California…her parents! What's her dad going to say?"

"Agh, Arthur. That man is intimating." Her eyes get big. "He is all about family respect, doing the right thing…he's someone you just don't piss off."

272

We see Clarissa walking back and try to change the subject. "Do you still want to go into the city today?" Olivia asks. "Can we go back for a nap first?"

I don't mind the quiet time since I'm just now starting to feel better from my hangover. I look at my phone for the first time today. I see I have a few unread messages from Jordan. I open them and read back to see where we left off.

Jord@n69: so you see what I'm saying? Btw, I see how you changed the subject when I asked if you were into me. So, comment or not, I know the answer ;)

Jord@n69: so now you don't say anything? ... I like girls who play hard to get

I smile. He's arrogant and it's so annoying. I have no idea what to say but I like the idea of making him wait. I set my phone down and close my eyes.

In the early afternoon, we ride the streetcar into the French quarter and wander through an outdoor market. We get in a very long line to buy powdered beignets and chicory coffee and eat them while walking around Louis Armstrong Park. Next, we walk down famous Bourbon Street. The smell of stale beer and vomit was a bit much for Clarissa's better sense of smell so we quickly walk through and finish at the Carousel bar.

"Are you sure you're okay with us being here?" Olivia asks Clarissa.

"Please just do what you would normally do. I'd like to pretend things are somewhat normal until this trip is over. When I'm home I'll deal with the reality."

Olivia and I each order a drink. I catch Clarissa glance at the bartender as she makes our drinks. This makes me feel like we shouldn't have come here.

"I guess this is where I order water," she says looking at us. "I can't even fathom this." She looks down at her stomach.

273

"But, one thing is for sure, I'm glad I'm with you guys right now."

I smile at her. "It's going to be okay. We'll help you through this."

"I don't even know what to do first or where to start."

"Make an appointment with your doctor. They'll tell you how far along you are." Olivia says. "You're not the first woman to have gotten pregnant and not know what to do. Your doctor will give you a bunch of information."

"Mo researches everything. If you have any questions, I'm sure she'll be a great source of information. She probably already has their name on the waiting list at the top daycare center in their area, even though they won't need one until like February."

"There's a waiting list to get into daycare?"

I swallow. Clarissa is the last person I would have ever imagined having an unplanned pregnancy.

"We'll buy some baby books. And there's tons of information online. Just start slow so you don't get overwhelmed." Olivia suggests.

"What are you going to do about Max?" I ask.

"It's crossed my mind to not even tell him...I mean not right away. I do not want to raise a baby by myself. It'd be shitty not to try to work things out with him right?"

"Are you even missing him? I feel like you've already moved on and it's only been a week."

"Of course I miss him. The thought of being alone sucks...hell, being alone sucks."

"Yeah being alone does suck but that doesn't mean you should give up everything. You don't have to be together to do a good job raising a baby. Co-parenting can work." Olivia says.

"We have some major issues. You guys don't even know the half of it," Clarissa says, shaking her head.

"So go to family counseling. Don't you think it would be easier to get on the same page before the baby comes? You can figure out a schedule that works for both of you even if you're apart."

"Riss, I think you should try making it work. You guys are good together. Every couple has their issues and I think the counseling is a really good idea." I suggest softly. "That way if it still doesn't work, then you know you tried."

"I have a friend who tries to make it work for the sake of her kids, and more often than not the father just does as he pleases. He leaves to go out with his friends and she's stuck home with the kids. She has no life. And they're both miserable because they don't even like each other. They had broken up once or twice before they found out they were pregnant the first time. I just can't picture that for you. If you get shared custody you can still have a social life. Do what you want, I know you will anyway," Olivia says with a smile, "but just think about putting yourself first. It might be the last time you get to."

Clarissa tips her head back and closes her eyes. She blows out a lungful of air. "What the fuck am I going to do?"

CHAPTER 20

We say goodbye to Olivia and thank her for her hospitality. I think how the idea behind this trip was for Clarissa and me to get our exes off our minds. For me, I'd say it helped. Clarissa though, not so lucky.

Now when we board it's Clarissa who looks bummed that we aren't seated together. I feel bad that I can't be next to her. After taking my seat, I look at my phone and contemplate sending Jordan a message. I decide to wait on it; if anything, I hope it makes him think of me. I shut my phone down and close my eyes.

Friday

Jordan and I meet at a place called Good Times. He had gotten us tickets for the comedy show. We order some drinks and within minutes he's slouched back in his seat with his arm around my seat.

"So, what do you do for fun, what are your hobbies?"

"I spend a lot of time in the shop working on my other bike. I'm on a dart league, that's pretty fun," he says nonchalantly. "What about you?"

I study him. I was nervous coming here tonight because I wasn't sure I'd be able to hang out with someone I didn't see a future with; outside the physical attraction, there is no spark or deeper feelings and it puts me at ease knowing I can't really screw up.

I clear my throat. "I like to spend time with my friends and family, I love a good book, I like to be active and trying new things."

"Nice," he says nodding.

His beer and my vodka cranberry are delivered. He sits forward to take a sip and then slouches back again. There's an ease to him. He's so relaxed and comfortable. Maybe too comfortable. But, it is kind of nice not trying. It feels somewhat easy because like him, I don't care if this goes anywhere.

The show starts and within the first few minutes we are deep in laughter. A few times I look over at him and he looks to really be enjoying himself, as am I. He orders us another round of drinks. The alcohol makes me loosen up even more and before I know it I'm slouched closer him. At intermission, he gives my knee a little squeeze and shoots me a sideway grin when he gets up to use the restroom. A little surge of energy shoots through me and I can't help but flirt back with my own playful smile. I feel good. This could really be fun.

After the show, we decide to walk to a neighboring bar. We cut through a back alley and when we turn the corner, Jordan grabs my hand and spins me towards him. He grabs my jacket and pulls me to him. He kisses me. When he releases me, I kiss him back. He gives me that same playful smirk as he did earlier.

"Let's go back to your place," he says kissing my neck.

I hesitate for just a moment. "Okay," I say and take his hand. We jog hand and hand back to my car like a bunch of kids. "Can you drive? I'm a little buzzed."

"Yeah, I've only had a couple beers."

I throw my keys to him.

Back at my apartment things heat up fast. Before I know it, Jordan has his shirt off and starts undressing me. His mouth is on my neck and his fingertips draw goosebumps when he unhooks my bra.

"Bedroom." He mouths. And there's just something so sexy about his confidence.

He climbs on top of me. And instead of kissing me raw and hard like he had been, he stops short and kisses my stomach. My stomach muscles tense and quiver as his lips brush against my skin making it tickle slightly.

"You on anything?" He asks, referring to birth control I imagine. The idea of becoming Clarissa in nine months crosses my mind. I'm praising myself for not stopping my contraceptive when Roo and I broke up.

"In the clear." I breathe into his ear. Knowing this is just sex I feel more confident and aggressive. I suck on the bottom part of his ear, my teeth graze his lobe and I gently bite, pulling it slightly.

"Oh, naughty girl. You just keep surprising me." He grins.

He runs his hands up my bare ribcage all the way to my wrist holding my arms down with one hand. I bite my lip and hold eye contact. He kisses me hard, then presses his pelvis against mine. The next hour is mind-blowingly amazing.

I wake the next morning to Jordan getting dressed.

"You want some breakfast before you go?" I ask in a hoarse voice.

"Nah, I'm good." He turns and glances at me with a quizzical look.

"What?" I ask, feeling pretty bad ass. I never thought I would be capable of having a solely sexual relationship with someone. Instead of sitting home self-loathing and paining myself over memories of Roo I had an enjoyable night of spontaneous sex with someone I find hot as hell.

"You're pretty hot, ya know that?"

I give him a flirty look, "thanks." I stretch, pushing the tangled mess of sheets from me and sit up.

"Sleep in, I got a buddy coming to pick me up." He nods.

"Will do." I smile and think that this might be the most considerate thing he's said to me thus far.

"I'll lock the door on the way out." He grins and gives me one on his famous winks. "Later babe."

I lie in the middle of my bed, a bit in shock. That went way better than I had imagined. As much as I like the idea of sleeping in on a Saturday morning, I find myself wide awake and in a really good mood. I feel like talking to someone. I think about possibly telling Emma about my night. I know it's safe to tell her and she's been dying to get together for weeks. I'll reach out this week for us to do something fun. But the main person that is on my mind is Clarissa. She will be up getting ready for work and I know she had an appointment yesterday; I'm dying to hear how it went.

Her doctor projects she's thirteen weeks along, and due in February. Olivia and I are still the only two that know. She tells me that she and Max have started to talk again and that it's going well. She wants to tell the girls but is unsure of when the time will be right. She's even more nervous about telling her parents but feels that she is starting to show. If she wears tight clothes a small round belly is noticeable, but for now she's been able to get away with baggy or loose tops. I've agreed to attend her next ultrasound appointment; she'll be able to find out the gender. We also discuss how she'll tell her parents and start to plan Kia's birthday before we hang up. I text Danielle after looking over my detailed note.

Jhett: Hey! Thinking about having Kia's birthday a weekend early so we can actually surprise her! Are you free next weekend?

Danielle: I'm open! Where ya thinking?

Jhett: There's a wine painting class at Marco's in the back room. I'll make plans with her and you and Clarissa can be there when we arrive.

Danielle: She loves those classes, that will be perfect!

Jhett: Starts at 7pm, we can take her out after. Clarissa said she can drive since she has the biggest vehicle.

I reassured Clarissa nobody would think twice about her not drinking if she agreed to be the DD. They know she's been careful since her DUI.

I text Kate next.

Jhett: Up for a drive?
Kate: I'd love to but I'm filling in at work.
Jhett: Alright- you better be free next time I ask ;)
Kate: hopefully…and sorry I can't, the overtime is really good!

I get in my car and drive to Mocha Joes. I cross my fingers the painting of the French bulldog is still there. Maybe I should have called first. But either way, I find myself enjoying the quiet drive. I step inside the familiar shop and smile to myself, releasing the breath of air I didn't know I was holding in. The painting is there hanging in the same place I'd last seen it. I place an order for an iced chocolate mint mocha and tell the barista that I'll be taking the painting as well. She offers to wrap it after finding out it's a gift; I smile and nod at the kind gesture.

I sit in an oversized leather chair and sip my drink through an eco-friendly straw. I couldn't help but think of Roo on the way here. Allowing myself to think of him, my thoughts start to spread like wildfire when I find I don't have a grasp on my feelings at all. All the hurt starts to come back as I've just re-opened the scab. I sit and think about what had happened. The weeks we were together went by so fast, and now it's been a month since we've last talked. Thinking about it all starts to put me in a funk. I had promised Clarissa I would not reach out to him and for more than just keeping the promise to her, I want to keep that promise to myself. I retrieve my phone and instead of checking Roo's Facebook, which he hasn't updated since our fight, or re-reading old messages, I send Jordan a message.

Jhettskii: You want to grab a drink tonight?
Jord@n69: Can't, got plans

Damn. It's Saturday and I have no plans. I feel a bit pathetic. A crazy thought comes to mind; I could drive to Roo's. Or maybe it's not crazy, maybe it's romantic to fight for him. Ugh, I hate the back and forth. I hate the pain in my chest and the headache that forms between my eyes when I think of him. It's painful and I'm sick of it. I just want to see him and if it is really over, I just need to hear it. I'd be there in just over an hour. But what if he's not there? Then I would really look like an idiot. I push the idea from my mind before I can talk myself into it.

Jhettskii: can you cancel them?

Jord@n69: Oh, someone had too much fun last night…

I roll my eyes. How can I reply without sounding desperate?

Jhettskii: I just want to grab a drink, what'd you say?!

Jord@n69: Sorry doll

I sigh, annoyed.

Jord@n69: tomorrow?

This takes me by surprise. He wants to hang out on a Sunday? Hmm, why not.

Jhettskii: Yes, bloodies at Marcos, 10 (am; just in case I have to make that clear)

Jord@n69: Why does everyone love that place? … but sure, see ya there

I don't know how I feel about these plans. I might actually be looking forward to them. But deep down, I think it's just the point of being with someone that is filling a void. I think I finally get why some people are okay with this kind of lifestyle. I finish my coffee, grab Kia's gift and head for home. I stop at a grocery store along the way. I fill my cart with a week's worth of food. On a whim, I grab a bottle of wine that's sectioned between the sweet reds and Moscato. When I get home, I throw a frozen pizza in the oven and crack open the wine. I did good; it's sweet and tastes as good as juice. I put on some yoga pants and an old worn t-shirt and plop down in front of the TV. I eat over half the pizza and drink the entire bottle of wine. I scroll on my phone for birthday party ideas for Kia. Around midnight my phone drops out of my hand waking me, I sulk half asleep to my bedroom and collapse on my bed.

I wake up covered in sweat. Oh my god, that can't be right. I feel like I've been asleep for hours but it's only three in the morning. My heart is beating so fast I feel like I might be having a panic attack. I reach for my phone; no new messages. I replay my dream. There's no way. I resist texting the only two people that would be able to confirm my nightmare because it's the middle of the night. And I highly doubt either is awake. I sit racking my brain on what to do. I feel a crease between my eyes. This can't be. In order to relax, I type out the texts and set them to send first thing in the morning. But boy, I hope I'm wrong.

Jhett: does Jordan go by JJ??
Jhett: is JJ's name Jordan??

CHAPTER 21

At 8:42am in the morning, Danielle replies to my message. While waiting I've chewed down my fingernails; a habit I had broken when I was nine. I reach for my phone with clammy hands scared to open the message.

Danielle: Good morning to you too, ha. Yeah, I think his friends call him JJ. Why?

My heart sinks. Shit, shit. I need to call Emma, or maybe I should just go see her in person.

Jhett: I'll explain later.

I send Emma another message even though I haven't heard from her yet.

Jhett: Can I see you today!?

I jump in the shower and rush to get dressed. Whether she responds or not, I decide I'm driving to her place.

I'm about ready to leave when I hear a ping from my phone.

Emma: Yes, I'd love to see you! And yep, Jordan!

I'm heartbroken by her enthusiasm. Especially since she's tried getting together with me for the past few weeks and I've blown her off. Now she thinks we are getting together for fun. This makes me feel terrible. I put my peanut butter and banana sandwich back on the counter. I doubt I'll be able to eat it; I'm about to break her heart.

Jhett: I'm headed to your place now if that's ok?

Emma: Sure, see you soon!

I pull up in front of Emma's place and the pit in my stomach tightens. I walk up to her door and she greets me before I knock. I can't help but smile at her contagious beaming face.

"Hey," I say nervously as the word is drawn out. But she's oblivious to my hesitation and throws her arms around me.

"I'm so happy you're here. I've missed you so much! Come in, come in!"

I try to swallow but my throat feels tight and dry, it's almost painful and feels as though I'm trying to get down a heavy stone. I recall the story of how her high school sweetheart cheated with her best friend and they had a frickin' baby together. I try slowly filling my lungs with air in the hopes it calms me down. My hands are shaking and my armpits are damp. I take a seat on her couch. She does the same, both of us sitting on the outside cushions so that the middle one is open between us.

"Are you and Jor…ah, JJ still together?"

"Yeah, we are!" Her smile bigger than the last. I look into her bright eyes and wonder what this is going to do to her.

I push myself to bite the bullet and just get on with it. "Is his last name Reyes?"

"Yeah, do you know him?" She asks, surprised.

"Yeah, I do. He's my friend Danielle's cousin."

"Oh, cool."

She waits patiently looking at me. I wish I knew what was going through her mind. Does she have any idea what I'm about to tell her? I watch as her eyebrows come together as if she knows I'm not done with the questions and is curious as to what I'll be asking next.

"When's the last time you saw him?" I ask picking at the cuticle on my thumbnail.

She thinks for just a moment. "He came over after my shift on Thursday. He was supposed to come over Friday too, but he wasn't feeling well."

Oh, no. He was with me Friday. I chew my lip and then think about what I thought her answer was going to be. "Wait, you weren't with him last night?" I ask, remembering he had plans.

"I think he was with a friend last night, he never told me who," she says casually.

I try my hardest to sound interested and not like I'm digging. "Do you know where he is now?" I ask knowing it's nine-thirty. Thirty minutes before he and I are supposed to meet for Bloody Marys.

"Um, I think he's probably at the shop by now," she says glancing at the time. "He messaged me last night that he'd be working on his bike most of the day. Why do you ask?" She looks at me more puzzled now. I'm not sure if she's reading my face and knows I'm about to deliver bad news, or if she's starting to register how random it was that I've sent a random text about the guy she's being seeing. Followed by an urgent visit and twenty-one questions. She stops smiling.

I swallow and slowly the words start to come out. "Emma, I had no idea, please believe me," I bring my sweaty palms together and fight to keep my eyes on her, "I went out with someone named Jordan Reyes on Friday night. We went to a comedy club." Emotion rises up inside me as she starts to shake her head back and forth. "I had no idea that he was JJ." It comes out almost as a whisper and my eyes dart around, finally settling on my lap. I feel cowardly not looking her in the eyes but seeing her anguished face as she takes in what I'm telling her is ripping me apart.

Her eyelids blink at a rapid speed and finally she says, "What?" And I can see she really doesn't understand. Or, maybe, she doesn't want to.

I clear my throat. "I met Jordan at Danielle's house a couple of weekends ago. He was there with another girl and they left together on his motorcycle. A couple days later we started talking and he told me he didn't have a girlfriend. We went out and…"

She cuts me off, "wait, what…what? You're joking right?" Her voice desperate. "Did he put you up to this?" She swallows hard. "He's always messing with me. He tells me I'm gullible like every other day."

I look down. I feel like crying and throwing up. I shake my head and bring myself to look at her again. "I'm so sorry. I swear I didn't know." The back of my eyes burn. It takes everything in my will power to keep the tears from spilling out.

She brings her fingertips to her forehead and rubs. I see her chest rise and fall. She stands and walks away from me. "I…I think I just need to call him." She presses her phone to her ear and after a few moments quietly says, "voicemail." Bringing the phone down she stares at the screen.

"Are you okay?" I ask. She's actually way calmer than I thought she'd be.

"I don't know. I'm really confused?" She says and it sounds like a question. "Are you sure we're talking about the same guy? I just don't know how this could happen," she says coming back to sit on the couch.

"I've thought about it all morning. The only thing he used to communicate with me is Snapchat. All messages delete, so there's no trace of him talking to someone else. Early on he asked if you were *only* seeing him, but he never said you were the only one he was seeing, right?"

"But you?"

And, here it comes. Her cheeks turn bright red. "How? How did you not know it was him?" I see the panicked look in her eyes.

"Emma, I never met him. I never saw him in person before Danielle's party. I would *never* do this to you."

She walks into the kitchen and carefully takes an ice pack from the freezer. She rests it against her chest. She closes her eyes, takes long, slow inhales through her nose, holds for a number of seconds and then expels them slowly through her mouth. It's dead silent, besides the release of her breath, for a few but very long minutes. I contemplate leaving. But what kind of state of mind would I be leaving her in? Should I call her parents? Then, slowly, she starts to talk.

With her eyes still closed, she softly and calmly says, "it makes sense. He would never let me take his picture, I was never allowed to go to his place, he always came here. He was secretive and he'd walk away to take calls. He'd say it was important, even though it would be weird hours like late at night. Sometimes he'd have to leave and I wouldn't hear from him until a day or two later. It was always, the shop, a friend, someone who needed his help. But most times if I asked questions, he'd change the subject or just get annoyed or angry." I stay quiet because I really don't know what to say. "I just…I, I need to know," her eyes shift, finding mine for a split second before she looks away, "what happened between you two?"

I shake my head and feel disgusted with myself. "We slept together." The words barely loud enough to be heard. My eyelids flutter shut. Do I tell her I don't have feelings for him? That it really meant nothing? That I used the person she loves as a rebound to fill a void? That I think he's arrogant, pigheaded and selfish and that she's better off without him? And that no matter how much she loves him and no matter what she does to make him happy he will always keep her at arm's length? If he's done this to her and countless other girls she'll never be enough for him? I won't say any of this because I know she's hurting enough. And it might even destroy our friendship. I want her to see what I see.

Yet, it would make me feel like a hypocrite and I know it's not my place. I know that Emma loves Jordan the way Sai loved me. I didn't cheat on Sai but the entire time I was with him I had known I needed more. So, I'm no better than Jordan, I just strung Sai along until I found someone better.

Someone I felt complete with, but then I screwed that up too. Emma's voice breaks my thoughts.

"At your place?" She questions.

"Yeah." Not knowing why this mattered. And without me asking she answers.

"We always hung out here too. I've never been invited to his place. Always thought that was a bit odd, ya know?" She walks back to the couch and takes a seat back down. "So, what now?"

Jord@n69: WTF just happened?
Jhettskii: I'm surprised you even have the balls to ask.

I call Danielle.

"Hey." She answers.

"Hey, you busy?"

"I just got home, what's up?"

"We need to talk."

"I hate that phrase, is everything okay?"

I sigh. "I think so. You were right about something and I'm ready to let you know about a huge mistake I made."

"Okay, but you better get here fast because now I'm going to be thinking up a hundred and one crazy scenarios. And let me guess, you're not going to say anything else until you get here?"

"You know me well. See ya soon." I hang up.

My phone pings. I glance at it, seeing I have another message from Jordan. This piques my interest. I am slightly intrigued at what he could possibly say that would be worthy of my time. Is he that arrogant that he thinks that what he did is even for a second forgivable? Or is he just that stupid? I've disliked his cocky, overconfidence from the beginning. His 'I'm so hot all women want me' mantra.

I see my reflection in the rear-view mirror and notice my forehead is creased and my eyes are squinted in a glaring fashion. I try relaxing my face as soon as I see it, reminding myself of what my great aunts told me about keeping my skin youthful as long as possible. Bad skin and deep facial wrinkles, they told me, are unfortunately hereditary, especially for the women in our family. I look closer at the areas of skin that had just been pinched together. Tiny red lines linger between my eyebrows and at the corners of my eyes; just like they had warned. Now I'm upset for allowing Jordan's actions to speed up the crow's feet and frown line wrinkles.

I don't knock. I walk straight in and join Danielle on the couch. She's folding towels and has a small stack on the floor. I grab one and fold it.

"I'm so sorry I didn't listen to you. I'm such a terrible person," I say spewing the words out.

"What could you have done that is that terrible? I'm sure you're being hard on yourself."

"I slept with Jordan."

"Oh!" Her eyes get big and she blinks hard. "Oh my gosh. What the hell, when did this happen? I didn't even know you were hanging out."

"We weren't really. I'm embarrassed to admit this." I take another towel and look away feeling foolish. "We started talking while I was in New Orleans. You know how I just wanted, or more needed to get Roo off my mind; I thought making the first move would give me a boost of confidence."

She brings her hand to her forehead, "I can't believe I'm hearing this. Ugh, he's such a player. And you? I can't believe you'd give him the time of day."

"I'm not proud. And the worst part..." I clear my throat, "Jordan, has been dating my old coworker Emma. I knew she was with a guy named JJ, and then this morning everything unraveled and now here I am.

"Wow. How is she taking it?"

"Actually, better than I thought she would. Sadly she's had a pretty shitty dating history. The girl has really bad luck."

Danielle looks at me with soft eyes. "How are you taking it?"

"Oh." I shake my head. "I… I knew Jordan and I weren't going to last," I say slowly.

"Well, even so, it's hard to find out the guy you're seeing is dating someone else."

"Yeah, that did suck. But I think I feel worse for Emma and that makes it less painful for me. I also think he's still seeing that girl he brought to your party. He wasn't with me or Emma last night and I'm not entirely convinced he was alone for the night."

"What a douchebag." She mutters under her breath. "How'd you find out?"

"Oddly enough, in a dream."

"How'd you bust him? And please tell me you put him in his place."

"We made plans to meet at Marcos for Bloody Marys. We were supposed to meet at 10am. He was pretty confused when Emma went in my place."

"Oh, I would have loved to have seen his face when he saw her and panicked. Do you think he figured it out right away?"

"He didn't. Emma had me secretively on the phone so I could hear everything. And I heard him asking what she was doing there and that he wasn't planning on seeing her today. That's when she confronted him. He was shocked. I ended the call after that to give her some privacy. I figured she might have questions and want some answers. After I hung up I decided to come see you."

"I'm guessing you haven't heard from Jordan then."

"I have actually! I was surprised to hear from him too. But, I'm sure now that everything is sinking in, I won't hear from him again."

Danielle gives me a look, "I'm sure you won't. He's a coward." She reaches for the last towel, "you want to stay and grab pizza for lunch? For old times' sake, we can get the taco special?"

"Raincheck if that's okay?"

"Of course."

"I need to go for a run. It's been too long and I'm hoping all of this craziness will get me some extra miles."

We hug goodbye and I head out the door. I drive to a trail I've always wanted to run. I wait for two teenage boys in cross-country shorts and tank tops to pass before changing into my running get-up. As expected, I start with great energy and my breathing falls into place by the second mile. The entire time my thoughts bounce around. The secret of Clarissa's pregnancy, Jordan and Emma, Kia's surprise party, Beck and Mo's baby shower, which evolves to what their baby will look like and then I start thinking about kids of my own. I daydream about my husband and within seconds Roo comes to mind. I find myself getting frustrated and there's an ache in my chest as I fight to keep him from my thoughts.

Typically, when I run, there comes a time when I feel accomplished, and in almost every scenario I feel better when I'm finished. But I can see my car in the distance and once back I will have hit six miles; the most I've run in weeks. Instead of feeling good from my sore and tired muscles, I feel hopeless and alone, but it's enough to fuel me and I sprint as hard as I can for the remainder of the distance.

By the time I cross the invisible finish line I'm completely breathless. I fold forward resting my forearms on the tops of my thighs trying to catch my breath. I pant loudly and force myself to stand straight and move so that I don't cramp. The sweat that dotted my hairline now begins to drip down my face. I go to my bag and grab a hand towel to dry my face and wipe my sweaty hands. When I'm able to catch my breath, I feel the heaviness of my mental exhaustion slightly start to melt away. I take a long slow deep breath and feel like I might be okay.

After a few minutes of cooling down and sipping water from my bottle, I slip into the driver's seat and glance at my reflection in the rearview mirror. My cheeks are so deep red they're almost purple and my hair that's pulled back into a scrunchie has lost a good portion of its strands. I redo my pony and make a mental note to run this trail again.

I stop for a sub and bag of chips on my way back to my apartment. I collapse onto a kitchen bar stool and devour the entire footlong. I also make sure every possible crumb makes it into my mouth by tapping the last few tiny pieces from the bag. I didn't realize how hungry I was until I had finished. I wipe my face and finish my can of seltzer water. I get up to throw my trash away when I hear my phone. A text from Kia.

Kia: We still on for our Saturday run?

Jhett: Yes! And I know it's counterproductive but would you want to go out to Marco's Sat night? I could really use some girl time...specifically Kia time, I miss you.

Kia: I'd love to and I miss you too! Should we make it a girls' day? We can shower and get ready at my place before Marcos?

Jhett: I'd love that!

CHAPTER 22

Saturday

"Hey, I'm here." I call out when I step into the entry way of Kia's duplex.

"I'm in back." She shouts back. "I'll just be a sec."

I take the few minutes to stretch out on the floor of Kia's living room. I place myself in the center of her plush gray rug that has a yellow accent design. I was with her when she bought it just over a year ago. I run my hand back and forth over the soft shaggy material remembering the first few days of its life. 'Please walk around the rug.' She would instruct. 'It wasn't cheap and I don't want it getting wrecked.'

Of course, Clarissa made fun of her for this while the rest of us snickered, but none of us dared to actually walk on it. It wasn't until two short weeks later that it had gotten its first stain. James came in late one night and passed out drunk on the couch. He didn't realize until the following morning when he woke to Kia screaming that he had knocked over a bottle of dark beer onto it. The beer had sat for hours leaving a deep brown stain the size of an eggplant.

Kia had threatened to break up with him if he didn't buy her a new one. So, the very next day James showed up with the exact replica of her beloved rug. But unlucky for him, Kia ran into James' mother days later at the grocery store. She asked how the rug was holding up and if she did a well enough job. Confused, Kia asked what she meant. Come to find out,

James had brought the original beer-soaked rug to his house and told his mom that if she could get the stain out and make the rug look as good as new, he would help her with any project around the house. His mother read the laundry tag, threw it into the washer, hung it to dry and that was it. Kia, furious that James had lied about buying her a new rug, had broken up with him for the second time in their relationship. The breakup only lasted a week; and in that week James held up his end of the bargain by helping his mom repaint their entire house. I smile at the thought of the whole situation.

"Hey, it's good to see you're smiling," Kia says in a smooth voice.

"Oh, hey, I didn't hear you." I smile. "Just thinking of when I wasn't allowed on this rug." I tease.

"Oh yeah, that rug is the best. Machine wash warm, gentle cycle, hang to dry." She chirps. "Comes out fresh and fluffy each time!"

"Yeah, my motivation to get up is pretty low now that I'm sitting here." I joke.

She laughs, "let's go, the sooner we go, the sooner we're done!"

We speed walk to the paved path and without acknowledging it we start a trot at the exact same moment. Kia and I have run together so many times that I think we can read each other's minds; at least when it comes to running. We start running while we chat on and off until soon enough, we're passing and slapping the high five tree.

Whipping around, we head back the way we came. We start talking about James, and Kia tells me his lease is up at the end of next month. They've discussed living together at Kia's duplex. She catches me up to speed on her parents too. Her mom has started volunteering now that she is fully retired and her dad has started walking in hopes to improve his health. They put in an offer on a first-floor condo in Falls and hope to be in by the end summer. The Jordan situation embarrasses me and I'm ashamed to admit what all went on, but I know eventually all the girls will find out so I ignore the hesitation and spill.

"I would have done the same the thing," she says, surprising me.

"Really?" I ask, relieved.

"Hell yeah, he is super-hot," she says, dragging out each word.

"Well, I'm glad I told you. And thanks for not judging. To be honest, I was thinking about not telling anyone because it's just kind of embarrassing, ya know?"

"Oh yeah, I get it. But you only live once. And we learn from mistakes. Mistakes named Jordan." She laughs. I grin and shake my head. "So, how are *you* doing?"

I get a little uncomfortable at this. We are best friends, yet I feel like I can't fully spill my emotions. I know she's here to support me and that's why she asked but I know I can't get over Roo if I keep talking about him.

"I'm doing better," I say.

She gives me a look and squints her eyes. "Tell me truthfully."

I smirk. "I'm okay. Thanks for asking." Just like I don't want to talk about Jordan, I have the exact opposite feeling about Roo. I could talk until I'm blue in the face.

We are both pretty pink-cheeked when we returned to where we had started. We walk to an artesian well and take turns sipping the crisp cold water. We take our time walking back to Kia's place, enjoying the easy summer day.

Coming out of the bathroom I wrap a towel around my hair and walk to the back patio to sit on a green metal chair. I smell and then taste a weirdly satisfying protein shake Kia blended up for us. I lean back and take in Kia's quiet, relaxing, fenced-in backyard. I can hear kids playing nearby. Their sweet voices and giggles make me smile and think of my own childhood.

I hear the back screen door open and Kia joins me.

"Pretty nice you get this place all to yourself," I say.

"I know!" She says running her fingers through her wet hair.

The other side of the duplex is rented out to a couple who travel for a living.

"I think they're back from Amsterdam in a week or two. Their next trip is Thailand; can you believe it?"

"Wow, can you imagine traveling with your significant other for a job? They literally vacation for a living."

"I know. But I've had conversations with them and there's so much that goes into it. It's not as glamorous as you'd think. And their side of the duplex is bare. They have a table and a few chairs, a bed and a few things in the pantry. It's like a hotel and not really a home at all," she says while working her hair into a side braid. "I wouldn't be able to travel with James like that, we'd kill each other by the end of the first week."

I laugh. "Yeah, no offense but I can see that."

Kia and I go in after we finish our shakes to finish getting ready. We have just over an hour before we need to leave for the paint and wine class. I text the other girls to see if everything is still on. Clarissa is planning on getting there early to tie balloons to Kia's chair and Danielle is picking up Kia's favorite dessert.

Kia walks out of her room in tight ripped jeans, a black top with an open back, and a pair of leopard print wedges.

"You look hot!" I say.

"So do you!" She says.

I check myself over once more before heading out of the bathroom. I'm wearing my new crop top that ties off to one side with a pair of high waist jeans and a pair of blush wedge booties.

"You ready?" She asks.

I grab my purse. "Ready!"

We climb into my vehicle and arrive at Marcos just before 7pm. We walk to the back where Clarissa and Danielle are waiting with flowers and gifts for Kia.

"Happy birthday!" They shout in unison.

"Oh my gosh!" Kia says with a giant grin. I can see the look of shock on her face. It was a successful surprise. "You guys!" Is all she says and envelops us in a hug.

"Welcome. You must be the birthday girl." The instructor of the class says coming over to introduce herself.

We take our seats and Demi walks in with three bottles of wine. A white, a red and a Rosé. "Just bring the empties up to the bar when you're ready for your next bottle," she instructs. The instructor starts with a short introduction of herself while circling the room pouring wine into glasses. She reaches Clarissa.

'What would you like dear?"

"I'm fine with water thanks," Clarissa says, gesturing to her full glass.

There's light conversation amongst the other girls in the class while the instructor juggles the three bottles trying to display their labels to each of us.

"Oh, it's included in the price," she says kindly.

"I'm driving." Clarissa responds and I can see she's trying to keep her patience with the woman.

Danielle proposes, "We'll probably be here a while, at least two hours, right?"

"At a minimum. You should be fine to drive. Maybe just one glass?"

I feel myself starting to get fidgety. Clarissa's face is starting to flush and I can see the look in her eyes that she wants to let this clueless woman have it.

"What'll it be?" She says with an obnoxious grin.

"Nothing!" She shouts, "because I'm fucking pregnant!" And her face gets three shades darker.

The woman looks embarrassed beyond belief. "I'm so sorry." She whispers and her cheeks match Clarissa's. The entire room is still. The woman's eyes drop to the floor and she steps on to Kia. She clears her throat.

Before having to speak, Kia helps her out by saying, "I'll have whatever's sweetest."

The four of us sit quietly for a few moments. I watch as Danielle and Kia shift their eyes from Clarissa to me and back to one another. Clarissa is looking straight ahead at the blank canvas set in front of her. I move in my seat trying to think of anything that could break the silence.

I watch Clarissa pull in her lips as if she'd just put gloss on.

She turns and looks at us. She swallows. "I'm pregnant," she says with no expression whatsoever.

"Oh my gosh, I...don't know what to say," Kia says.

Clarissa glances down and we sit without talking for another long minute.

"You're keeping it right?" Danielle finally says.

"Yes."

"What about Max?" Kia asks, a look of surprise still on her face.

"He doesn't know yet. But we've been talking and things are going okay."

"When did you find out?" Danielle asks.

"When we were in New Orleans," Clarissa says nodding in my direction. The girls' eyes follow and look at me. "It's fine. Really. Of course, this was completely unplanned, but it will be okay."

"Okay, if everyone is now ready to begin, I'd like you to start with your large brush." The instructor says holding up her brush, waving it around above her head.

We follow the first few steps as we're instructed and sit mostly in silence. After the first half-hour we have our background completed and the base of a tree. We're shown how to create a leaf quickly and easily with the brush and are instructed to, 'paint as we please'.

"I'm going to run to the restroom." Clarissa mouths to us.

"Do you want me to come with?" I ask.

"Only if you have to go." She replies a bit sharply. I shrug and shake my head no.

After she leaves the room Danielle says, "She still sounds upset."

"Bitchy is more like it." Kia adds.

"Honestly, I'm glad to see she's back to her old self. She's been a bit off since she's found out. I think you not knowing was really stressing her out."

Danielle leans towards me and whispers, "I don't know what to say to her. Like, do we act happy?"

"Just be supportive. And let's stop whispering, if she walks in she's going to know we are talking about her," I say glancing over my shoulder.

"I can't believe you knew," Kia says.

"It wasn't easy." I stress. "She was planning on telling you guys soon."

Kia lifts her glass at the instructor who is making her rounds refilling glasses.

She hurries over, "Are you ladies having fun?"

"Yeah of course," Danielle says in her most optimistic voice.

Out of the corner of my eye I see Clarissa walk back into the room. Within seconds my glass is filled and the woman is gone; most likely because she's still embarrassed.

Clarissa takes her seat and the vibe turns awkward.

"Okay, this," she says creating a circular motion between the four of us, "cannot happen. I need things to be as normal as possible or I'll lose my mind."

Danielle is the first to speak. "Okay. So, I can ask questions?"

"Of course. Please! Anything is better than silence."

"When are you due?" Danielle's mouth turns into a smile and I think we all relax a bit.

"February third," she says.

"Boy or girl?" Kia probes.

"I'll find out at my next ultrasound appointment. I'll let you all know right away."

"Oh, I can't wait!" Kia says smiling and I notice we all are.

A full hour later we are all making our finishing touches before turning in our brushes. I'm pleased with my painting so I sneak away to retrieve Kia's gift from the trunk of my car. When I get back inside I notice everyone has dumped their dingy brown water and handed in their brushes. We take a final group photo and people from the group start to leave.

"Demi said we could stay in here as long as we'd like, there are no other parties tonight." Danielle informs us.

"Great, I'll get us another bottle. Kia, what was your favorite?"

"I liked the rosé."

"You got it." I hand her the gift bag. "Don't open this until I return."

With each of us with a glass of wine and Clarissa drinking ginger ale we sit around and watch Kia open her gifts. A colorful array of succulents in a hedgehog planter and a pair of geometric earrings from Danielle, a pair of soft avocado socks, the newest book by her favorite author and a coffee mug with cartoon avocado and toast holding hands from Clarissa. At last, she opens the French bulldog painting from me.

"Oh my gosh, you all know me so well!" Kia shrieks.

"Do you still eat avocado toast for breakfast every morning?" Danielle asks.

"At least five days a week. And did you go back to Mocha Joe's for this?" She asks me.

"As soon as you commented on it, I knew I'd be back for it."

"You ladies are the best!" She says hugging each one of us.

302

We all end up at Kia's duplex just after eleven. Within ten minutes of being at Kia's, Clarissa starts to yawn and we suggest she go to bed. She doesn't fight it and tells us she's going home to sleep in her own bed.

When we say goodbye I overhear Kia say, "congrats, by the way" and I see her squeeze her hand as she walks her to the door. They hug and I see relief on Clarissa's face.

When she's out of the driveway Danielle says, "wow, I'm still in shock. She's having a freaking kid!"

"No shit, right!" Kia says. "Her parents are going to flip out."

"I just hope Max stays in the picture. I don't want her to struggle as a single mom," I say.

"She will have us," Danielle says.

"She does, but that's not enough. Even with her parents' help, which might only be financial, she'll never get sleep and she won't be able to hang out with us like she does now."

"So, let's not let her bail on us. She can just bring the baby with and we can take turns holding it."

"Danielle, babies can't hang out in a bar," Kia says.

"I didn't mean in the bar, we'll just have to stay in and do more of this kind of stuff."

Catching me off guard, my phone flashes. I pick it up and see I have a message.

Jord@n69: hey girl, I miss you, whatcha up to?

I freeze.

"What?" Danielle asks.

"Jordan just sent me a message."

"A booty call?" Kia makes a look of disgust.

"How does he have the nerve?" I ask.

"That's Jordan. He might not even expect you to answer, he most likely texted you and three other girls," Danielle says shaking her head.

"How's your friend Emma doing?" Danielle asks.

"She's heartbroken. She says she has some regrets, like not having better communication with him, something she's learned a lot about in the last few months at therapy."

"If I were her, I wouldn't have let him walk out of Marco's without a black eye," Kia says.

"I'll drink to that!" Danielle says.

We raise our glasses, touch them together and drink. Setting her glass down Danielle reaches for her phone. Her eyebrows rise and she looks at me. "I just got a text from Jordan. He's asking about you."

"Are you serious? What did he say?"

"He wants to know if I'm with you or if I know where you are."

"Alright, I'm just going to end this now," I say, picking up my phone.

Jhettskii: Hey listen, we're done. I don't want to hear from you again.

There are a few minutes that Danielle, Kia and I hover over my phone waiting for his response. It's agonizing as we watch the three little dancing dots show up letting us know he's writing a message, when moments later they disappear.

"I can't take this. Why am I allowing him to do this to me?"

"Right, let's put it away," Kia says with her eyes on my screen.

But just as she says it and after the third time of seeing the dots appear, he sends his response.

Jord@n69: Hey, I had a really good time with you. I know I messed up but, I like you...

Anger makes my muscles tense. "I really wish I could punch him right now," I say, getting ready to respond.

Jhettskii: a smart man would have started with, I'm sorry, I'm an idiot and I need to realize I'm not the hot shit I think I am. And for the record, it was all for fun, I wasn't that into you to begin with.

"Ouch" Danielle says. "But that's good, he needs to hear it."

Jord@n69: You're right. I'm sorry. I am an idiot and I'm not a hot shit, I'm an asshole. I broke things off with Mandy, the girl I brought to Dani's. And of course, you know things are over with Emma. It's not an excuse but I was going to end it soon anyway. I want to see you again. I've never dated a girl like you before.

Jhettskii: That's because a girl like me doesn't go for a guy like you. I know I can do better and in normal circumstances, I wouldn't have given you the time of day. Just like I shouldn't be right now.

Jord@n69: Let me take you out again

Jhettskii: NO

Jord@n69: Jhett, just think about it

Danielle sits back in her chair. "Jhett, he's into you." She puts one hand up to keep me from commenting. "You probably think he talks like this when he's in the hot seat, but he doesn't. He just ends it when any little thing goes wrong and moves onto the next girl. And I've never heard him apologize to anyone other than Lola; our grandmother. And to me," she says touching her chest, "I'm surprised he's still trying. Believe me, Jordan doesn't try this hard."

"So, are you saying she should give him a shot?" Kia asks, concerned.

"Absolutely not! I just think it's fair for her to know that he actually likes her. And clearly, I don't blame him. She's amazing." She looks over at me. "Why wouldn't he want another shot with you?"

"Um...maybe because, how could I ever trust him? People don't change overnight. And it just drives me wild that he thinks he can ask for another chance even though he was dating two other women at the same time he was seeing me."

"No, I get it. It's just not like him. So, do what you want, but know he thinks you're worth it. And maybe he'd surprise you."

"You told me to steer clear of him, remember?"

"I do." She nods.

"That's what I'm going to do. Being fun was the only box checked for potential dating material. I need a minimum of four to consider someone to be dating potential, because of course when you first meet someone you won't know right away if they'll meet those requirements. And for marriage it needs to be all five. For Jordan, like I've said before, I knew this wasn't going anywhere. It was just shorter-lived than I had expected."

"Oh my gosh, I love this, tell me what your criteria are!" Kia beams scooting to the edge of her seat.

"One," I say touching my index finger, "trust, no brainer it needs to be there. Two," moving onto my middle finger, "compromise, if he can't compromise, it'll just never work; imagine all the fighting and frustration. Three, spark; as attractive as he may be, there needs to be more. There needs to be something that drives the passion and that will make you want to fight for the relationship when things get tough. Four," I continue to my pinky finger, "Mystery, in Jordan's case this is what he had going for him. There needs to be something that keeps me curious.

I don't want to get bored after the honeymoon stage or worse after we become empty nesters; I've heard about that. And five," I say and I feel like I'm giving a TED talk to two of my best friends. They're so intrigued and look so serious. I continue, "Priorities. He's gotta have his shit together. I don't want to date some twenty-something-year-old that lives with his parents and plays video games when the suns out. I have no time for that."

Danielle starts clapping.

"Impressive! I can't believe we haven't talked about this sooner. Can I steal it?" Kia asks.

I laugh, "of course." But it makes me think and anxiously I ask, hoping I don't cause a problem, "does James check these off?"

She considers this. "You know, when you were going over them, I wasn't picturing James at all. I was picturing this perfect dream guy. And it's not that I don't love your list, because I do, but does a guy like that exist? Like really?" She scrunches up her nose.

He does. Roo, I want to say, but I bite my tongue and don't go there.

Kia looks up and her fist goes under her chin like she's thinking hard. "Okay, I trust him and there's spark, but compromise, no, I cave way more often than he does. It's like ten to one. And I'd say there is a little mystery but not much," she says, stressing the word not. "And priorities...he didn't finish college but he makes pretty good money so that doesn't bother me really."

"I think it's a good thing you're being realistic." Danielle shrugs. "So, the main thing would be the compromise. Do you think over time it will get better or worse?"

"I want to say it will get better because I want it to, but if I'm being honest, I really think it will get worse. And I say that because he tried so much more in the beginning. He hardly tries at all anymore, I don't see him suddenly wanting to start compromising. You know what I mean?"

Danielle makes a face. "Yeah, I do, that was an issue for me and Ben."

"One thing I know for sure, James would never plan a surprise party for me. Thank you for a very nice birthday celebration, you guys are the best! Now," she says standing, "anyone want to share that tiramisu?"

"Yes! But just a few bites, I have an early morning planned with my dad," Danielle says getting to her feet and we follow Kia into the kitchen.

We take turns forking off chunks of the spongy layered cake. There isn't a sound aside from our moans at how good it is. Now I know why it's her favorite. We don't stop until it's gone. But Danielle and I back off so Kia can enjoy the last few bites of her cake. I can tell we are nearing the end of our night. Just as Danielle said, she grabs her things and says goodbye. I'm feeling tired myself and plan to stay in the guest room like Kia and I had planned all along.

"Tired?" I ask as Kia yawns.

"I'm ready for bed," she says.

"Me too. Happy early birthday my friend." I wrap my arms around her.

"Thank you." She smiles back.

"How long have we've known each other?" I ask, trying to do the math.

"Fourteen years?" She says getting to the number before I do.

"Wow, that's pretty amazing," I say thinking about the start of our friendship. "If I wake before you, I'll make breakfast." I smile.

"And if I wake before you?" She asks curiously.

"We both know I'll be up first." I laugh.

"How about you move in and James doesn't." She laughs back. "Goodnight Jhett."

"Night birthday girl."

I close the door and get changed into a loose tank top and shorts. I turn on a fan after I finish my nighttime routine and get under the bedsheet. I start to scroll on Facebook to see what I've missed from today. I heart the pictures that Kia posted from the painting class and a selfie of the four of us that we snapped before Clarissa took off. I move onto the next picture and it's of a couple I don't recognize. I enlarge the picture and look closer at their faces before checking the names. Raegan Smith is with Alexander Harris and two others.

I remember now, Alex is Roo's brother. I read the caption; *Today I said YES to the man of my dreams! Thank you for everyone who made this possible!* I scroll slowly through the pictures and stare at each one. Roo is in two of the posted photos. The only photos that have been posted of him since the last one I had tagged and shared. The first photo is of the couple on top a hill with a breathtaking background of the sun setting behind them with a burst of beautiful colors. Alex is down on one knee in the center of a blanket smiling up at Raegan. Raegan's hands are to the sides of her face and you can tell by her body language she is both surprised and very happy. There's a picnic basket, pillows, and a lantern that helps create the perfect picture.

I look at every inch of the picture to find something that's not perfect. As happy as they look, I don't smile. I feel my heart thumping in my chest. I can't really be happy for them. I move onto the next photo. Alex is holding the picnic basket with one lid open; Raegan is pulling out a bottle of champagne with one hand and cradling two champagne flutes with the other. Big expressive smiles cover their faces. The next photo is the two of them twisting their arms around one another as they take their first sip of champagne together. A few more are shots of Raegan admiring her ring and the couple standing in different poses. The first photo that Roo is a part of is the group photo that reads, *Many thanks to our meteorologist friend Paul, who helped Alex pick the perfect night for a clear sky. He had to wait three days!!! And Stella for capturing these priceless photos!*

No mention of Roo's roll until the last photo where he is hugging his brother in a profile shot. Thankfully he's facing the camera, giving me a view of his face. His eyes are closed as tight as the hug looks to be. The caption under it reads, *And it couldn't have happened without my wonderful future bro-in-law being on stand-by for the past three days to set up this picture-perfect scene! Roo, you made this so special for us! We love you!*

A tear rolls down my cheek. I love him. I miss him. I wipe the drop away. I can envision him fluffing out the blanket to make sure it was just right and chilling the champagne in a bucket of ice until he got word they were getting close. I know he would have snapped off a few photos from his own camera during those heart-throbbing moments. I blink until my eyes are clear and no longer dripping. I go to the comments section and type, *So happy for you, congrats!*

CHAPTER 23

The first thing I notice when I wake up, after reading the time on my phone, is two missed calls and a voicemail from Danielle. I see she has texted me so I open the text first.

Danielle: Hey, everything is good. I found a ride!

I listen to her voicemail and learn that her car broke down just a few minutes from her house. But because it was raining, she called to get a ride. Jordan was the first person who answered and gave her a ride home. I imagine like me, everyone else she tried calling had silenced their phone before they went to bed. I call her.

"Hi." She answers.

"Hey, how are you? I'm really sorry I missed your calls."

"Oh, I'm fine. I only had to wait about twenty minutes for Jordan to get there. And the tow truck driver, Davis, stayed and waited with me."

"Oh, but that can be kind of scary. I'm sorry."

"It wasn't at all. My dad stayed on the phone with me; he was still driving back from Milwaukee and wanted to make sure I was safe. But I felt fine and I ended up telling him Jordan was there…even though he wasn't because I felt safe and I was having a nice conversation with Davis."

"Danielle, you can never be too safe, I can't believe you did that."

"Well, I'm alive and well." She laughs. "Did you stay over at Kia's?"

"Yep, just woke up actually. And that reminds me, I better get started on breakfast."

"You two have a nice morning, I need to get going anyway, I think my dad is ready to put me to work."

We say goodbye and end the call.

I finish mashing two avocados in a small glass bowl before I grab the spatula and check the scrambled eggs. Just a minute to go. I sprinkle a generous amount of Monterey jack over them. I thinly slice a plump red tomato and layer the ingredients. I add salt and pepper and place the stacked toast on a heavy china plate. I grab the açai bowl out of the fridge that I'd put together before starting the eggs and make way to Kia's bedroom. I set the tray down, run back to the kitchen for two glasses of orange juice and knock gently on Kia's door.

It takes a bit but eventually I hear a groggy, "come in."

"Good morning!" I say cheerfully but quietly because I don't want to be too loud first thing in the morning.

"Oh my gosh, are you for real, breakfast in bed?" She smiles and yawns.

"Well I wasn't sure if you'd want to eat up here but I didn't want your toast getting cold and soggy.

"You are so sweet. And this is so much food, you're going to help me, right?"

"I sure am," I say, grabbing one of the two spoons.

Kia scoops a spoonful of açai out of the bowl and brings it to her mouth. She has the perfect ratio of puree topped with a strawberry slice and a sprinkle of granola that I drizzled with chocolate syrup.

She closes her eyes, "this is so good! Thank you so much for doing this for me." She smiles sweetly.

"You're welcome. I'm just glad you have a stocked kitchen." I smile.

After pulling away from Kia's duplex I head in the direction of my apartment. I need to shower before meeting up with Clarissa. We'd asked her and Danielle to join us at the beach, where Kia and I had spent the last four hours and both gotten a little pink. Danielle was still working on house projects and Clarissa said she wasn't feeling up for it. She did however ask me to meet her at her parents' house. Now that the girls know about the pregnancy, she said it's time to tell her parents. Because she doesn't know how it will go over, she really wants me to be there. After a quick check and food replenishment for Patches, I head out in the direction of the Thomas household.

I'm greeted by Clarissa's mother and I follow her into their massive kitchen.

"Can I get you something to drink?" She asks kindly.

"Water would be great, thank you," I say, feeling my mouth starting to go dry.

She reaches into the fridge and ejects a bottle of water. Smiling, she sets it down in front of me. Clarissa turns into the kitchen looking a little stressed.

"Hey, I'm glad you're here." She walks towards me tucking a strand of hair behind her ear.

When her mother's turned and reaching into the pantry, Clarissa mouths, "I'm freaking out."

"You are strong and you can do this." I mouth back. Her mother finds what she was looking for and closes the pantry door.

"Can we all go into the sitting room?" She asks.

Her nervous energy has me a bit anxious. Why did I agree to this? I know it's easier for her with me being here, but I feel out of place. Knowing the news that she's about to drop is giving me clammy hands and sweaty armpits. I walk in behind Clarissa and search for the best seat option. I sit in a leather chair with wooden legs. It's not the closest to the door but I'm directly across from it and I feel more comfortable being able to see the exit.

"What's this about Clarissa?" Her mother asks.

I see Clarissa swallow. "Can you just call Daddy in? I need to talk to you about this Fall," she says with a tremor in her voice, but her mother doesn't seem to notice.

A moment later, Arthur walks in to join us. I'm not sure he sees me because he doesn't pay any attention to me at all, and right now I am more than fine with that.

"I've only got a minute, what is it honey?"

Clarissa sits at the edge of her chair to my left. She starts out looking at her parents but as soon as she starts talking her eyes bounce around until she focuses on the coffee table. "I'm not going to UCLA…"

Her dad shakes his head and frowns. "And why is that?" He says in a stern voice. "You know I will only be covering that beach condo if you're there for education."

"Sorry, I mean I'm not going to California. You'll need to cancel the lease."

Clarissa is sitting across from her mother, ten or so feet apart. Her mother raises her hand as if she's asking a question but doesn't wait to speak, her tone comes out motherly, "I know something like this can be stressful and it will be hard to leave your friends but-"

Clarissa cuts her off. "No, mom, it's not that," she says in a sharp tone. Besides Clarissa's thumb and index finger futzing with the bottom of her baggy top, she is still with perfect posture. Her parents are seated the same way but completely still.

I look down at my own trembling hands and wish I could just vanish from this room. I tuck them under my butt to keep them still, and pray this is all over soon. As the thought goes through my mind, Clarissa continues.

"I'm pregnant. That's why I'm not going." The words hang in the air. Moments go by and her parents look stunned.

Her mother swallows hard and then says, "What?" as if Clarissa just insulted them.

"You," Arthur says pointing at me and then the door, "Leave!" I'm sure I turn as white as a ghost. "This is a family matter," he says with authority.

"She's not leaving," Clarissa says back with the same strong tone as her father. Now I see where she gets it from. No longer nervous like she had been moments earlier, she suddenly has strength and I feel an argument coming on.

"Jhett, would you please give us a minute?" Her mother asks. Without looking at Clarissa I swiftly allow her to usher me into the nearby room. Her mother walks out without saying a word and closes the door behind her. Through the wall I can hear the conversation continue.

"And what does Max have to say about all of this?" Arthur asks as if he's disgusted.

"Max doesn't know yet. Things weren't going so well between us, but we're working on it and I plan to tell him soon."

"Oh, for fuck's suck." Her father bellows.

I hear Clarissa's mom, "Oh Clarissa...your dreams, your school. You wanted UCLA so bad. That's where you're supposed to be." She starts sobbing.

"What happens if the two of you don't work out?" Arthur growls showing no mercy.

Clarissa doesn't answer.

"What's your plan if he doesn't want to be a part of this kid's life? How's he going to pay for child support? Is he even working? I know he doesn't have any real ambitions." He adds and I can only imagine the hurt and sadness Clarissa must be feeling to not have supportive parents. Her father continues, "You don't pay your own bills, you don't know how to cook a meal, can you even cut your own grass? How are you going to raise a child? You've never even held a job longer than three months."

"And that's my fault?" Clarissa raises her voice. Surprising me, her parents say nothing to this. "By the time the two of you met, you were already established. You had one full-time nanny and a housekeeper after I was born. Mom never cooked meals, she'd send the housekeeper to pick up dinner. And you always had me in piano classes, gymnastics, tennis lessons or swim camp; nothing that could actually prepare me for real life. You've threatened to cut me off so many times but you've never taught me how to do things for myself. I've been spoiled with these lavish vacations and I've had people do things for me since I was born. You chose that for me. I know what my reality is and I'm trying to deal with it the best I can."

"You were as lazy of a child as they come," Arthur says. "We kept you busy with all that shit because you would have just sat around. That's all you ever wanted to do and I couldn't stand the mopiness, it was depressing."

"I was hoping for your support but if I can't get that from you, then you don't have to be a part of this child's life."

"That's not what we're saying Clarissa." Her mother interjects.

"Whether Max is with me or not, I don't need you. I can do this on my own."

Her father laughs a taunting laugh. "Yeah, with what money? Raising a child is not easy, and with your lifestyle and no money it's going to be nearly impossible."

CHAPTER 24

"I told Max." Clarissa tells me on the phone.

"How did it go?"

"Better than it did with my parents. He asked if it's why I wanted to give our relationship another try. I didn't see any point in lying so I was honest and told him it was."

"What about his drinking?"

"He said he slowed down after we started talking again. I guess he'd been getting wasted nearly every night after we broke up."

"Wow. Are you concerned that he might have a problem?" I ask thinking back to her comments at Danielle's house.

"It's hard to say. He's twenty-five and hangs out with his buddies four nights a week. Of course, they're going to drink. I just don't know how to tell if it's out of his control, ya know?" It's silent for a few beats and then she adds, "I told him that if he's going to be a dad, he can't pick and choose when to be there. Things will change after the baby comes and if he's going to be in this kid's life, it's going to be for good; whether we stay together or not. He will keep his promises and follow through. He can't just pop in as he pleases. I will not tolerate him being a deadbeat dad."

My eyes widen although I know Clarissa can't see me. "How'd he respond to that?"

"He said he wants to be a part of our lives no matter what. He sounded pretty serious when he said he will do whatever it takes."

"How has your relationship been since we got back from New Orleans?"

"Things have actually been good for us. And I wanted things to be okay before telling him about the pregnancy."

"So, now what?"

"Well, we had a long conversation. He's going to enroll in online classes so he can still work. He has three semesters left until he completes his bachelor's. And I'm going to look for something else. I'm not making any money at Redds. I've been getting a dumpy twenty hours a week, so keep your eyes open and let me know if you see anything."

"I will, and Clarissa, I'm so happy he's being supportive. I think you guys are going to be fine."

Clarissa: Emergency meetup needed (not really an emergency). Let's meet at the Mexican restaurant in an hour.
Kia: K
Danielle: I'll be there if Jhett can pick me up along the way?? My car is acting up and I'm worried it might break down again.
Jhett: Yes Dani. See you all soon.

Danielle and I walk in and see Kia and Clarissa at the bar. We walk over and I look at Clarissa to read her face.

"Is everything okay?" I ask.

"Yeah," after a split second she adds, "baby is fine." She places her hand on her tiny tummy. "And it's so much nicer now that everyone knows."

We look at her and wait. We've been friends long enough to know that you only text 'emergency' if there's a legit reason. But looking at Clarissa crunching away on chips, I'd say everything seems just fine.

Reading my thoughts Kia asks, "So, why'd you call us here?"

"So we could all be together. Dive in!" She holds up the bowl of salsa.

"You can't just scare us all half to death whenever you have a craving and want us with you." She rolls her eyes.

318

Clarissa laughs. "You said you'd be there to support me. I just wanted to get something to eat with my girls. And so we're clear, I said it wasn't really an emergency."

"You've got to be kidding me, I was in the middle of a workout," Kia says, looking pissed.

I find myself annoyed too. "You know you could have just asked one of us. Riss, you actually had me worried."

"Us...we were all worried," Danielle says.

Clarissa continues to consume chips as if she has no care in the world.

"Well fuck, I'm going back home to finish my workout," Kia says throwing up her arms.

"No, stay, get a margarita."

"Are you serious right now?" Kia's squinting her eyes at Clarissa.

"We need to celebrate." Clarissa chimes.

"Celebrate what?" Kia asks with some attitude.

"My engagement!" Clarissa says scooping up another glop of salsa.

"What?" I say grabbing her by the shoulders to make her face me. "Are you kidding right now?"

Clarissa drops the chip as Danielle grabs her by the wrist and yanks her left hand up for us to examine it.

"No ring?" Danielle announces the obvious.

"Not yet, we're going to look tomorrow." She smiles.

We each step forward to hug her and soon she's in the middle of a group bear hug.

"Ugh, stop. You know I don't like all that touching," she says pushing us away.

"You did this to yourself," Danielle says with a big happy smile plastered on her face.

"Congrats you loser," Kia says laughing.

Clarissa is laughing too. "You should have seen how pissed you all looked. I couldn't even face you; I think I would have pissed myself with laughter."

319

"Tell us how he did it?" I say bouncing on my toes.

"Why don't you sit and order a margarita. Please drink one for me and we can enjoy this moment together."

"Good idea, I'll drink to that!" I look at the special of the month board. Kiwi Strawberry. "I'll take the special." The bartender responds with a nod.

"After I got off the phone with you last night, Max asked me to come over. When I got there, his place was super clean, he had my favorite music channel on and he had a bunch of candles lit. He gave me a dozen red roses and made me dinner. I thought he was doing it to show me things were going to be different. After dinner, he rubbed my feet and we just talked. It was really nice.

"Then, nonchalantly he asked if I wanted dessert. I'd actually turned it down because I was tired and ready for bed. He asked if I'd mind him eating it in front of me. Of course I didn't care, so he came over holding a cardboard cupcake box. He set it down and opened the lid. I couldn't see inside the box because the lid was blocking my view. He took out a red velvet cupcake saying that one was his and then set it down. Then he said, 'and this is for you.' He took out a white leather ring box. My blood turned cold and I felt goosebumps over my entire body. I think my expression was somewhere between a shock and a smile, but I don't really know for sure.

"He got down on one knee, which was pretty cute because by this point, he looked super nervous. And then he said he was going to try harder at making us work than anything else he's ever done and that he wants to be the greatest dad ever. Then he opened the box, and inside was a red stoned ring; not a ruby. When I looked at the ring he said, 'This is only temporary, I didn't have time to go ring shopping, I'm sorry'. He took the ring out and held it out to me and asked me to marry him. And, I said yes." Clarissa is glowing and looks so beautiful as she describes their engagement story.

"I'm so happy for you," Danielle says. "Let's toast," she says, raising her margarita, "to Clarissa and Max...and baby and happily ever after!"

We raise our glasses and cheers.

"So, why aren't you wearing your temporary engagement ring?" I ask.

"I don't need my finger turning green." She smiles. "I might hold onto it for costume jewelry but probably not, it's pretty gaudy. And I think I can wait the one week or however long it takes to get my ring in. Also, I don't want to say I told you so," Clarissa says raising an eyebrow, "but that psychic got it all wrong, she said you'd be married first," she says pointing at Danielle.

"Well, not necessarily," Kia says, "you really weren't apart of the reading. So, when we asked, it was between the three of us." Kia points a finger to Danielle, me and herself making an invisible triangle.

"Believe what you want my dear." She smirks. "Onto the next topic. You will be my bridesmaids plus Olivia."

"Yay!" Danielle says clapping.

"I want to know when you're getting married."

"I'd really like to get married before the baby comes. And Max wants something post-baby. I told him how my parents reacted to the pregnancy and how upset they still are. He's hoping to smooth things over with them but they've ignored his calls...so they don't even know about the engagement yet. Getting married before the baby comes will lessen the friction with my parents and I think in time they will come around. But hearing that upset him. And I understand why, it's not their wedding it's ours."

"Wow, that's hard. And unless you have a shotgun wedding, you could be super pregnant for your I do's. I'm not trying to be a bitch but you're already starting to show," Kia says.

For the first time since finding out she was expecting, Clarissa is wearing something fitted.

"Thanks for your concern but that's sort of the least of my problems. If we get married before the baby comes, I think my dad will pay for it. Together Max and I have no money, so getting married after the baby is here, we might really be on our own. Even if we do get better jobs, things will be tight and I can't see being able to pay for our own wedding."

"Give it a little time, things could be very different in a week."

CHAPTER 25

Jhett: Happy birthday to the world's best neighbor! You still having people over tonight?

   Jillian: Thank you! Yes, you're still coming right?

   Jhett: Yep, see you in a few hours!

When I leave the humane society from walking dogs with Clarissa, I head to the grocery store. I get my usual groceries plus a few extras just because. Once back at the apartment I make cream cheese bars to bring to Jillian's. I grab my phone to text my sister.

   Jhett: Meet for coffee tomorrow?

   Kate: Sure, 10?

   Jhett: Perfect!

As I walk past Jillian's to grab my laundry, I hear music. I look at the time and decide that after putting away this basket of clothes I'll go over. I walk in after knocking twice because I don't think anyone could hear me over the music. A few unfamiliar faces look up when I walk in.

"Hi," I say waving, "I'm Jhett, the neighbor."

A few friendly hellos come my way until I spot Jillian with another small group of people.

"She's here!" Jillian says and takes the pan of bars I offer.

I smile and nod as she goes around the room introducing me to her fellow coworkers.

"We're not all teachers, but we all work at South," she says.

I take an open seat in her living room feeling a little timid. A fourth-grade teacher walks over offering me a cocktail.

"Hi, I'm Margaret. I came over a little early to experiment with Jillian. We agree this drink turned out the best."

"Thanks," I say, reaching for it. "What is it?"

"Lavender Collins."

"Lavender?" I wrinkle up my nose. "In a drink?"

"I was hesitant too, but you might be surprised by how good it is."

Imagining the floral scent of the flower I bring the glass to my lips and take a small sip. "Hmm, that is way better than I expected," I say taking another drink.

"So, as tradition has it, we will be playing the teacher's version of 'Would You Rather' once Leon and Gavin get here." She tells me. "I'll help you out if you need it."

Margaret and I are two drinks deep and in the midst of getting to know each other when the apartment door swings open. Two men dressed in basketball shorts and t-shirts walk in.

"Leon and Gavin," Margaret says quietly.

I look at her, giving her a pleased smile. "Who is the one on the right?"

"Leon," she says. "He's a favorite around the school...if you know what I mean." She winks at me.

"Wait, has he dated a bunch of teachers?"

"Oh no, he doesn't date teachers...well, not at our school. My friend Penny," she lowers her hand and points to a woman in a yellow dress, "she can be pretty bold. She asked him out at the end of the year but he turned her down, saying he doesn't date coworkers. And trust me, more than just Penny had been eyeing him up."

"What does he teach?"

"P.E. And he's so good with the kids, makes him even more attractive." She starts giggling.

"What?" I ask, curious about her laughter.

"Don't let him catch you staring."

"I'm not," I say, but know I'm totally guilty. "And he works with kids, that's so charming," I say, giving her a sideways glance.

"Last call, who needs a refill before we start?" Jillian shouts making her way into the living room. I can tell she's a bit tipsy by how she's walking. Margaret and I both lift our almost empty glasses as she makes her way past us.

We arrange our chairs so that we are sitting in a circle.

"Okay the rule is, if both people around you answer differently than you do, you must drink. Margaret and I made up a bunch of questions earlier today but if you'd like to create your own there are blank cards in the box. Penny, let's start with you." She hands her the box.

"Okay, would you rather, teach an eight-hour day in a subject you love, or a six-hour day in subject you hate?" Penny snorts, "Oh my God that's so easy, definitely a six-hour day! I'd do just about anything to have more free time."

And just like that I can see why Leon turned her down. Whether his reason of not dating a coworker is legit or not, she is obnoxious and her high-pitched voice makes you want to plug your ears when she speaks.

The box of cards gets passed around and the laughter gets louder with each card drawn. Jillian grabs the next card. "Would you rather make-out with Todd the bus driver or Leon?" She bursts out laughing so hard she spills some of her drink. At the same time, Leon's eyes go big. Everyone in the room is busting a gut including myself.

"I did not put this card in there," Jillian says, through giggles.

I look over at Penny, she is the only one composing herself and has a sour expression across her face. She clearly did not put that card in either.

"Please, please don't answer that." Leon says as the room around him is trying to slow their laughs.

"Maybe this is a good time for a break," Jillian says. "Please, everyone make sure you get something to eat."

A few people get up and make their way into the kitchen.

"Can I get you another?" Margaret asks, pointing to my glass.

"Yeah, thanks," I say, handing it over to her.

"Hi, I'm Leon," Leon says, swiftly sliding into Gavin's now open chair.

"Hi," I say, feeling some excitement, "I'm Jhett." We shake hands. His grip has the right amount of pressure.

"I'm sure you've already figured it out but I work at the school with Jillian. How do you know her?"

"I live right next door," I say waving my thumb in the direction of my apartment.

"I've never been down this block before; it seems to be a very well-kept area."

"I believe this area is newer to the city. These apartments are only a few years old."

We have a few more minutes to ourselves before Margaret shouts, "It's cake time!" She comes from the spare bedroom holding a platter of cupcakes. Margaret breaks out in Happy Birthday and we follow along, singing offkey.

"I brought you one," Leon says, holding two cupcakes. He takes the seat next to me once again.

"Thank you."

"You do like sweets, don't you?" He asks, grinning.

"Love them!" I say and to prove it to him I peel back the cupcake wrapper and take a bite.

"Then you'll love those bars up there. You'll have to try one of those next."

"In the glass pan?" I ask. "The cream cheese ones?"

"Yeah, have you had one?"

I laugh, "I made them, I'm glad you like them."

"I'm not sure if I should admit this, but I had four. I couldn't stop."

326

"Wow, well I'd say you like sweets too."

"It's one of the reasons why I wanted to be a Phy-Ed teacher. Growing up with a sweet tooth and a love for sports I knew if I was to stay in shape, I had to do something that would keep me fit physically."

"So, is your job as a P.E. teacher all you thought it'd be?"

"Oh, I love it. I goof around all day."

I grin at him and he smiles back. We're still like this for just a moment.

"Hey, do you…have plans after this?" He asks.

"Um, no." I shrug.

"Would you want to grab a drink?" He asks, giving me a quizzical look.

Kia would describe this guy as dreamy. And part of me thinks I am dreaming. With my heartbeat matching the beat of the music I answer him. "Sure, where would you like to go?"

After a quick search, on his phone he finds a bar within walking distance. I know I could suggest Marcos but for the first time I don't have the impulse to go there. I don't think it would be wise to bring Leon to a place that is filled with Roo memories.

We get a mix of curious looks and one glare; from Penny, as we say goodbye and leave Jillian's. I had a few moments alone with Jillian to thank her for the invite and to say goodbye. She let slip that she had mentioned my name a few times in the past few weeks when she had been around Leon. I naturally insisted on more information and needed to know if he was in on it. Was this some sort of blind set up that I wasn't in on? She assured me it was not. Her plan was just to plant the seed. Whenever Leon was in earshot, she would find a way to mention her good looking, sweet and fun neighbor whenever possible. I teasingly glare at her but I think she and I both know I'm excited to spend some more time with him.

Leon opens the door to the bar and we walk in. It's dark and since I've never been here before I'm hesitant to pick a direction.

"I think I see two open stools over there," he says pointing to the left side of the room.

I follow his lead, noticing some of the women who turn to their friends and whisper. I see others hold their gaze for that extra second before looking away. I can't blame them; from what I can tell he's the best eye candy in this bar. The attention he gets does make me a bit jealous, but it goes away as soon as we cozy up next to each other on the bar stools.

"Have you ever been here?" I ask.

"No, you?" He says catching the eye of a bartender.

"First time. Hard to believe with it being so close to my place, right?"

"For sure. Why haven't you stopped in before?"

"I knew it was here, but it just didn't stand out."

"Looks like it's the place to be. Maybe it will become your new go-to spot," he says with a flirtatious smirk.

"What can I get for you?" The bartender asks.

Leon turns towards me and waits for me to order.

"Vodka cranberry," I say.

"Nice," he says approvingly. "Vodka tonic for me please." He sets his credit card down. "Keep it open," he says and turns back to me.

His slightly messed sandy blond hair, tan skin, and ocean blue eyes make him look like he's just come back from a surfing trip with his buddies. His good looks make it hard to concentrate on our conversation.

Three drinks later and a stumbly trip back from the restroom, I hear, "Last call!"

"Wow already?" Leon looks up to the bar clock and I can see he's just as surprised as I am that it's thirty minutes to bar close. "You're not ready to go home yet, are you?"

I grin and slap my hand on his knee. "As much as I'd love to stay out and continue our conversation," I say a bit slurred, "it's been a long day and I should go home."

"You know what they say about the word, 'should' don't you?" He asks.

"No, what?"

He hesitates, "I don't remember." He starts laughing and I trail with some of my own drunken giggles. "Well, okay," he says slowly, "I guess I better walk you home."

"Is your car at my apartment?"

"Gavin drove us. No worries though, I'll grab an Uber."

When we get to my door, we are laughing so hard we can't keep our balance.

"Tonight, was really a good time. Thanks, for getting that drink with me."

"I'm glad I did."

"Would you want to do it again sometime? Maybe we can get dinner beforehand?"

"Yes, I would."

He leans in to kiss me but when we touch, we stumble back and I hit my head on my door. It makes a loud thud and I start laughing.

"Oh, my gosh are you okay?" He laughs.

"I'm fine," I say, rubbing the back of my head, knowing if this had happened with Roo he'd cradle my head with both hands and kiss me gently, just to make sure it didn't happen again.

Leon kisses me, "Goodnight."

"Goodnight," I say.

CHAPTER 26

"Oh my gosh, this guy sounds like a piece of heaven!" Kate says.

"I know! He works with kids and he's fun and really good looking." I gush.

Kate smiles and takes a drink of her macchiato. "I'm happy for you. This is really exciting. You'll have to thank Jillian for planting the seed."

"I got a text from her this morning saying she heard us come up the stairs last night. I guess we were loud and she admitted she looked out the peephole just to make sure it was us." I give Kate a look. "Do you think she watched for a while? I think I would have if roles were reversed," I say, shrugging.

"Yes. Especially since she knows both of you."

"I'll have to question her later about that," I say.

"I've actually met someone too," Kate says a little apprehensively.

"You have? Oh my gosh, I have so many questions," I say surprised.

She smiles.

"When, where?" I ask when she gets quiet.

"I met him at work, he's in another department."

"Okay, so I need more. Why are you being hesitant?"

"Well, he's my manager. And although there's nothing against coworkers dating, it states in our handbook that titled employees cannot be in a relationship with coworkers. And I get it, it could cause problems."

"Okay, so are you secretly dating?"

"I wouldn't say that," she says, bringing her legs up, tucking them under herself. "I don't really know how to describe our relationship. We know we want to be together, but we just don't know if we want to risk our jobs. We're both really happy with where we're at."

"Aw, Kate, I'm sorry. That's got to be hard."

"It is. I want a normal relationship. I don't want to hide anything and it would be really hard keeping it from the other coworkers."

"How did this start?"

"With all the extra hours I've been taking, we've just been together more. I helped him with a few projects and things just started to take off." She shakes her head. "Last week he looked at transferring to our sister company but they aren't hiring. And I thought about taking a different shift so I'd be under a different manager but that was a dead end too."

Kate and I go back and forth trying to think of different situations until my phone rings. I get goosebumps when his name comes across the screen.

"Oh my gosh he's calling," I say flashing the phone to Kate.

Her eyes go big. "Take it!"

CHAPTER 27

February - Six months later

Clarissa: It's happening! When will you be here?!

The text came through at 12:02am. We all agreed to go to the hospital and wait in the family and friends area until Max would come to get us.

Kia: I'm so happy and excited for you but why couldn't you wait until I was back in town? I'll see you as soon as I can!! EEK!!

Danielle: I'll come straight there after work tomor. Love You!

I send my reply at 7am.

Jhett: I'm so sorry. I didn't hear my phone. I'm on my way! <3

I race around my apartment, trying to move as quickly as I can. My heart is beating rapidly in my chest like I slammed an energy drink. Pulling into the first open parking space near the entrance to the hospital, I slam my gear shaft into park. Rushing to get out of my vehicle, my purse catches on the parking brake and yanks me back. I grumble to myself and roughly pull it free.

I half run-walk to the entrance doors while checking the room number for the third time, #115. After getting buzzed in through the intercom, I walk briskly through the hallway. I read every door number and look into each room, even though I know I have a way to go until I reach Clarissa's. The further I walk, the stronger the familiar baby ward smell gets. Chills cover my skin and tears fill my eyes when I see room #115. After getting here as fast as I could, I freeze in front of the closed door. Do I knock? Barge in? Is Clarissa sleeping? Nursing? She is a private person, so I understand it being closed. I finally knock gently and push open the door.

"Come in." I hear her hoarse response.

The smile on my face lessons a bit when I look at Clarissa. Her hair's messed up, there are dark circles under her red eyes, and she's wearing a deeply exhausted expression.

"Are you okay?" I ask.

She barely nods. I lean in to hug her. We are the only two in the room. I see a beautiful bouquet of flowers and a gathering of helium and latex balloons placed on the windowsill. I see a small whiteboard with birth information and a bassinet a few feet away. I get up to look inside; it's empty.

I read the little white card displayed on the bassinette.

Congratulations, it's a BOY!

My name: Ezra

My birthday: February 2nd 2020

Time: 5:04am

Weight: 7lbs 2oz

Length: 19 ¼"

"The nurse just took him. Routine testing, she said she'll be right back."

I feel my body relax when I take in that the baby is okay, but her voice lets on that there's more. Something is off.

"How was the delivery, did everything go okay?" I ask, gently sitting beside her on the bed.

"I labored at home for a few hours before Max drove us in. My water broke in the car and I had him early this morning," she says, with sadness in her eyes.

I don't know what it's like to be a first-time mom, but Clarissa is not acting normal and I wonder how long it takes postpartum depression to set in.

"Did your mom make it in time?

She nods her head again. "My mom and Max were both here for the delivery."

"Where is everyone?" I ask, confused.

Clarissa adjusts the top of her cotton hospital gown. "My mom left shortly after he was born and Max..." she trails off.

Just then a grey-haired nurse walks in holding a swaddled baby. "His numbers look good, Momma," she says softly. She walks over to Clarissa's side and asks, "Do you want to try nursing again?" After Clarissa hesitates to answer, she adds, "I think he did better last time, it just takes some practice."

"Is he sleeping?" she asks.

"He is."

"Then, maybe when he wakes," she says.

The nurse looks to me with a warm smile and then turns to place Ezra in the bassinet. "Just buzz if you need anything," she says, closing the door behind her.

I get up and slowly walk over to the bassinet. A little wiggle from Ezra but then back to perfectly still. I place my hand on the side of his bed and look at his tiny, round face. Slowly, my lips part and I'm at a loss for words. My mouth goes dry as I try to think of what to say. What to ask. I turn to look at Clarissa but to my surprise she is not watching for my reaction, she is staring straight ahead with a blank expression on her face.

CHAPTER 28

"Clarissa? What happened?"

I watch a silent tear fall from her eye as she turns to me. She shakes her head. "I screwed up."

Walking over, I sit on the bed and place my hand on her shoulder. "I am here for you, I will support you. I will do whatever you need me to do."

She takes my hand. "I lied. I lied and I knew when I first found out I was pregnant that this was going to happen. I just knew."

I stay with Clarissa for hours. I help her into the shower, braid her hair, and force her to walk the halls with me. I rub her back as she cries harder each time she tries to get Ezra to latch to her sore, tender nipples. When she falls in and out of sleep, I hold him and rock him. I order her meals from the cafeteria and encourage her to keep eating so she can keep up her energy. By the time 5pm rolls around, I feel the need for some fresh air.

"Do you mind if I go make a call?" I ask quietly.

"I'll be okay. I'm kind of tired anyway," she says closing her eyes.

As soon as I'm in the hall, I message Kia and Danielle.

Jhett: Are you guys almost here?

Kia: Yeah, just mins away.

Jhett: I'll meet you outside.

I noticed I had two missed calls before texting the girls. I look at my call log. The words, *My Love,* in red indicating a missed call. I hit the phone icon.

"Hey babe, is everything okay? What's going on?"

"Um, it's hard to say. Baby Ezra is…beautiful but there's something else that's just going to be hard for Clarissa." I look up to see Danielle and Kia walking towards me. "Are you at the apartment?"

"Yeah, I'm here. So, what's the problem, her parents? Did they not show up?"

"I'll fill you in when I get back. I'm going to talk to the girls and then come right home."

"Okay, I love you," he says.

"I love you too, I'll see you soon."

"Oh my gosh, how is she?" Kia asks.

I shake my head. "Not the best."

"I could tell from your texts that something is not okay with Ezra, but I was too afraid to ask over the phone. Is he okay?" Danielle asks.

"Ezra's fine. He's healthy and so sweet; you guys will love him." I struggle to continue, but I promised Clarissa I would tell them because she doesn't have the strength to talk about it. I force myself to muster up the courage to tell them. Slowly the words come out. "Max is not the father."

They stare at me like I'm speaking a different language.

"Huh?" Kia says looking shocked.

"Think back to when Clarissa went to Barbados with her parents." I give them a moment. "Remember Alejandro? The sexy guy she spent the evenings with; the one she told us she only had kissed?"

I walk up the steps to my apartment and open the door. A delicious smell hits my nose and I see Chinese takeout boxes on the counter.

"Hey sweetheart. I hope you're hungry."

"I'm starving. I didn't realize that while I was encouraging Clarissa to eat, I wasn't feeding myself." I take the open seat at the counter and turn to him. "Roo, you're not going to believe this."

He sweeps me into a tight hug, and kisses my forehead. "Tell me everything."

Book two coming soon!
For updates about the sequel, follow Ellison Clark below.

I would love to know what you thought of *With You*!
Please leave a review at:
- Amazon
- Goodreads
- Facebook

Connect with Ellison Clark:
Instagram: ellison.books
Facebook: Ellison Clark Books
Email: ellisonbooks@gmail.com

Ellison Clark lives in Northern Wisconsin with her husband and two children. 'With You' is her first novel.

Made in the USA
Columbia, SC
21 September 2021

45211828R00205